THE
SANCTUARY

GARY RIEDL

Pleasant W●rd

Pleasant Word (a division of WinePress Publishing, PO Box 428, Enumclaw, WA 98022) functions only as book publisher. As such, the ultimate design, content, editorial accuracy, and views expressed or implied in this work are those of the author.

Unless otherwise noted, all Scriptures are taken from the Holy Bible, New International Version, Copyright © 1973, 1978, 1984 by the International Bible Society. Used by permission of Zondervan Publishing House. The "NIV" and "New International Version" trademarks are registered in the United States Patent and Trademark Office by International Bible Society.

Scripture references marked NASB are taken from the New American Standard Bible, © 1960, 1963, 1968, 1971, 1972, 1973, 1975, 1977 by The Lockman Foundation. Used by permission.

Scripture references marked KJV are taken from the King James Version of the Bible.

ISBN 13: 978-1-4141-0922-0
ISBN 10: 1-4141-0922-9
Library of Congress Catalog Card Number: 2006910994

TABLE OF CONTENTS

ACKNOWLEDGMENTS

First, I thank my wife, Emily, for clarifying my ideas. Next, many thanks goes out to Donna Fleisher for her advice regarding writing techniques, to Heather Schroeder and Darlene Paxson for editing assistance, Tom Gray for technical assistance, and to the hundreds of readers who have given me added insights.

In addition, I am indebted to the experts of specialized resource materials. They brought to my doorstep the distant lands that I could not visit in person, and allowed me to bring recorded history to life.

Finally, I thank God; the same One known in ancient times, as is today, and will be forever.

CHAPTER 1

ATLANTA, GEORGIA, U.S.A.

Rebecca bit into her energy bar just as a scream rang out through Concourse T of Hartsfield International Airport. She dropped the bar and instinctively turned toward the source of the outcry. It came from a sobbing, young, colorfully dressed Zambian woman who was crouched down and searching for something valuable. The woman discovered a rag doll, and then continued her search repeating the words *"mwana munono!"* A crowd gathered around to attend to the distraught woman's dilemma.

Rebecca scanned the area for what might be the cause. She caught sight of a man awkwardly cradling a young black girl, his hand over her mouth, in a fast walk toward the baggage claim area. She waved a hand at the man. "Hey, mister!"

He didn't flinch.

Rebecca glanced down at her watch. Only ten minutes before her flight started boarding. "Wonderful!" she groaned. "I knew I should have taken that flight through Orlando instead." She bid good-bye to the boarding gate, then sprinted toward the man, her brown ponytail flying behind. "Hey, you!" she shouted again, quickly gaining on him.

The man's guilt was confirmed when he went from a jog to a run.

As Rebecca closed in on him, tears trickled out from the corner of her eyes and across her cheeks. *I must be crazy!* "Hey, you! Stop!"

The man glanced back at his nemesis and dashed toward the exit, clutching his hostage to his chest. Bystanders unknowingly cleared a path for the kidnapper, closed ranks, then parted again for Rebecca, who was in pursuit. She looked around for something to throw, but knew that if she stopped for even a second the man would assuredly escape. *Where are the security police? Probably at the boarding gate...where I ought to be.*

The man panted heavily just a step ahead of her. She reached out to grab the back of his shirt. *What am I doing? If he has a gun, he could kill me!* The man glanced back with wild anxious eyes, then without a word, dropped the girl, dodged a few luggage carts, and disappeared through the crowded airport exit.

The little girl bounced down on her padded behind and whacked her head on the tile floor. Trying to rein in her momentum, Rebecca leaped over the child then turned quickly to check on the girl's condition. The child, not more than three years old, held a chubby hand in her mouth and cried from the bump on her head. Rebecca squatted down and with open arms successfully invited the trembling child to come to her.

Rebecca scooped up the girl and stroked her head for a moment, then slid the girl to her hip to check her watch. "Oh, for goodness sakes!"

Rebecca turned around and jogged with the child in her arms, backtracking to find the mother. It wasn't long before she spotted the mother and hastily presented the child to her. The mother's eyes lit up with hysterical pleasure and squeezed her daughter passionately. At that instant, the last call to board the flight to Houston was announced.

Rebecca glanced in the direction of the boarding gate. The young mother blathered compliments and tried to kiss Rebecca's hand, who only nodded and smiled while backing away toward her flight. With a quick wave, she turned and darted away at full speed to swoop up her backpack on her way to the gate. Before the flight attendant had fully closed the Jetway door, Rebecca grabbed the handle and yanked it open, flashed her ticket, and heaved a sigh of relief when the attendant waved her in.

Inside the jet, a flustered heavyset man in a business suit—her supervisor—alternated between reading his newspaper and glancing down the aisle for her. Rebecca greeted him with an apologetic shrug.

He laid his newspaper in his lap and let his tardy associate squeeze by to the window seat. "Where did you run off to?" he asked with a frown. "You almost lost an opportunity to meet with the C.E.O...of Terra Petroleum!"

Rebecca patted his hand and slumped down in her seat. "Run off to? You wouldn't believe how accurate that statement is. I'll explain shortly. Give me a minute." She blew out a deep breath and replayed the dramatic events in her mind.

"It had better be good. Because this job is for someone responsible...someone we can count on to follow through with a tough and complicated situation."

"I'm sorry. It won't happen again." Rebecca rested her chin on her palm and leaned against the bulkhead. The adrenaline in her veins faded and her heart rate slowed. Tilting her gaze out the window, she watched the ear-protected ramp agent signal the plane with orange flashlight wands. As the jet revved up its engines and slowly pushed backward, Rebecca stared across the Tarmac into the big terminal windows. She caught sight of the young mother still squeezing the child, smothering her with kisses. Rebecca grew a smile that filled the edge of each cheek. Her heart welled up with joy and she whispered, "Thank you, Jesus!"

CHAPTER 2

TREASURE AT LAKE SEVAN

Jamal Ramezani was having the time of his life. He hadn't seen his family since starting his graduate studies at the University of Tehran. His aunt had fed him more exquisite food in a week here at Sevan, Armenia, than he normally ate in a month. Jamal speculated that his aunt had stuffed him like a pig to offset any possible substandard bachelor eating habits. Jamal looked out the window to see that the relentless rains had finally let up. He convinced his two cousins that they should walk off some of their feast.

The threesome went down to the shores of Lake Sevan and gawked awhile at voluptuous women in their skimpy bathing suits, a scene unheard of in his native Iran. Jamal's cousins had convinced him to take a shipboard sightseeing trip on Katrina, the newest addition to the Lake Sevan's tours. His cousins sped ahead of him on a race to reach the new, gleaming, blue and white, 35 meter, 145-passenger ship.

"Wait up for me!" Jamal shouted.

They laughed as they ran. "You are slow, Jamal! You sit and read too much!"

Heaving and panting, Jamal eventually caught up to his cousins at the dock. He bent over and leaned on his knees, trying to catch his breath. "I am just unused to the high elevation." He was a strong and wiry man, with dashing green eyes, yet his heart and lungs were nothing to aspire to.

They laughed and jeered at him, but it didn't matter to Jamal, he was with family. When Mohammad Reza, the Shah of Iran, was exiled from his autocratic rule of power, many people closely aligned to the president were killed or chased out of the country. Jamal's noble parents were hounded by religious vigilantes and killed in the process, but his uncles and aunts survived to live in Armenia. Jamal had grown up knowing two worlds, one Christian and one Muslim. He accepted both.

The young men paid for their ride on the ship, then stepped back to the end of the queue to come aboard. Seeing it may be a long wait, one of the cousins brought out a small, portable game of chess.

"It is believed that in the 9th century chess flourished in Persia and then to Arabia," said Jamal as they set up the tiny pieces. "Some believe chess originated in India around 600 A.D., but many think it began in Persia first."

One of the cousins rolled his eyes. "Thanks for the history lesson, Jamal, now will you let us play without a commentary?"

"Only if I get to play the winner."

Jamal had successfully completed his graduate studies in history—top of his class, thanks be to Allah! He had to decide whether to continue into the doctorate program or take the teaching position offered by the state. He had all summer to decide. The weather was hot and beautiful, and this day was going to be a fortunate one. Jamal knew that something special was about to come his way.

A week earlier in the mountains above Lake Sevan, an unsuccessful middle-aged antique dealer from Germany trudged in and out of caves throughout the rugged terrain. He had read an article in the Hamburg *Morganpost* newspaper about an obscure myth that referred to a lost treasure, and he was determined to capitalize on it. He was only an amateur archaeologist, but never refused an opportunity that might bring fame and fortune.

The endless rain would have put off the average treasure hunter, but the stubborn German dismissed the option of giving up. Thus, he persisted to slosh through the muddy terrain searching for hidden riches. However, as the days marched onward, he still had nothing to show for himself.

One drippy morning, the solitary treasure hunter sat inside his tiny tent pitched on a hard, bumpy floor. He arched his aching back and stared out at the endless mountain drizzle and streams of water running across the front door flap. The explorer had meticulously combed the northern hillside in a very methodical grid for ancient artifacts and only found a rusted, crumbling medieval shovel.

The man sat down on the floor and crossed off the last of the leads of the many maps that were strewn across the floor. He looked into his backpack with only a few provisions left and suddenly jumped upon the shovel. He stomped and stomped until it was in pieces. He threw down a stale piece of bread, swallowed the last of some bitter coffee, and started to pack up and leave the area permanently.

After stuffing his backpack and slipping it over his shoulders, the German traveled restlessly along a trail on the north side of the basin. He trekked two miles through the woods with sweat trickling down his face, until he found a lake-facing boulder to rest upon. The rains tapered off and cumulous clouds parted slightly to allow a few rays of sunshine to poke through. While he gazed upon the beauty of Lake Sevan's turquoise waters from above, the forest became very quiet…strangely quiet. He cocked his head to listen more carefully to the sounds of nature, but there was nothing. No birds singing or animal noises. Even the rustling wind that was blowing through the trees had stopped.

Without warning, a small tremor rippled beneath the man's feet. He lost his balance and instinctively clung to the nearest pine tree to steady himself. A landslide tumbled thunderously close to him, loosing mud, stones, and rivulets of water from the mountainside. He held his breath and tightened his grip on the tree as the ground beneath him dropped away. The earthquake continued and the pine tree shifted. He clutched onto the branches for dear life and glanced down at the sheer drop as the tree angled out over the edge.

Fortunately, the violent earthquake subsided and the tree's roots held in place. The German clung to the branches and hung precariously over the embankment, his legs dangling in midair. He frantically started to bargain with God. All was still, all was calm, and the tree held its position. He carefully pulled himself and his backpack up to the almost horizontal tree and sat down to calm his shaking body.

After a moment, he made his way through vertical branches, and cautiously crossed the large trunk to solid ground. He scrambled up the loose embankment to a flat area and lay flat on his back to rest a moment longer.

With the collar of his undershirt, the German wiped sweat from his face and picked up his gear. He stepped around some fallen boulders and tried to retrace his steps back to the trail.

Something glittering from within a newly formed opening in the hillside caught his eye. Warily, the explorer climbed over the rocks and peered into a narrow crevasse. He took out a flashlight and spotted what looked like a knife poking through the seam of an animal hide. It was only a few feet from him, so he tore off a long stick with a nub on the end and fished out the bundle. The hide was dried out and held together with a thin piece of leather. Undoing the lacing around the hide, he discovered a bone-handled knife. Next to the knife was a box inlayed with various colored wood strips. After a brief examination, there seemed to be no apparent way to open it. Stuffing the box into his pack, the German beamed at his unexpected treasure.

It took several hours by bus for the treasure hunter to travel from Lake Sevan to the capital city of Yerevan. There he inquired at the National History Museum to determine the value of the artifacts. The German approached the curator of the museum, who wore a crisp, blue business suit that covered his rotund frame. The curator held a distant gaze, looking somewhere in the depths of art history. The dirty, excited explorer presented the box to the expert and asked for his opinion of the artifact. The curator accepted the box casually, and proceeded to turn it over and around to examine it without any apparent regard. Two men standing idly nearby, one short and one tall, nodded to the German. After a moment or two, the curator gave it a worthless assessment and handed it back. Positive that the curator had made a mistake, and undeterred, he decided to take it to another expert.

Eager to get a serious analysis before returning to his homeland, the German struck out for the Matenadaran Manuscript Museum. Unfortunately, when he arrived the director told him the museum was interested only in manuscripts. However, the director recognized the box's special qualities and recommended that he talk to an artifacts expert who happened to be staying on the north shore of Lake Sevan that very week. The exhausted explorer slumped at the comment, but left to look for the nearest bus. The shops were starting to close and he took the last bus back to Sevan.

It was dark when the German arrived at the Blue Sevan hotel. He purchased a small room, set his backpack on the end table, and then flopped down on a soft bed to rest. After several minutes splayed out on his back, he reached inside the backpack to examine the wooden box. He took out a magnifying glass to more closely inspect the container, scrutinizing it for some identification markings. When there were none to be found, he fumbled around for a lever of some kind in order to open it up, but he was unsuccessful.

He reached into his backpack to find the knife that accompanied the box. The knife was so unusual, with its simple asymmetric metal blade and bone handle. He held it up to the light and reverently set it aside with the box. Tired from his eventful day, he turned off the light on the nightstand to get some sleep. With his hands behind his head he looked wishfully at the ceiling.

The following morning, two men from the National History Museum stood around the corner and waited for the German to exit his hotel. The smaller man was husky and built like a small truck. The taller, slick-looking man wore a casual gray suit.

"There he is, Erol," whispered the shorter man.

"OK, Berk, give the German some room, we don't want him to know we are following him."

"How do you know he is German?"

"Open your eyes and ears," Erol whispered harshly. "He has blond hair and spoke with a German accent at the museum."

The short, thick man nodded. They followed their target down the alley, over to another hotel, and peeked around the corner to eavesdrop as the German was speaking to the desk clerk. He lay the knife and the box on the counter and was requesting something about meeting with an expert.

"He just left to board the Katrina," said the woman at the desk. "If you wish to catch it, the boat is to leave in ten minutes."

Erol watched as the German thanked the woman, slid the knife in his belt, grabbed the box, and rushed down to the water's edge. Erol and Berk ran to catch up. The German paid for a ticket at a small booth, and ran up the gangplank as the quartermaster gave the last call to board. Erol and Berk ran past the booth, and caught the ride just before the ropes were cast off. Erol slapped a five thousand dram bill into the deckhand's palm for his troubles.

As the large craft plowed through the white-tipped waves, they followed behind their suspect, who was scanning the crowd for something. "I'm going to keep an eye on our friend, you go below and, well you know what to do."

Berk smiled and skulked to the lower deck, while Erol lit up a cigarette then leaned against the bulkhead. He watched the German ask questions to passengers...one after another.

The German threw up his hands and pulled aside one of the crew members. He seemed to be asking the crew about making an announcement to the passengers. Before the crewman could answer, dark fingers of smoke suddenly arose from the deck's lower hatches.

An alarm sounded and the crewman quickly excused himself. As the crew members scrambled for fire extinguishers, gasps and worried murmurs soon spread around the ship like a contagious virus. The smoke thickened and the treasure hunter backed up between two lifeboats with his treasure in one arm and a handkerchief to his face.

With the diversion set, Erol took advantage of his prey. The husky Berk showed up wiping his oily hands with a rag. Erol straightened his suit and stepped in front of the German with a cold, callous expression.

The German lowered his handkerchief. "Didn't I see you men at the museum?"

Erol stuck out an open palm and wiggled his fingers. "Give us the box," he demanded, in Armenian.

The German, who knew little of the language, had no problem understanding the universal give-it-to-me gesture. He shook his head, gripped the box even tighter, and dished out derogatory remarks from his Germanic tongue.

Silently and coolly, Erol glanced around to ensure they were alone and gave a signal to his associate. Berk swiftly grabbed the German's own knife from his belt and thrust the blade deeply under his rib cage.

Erol crossed his arms across his chest, and a tiny, evil smile curled up the side of his lip. "You have learned too late that I do not give second chances."

The injured explorer dropped the box on the deck and clutched his wound. He stood motionless for a moment, and stared at the gash with eyes wide and mouth open. His shirt oozed blood and quickly turned from white to red. Their victim looked up to his attackers, mouthing silent nothings. He tried to scream for help, but only let out a wheezy groan. His face grew pale and within seconds he passed out, crumpled down sideways on the deck.

Berk stashed the knife in his vest, found a heavy chain wound neatly near a lifeboat, tied it around the German's body, and then casually pushed him over the side. With all the commotion and smoke, no one even noticed the foreigner falling limply overboard to the depths of the lake.

The men smiled at their victory and walked over to pick up the box that had fallen to the deck. The engines of the vessel suddenly stopped and the boat pitched and rolled helplessly in the lake's swells. The box slid along the deck, under the guardrail, and into the water. They dove for the box but were a second too late. Lying prone on the deck, the thieves reached out for the box while the boat bobbed up and down in the water. A gold crucifix dangled from around the neck of the taller man, as he stretched out to grab the elusive box.

After a series of waves smacked against the side of the hull and into their faces, the men cursed their loss and got up from the deck. They spotted a lifeboat and made a dash for it. Erol unwound a crank and began to lower the boat, while his husky associate rolled back the canvas boat cover.

A crewman passing by, noticed their strange behavior. "May I ask what you men are doing?" he demanded.

The two criminals stopped what they were doing and turned around. Erol combed his straight black hair back with his fingers, stuffed the gold crucifix back into his shirt, and then composed himself. "We lost something of ours overboard and we need this boat to retrieve it."

"I am sorry, sir, but we cannot allow you to lower the captain's gig. You can report your loss and we will make every effort to retrieve it later; but you cannot take this boat."

"I can pay you well if you let us borrow it, *now*," he asserted.

"You cannot pay me enough if it means not being able to save our passengers." The crewman waved them aft where the rest of the passengers huddled near the railing. They gave a reluctant nod, grumbled a bit, and moved slowly toward the others.

The taller man turned to his compatriot. "Berk, if you jump in, you could swim for it and they would have to throw a life preserver to you."

"But Erol, you know I do not swim well." He looked down at the water. "I may sink before I get to it."

"Are you a coward?"

"Are you?" retorted the shorter thug. "I got the smoke started for the diversion, didn't I?"

Erol tried to see where the box had floated off to. He waved smoke away from his face and sidestepped along the guardrail, hoping to catch sight of their loss. He straightened his suit. "Nevermind! When we get to shore, we will rent a skiff and retrieve it then."

Some time passed and it was determined that there were no apparent damages to the engines, but the captain concluded they should return to shore for a full inspection. After the vessel landed, the two men quickly made their way to the nearest boat rental to get back out to the lake. The men got into the skiff, started the small motor, and pushed off from the dock.

While Berk increased the throttle of the small boat, Erol watched as the rest of the passengers departed the Katrina. Three young adult males striding down the plank caught his eyes. "Jamal! Wait up!" his friends called out. Erol looked closer and saw a young man with a silly grin on his face, holding up a box and waving it to his friends.

Erol backslapped his associate's arm. "Did you see that?"

"What?"

"That!" He pointed to the young man with the box. "It looks just like the one we are after. How did he get it? It fell into the water."

"It doesn't matter. Follow him, idiot!" the self-appointed leader yelled.

"Don't call me an idiot, or I won't follow him!"

"Fine, *Saint Mashdotz*! Follow him!"

Berk beamed grandly. Mesrob Mashdotz was the creator of Armenia's alphabet in 406 A.D. and later canonized by the Catholic

Church. Berk swiveled the motor and the boat made a U-turn back to the dock.

Erol tied up the craft while his stout friend ran to catch up with the young man named Jamal. He waded through the tourists, but lost the young man in a throng of people clogged up at the beach entrance. After Berk breached the bottleneck, he tried to pick up the track of the young man. It was no use; Jamal and the box had disappeared and Berk returned empty-handed.

The slick-looking associate, smoking a cigarette, leaned against a lamppost at the ramp to the pier. "Where is it?"

The husky brute could hardly raise his head. "I lost him."

Erol walked over to get in his associate's face. "What?! You idiot! How could you lose the boy? Do you not know of the bonus we were promised?"

"I said do not call me an idiot!"

Erol flung the half-burned cigarette to the ground. "Never mind—I have an idea. Come with me."

He led his associate up the plank to the booth, where tickets to the Kartina were sold. A young woman was in the booth sorting papers.

"Excuse me, miss," Erol asked. "I just lost a friend of mine and I don't know where to find him. Would you look in your manifest for me and see if there is an address?"

"What was his name, sir?"

"Jamal." He winked at his friend, proud that he overheard the name.

"Does Jamal have a last name?" she asked.

"Yes, of course—are you saying there was more than one Jamal on board?" Erol turned around and closed his eyes, hoping there wasn't.

"You are right, there is only one. Jamal Ramezani. Is that your friend?"

He turned and pretended to examine the name for authenticity. "Yes, that's him."

She looked through the papers. "He does not have an address here, just his home in Tehran; but you probably knew his home address," she said with a smile.

21

"Yes, certainly. But miss, I also think I lost a package on your boat. Could my friend take a look for it? I think it was near the Captain's boat."

"I think that would be all right."

"What did you lose?" Berk asked, looking confused.

Erol hoped to buy some time to look at the address in the ship's manifest. "You know…the *pack-age*."

Berk furrowed his brows for an instant, then caught on. "Oh… the package, sure."

After the woman escorted Berk to the gig, he pretended to be searching for "the package," while Erol read through the manifest. When she and Berk returned empty-handed Erol thanked the woman for her assistance anyway, and gave her a tip for her efforts. He then took the pinched address information and headed back to the National History Museum.

Once there, they found the curator in an alcove scrutinizing some historic documents. Mr. Damec heard their footsteps and glanced up from his work to see the two men empty-handed.

"Where is it?" Mr. Damec asked, with one raised eyebrow.

Erol sighed. "I am not sure. Van Wilpe, still had it—."

"Who?" Mr. Damec asked.

"The German we followed to the Blue Sevan was registered as Van Wilpe. But he does not have it now."

"Where is it then?"

"I don't know how he got it, but it's in the hands of some young guy from Tehran and…*Mashdotz* here lost him." Mr. Damec held back a chuckle. Erol knew that Mr. Damec would understand the irony between Berk and the revered St. Mashdotz.

"Don't blame it on me," challenged Berk, stepping close to Erol for a fight.

"Stop it!" the curator shouted. He looked around the room and gave a pained smile to a customer who overheard him. He leaned over the desk to whisper harshly to them. "Do you have this young man's name?"

"Yes. Jamal Ramezani. I have his address at Tehran University—and this." He presented the ancient knife. "Van Wilpe carried this too. It is one of the things Berk managed to hang on to. Is it worth anything?" Erol hoped the shrewd yet fair Mr. Damec would appraise it high enough to assign a good commission.

The curator pulled out a magnifying glass from the drawer to scrutinize the knife. "Hmmm, interesting—I will have this dated." He paused and tapped the magnifying glass in his hand. "I now remember Van Wilpe, or his associate rather. They cheated me out of a medieval sword last year." Mr. Damec opened a file cabinet and thumbed through it. "Here it is. Van Wilpe is an antique dealer in Germany. There is some background information on him in here." He handed Erol the file. "Do you think you will need this? He may be trouble."

Erol shrugged and glanced at Berk knowingly. "Let's just say we made our point and he didn't argue. You won't hear from him again." Erol knew Mr. Damec was experienced enough in these matters not to delve into the details.

Mr. Damec didn't even blink before answering. "Then I want you two to go to Tehran and find this Jamal Razemani. Do not return without good news."

Erol glanced through the file and noticed something peculiar, but said nothing to his boss.

"How much will we get for this one?" Berk asked.

The curator stared at him sternly. "Do not concern yourself with such trivial things. I will make sure you are duly compensated. Now—get the box! Do I make myself clear?"

"Yes, sir," the two men replied in unison.

CHAPTER 3

GETTING UNDERWAY

Rebecca Belmont's heroics traveled swiftly through Terra Petroleum's exploration office in Houston, and her new position to work under the general manager in Azerbaijan was easily approved. Azerbaijan and Terra Petroleum held a joint venture in developing the oil rich Caspian Sea, where valuable hydrocarbon reserves lay undeveloped. Russia, Kazakhstan, Turkmenistan, and Iran were also in competition for oil and gas exploration, causing territorial disputes. Most conflicts were resolved through politics, but recent physical confrontations had presented Terra with setbacks. It would be up to savvy and resourceful individuals, such as Rebecca, to conduct productive field research and at the same time avoid territorial disputes.

Weeks later, Rebecca stared mechanically out the window as the Airbus 310 finished the last leg of a long, bumpy flight from Prague to the Azerbaijan Airport in Baku. When the jet landed, the lean, athletic young woman eagerly jumped up, grabbed her daypack, and jogged down to the baggage terminal. She wiped the sweat from her face with a scarf and mused at the contrast of temperature between chilly Prague and sultry Baku.

While waiting for her belongings, Rebecca stretched out: reaching high, touching her toes, twisting around. When the luggage arrived, she grabbed her father's old military duffle bag and hoisted it up to her shoulder, then proceeded to the nearest window to buy the additional business visa required for Azerbaijan. With her visa in hand, she left the terminal and flagged down an old Russian taxi that was no doubt left over from the Soviet occupation era. Rebecca quickly scanned the cab's insides for cleanliness to gauge whether the vehicle met her standards of respectability. In her mind, cleanliness indicated reliability. With her approval she gave the driver her destination, then opened the windows to compensate for the humidity.

As Rebecca leaned out of the cab to let the wind cool her down, the driver rambled on about the ancient minarets and medieval palaces and their historical significance in Baku. The driver looked in the rearview mirror. "I see you are a woman of knowledge. Maybe you would like to see the sites of ancient history. On the Apsheron peninsula there are the famous cup marks, sacrificial holes, and burial sites. We even have ancient grooves known as the cart ruts, which are etched into the land and down to the sea to where some say was an ancient city."

"I'll keep that in mind," she replied, half-listening.

"You must see the Maiden's Tower," the driver advised. "It got its name from the legend of a girl who threw herself off the tower because of an unfortunate love."

"Thank you, I'll remember that too," said Rebecca. She tried to listen politely to his knowledgeable commentary of Moresque, Gothic, and Baroque architecture, but her mind wandered to thoughts of her new job on the open water. It would be a big step in her career and she hoped she was making the right move. After the breakup with her fiancé, this was about as far away from Texas as she could go and get paid for it.

When Rebecca arrived at the port of Baku there was a cool easterly breeze blowing into the harbor. She sat in the cab a moment and examined the majestic research ship which was to be her new home for the next several weeks. Above the pier, the crew brought food stores onto the 275-foot-long, 3500-ton ship called the *Bering*. It was deep red from the main deck down and pearl white up to the superstructure. A large, A-framed crane was mounted at the aft end of the ship for use in lifting the underwater vehicles. The ship carried all the latest electronic equipment needed for precise evaluation of the seafloor and the geology below the seafloor. Workmen looked like a line of ants as they carried boxes of food to the ship.

Rebecca stepped out of the taxi and adjusted her ponytail to stick through the back of a California Angel's baseball cap. She unzipped her travel purse and paid the driver the few thousand mantas they had negotiated on. The man opened the trunk of the car and helped her load her canvas bag onto her shoulder. Rebecca thanked the driver, then waited for a space between the workers to go up the ramp. She saw a man with a cowboy hat at the top of the ramp dutifully checking off the items on his clipboard and assumed he was in charge.

The cab driver tapped her on the shoulder and Rebecca turned around. "Miss? Here is my card if you wish to have a guided tour."

She smiled politely. "You're very kind. Thanks again," she looked down at the card, "Dimitri. I'll call you if I decide to see the sights." Dimitri bowed slightly and got back in his car.

Rebecca found a gap in the line of workers and proceeded to climb the ramp. When she reached the top, she dropped her bag and saluted. "Permission to come aboard?" she stated playfully to the man checking the shipboard stores.

The man was tall and muscular, a few years her senior, wearing a sleeveless T-shirt, cutoff-jeans, and hiking boots. He quickly scanned her red, zip-neck polo shirt and tight blue jeans, then extended his hand. "I'm Tony Hansen. Permission granted, darlin'," he replied in a Texas accent. "Nice to have you aboard. You're the prettiest thing I've seen all day," he added with a handsome grin.

Rebecca Belmont smiled sweetly and shook his hand. She handed him a letter from Houston and looked around as he skimmed it quickly.

"Let's see…Rebecca Belmont. Where are you from, Rebecca?"

"Most people call me Becca."

"OK, Becca, where are you from?"

"Mecca, California."

He leaned forward. "No foolin'? Becca, from Mecca?" She nodded slowly. "Ha!" he smirked.

Rebecca smiled painfully but said nothing. She could usually size up a person based on his or her response when she mentioned her hometown. Rebecca determined the muscular man could be self-centered. She kept up her guard. Then again, she still had some residual anger directed at men in general, which she had promised herself to work out.

A look of recognition came over Tony. "Hey, wait a minute. I think I saw you in the Olympic trials…for running or something."

"It was the heptathlon, but I didn't make it." She looked down and patted her knee. "I had to have a little surgery."

"Oh. Tough break. Are you OK?"

"Yeah, it's as good as new. So where do I put my bags, I'm anxious to get started."

Tony stuck the letter to his clipboard. "Glad to hear it. Well Becca, Bob McCray has been expecting you. Follow me and I'll take you to his cabin." He laid the clipboard on her duffle bag and picked it up. "Watch your head," he cautioned, unnecessarily pressing her head down through the door hatch, like a cop helping a suspect into a squad car. Tony led her through a series of hatches and passageways and up some ladders toward Robert McCray's stateroom. Rebecca felt several male eyes staring at her as she followed Tony. Other than a robust Azeri woman in the galley in charge of food preparation, Rebecca was the only female on board.

"This is a beautiful ship. It seems a little big to conduct only scans of the seafloor. What else will the ship be used for?"

"I just take orders. You'll have to ask Doc about that."

"It reminds me of the ship *Atlantis*...from the Wood's Hole Oceanographic Institute."

"You have a good eye, Becca. The Russians couldn't be outdone, so they came up with a research ship a lot like the Atlantis. We were lucky enough to lease her for half the price of the American counterpart." He stopped briefly in the passage. "It *is* Miss, isn't it?"

"Yes, it is." Rebecca didn't have to ask why he inquired. She was old enough to determine his intentions. "So where did they get the name *Bering?*"

Tony continued walking. "Vitus Bering was some fancy explorer who was commissioned by Peter the Great to lead an expedition to determine whether there was a land bridge between Russia and America. You've heard of the Bering Straits?" Tony didn't wait for her answer. "Well, there ya go. Yeah, it was in 1728 when Bering became a big hero and discovered that Asia and America were separate continents. They say that as 'Columbus tied together the world to the west, Bering tied it together to the east.'"

Rebecca was impressed. "Are you required to learn this information?"

"Nah. When I get bored in the cafeteria, I just read the historical plaques up on the bulkheads."

"Have you been with Dr. McCray long?" she asked, wondering about his role aboard the ship.

"Oh, yeah. Me and the Doc go way back. He got educated in London, but we grew up in the same Texan town. He knew I could fix just about anything, which is why I'm here now." Tony glanced back over his shoulder to catch a glimpse of cleavage from her v-neck T-shirt as they went up some steps. "Ya know, if you get lonely out here—bein' so far away from home and all—I'm always available."

She caught his roaming eyes. "Thank you," she replied politely.

"No problem; I aim to please."

"Hmmm, I bet you do," she said, under her breath.

They finally reached the staterooms near the captain's cabin and Tony knocked two slow taps, followed by three fast, and then two more slow ones. They waited a moment and heard a muffled curse word.

"Come in!" A hoarse voice called out from within.

"Sorry to wake you, Doc, but you asked me to get ya when your assistant came aboard. This is Rebecca Belmont. She goes by Becca."

Dr. McCray, Terra Petroleum's most respected field geoscientist, sat at the edge of his bunk. He combed his fingers through his dark hair—cut short, military style. He looked ruddy and powerful, with a barrel chest filling his forest green T-shirt. She sized up the room while her new boss rubbed his eyes to adjust to the light. A copy of Shackleton's Antarctic Expedition lay on his impeccably clean desk, a pad and pencil to the side. The rest of the room was spotless.

"I was about to give up on you." He put up his hand to his mouth to stifle a yawn then stood up and reached out to shake her hand.

Rebecca tried to reciprocate a firm handshake.

"I expected you yesterday."

Within the last few days, Dr. McCray had managed little time to sleep in order to prepare for the voyage. He was a sturdy man of forty-two, who liked his routine of a jigger of whiskey before bed followed by a typical seven-hour slumber.

"I'm sorry, sir. My flight was delayed in Prague."

He waved her off. "No problem, two hour's sleep in three days is better than none. So you have come to take over the administrative tasks Houston thinks I can't handle? Maybe do some wirelog interpretations?"

"Yes, sir."

"Well, I hope you are up for it."

She detected a bit of skepticism in his voice. "I'll do my best, Dr. McCray."

"Tony will show you to your quarters and we will talk later on the bridge...say 1300? That's one o'clock."

Rebecca nodded and stepped outside in the passageway. The door was cracked open and she pretended she couldn't hear them whispering.

Robert McCray grabbed Tony by the arm. "*She* is my new assistant?"

She could feel Tony's eyes checking her out. "She's a beaut, ain't she? Fragrant and full bodied, like a good whiskey."

"You mean, like a good wine," corrected McCray.

Tony clicked through the side of his mouth and winked. "That'll do too—But she's My-T-Fine."

Dr. McCray shook his head. "She'd better have more to her than good looks and perfume. We don't need distractions on the ship."

"Speak for yourself, Doc."

Tony exited Dr. McCray's quarters and escorted Rebecca to her room. He pointed to a layout of the ship on the bulkhead so she could find her way about. She quickly examined her new home away from home. The air conditioning was not working properly and a fan hung in the corner of her room, which helped only to move the humidity from one wall to the other. There was a small porthole that shone light on the calming color of light green walls. Below the porthole were two bunks with traditional cotton mattresses and at the opposite wall stood metal storage lockers. Luckily for Rebecca, she had plenty of space and a private shower.

Rebecca knew that Tony wanted to stay and chat, but she gracefully got rid of him so she could unpack her things. Rebecca loved the open water and hoped Tony wouldn't be a pest during the voyage, like so many of the wild and crazy oil workers she had met in Texas. She was determined that being a female wasn't going to be an issue. Rebecca had been a traveler ever since she could remember. Being towed behind her parents when they went on Christian mission trips had had a notable impact on her. Living in other countries had given her the taste of varied cultures and a desire to learn and understand their beliefs and lifestyles. Although Rebecca held close to her faith, she usually didn't advertise her beliefs.

Jet lag was setting in, so she lay down on her bunk for a cat nap before the meeting. Every few seconds, the fan blade above her would lightly tap the side of the metal housing in a rhythm that put her to sleep. Waking to the sounds of engines revving, Rebecca jumped up and looked out the porthole to see the ship starting to move away from the pier. She glanced at the marine clock on the wall to see the little hand at the 1300 mark and the big hand at 1305 and realized she was late. After scanning the layout map of the ship on the bulkhead, Rebecca opened the cabin door half expecting to see Tony still in the passageway. With no one around, she turned right and followed the map now engrained in her mind. Confidently opening hatches and skipping up ladders to the main deck, she eventually sighted the bridge.

Inside, Dr. McCray and his men were going over protocol for operating equipment when he caught sight of Rebecca stepping quietly into the room.

"Here she is now," said McCray with a nod. The other men turned around to see their newest staff member and each raised a hand as they were introduced. "Rebecca Belmont, I'd like to introduce you to my support team: John Schmitt-geophysics, the best-looking man here and a sharp mind to go with it; Chuck Gohn-engineering, largely trustworthy, just like his belly." The men chuckled. "Rick Klocke-computers, a lean not-so-mean thinking machine; Joe Hanak, our friendly and dependable master diver; Yakov Comaneci-Underwater Submersible, he's cousin to the famous gymnast; and you've met Tony, our repair technician. Oh, and Captain Vladimir Kovacheski will be piloting the ship." The men nodded as they were addressed and she reciprocated. "Not present are some marine technicians and several Azeris to help with food and general shipboard duties. You can meet them later. We were just discussing the survey plan when we reach the Guneshli field. Terra wants us to investigate this area here." He pointed to a seafloor topographical map that was selected to conduct a shallow hazard survey sixty miles east of the port. "We will study this shallow area, then go farther and deeper using some high-resolution imaging of the subsurface. Are you familiar with this type of survey, Ms. Belmont?" Dr. McCray posed.

Rebecca assumed he was trying to test her knowledge of the equipment. "Yes, sir."

"Please…call me Doctor, Mr. McCray, or even Bob, but when you call me sir I think of my old man. As you were saying, Ms. Belmont?"

"Well, sir, I mean Dr. McCray, I am familiar with most bathymetric sonar systems and acoustic Doppler profilers as well as quantitative modeling to evaluate the migration and accumulation of hydrocarbons. Additionally, I've had many hours with the Cyclo-Log mathematical software designed for geological interpretation of wireline logs, and particularly for stratigraphic analysis of log data. I see by our equipment we're using the 9C-3D and capable of the 4-D technology. I'm assuming that the shallow hazard survey requirements down to a thousand feet will be the standard: accurate navigation, a dense survey grid, side scans, and MCS (multi-channel seismic) imaging of the subsurface."[1]

She gave a few more detailed descriptions of the equipment in question, not only with accuracy but with boldness and confidence. Men who thought of her only as cute were soon enlightened when she spilled out information from her uncanny memory.

Tony whispered to his boss. "She's got tongue enough for ten rows of teeth, Doc."

Bob McCray, both an exploration geologist and geophysicist (or explorationist) was quiet for a moment as he scratched his unshaven chin.

"I read that you graduated at MIT with honors, with two undergraduate degrees from MIT in ocean engineering and computer science, and earned a master's degree in ocean systems

---

1 The survey is looking for the types of formations associated with traps for oil and gas accumulation. Shallow hazard surveys cover a smaller area looking for things that might interfere with drilling activity or development activity. This would include things like shipwrecks, reefs, old bombs and mines, and other archaeological sites. Surveys also evaluate hazards that could be just below the sea floor, like reefs or shallow gas accumulations.

management." As she smiled proudly, he leaned on the table with both hands and drummed his fingers slowly. "Most of these men also have equal or greater academic credentials. The real test is how you conduct yourself in the field."

Rebecca caught the men's snickers. *I hope he doesn't doubt me because I'm a woman. I've proven myself in Houston and everywhere else the company has sent me.* She wasn't afraid to speak up, but she knew that humility was something she constantly had to wrestle with and wouldn't let a little thing like this get to her. Rebecca had worked hard…twice as hard as her other colleagues. Her father always said that to achieve great things, she had to "labor above the best."

It was common knowledge that Bob McCray didn't like to waste time letting people expound their wisdom. His motto was "Speak short and sweet—surplus is swill."

"I was told you were an expert data analyst and you coordinated a good team on the Gulf surveys associated with the Geronimo Field. I don't expect you to disappoint me."

"I won't, si—Dr. McCray. The Gulf survey was a very rewarding experience. I know it is not associated with this type of survey boat work, but I'm sure I can use here what I have learned from there."

"We also have an ROV and AUV on board…the remote and autonomous underwater vehicles. Are you familiar with them as well?"

"I spent a little time with them, Dr. McCray." She cut her response, so as not to espouse any more knowledge unless he asked.

"Good." McCray turned to the crew and looked at his watch. "We'll be casting off for the Guneshli field in an hour to lay out the hydrophone array. We'll start with the two dimensional seismic survey and see what we come up with. Spending half a million bucks per square kilometer on 3-D at this point would just be frivolous. So unless there is anything else, you're excused." As the men dispersed, he caught Rebecca before she left. "Belmont, I want you to stay with the captain and call me when we near our first survey site…Vladimir knows the coordinates. I'm going to my cabin to look over a few charts. Oh, and forget the perfume, we're not at a dance." He raised an eyebrow, then stepped through the hatch.

"Yes, Mr. McCray," she replied, to his back. *I didn't like that scent anyway.*

Moments later, the room emptied and Rebecca and the captain were left alone. She peered through the window toward the prow of the ship where Tony stood inspecting some diving equipment, his blond hair blowing in the wind. He took off his shirt and tucked it in the back of his pants, then caught sight of her. Tony plastered a Cheshire grin on his face and flexed his muscles briefly, then laughed while he returned to rearranging some equipment on deck.

Rebecca groaned. *Yep, he's the self-centered type all right.*

CHAPTER 4

DATE WITH A CRIMINAL

E rol and Berk took the first flight they could to Tehran since learning Jamal Razemani attended the University of Tehran. When they arrived at the university, they strode under the main archway, through a beautiful garden, and up to the administration office. A fat young man was entering some data into the computer at the front desk. They inquired about Jamal under the auspice that they had a nephew in Armenia who was thinking of attending the university.

"I know Jamal," said the young man. "He lives in the dormitories, but you just missed him. Jamal went to make an appointment with Dr. Witherspoon. His office is in the Department of Archaeology."

"Where is the Department of Archaeology?" asked Erol.

The young man gave him a layout of the campus and circled the destination. Erol thanked him and walked a few paces. He turned to his compatriot, then pulled out the file that Mr. Damec gave him. A sly grin crept up his face.

"Berk, you would not believe what I have just learned."

"What is it?"

"There is a woman named Mary in Dr. Witherspoon's office."

"Yeah. What about her?"

35

"Let's just say that the world of archaeology is smaller than I thought."

Erol divulged his plan on the way to Dr. Witherspoon's office. When they entered the office a woman about forty with a plain headscarf was typing on the computer. Erol smiled, and she reciprocated.

"Hello, my name is Erol, and you are…"

She looked up from her work. "I am the administrative assistant of Dr. Witherspoon, Mary."

Erol glanced back at Berk to wink, then focused his attention on Mary. "I am looking for a Jamal Razemani. My nephew is applying for placement and I thought Jamal might be able to help him."

"I spoke to Jamal not five minutes ago. He will be back in a week for an appointment with the professor. You may be able to catch up with him."

Berk trotted to the door and left the room. Erol sat on her desk like he was at home. The suave Armenian tapped on a photo at the corner of her desk. "Is this your boss?" He pointed to a picture of a spry, studious man, in his sixties, hair somewhat disheveled.

The secretary stopped examining some papers and lowered her reading glasses. "Yes, that is Dr. Witherspoon." She smiled meekly at Erol then started to type something on the computer.

Berk came back in and Erol turned around to see Berk shaking his head in disappointment.

Erol reexamined the photo. "Look's like a nice guy. So Mary…" He said with an inviting smile.

The assistant looked up from her work. "That is a beautiful name. How is it that someone as lovely as you spends all her time in a stuffy place such as this?"

Berk had plopped down on a couch, rolled his eyes, and found a magazine to occupy himself with.

Mary blushed, squirmed slightly, then adjusted her glasses and the drab hijab over her head. "No one has ever called me lovely." She straightened up. "Is there anything else I can do for you? Would you like me to tell Jamal Razemani you were here?"

"No, no, that would not be necessary. I better talk to my nephew before I try to use Jamal's influence to get him into the university." He rested his hands on her desk and leaned over assertively. "But there is something you could do to help…have dinner with me." He had seen she had no wedding ring on her finger, but even if she had he would have tried anyway.

She put her hand on her chest. "You do not mean it."

"Yes, I do. I see something about you that begs me to learn more of." Erol saw her glance at his custom suit and expensive gold watch and calculated he had her.

She looked around to see if any of the staff saw them. "I do not even know you."

But he knew her type: starved for attention; a dreary, monotonous academic routine. Erol stood back and put his hands on his hips, waiting, with a wry smile for the inevitable.

"I guess I could have lunch near the university," she finally responded. "That would be respectable." Erol's smile broadened. He arranged to meet with her the next day at a café near the university.

Erol thanked her and in the proceeding hours weaved out a strategy to get information. The next day, lunch went as well as could be expected. He fostered her trust with pleasant conversation and she surprised him by revealing much about her life. As they talked, she gave out private information about; how she was orphaned at a young age when her parents died in an auto accident, and that she had not seen her husband in over two years. She seemed relieved and open to talk of her past, which was exactly what Erol had in mind. Erol let her speak freely and with candor, yet he kept his own past concealed. He thought it would indicate to her that he was a good listener.

Mary even commented on it. "Most men only want to talk about themselves. Thank you for letting me speak."

"It is nothing," replied Erol. He wore a humble façade and continued with his favorite strategy—flattery. "Why would I not let a beautiful woman speak?" Then, as he predicted, he asked her to dinner and she accepted.

When Mary got home from the university, she hurried to get ready for her date. She put on just enough makeup not to cause attention, with a dash of her favorite Al Shams perfume. Her stomach churned with excitement. It had been a long while since a man even looked at her with interest; and at forty she knew time was not on her side. She was gifted with a shapely body and wasn't about to waste it when an opportunity presented itself. Mary stood back from the mirror and smoothed the sides of her snug and flimsy pink pastel smock.

"I am glad this is Tehran. The police would not have approved of this outside the city," she informed the image in the mirror.

She started to look for her plain hijab, worn every day to the university, but instead changed her mind and put on a translucent blue headscarf with white cherry blossoms. The university secretary looked at her ordinary face in the mirror, then playfully stuck out her tongue and opted to add a little more red lipstick.

Mary was turning from side to side in front of the mirror to evaluate herself when she heard three quick knocks on the door. Peeking through a slot, she saw it was her date. "Am I up for this? I do not even know him, and technically, I am still married," she muttered under her breath. But something propelled her to continue. "Oh, but to be looked upon with desire from a man!"

She put on a white manteau cloak with a waist-high slit, and then opened the door. On the stoop was her date, with his gelled black hair, combed from front to back, and wearing an impressive dark blue, double-breasted Armani suit.

Erol stepped back to take in her striking figure and the pleasant addition of makeup. "My, my, you are as lovely as these flowers." He gave a quick scan of her dress and handed her a bouquet of red roses. "And the scent of an angel."

Mary bowed modestly and placed one hand on her heart. "Thank you, but I really am nothing compared to those beautiful roses." She sniffed their aroma and walked back to the kitchen to find a vase.

"I disagree; you will indeed make men look twice. Aren't you afraid of the 'social morality' police I have heard so much about? That headscarf alone might draw attention. In fact, I heard of a public flogging just last week."

She giggled. "Maybe the Lebas Shakhs-iha vigilante paramilitary will use a squad to arrest me for my dashing hijab?" She paused. "Sometimes we must live dangerously," she replied theatrically, brushing back some of the exposed locks from her forehead.

"Ha!" He handed her the flowers. "A woman after my own heart," he said with a sly grin. He glanced inside the small apartment. "You live alone?"

She filled a vase with water and adjusted the flowers. "Yes. Why do you ask?"

"It would seem that a lovely woman as yourself would have a roommate...." She eyed him for an instant. "Or you might have family?"

"Actually, I have a twelve-year-old daughter named Goli. She lives at the blind school most of the year." She waited for his response, but he beheld a poker-faced expression and said nothing. "Does that bother you?"

"Why should that bother me? Did you think I would run away, Mary?" He didn't wait for an answer. "Are you ready to go?"

Mary relaxed with a smile. "Yes, let me get my bag." She picked up her purse and put her keys inside, then followed him to his rented Mercedes. He opened the door for her and trotted around to the driver's side. Soon they wound their way through the evening streets of Tehran to the Shar restaurant. There, they were seated in one of the terraces with a hint of a breeze that seemed to magically change the smoggy city into an enchanted metropolis.

Mary put her hand to her chest and dropped her mouth as she looked around. "This restaurant is beautiful!"

Erol put a napkin on his lap. "I like to treat myself to nice things. I'm sure you would agree?" Mary gave a shy yet impish nod.

Mary was served chicken with small, red, sour berries called *zeresh*, and eggplant stuffed with ground lamb and raisins. Erol had the traditional beef kabob. The surroundings were exquisite, the food wonderful, and like his meal, Erol routinely peppered Mary with flattery. She didn't mind one bit.

The Armenian impressed Mary. "Your Farsi is very good. Have you ever lived in Iran?"

"Thank you. I know a few languages. It helps in my travels. And no, I have not had the fortune to reside here." Erol gracefully steered the topic back to her work. "Please tell me more about your work. Is it a good or bad job?"

"I love my job. Professor Witherspoon has been the kindest man I have ever worked for."

"He sounds like a good man." Erol glanced at a keyring with several keys in her purse. "You must be a responsible person. I noticed you carry quite a set of keys. Why do you need so many?"

Mary pulled them out of her purse and highlighted them one by one. "This is to my office—I mean Professor Witherspoon's office; this one is to the storage room; this is to the toilet room"—she giggled "and this one is to where artifacts are stored."

His eyebrows rose. "Artifacts?"

"Yes, the items retrieved from archaeological excavations."

"Ah," he nodded. "Tell me more about these excavations. Do you go on these?"

She chuckled. "No, of course not. I help the professor with administrative tasks: communicating with other adjunct professors or colleagues in the field, sending off documents, coordinating inventory of artifacts, that sort of thing."

"I see we have some things in common. I am fascinated with history! I am a buyer of antiquities and am always looking for new relics. I believe it helps us link the past with the present to help us better understand ourselves."

Mary sat back. "That is very true." She sipped on her pomegranate tea. "I did not know you were interested in history. That is why you travel?"

"Yes. I buy and sell ancient wares…but I am more interested in displaying them to mankind than in making millions of rials."

She rested her chin on her hand and leaned forward. "My husband had only wanted money and prestige, and had little time for the more cultured ways of thinking. He was always off on some adventure that required me to stay home...." Mary gulped and dropped her head.

Erol tried to peek under to see her face. "Thank you for being so open with me. I promise I will keep your statement confidential." Mary looked up, smiled weakly, and sighed. She had wanted to get that off her chest for a long time and was glad he was the one she had confided in.

After dinner, Erol brought her back to her apartment and kissed her hand. He didn't push himself on her but did ask her out again. The weekend was approaching and she accepted the offer.

The next days were progressing as Erol had predicted. He took her to the People's Parks, the Bazaars, the Zoo, and just simple walks together and she would mention some of the activities back at the university. She divulged that a box contained a parchment that was very unusual and that the writings were of unknown origin. This was a great encouragement to Erol.

Erol had his associate Berk conduct a background check on Mary's life for even greater leverage. Berk had heard university gossip that she would not admit her marriage was a failure, even though her elusive husband was considered to have abandoned her. Erol hoped that he could use her husband's years of vacancy as a tool to fill the gap.

The whirlwind romance had taken hold when he took advantage of one particular evening. After a wonderful day together, Mary opened the door to her apartment and he reached around the small of her back and slowly pulled her close. His close-cropped beard was inches from her smooth perfume-scented face. Her body tensed. Erol assumed that it had been a long time since she had been with a man and hoped that she would welcome the sign of affection. He pressed his lips to hers and she received his passionate kiss willingly.

Mary pulled slowly away. "Would you like to stay awhile, Erol?"

"You know, rumors in the neighborhood would most certainly get around," he warned.

She pulled him close and shut the door. "I don't care."

Erol left the next morning, but arranged to have lunch with her. At noon they met at the café and Mary was in a joyous mood. She mentioned that Dr. Witherspoon was in the process of analyzing the puzzle box that Jamal had found. Before Mary continued, she passed a package across the table to Erol. "What is this?" asked Erol picking up the small rectangular gift.

"Something my father gave me, just before he passed away."

Erol opened the package. It was a shiny gold butane lighter. "This is beautiful." Erol clicked open the top and flicked the flintwheel. The flame popped up at the first strike. He brought his gaze back to Mary. "I could not take this. It is too expensive."

Erol started to hand it back but Mary closed his fingers over the lighter. "No. I want you to have it. It will not do me any good gathering dust at home. It matches the golden cross on your neck."

Erol pulled out the crucifix and held it next to the lighter. "So it does," he admired. Erol took her hand and kissed it. "Thank you, my dear. I will think of you every time I use it."

"I was hoping you would, Erol."

Erol tucked it in his breast pocket and patted it for safe keeping. "Speaking of precious gifts, Mary, has your professor friend determined the age of the ancient box and the parchment?"

"Not yet, but the professor seems to think it is very valuable. He speculates that the parchment is at least five thousand years old."

Erol was amazed. "Over five thousand years old? This is something that will have to be shown to the world. Why does your professor hide it in the university?"

She shifted awkwardly. "There *is* procedure, and I do not think we should discredit the professor's methods. They still have to determine the authenticity of them."

"Or are they trying to hide something?"

Mary's face drooped slightly; her eyes looked down to her lap. "Dr. Witherspoon is a good man."

Erol pulled back to surrender. "I didn't say he wasn't. But if this is as important as I think it is, he cannot keep it hidden. I guess I cannot blame you if the department wants to keep it to itself. They are there to make money, and seeing only the aesthetic value to mankind can be a weakness of mine." He had used these lines a thousand times. A businessman would only laugh, but it always seemed to connect well with academics.

"No, I agree with you. I want others to know of this too. Tell me what I should do."

Erol hid a wicked micro-smile while he slowly sipped his tea. Setting his cup down, he presented his logic. "It is simple. When you are in a room while the professor is working with a colleague, stay in the room and listen a few minutes longer…the information you give me will be confidential, I assure you. I will then speak to my associates as to the best course of action." Erol's cell phone chirped a brief Tchaikovsky ballad. "Excuse me, my dear."

Erol gave her a wink then stepped into the lobby to answer the phone. "Yes?"

"It's me—Berk."

"Well, what is it? I am busy," he replied curtly.

"I haven't been able to get the box. The kid must have taken it out of the dormitory and put it somewhere else. Mr. Damec is getting tired of waiting. He says the knife you gave him is very old and suspects the same for the box. What should I tell him?"

"Have you not found out anything about Ramezani and Witherspoon?"

Berk lit up. "Yes! I bribed a man in the archaeology department, and he said that a small chip from the box was sent outside the country to determine if it was authentic. From what he said, they also found some sort of old writings inside."

"I have learned of the parchment too. Have you told Mr. Damec of this yet?"

"No, I was waiting to tell you first."

"Perhaps you aren't such an idiot after all, Berk. I already have a plan and will tell Mr. Damec of it soon." Erol suspected that Berk would only get in the way at this point and worried he may even expose himself. "You have done all you can do, Berk There is no need for you to stay on here. Go back to Yerevan. I will call you if I need you."

Erol hung up and went back to the table where Mary waited. "Business?" Mary inquired.

He nodded. "Yes. My associates never seem to be able to do anything without my approval. It would only bore you. Now what were you saying, my dear?"

Mary told Erol that she respected his vision of gifting the world with ancient discoveries and would help him in anyway she could. He flattered her for her higher standards…and her dazzling figure, for good measure. Things were proceeding as the Armenian expected. If Mr. Damec considered the knife ancient, so too should the box. And the more ancient it was, the more expensive it would be. Erol was eager to learn more about the parchment as well. If it was a gospel to a primitive religion, or a description of an ancient culture, it would only make the artifact that much more valuable.

The following day was not as Erol had expected. Mary called and said that she had received a call from the police in Armenia. Her voice cracked as she made clear that it was important they talk. Erol hung up the phone and worried that somehow the Yerevan police might have revealed his past to her. He wondered if the charade was up, and all his hard work wasted. They agreed to meet at a local coffee house on Vali-e-Asr Avenue by the National Museum of Iran.

When he arrived at the coffee house, he saw Mary sitting at a table alone. Erol looked around to see if he was being followed, then sat down. Mary glanced up to acknowledge him but looked back down at the table quiet and somber. Erol carefully watched her for a moment to determine if his schemes were detected.

Then without warning she dropped her head into her hands and started to cry.

For the first time, Erol felt a genuine concern. "What is it, Mary?"

"I just got word my husband was killed," she cried out through bitter tears.

Erol thought back to the file that Mr. Damec had given him. He had known all along that Mary was married to Van Wilpe, the German. But now the truth was out. *She is to confront me on this. Should I leave? She may be angry with me. Be patient, Erol.*

Erol played it cool and handed her a handkerchief. "How did he die?"

"He drowned in Lake Sevan, Armenia."

"What did you say your husband's name was?" he asked for confirmation of what he knew.

She paused and dabbed her eyes. "Johan. Johan Van Wilpe."

He blinked slowly. "Van Wilpe?"

"Yes. Did you know of him?"

Erol fidgeted in his seat. "Um, no. However, I have passed through Lake Sevan many times and I may have seen him." *She doesn't know of my involvement in Van Wilpe's death, but does anyone else know?* "What else did the police say?"

She looked down through the table to distant memories. "Actually, I was told he was murdered—stabbed! The police said a fisherman found him floating in the water." She shook her head in disbelief. "Why would someone want to kill *him*?"

Erol's heart thumped faster. "I do not know, but it must have been awful to die like that. Do they have any leads?"

"No. They said there was little evidence, but would continue to pursue the case." She grunted with irritation. "It does not matter. He was always up to bad dealings. I knew Johan would end up dead some day."

Erol breathed easy, but kept up a sympathetic appearance. He reached out to squeeze her hand gently. "Did you have feelings for him?" Mary looked longingly at her new friend. Erol could only surmise that she didn't care for her deceased husband, since she was dating a new man.

"We have not seen each other in years…he left me." She paused.

Erol tried to anticipate what she might be thinking. *Could she trust me to take her husband's place? How desperate is she to let another man into her life? She's got to be thinking of her blind kid, Goli, and if I could support them?* He stayed silent, pretending to be empathetic.

"Thank you for listening to me."

On the one hand, Erol felt estatic that he had her trust and determined he could continue to use the opportunity to deceive her with his charm. On the other hand, Erol felt awkward with Mary. He had cultivated a relationship with the woman who was married to the same man he commanded Berk to kill. This world of archaeology and antiques really is a small one.

After their talk at the coffee shop, they took a walk together at the park. She rested her head on his shoulder and talked about mindless superficialities. The death of Mary's husband was thera-peutic for her. She seemed much more relaxed and free to express her feelings toward Erol. He had nurtured their relationship with a habit of entertaining her to dinners and more intimate acquies-cence, and Erol was confident he could continue to manage the charade.

Ultimately, Erol's "research" had finally paid off when he re-ceived a photocopy from Mary of the parchment. She told Erol that she overheard the professor confirm that the parchment had combined pictographs, hieroglyphs, and a phonetic alphabet and that it was not five thousand, but over seven thousand years old. Erol kept a calm exterior as he held the parchment replica, but inside he was ecstatic. Mary also stated that Dr. Witherspoon and Jamal had a breakthrough on deciphering the ancient language. The Armenian's pleasure was running high until she added that the university was expected to let the public know of the findings at the end of the week. This was sobering news to say the least.

Erol found a reason to excuse himself and wasted no time calling up the curator of the National History Museum in Yerevan. "Mr. Damec?"

"Yes, Mr. Chenian?"

"I have some good news for you."

"I hope you're going to tell me my money isn't being wasted on your 'vacation' in Iran."

"Do not worry about me spending your money, this could be worth millions!" Erol calmed himself and glanced around. "Are you alone, sir?"

"I am. What is it?"

"Berk must have told you by now about the parchment inside the box with an unknown language."

"Yes, he mentioned it. I am glad to hear it verified by your mouth."

"My source tells me that the parchment and box are over seven thousand years old."

"Why is this parchment so special?"

"Because a professor Witherspoon has deciphered much of it and he has determined that it is from an unknown language."

"Is this true?"

Erol cradled the phone with his shoulder and looked at his watch. "Yes, sir, I guarantee it. Mary—I mean my source—is impeccable. And although this Dr. Witherspoon has already deciphered much of the parchment, he is about to go public with it. I am told the professor is to have a celebration in a few days and then present the artifacts to the press. If we don't retrieve the objects from him soon, it will be too late."

"Then we shouldn't wait any longer. Do what you must, but remember, if you are sloppy and get caught I will not have anything to do with you."

"Yes, sir, I agree. I will grab the disk of the deciphered parchment and the box while they are at the party. But won't the professor make quite a stink about the theft?"

"Don't worry. I will take care of it. Just get me the artifacts."

"Yes, sir. I will call you once I have them."

Erol hung up and looked at his watch again. *Dr. Witherspoon mustn't be the first to let the public know. Mary said they were about to announce the news of the box to the press this Friday.* He laughed to himself. *But knowing Mr. Damec, I suspect they may have an unfortunate delay.*

CHAPTER 5

FRAMED

With the first set of writings deciphered, Dr. Harold Witherspoon asked permission from the president of the university to release their findings to the media. President Massoud Yassin questioned the professor about the confidence of his findings before exposing the university to worldwide critique. Dr. Witherspoon was undaunted. He virtually guaranteed Yassin that it would bring credibility to the Department of Archaeology and raise Tehran University to a respected position in academia; something like this comes along only once a century. Yassin enthusiastically gave his approval.

The professor invited Mary, Jamal, and the associates who worked in the Tigris site excavations to celebrate the recent advancements. That evening, his guests mingled snuggly about in the modest contemporary Iranian home, discussing archaeology, punctuated with the typical spirited political conversation. Jamal took advantage of the professor's British citizenship to play reggae music.

Mary set out plenty of rice, and a thick stew of poultry with ground walnuts and pomegranate syrup, known as *khoresht*. Also on hand were flat, thin, circular breads known as *lavash* and dishes of caviar fresh from the Caspian sea. Side dishes of soup and salad filled out the meal. For dessert they had their choice of Iranian ice cream flavored with saffron, rosewater, and nuts, or fruit slices, but most ate both. The guests devoured Mary's food with considerable pleasure.

Toward the end of the joyous festivity, Dr. Witherspoon espoused his gratitude to all his colleagues for their participation in what he believed would bring notable standing to the university. It was late when the guests left his home, leaving Dr. Witherspoon, Mary, and Jamal alone. Mary adjusted her headscarf and picked up her purse.

The professor walked her to the door. "Thank you, Mary, for putting up with me in the last few months. These latest discoveries have made me tense. I hope I haven't been too hard on you."

"You have been nothing but kind to me, Professor. I am glad that you will show the world your discoveries."

"Indeed we will," said the professor.

Mary put her hand to her chest and spoke confidentially. "And they liked my cooking, Professor."

"I believe you may have a calling in another profession, my dear."

He waved to Mary as she walked happily through the courtyard and down his walkway. The only guest left was Jamal, who sat on the couch, cradling the ancient box. He studied his student, who reminded him of himself decades earlier.

Dr. Witherspoon sat down next to him, eyed the box and shook his head. "I am proud of you, son. You have proved to be a worthy student and we have come far in this project. Moreover, I am proud of your decision to continue with your doctorate studies in history. But I must admonish you for carrying around an antiquity outside the university. You cannot think of it as your own. It is too easy to be consumed by a project and let it become the main focus in one's life."

Jamal looked down at the box like it was a pet. "Yes, Professor. I will take it back to the university tomorrow."

"Good, because this is a special time and we do not want anything to happen to it before we show it to the public."

In the middle of the professor's conversation, footsteps thundered rapidly outside. *Boom! Boom!* The sound of heavy thuds slammed against the door. Dr Witherspoon had no more than finished his last sentence when the door burst open. Jamal jumped back to allow room for the three Iranian police armed with AK-47 rifles and one dignified official with legal papers. The official ignored the student and walked directly up to the professor.

"Are you Dr. Witherspoon?"

"Yes," he acknowledged, annoyed that instead of knocking, they ruined a perfectly good door.

"Come with us immediately," the officer demanded.

"May I ask what this is all about? I think you have made a mistake. And don't tell me it was the reggae music."

"You are the Dr. Witherspoon that teaches at Tehran University?"

"Yes, that is me."

"Then we have not made a mistake. Come." A soldier jabbed his rifle into the professor's back to encourage him.

The professor brushed away the nozzle of the rifle and faced the official. "What have I done?"

The officer waved the documents in front of the professor. "You will find out soon enough. My orders say only to bring you to the station."

As the professor was being ushered out, he called over his shoulder to his assistant. "Jamal, tell President Yassin of my predicament. I doubt I will be available for tea tomorrow." Jamal watched as Dr. Witherspoon was escorted into the police car, then immediately sent word to the president of the circumstances.

The next day, Jamal brought President Yassin to the prison to speak with the commander in charge. The commander wouldn't reveal the particulars of the professor's incarceration but they were allowed to speak to him for a few minutes. They found themselves in front of a dingy cell with a small window and Dr. Witherspoon sitting in thought with his elbows on his knees and hands on his chin. The professor's eyes brightened when he saw them approaching.

"Harold, what is this all about?" asked the president.

"I do not have the vaguest idea, Massoud. They tell me nothing. I have worked faithfully with the university for several years; how could they think I am a criminal?"

"The police commander said someone accused you of appropriating artifacts illegally."

The professor blustered. "That is ridiculous!"

Jamal stepped back with a soured look on his face.

Yassin nodded. "I told the police the same thing."

Witherspoon became introspective. "Wait, Massoud. The box that Jamal found was taken from Armenia. Although it was found in the lake, technically the origin of it would be from that country. I had sent a letter to the authorities in Armenia, but never received confirmation. I was too determined to decipher the parchment in the box...but I assure you, Massoud, the scientific community would have contacted me if there was an irregularity."

"I believe you would, Harold. But why would they accuse you of stealing it?"

"That is what I would like to know."

"Do not worry, my friend, stay calm. I will get some answers." The president reached through the bars to pat the professor's shoulder.

Jamal hung on the steel bars nearby, listening.

"I will be in touch," said the president as he turned to leave. The professor turned to Jamal with a serious frown and spoke quietly. "Jamal, is the box safe?"

"Yes, Professor. I put it back in my room."

"Good. Take it and put it in the vault. We have no choice but to return the box to Armenia with our apologies. I'll think of something to say. Also, I want you to delete all the computer files at the university," he whispered.

"What? Why?"

"Do as I say, I have a back-up at home. I will explain later."

"Yes, sir. I will do it right away."

Dr. Witherspoon sighed. "Good, because I detect something rotten in all this hubbub."

Jamal quickly made his way back to the university to do as he was told. He remembered his puzzle box he left in his dormitory room and went to check on it. Upon entering the room he found his room ransacked. Books were strewn across the floor, his bed was disheveled, and drawers to a bureau were pulled completely out. His heart fluttered. Dashing to the closet where he kept the puzzle box, Jamal flung open the doors and stood gaping at the broken latch on his locked drawer. He pulled out the drawer, fumed at the empty contents, and threw it across the room.

"In the name of Allah, what have I done to deserve this!?" he shouted at the ceiling.

Jamal held his head in his hands for a moment and moaned. "The professor was right! Why did I not lock it up in the vault? My parents would think me irresponsible for letting down the university and their good name. How can I replace it?"

Jamal felt alone. He crouched in a ball hugging his knees, weighing the options he could and should have taken. Eventually he collected himself and decided he should get some advice from the professor's secretary, Mary. He went to the office and explained what had happened.

"What do we do now, Mary?"

"I was shocked to hear that Dr. Witherspoon had been arrested. Why would he be arrested for a minor discrepancy? I am sorry to hear about the stolen artifact. I will report the theft to security, and I assure you, they will find it."

Jamal breathed easier, but doubted how Mary could make such a guarantee.

The next day Mary and a few of Dr. Witherspoon's colleagues checked to see if any other artifacts were stolen. To their relief nothing else was taken. She knew that the professor was innocent, but wondered who could have done this reprehensible thing. Mary left the university that afternoon and decided to get some advice from Erol. He was widely traveled and may be able to give her some advice in how they may be able to retrieve the stolen articles.

Arriving at his hotel, she found him packing his bags. "Oh, Mary, I am glad you are here. It will save me a trip to your apartment."

She looked at his luggage. "Where are you going?"

"It is a business trip. I will not be back for a while." He stood awkwardly, hesitated, then went to embrace her.

As Mary held him, she closed her eyes and sighed, disappointed that he was leaving. She hoped he wouldn't be gone long, he was such a comfort to her. When Mary opened her eyes to tell him of the situation at the university, she noticed something familiar next to his suitcase. It was the missing puzzle box on top of a manila folder containing the parchment she had given him. She pulled back in horror and stared at the stolen artifact with her hand over her mouth. A flood of images of him asking questions about her work came back to her. Suddenly, it all made sense. She stared at her newfound love in disbelief.

Mary rested her hand on the bureau to steady herself. "It was you?"

Erol held out his hands and hunched his shoulders slightly. "I don't know what you are speaking of."

"Stop it! It *was* you! How could you! I trusted you!" Erol tried to quiet her by putting his finger to his lips, but she only shouted louder. "Do not deny it!"

She started for the box, but he warned her gruffly, "Leave it, Mary."

The door was ajar and an attendant walking by slowly opened the door. "Is there a problem?"

Erol looked desperate for a second, then smiled confidently at the worker. "Yes, yes, she is my mut'ah wife and today was our last day...you know." Erol nudged the man with his elbow and smirked. The man nodded knowingly and closed the door. Mary stood enraged, with her fists tightened and her arms stiff at her sides.

"Mut'ah! You think of me as your mut'ah wife! I never want to see you again!" She reached up and ripped off the necklace he had given her and threw it to him in pieces. She ran from the room and down the hall with tears streaming down her cheeks. Her hijab had fallen back and the desk clerk in the lobby started to complain about her indecency. "Leave me alone!" she shouted over her shoulder.

Mary wailed her way out of the building and onto the sidewalk, crying loudly with her long, brown hair streaming behind. A dark bearded policeman, with bright blue eyes, in green was standing next to his police car when she ran by him. He reached out and grabbed her by the arm. Others walking by were sure she was going to be taken and be flogged.

"He may as well have called me a prostitute!" she cried out between sobs. The policeman pulled her aside and took her into his car to calm her down. "How could he say I am his mut'ah wife?" she asked the officer.

"Are you?" he asked directly. "I know many men with other wives—"

"NO! I knew what he meant!" Her shout dropped to a whimper. "I thought he loved me. I feel like dirt."

"Hmmm." The policeman sat in thought for a moment then looked at her closer with his unusually bright blue eyes. "Do you work at Tehran University?" he asked, handing her a napkin left over from his lunch. She nodded as she raised the napkin to her face to wipe the tears. "I thought I had seen you there. Where do you live and I will take you home."

He opened the car door for Mary and she sat down in the seat sniffling. She told him the address, and he drove slowly back to her apartment. By the time they arrived she had calmed down. He escorted her into the apartment and inquired for more information about her situation.

"Who was this man you were with?"

"Erol. Erol Chenian. He is from Armenia and buys antiques."

"Hmmm. Erol Chenian …Antiques?" He made a mental note. "And how long have you known him?"

"Since this summer."

Mary was wrestling with whether to tell the policeman about the theft. She believed that Erol would not have stolen the puzzle box if she hadn't given out so much information. And if the authorities found out about her involvement with Erol, she may be considered an accomplice. In hindsight, she wished she had grabbed the box from him.

"Did he beat you?"

"No."

"You may have led him on. Women are revealing themselves too much today." The policeman waited a long moment and glanced around the room. "Is there anything else I should know?"

She suspected that the policeman knew more than he portrayed. "I cannot think right now," she replied, unconvincingly.

He stood up and handed her a card. "Call this number if you have more information." She took the card and held it in her lap. "Are you all right?"

"Yes, thank you, sir." She led him to the door and waved to him as he left. She felt sick. *This all may be because of me.*

Erol packed his things and drove to the airport. He strode toward the airplane with his cell phone to his ear. "Mr. Damec, I've got the box, but the secretary may go to the police."

"As long as it is in our possession it won't be a problem. It has always been the property of Armenia anyway."

The thief nodded and stepped up the mobile stairway to the aircraft. "I'll be in the country tonight. Can I expect payment tomorrow?"

"Bring it and the copy of the disk and you will be paid well."

Erol hung up his phone and boarded his flight, with a couple more relics to add to his luggage. He took advantage of the first class seating and the free alcoholic beverages. Several hours later, the plane landed in Yerevan and he took a cab back to the museum. It was evening and the museum was closed, but Erol saw the light on in Mr. Damec's office.

Erol unlocked the museum door and strode through the lobby with a newspaper wrapped around the box under his arm. He knocked on Mr. Damec's office door.

"Come in," said the voice inside.

Erol stepped inside and saw Mr. Damec seated in a leather chair, waiting for him with a wry smile. "You have it?"

Erol nodded, and set the object on the desk. He reached into his jacket and pulled out a computer disk. "The parchment could not be obtained, but I have a copy of it. And this disk has all the most recent analysis of the ancient language."

Mr. Damec finally smiled for once and put the disk in a drawer. "You have done well, Mr. Chenian. I will pay you half now for the box and the remainder when we retrieve the parchment." Erol frowned. "Don't worry, It will be easy to get the parchment back now that we have the box," assured Mr. Damec.

"Fair enough," agreed Erol.

The curator sat back in his padded, high-back chair. "Professor Witherspoon has been detained by the police. This will give us some time to prepare ourselves for our own press release, but we must hurry. We don't want to be second with this historic find."

Erol grinned through one side of his mouth. "My thoughts exactly, sir."

CHAPTER 6

JAILED

J amal had shown up for one of his daily visits to inform his teacher of an article from the newspaper. Dr. Witherspoon had spent more than a week incarcerated in the Tehran prison and Jamal felt obligated to entertain him. Jamal paraphrased to the professor that the Armenian museum was stating they had in their possession a 7,500-year-old box found in the hills around Lake Sevan and that they will consider putting it up for auction. The article said it may be worth millions.

"I assume they are referring to the box we had been evaluating," said the professor.

Jamal sighed, then lowered the newspaper. "It was my fault, Professor. I should never have left the box in my room. My parents have forgiven me, but I haven't forgiven myself."

Dr. Witherspoon picked up the newspaper and scanned the article. "Don't worry, son. If they really wanted to, they could have gotten their hands on some other rare artifacts we kept at the university. Although, I am a little concerned about the stolen disk. They have acquired the data on the ancient language that we worked so tirelessly on. To challenge them in the judicial process would be fruitless, considering we will eventually have to hand over the parchment anyway."

Jamal smiled, like a mischievous pixie. "I do not think you should be worried about them producing the language translations."

Dr. Witherspoon squinted. "Jamal? What do you have up your sleeve, young man?"

"Every time they open the disk, it will spread a little virus," he snickered. "Soon they may even loose their hard drive."

"You rascal, you! That is the best news I've heard all week."

Jamal had gained back some respect from the professor. But it was bittersweet. Jamal had lost his box to some thieves and contributed to the demise of his professor. "I really should be the one in prison, Dr. Witherspoon. I am the one that took the box from Lake Sevan."

"Don't be silly, son. You didn't know what you were taking. You didn't know the protocol. Besides, I doubt I will have to endure this beastly place much longer. I am banking on President Yassin's influence in this city. But there is something I need for you to do."

"Anything, sir."

"Tell Mary I wish to see her. I am going stir crazy and need her to drop off some documents for me to evaluate."

Jamal thought for a moment. "I have not seen Mary at the university since she reported the theft. She could be sick."

"Hmmm. I haven't seen her sick in three years. Jamal, go check her flat and let me know if there's a problem."

"Yes, Professor."

"Oh and Jamal, try not to weigh yourself down with guilt. Men do desperate things in desperate situations...it could have been your life they took and not just a box." Jamal nodded in agreement; although for a while, Jamal felt death would have been better than facing his relatives.

Jamal left the building and caught a bus to Mary's place. He knocked on the door of her apartment, but there was no answer. He knocked again, and again no answer. Finally, he tapped on the door with a coin to accent the sound before giving up. As he turned to leave, Mary cracked the door open. Upon seeing Jamal, she let him in. Mary was pale and unkempt. She pointed to a sofa for him to sit and went to fix some tea.

"Are you ill, Mary? I have not seen you at the university."

She shrugged, then turned the heat up on the kettle. Soon she returned with some tea for Jamal, handed him a cup, and slumped down in a chair. "Yes."

Jamal leaned toward her with the tea cup in his hands. "With what?"

Mary bent forward and put her head in her hands. "I am not sure."

"Have you visited the doctor?"

"No."

"Can I get you something?" Jamal looked around the room and noticed it was untidy and the dishes were piling up in the kitchen. He knew she had few friends; the rumors of her German husband abandoning her left quite a stigma on her. Many said that she shouldn't have married someone outside Islam, but Jamal never made a judgment. "How can I help you?"

She put her hands on her lap, but didn't look up. "There is nothing you can do. Thank you."

"Dr. Witherspoon wanted to see you. Are you well enough to talk with him?"

"Maybe."

Jamal knew there was something else she wasn't telling him. He spoke softly to her. "It seems as though your illness is in your heart. Maybe Dr. Witherspoon can help. He has said many good things about you."

Her eyes started tearing. "You must go now."

Jamal felt empathetic, but wasn't sure how to console her. Instead, he quietly nodded, set the tea down, and got up to leave. She led him to the door and thanked him for coming.

Mary started to close the door, then stopped. "Jamal could you take me to the professor?"

Jamal drove Mary back to the prison and asked to see the professor. Dr. Witherspoon was examining a piece of stone on the windowsill, when Jamal and Mary were escorted to his cell. The professor seemed pleasantly surprised to see Mary. The guard left them alone and Jamal stood aside to let the professor visit with Mary.

"Hello, Professor," said Mary meekly. The two stood awkwardly with jail bars between them.

"Jamal said you might be ill."

Her eyes started tearing again. "I am a failure!" she blurted out.

Jamal quietly handed her a handkerchief. He gave them some room to talk, but stayed close enough to find out what was bothering her.

"At what? You are the best secretary I have ever had."

Mary dabbed her eyes. "Erol told me he loved the ancient artifacts and just wanted to look at them. So I let him into the storage rooms."

"Oh."

Jamal watched as the professor turned a little pale, then quickly gather himself.

"Erol; the man from Armenia you were seeing. So that's where the artifact ran off to."

"I saw him with the box before he left Tehran. And…and…he *used* me." She spit on the ground. "Just like Johan."

The professor spoke soft and gently. "Mary. It wasn't your fault."

A tear trickled down her cheek and a small whine crept out. "You must hate me."

"I could never hate you, Mary." He reached out to touch her tears and she coughed joyfully at his words.

"Look what I have done to you." She turned to Jamal. "And I have lost the box that you cherished." Jamal shrugged his shoulders. Mary turned back to the cell. "What will you do now, Professor?" she asked, wiping her face with Jamal's handkerchief.

"It will all work itself out, my dear, you'll see." The professor lowered his voice and glanced down the hall through the bars and winked at Jamal. "Mary, chin up, there *is* some good news. Although the box has migrated back to its country of origin, the Armenian also has taken a sickly computer disk with it."

"I do not understand."

"It has a little virus, thanks to Jamal, and by now has rendered the software useless to them. They will have to decipher the parchment the old fashioned way...with honest hard work."

She looked over at Jamal. "You loved that box and now Erol has it."

"Do you have to keep reminding me of it? It only salts my wound." Jamal hung on the jail bars with his head between the metal rods. He didn't know whether to blame her for being an accomplice or blame himself for finding the box in the first place and causing all this trouble.

Dr. Witherspoon swatted a hand into the air. "There will be more boxes."

Mary looked down at the handkerchief and spoke softly. "I haven't told the police of my involvement with Erol. I thought they might think I was with him."

"I wish I could vouch for you, Mary, but my credibility is less than stellar at the moment. Normally, I would recommend being honest with the police, but that is up to you."

She reached into her purse and pulled out the card the policeman gave her. "I will call this man. He was very kind to me."

"Who?" the professor inquired.

"A policeman that I met."

"Good show, Mary."

Mary's face waned. "Here you are in prison and you are encouraging me. I feel so ashamed."

"He reached out to pat her hand. "Do not feel ashamed. I have always respected you, from the moment I hired you till today. Don't let all this froth and bubble keep us from pushing onward."

She studied him a moment and started to choke up. "You have been so kind to me. I do not deserve it."

He pulled back to scold her. "Hush, Mary. Try not to get so emotional or I will weep as well."

Mary started down the hall. "I am sorry. I must go. Come, Jamal."

The professor whispered at Jamal, "Could you get her to send me some of my work to read?"

Jamal smiled and nodded, then caught up with her.

When Mary reached the end of the hallway, she signaled the guard and he opened the door to let her and Jamal out. They climbed the steps to the main lobby of the police station and approached the officer at the main desk. The policeman was rapidly sorting papers and typing on the computer.

"Where can I reach this man?" she asked, handing the policeman the card given to her earlier.

The officer didn't look up quickly, but eventually took the card and set it on the counter. "Mohammad Jalil?" noted the policeman. "One moment." He checked the computer database to see what part of the city he may work out of. "There is a director of scientific information by that name, but I see no policeman."

Mary tapped on the business card. "But he gave me this for identification."

"Perhaps he works outside of Tehran. You have his number, call him." The officer was busy and Mary decided to follow his advice and call the number when she got home.

Jamal took her back to her apartment and sat with her. "What do you plan on doing, Mary?"

"I will have to explain everything. The truth will come out somehow. It is better for me to tell it to the police in my own way than have them find out some other way."

Jamal looked closely at the card. "But the police did not know this man. Who is he? Do you think he works with Erol?"

"No, he had a police car and took me home. I must call him again."

Jamal not only desired to help Mary, but wanted to stay and learn more details about this intriguing affair. "I will stay and help you if you wish."

Mary squinted and waved a finger in the air. "I have an idea… yes, I could use your help." She got up enough nerve and made her call. After a few rings the only answer was from Mr. Jalil's voice message. Mary left a message for him to call her, then sat and summarized the past few months of her life to Jamal. Within a half hour, the phone rang.

She smoothed out her dress, then answered the phone. "Yes?" she stated with trepidation.

"Mary? Mary Van Wilpe?"

"Yes?"

"This is Mohammad Jalil. I received your message. How may I help you?"

"I have decided to tell you everything I know about Erol, Erol Chenian. Should I meet you at the police station?" She whispered to Jamal with her hand on the receiver. "I want to find out what station he works out of."

"No, I will come to your place and we can discuss this some more," said the man.

Mary's eyes narrowed. "You *do* work for the Tehran police?" There was silence on the other end of the phone. "I ask this, because a policeman at the prison said your name was not on file."

Mohammad Jalil sighed, then spoke coolly. "I will explain more when I see you in person, Mary. I cannot explain this over the phone."

"Then let us meet in Baharan Park. I have become wary of men in my home lately."

"I understand. I will see you at the south entrance in thirty minutes."

Mary hung up. "I can't let another man take advantage of me, so could you be with me at the park?"

"I am at your service." Jamal tried to sound humble, but the intrigue was starting to pique his interest. "I will pretend not to know you and be nearby just in case he tries to hurt you." Mary agreed.

Jamal drove Mary in his little blue Alfa Romeo up to the park, then they split up. He strategically seated himself on a bench eating a bag of ajeel, pretending to read a book, while she walked slowly from the entrance. Jamal saw a man with dark glasses following her and tightened his muscles in case he had to spring into action.

The officer caught up to her and escorted her to a nearby fountain. He scanned the area quickly, took off his sunglasses, and sat down on one of many flat stones that surrounded the rippling water. She glanced one more time toward Jamal before sitting down next to the officer with the bright blue eyes.

"Mary, you were right. I am not a policeman."

"Are you with the Lebas Shakhsiha?" she asked in a whisper. He shook his head no. "With the Revolutionary Guards?" Again he shook his head.

"I am an Iranian intelligence agent with the Interior Ministry. I have been watching your Armenian friend for months now and we believe he is an international art thief...a very slippery one."

Her mouth dropped open as he spoke. "Why did you not arrest him?"

"I am working with Interpol to locate some stolen art and get enough evidence to convict him. We believe he has stolen a venerated document of the Qur'an dating back to 1091, a mosaic from the Roman era, a five-thousand-year-old Elamite bronze vase, a gold Byzantine cross from the Vatican, and others. He deals in antiquities, as you have come to know...but not how you might have thought."

Mary dropped her head and the muscles in her jaw tightened. She brought her attention back to the agent. "You must know I have only known him a short while."

"I know," he replied, with a quick smile. "And I have made sure the Tehran police do not investigate you. I only tell you all of this because Erol Chenian, if that is his real name, may want to contact you again. If he does, you must call me immediately. But you must keep my identity secret or it may jeopardize my work. If you need confirmation on my identity, I will give you the name of my superior in the Interior Ministry who can verify everything I have said."

Mr. Jalil stood to go. Mary thanked him and returned to Jamal, who sat on the bench spitting pumpkin seeds to record distances. She stepped on a small pile of husks and shells to sit down next to her friend. Jamal popped a handful of watermelon seeds, almonds, and hazelnuts into his mouth.

"Is everything all right? I made sure he didn't even touch you," he asked, his mouth half full.

Mary chuckled. "Yes, everything is fine. You will not believe what we got ourselves into Jamal. I can hardly believe it myself."

CHAPTER 7

ANCIENT RUINS

Rebecca examined the seafloor charts on the bridge as the survey ship propelled its way out of Baku harbor past some rusty oil platforms at ten knots. She rocked in her seat as the ship moved into open water where sea swells gently pitched the vessel. Captain Kovacheski navigated around an oil derrick operated by their Russian competitor, Lukoil, and preceded toward the east end of the Guneshli Shallows. It was late afternoon when the captain pointed out to her that the ship had neared the coordinates for the initial seismic tests. Rebecca promptly sent word to Dr. McCray of their arrival.

Rebecca had been narrowing in on the charts when McCray entered the bridge. She tapped on the seafloor map. "We are at the western edge of where you wanted to lay out the grid, doctor."

McCray nodded to Rebecca and turned to the captain. "We'll anchor here and get started with the preliminary scans in the morning. Are you ready for this, Ms. Belmont?"

"Ready as I'd ever be, Dr. McCray."

"Good—it's time to tell the others."

A puzzled wrinkle crossed her forehead. "Shouldn't you tell them?"

"I thought you were hired to assist me."

"Yes, but…"

"Well, my theory is that if I have someone to do the mundane work for me, I'll use 'em. And you just happen to be that person."

"OK, you're the boss," Rebecca replied, not daring to reveal her hesitance.

She felt like she was violating a rule—giving directions to a crew that seemed very attached to her boss. Most men in the world are reluctant to take orders from an unknown female. However, she wasn't going to let her own fear dictate her obligations. She was confident she could prove herself among all these oil company men. With her stomach doing backflips, Rebecca found the staff members and dutifully told them of Dr. McCray's plan. The crew was congenial and gave no sly comments to her, which was a pleasant surprise. By the time she lay down to sleep, she and her stomach had finally relaxed.

The next morning a helicopter whirled overhead and John Schmitt stepped into a basket and was hauled upward. The crew gathered around to see the geophysicist leave. Dr. McCray waved his crew around to make an announcement.

"Schmitt's wife is going into labor and he has to leave for the States, so we'll have to do without him. He's a good man…hate to lose him. That's OK, we've got another expert in Ms. Belmont." Rebecca held back a groan. The thought of being the only one on board eminently qualified to interpret the scans meant double duty. She assumed that her boss's cavalier attitude meant that he wanted to see her fail.

McCray didn't seem to want to procrastinate and promptly instructed the team to initiate the seismic survey scans. The crew set up the hydrophones in an array to be towed behind the ship for a three dimensional reading. Once the array was streaming along behind the ship, an air gun was set off to release bursts of compressed air underwater, which was then checked for speed and volume of the reflected sound through the earth's crust. After repeating this process a few times, they developed a picture of subsurface formations. Rebecca scrutinized the process, and made mental notes as to what they could do to be more efficient in the future.

The ship slowed to a crawl. Rebecca saw Tony on his knees fixing some equipment and decided to be civil with him. "Hey, Tony, if that Russian company, Lukoil, has the development contracts for the Guneshli Shallows, why aren't they doing the survey?" She positioned herself on the opposite side of the aft control station from him.

The powerful man stood up and swaggered over next to her. "Well seein' as Terra has better exploration equipment, maybe the Azeris divvied out a portion for us." He laid down a wrench and wiped some sweat from his brow with the back of his wrist. "So Becca, when we pull into port, how 'bout you and me paint the town red?"

"Thanks for the offer, Tony, but I don't drink."

"No? It seems like a feisty young thing such as yourself wouldn't be afraid of a little brew."

"I'm a Christian," she announced, as if that would somehow settle the matter.

"So what? Jesus turned water into wine."

"What I mean is I don't get drunk. I have a relationship with God, so I try to follow his word in the Bible."

"Oh, I get it. You've been branded."

"Branded?"

"Yeah, you know, 'born again.'"

"Hmmm. I guess I have. I hadn't thought about it that way."

"Since you have religion and all, maybe you could tell me something. When Jesus fed the five thousand with two fish, were they bass or catfish?"

Rebecca almost smiled, but knew better. *How Dr. McCray ever decided to hire Tony is beyond me.* "I think we better concentrate on our work." Rebecca had a strange feeling that even though she revealed her spiritual convictions to Tony, it probably wouldn't stop him from attempting to seduce her.

"What ever you say, darlin', but we're not done talkin'," he vowed, picking up his wrench and pointing it at her. He went back

69

to tightening some bolts and Rebecca walked over to where a small monitor was set up near the control station. Yakov Comenici had been conducting a test on the R.O.V. and left the submersible's digital camera to free up a tangled line.

Rebecca happened to spot something on the remote monitor, then motioned to her coworker. "Hey, Tony, stop what you're doing and take a look at this."

He scooted around to the monitor and tipped his head left, then right, then left again. The object had moved out of view. "What was it?"

"It was long and smooth and definitely not a natural formation. We must be only thirty-five meters deep here. But according to the charts, we should be at least fifty." She ran up to the computer room to check the seismic readings, then called Dr. McCray's stateroom.

"Dr. McCray? This is Becca. We have something on the bathymetric scans that I think you ought to see."

"I'll meet you up in the computer room," replied McCray.

Tony and Yakov followed Rebecca up to the computer room, where the primary monitoring equipment was, and a few minutes later Dr. McCray entered the compartment. Rebecca showed him the scans taken of the strange object and replayed the video on the submersible's camera. Their boss puzzled over it for a moment, then decided to take some time to investigate. McCray ordered the captain to circle the *Bering* back to the area where they spotted the object. Once they neared the coordinates, McCray then directed Yakov to move the submersible with its cameras over the designated site for a closer look.

As the R.O.V. circled the area, it relayed colored pictures of rectangular stone debris. "Isn't it unusually shallow here?" Rebecca asked her boss.

"Yes," he mused. "These scans show a barrier running east to west about thirty-five meters. That's uncommon in this area, because on each side of the ridge the Caspian drops down to about five hundred meters."

"I guess that's why they call it the Guneshli Shallows," added Tony.

Rebecca ignored Tony. "Someone must have discovered this before."

"Not necessarily," McCray pointed out. "When Azerbaijan was part of the Soviet Union, much of this area was neglected for exploration. Now that the Azeris are free from the Russians, they have been systematically exploring subfloor opportunities branching out from the shore. It very well may be that this spot was overlooked."

Rebecca pointed to the rectangular shapes on the sonar screen. "The sonar is picking up some large configurations...we should see them on the video screen in a few seconds." The R.O.V. closed in on the coordinates. "There it is!" she announced, tapping on the monitor at a distant object that looked like a broken pencil. "That's what I saw!"

With the cameras rolling, the scientists froze in anticipation. Some geometric structures grew larger in the screen as the team leaned forward for a closer look. Yakov drove the R.O.V. closer, zooming in slowly to the pencil-like object. The structure was a long, rectangular obelisk that had been split in two and rested on its side.

"Would ya look at that!" whistled Tony. "...just like the Washington Monument—but only broken. There's something even bigger next to it. That is not natural! It's a building of some kind. Even with those rocks and plant life all over it, you can see steps moving up in a pyramid formation."

"A Ziggurat?" Dr. McCray unintentionally said aloud.

"A what?" asked Tony.

"A step type of pyramid. You made a good find, Ms. Belmont. This kind of thing is very rare."

Rebecca was beaming. "Thank you, sir."

"But don't let this accidental find get to your head," he warned.

Tony put his arm around her and gave her a squeeze while she sat facing the monitor. "Nice job, sweetheart."

"Thanks, Tony," she forced out heroically. With his arm still resting on her shoulder, Rebecca gracefully swiveled the chair to release his touch, and then made an adjustment to the R.O.V. camera. She noticed something near the underwater structure. "Dr. McCray? Can we get closer to that block of stone just next to the obelisk?" she asked.

Bob McCray nodded an OK to Yakov, who maneuvered the craft to her new coordinates. The seafloor silt was stirred up by the propellers on the machine, causing murky visibility. He slowed the speed of the submersible to a crawl until it stopped in front of a thin, flat stone, about a meter wide. When the sediment settled, the staff whispered with awe, as etched symbols could be clearly seen on the stone.

"OK, I've seen enough," said Dr. McCray, standing up to peer out the porthole. "Tony, we need to get a couple divers to see if we can hoist the slab aboard without damaging it. Get someone to assist you and make it happen."

"Yes, sir, J. Bob."

Tony enlisted the help of the master diver, Joe Hanak, and wasted no time getting to the slab. They brought some reinforced netting and tipped the stone tablet onto it carefully. They attached a carabiner to a heavy cable and signaled the operator of the boom crane to lift it from the seafloor. Within minutes, the crew carefully and methodically brought the dripping stone slab on board, guiding it over to a secured area. Virtually everyone on board was present to view the spectacle of the heavy artifact pulled from the sea. After it rested gently on the deck, one of the scientists brushed off the excess soil to reveal clearly chiseled symbols.

"Get Houston on the phone!" McCray yelled to the communications technician.

It was early in the morning and Lee Thompson, the chief executive officer of Terra Exploration, answered the call back in Texas. Mr. Thompson saw the caller I.D. and recognized the number of the iridium phone system used by their company. He talked with the technician briefly before Dr. McCray got on the line.

"Yes, Bob, what's the big tado?"

"Lee, we found some very unusual ruins in the Shallows when we were starting our survey. I thought you might be interested in it, so I am sending some attached photos to your email as we speak." Dr. McCray continued to describe the accidental discovery to his boss, while Lee Thompson accessed his computer. "I didn't know whether we should continue with the survey or spend more time pulling up artifacts."

"Pull up old artifacts?" Thompson asked. "That rings like a negative profit bell, Bob."

"Hold on, Lee. We have a slab of stone with some inscriptions on it for solid proof of the ruins. This could be big news."

The CEO flipped through the emailed photos as they spoke. It was his job to weigh out the costs of lost oil survey productivity with high profile exposure of this ancient discovery. "I am not sure, Bob. However, don't go any further until the Azerbaijan government is informed about it. I have an old friend who teaches archaeology in Tehran… Harold Witherspoon. He's an expert in just this kind of thing and would give credibility to the excavation. I want you to get a hold of him and see if he would take an all expenses paid trip to the Guneshli field. Contact the Terra office in Baku and inform them of the situation. They will get permission from the government of Azerbaijan to continue additional expeditions. Once Dr. Witherspoon evaluates the viability of the ruins, we will be in a better position to determine whether to continue or not."

"I'll get right on it, Lee."

"J. Bob, I know you don't have all the proper equipment for this kind of thing. Tell me what you need. If they don't have it in Baku, I will send it to you as soon as possible. In the meantime, send me the video of your underwater movie so we can keep the big guy in London up to speed, and he can make a decision on whether or not to pass it on to the media. Also, get some 3-D imaging and send them. I want our team here to use the virtual vision room to get some detail on the structures."

"I understand," replied McCray. He hung up the phone and went back to where scientists and deckhands alike stood hovering over the slab of stone to get a glimpse of the discovery. "OK, break it up. I need to make an announcement." The men moved out to let McCray in the center of the circle. "The survey is suspended until further notice. Houston gave us permission to investigate these ruins further." Several of the men hooted and gave high-fives, anxious to be involved with an expedition that didn't have the word *oil* attached to it. "To evaluate this properly, we'll need to pick up an expert in archaeology. We also have to wait for the Azeri government to give us their blessing, so pack up the survey equipment…we're headed back to Baku."

As the men straggled back to their duties, Dr. McCray gazed down at the stone slab and shook his head in disbelief. *In all my years, I've never been lucky enough to find something like this. And this is Belmont's first day,* he thought with a tinge of jealousy. Later in the evening, he was still pouring over the pictures of the ruins, spellbound by thoughts of an unknown civilization.

CHAPTER 8

FREE TO EXPLORE

The prison guards moved the professor into a private yet dismal room, complete with rock walls, a tiny barred window, and a thick, solid oak door. Nevertheless, the science part of him wasn't deterred, even by the barest of surroundings. In no time he was scrutinizing the composition of the walls. Dr. Witherspoon took a spoon from his lunch tray, scraped off the surface of a stone, and adjusted his spectacles for a closer look. He jumped up and danced a little jig, oblivious to standard demoralized jailhouse behavior.

"I know where this limestone came from! It has to be from a quarry on the eastern border of Kurdistan!"

The energetic educator had spoken aloud, as if someone were assisting him on the project, and was smiling grandly at his find, when a guard unlocked the heavy door. The heavyset guard interrupted the professor from his scrapings and handed him a cordless phone.

Dr. Witherspoon accepted it, then spoke into the receiver. "This is Harold Witherspoon." A fuzzy static greeted him on the other end, so he talked louder. "Hello? Hello?"

The static cleared. "Hello, Professor Harold Witherspoon?"

"Yes?"

"Professor, I am Dr. J. Robert McCray of Terra Petroleum Industries. The president of Tehran University, Massoud Yassin, told me I could reach you here."

Dr. Witherspoon sat down on his bunk while the guard leaned leisurely against the wall. "You have my undivided attention. I'm available at the moment," he replied, winking at the pan-faced guard.

"We need your expertise to help evaluate some ruins we accidentally discovered in the Caspian Sea, just east of Baku. I was told of your work in the Tigris and how your knowledge may be vital to our findings."

The professor snickered. "I am a little preoccupied at the moment. You may have to make an appointment with the local Iranian authorities."

"I am well aware of your situation, Mr. Witherspoon, and my recent contribution to the police should result in your quick release."

"Oh...I see...well, thank you, my good man."

"The commander of the police said he would make arrangements for you to be on a plane to Baku tomorrow. I won't discuss the particulars on this line, but you can find out more from the president of your university."

"I don't know how to thank you, Mr. McCray. So why me and not a marine archaeologist?"

"You can thank the president of Terra Exploration, Lee Thompson, for that. He knows and trusts you." Static weaved in and out of the phone line.

"Did you say Lee? Lee Thompson? I haven't seen him in years! How did he know—"

"I don't mean to be rude, Professor, but we can talk more when you get here. I'm afraid I may lose the connection."

Dr. Witherspoon nodded to the receiver. "Quite right! I will see you soon. May I bring an assistant?"

"By all means. And anything else that will aid you in this venture. Goodbye for now...."

The professor handed the phone back to the guard. "Well, my good man, I believe it is time we said our own goodbyes. I am afraid I won't have the pleasure of visiting you again very soon." The guard gave no impression that he enjoyed the professor's presence and left the room without a word.

Terra management agreed to let the public in on the discovery and it didn't take long for the major news stations to announce it to the world. Rebecca and some of the other crew were intently watching news of the ruins in the computer room. Robert McCray leaned back against the bulkhead, smoking his pipe. The monitor flashed images of the ancient ruins that Dr. McCray's team sent to them via the Internet, as the news anchor reported the story.

"Terra Petroleum of Azerbaijan announced last week that they had discovered an ancient artifact in the Caspian Sea. The artifact was found by accident when the survey team was conducting a shallow hazard survey about sixty miles east of Baku," said the reporter.

As the news report continued, a seaman interrupted McCray's attention on the T.V. to inform him that his guests had arrived.

Rebecca was taking some notes as she watched T.V. on the corner near the ceiling. Her eye caught Dr. McCray at the door to the cafeteria. He waved her to come to him. She stuck the pad and pencil into a small backpack and jogged over.

"What's up, Doc...tor McCray."

He shook his head. "Oh, that's bad."

She giggled. "I'm sorry, it just came out."

"I want you to meet some new arrivals—archaeologists, to be exact. Lee Thompson said we could trust these men. I know Terra is going to get some good publicity off the story, but it also may become a breeding ground for the curious. Other than extreme environmentalists, we rarely get attention from the public and I like it that way. But I don't know if this is going to be an asset or a liability."

"Hey, who knows? Maybe you'll get boatloads of email from some fans."

"I really don't have the time or inclination for that sort of thing. That's why you're around."

The right side of Rebecca's lip curled up. "Oh, thanks, Dr. McCray."

"It may be easier on me if you called me Robert, Bob, or even just McCray."

She nodded. "Oh, right. Tony called you J. Bob. What's the J stand for?"

He sneered slightly. "I'll tell you some other time," he said as he sighted his guests amidships.

Rebecca looked up at her boss. "Do we really have the expertise for this kind of exploration?"

McCray nodded for her to follow him. "Well, most oil companies would subcontract for this, but since we have John Hanak and his dive team aboard, we have plenty of expertise."

They met up with a frumpy, gray-haired gentleman with glasses who was being escorted by a young, well-dressed, Middle Eastern man. The two men both had a suitcase in each hand and set them down when they stopped in front of Rebecca and McCray. A dusty wind blew on the port side and the four moved to a sheltered corridor.

Dr. McCray reached out to shake the older guest's hand. "Professor Witherspoon, I presume? I'm Bob McCray. We talked on the phone the other day."

"Yes, yes, it is a pleasure to meet you, sir. I am in your debt for bailing me out of prison. Nevertheless, aren't contributions to the police for a prisoner's release prohibited by law? Or do you not wish to talk of this?"

McCray smiled. "Your release could be considered a bribe, or what we in the industry call a grease payment. I prefer the word *donation*. I should thank you, Professor. We could really use your expertise in a situation like this."

Dr. Witherspoon balked at the compliment. "If what you tell me about the ruins is true, I believe I will be the one to be passing out the thanks.

"Witherspoon then turned to his assistant. "This is Jamal, a doctoral studies student of history at the university. He has been a great assistance in gaining knowledge about an unknown people group we have been studying."

Jamal reached out to shake Dr. McCray's hand.

"Speaking of assistants, this is mine, Rebecca Belmont. She will be helping us with decoding some of the underwater readings near the site."

Rebecca shook the professor and Jamal's hands. "Nice to meet you, sir, and Jamal. Call me Becca." They smiled and nodded politely.

"My men will take your luggage and equipment to your room. I hope the room will be satisfactory," McCray offered.

"Compared to my latest flat, I have no doubt it will be," chuckled the British archaeologist. "So how is Lee doing? I haven't seen him in years."

"He is doing quite well. Unfortunately, you won't be able to meet him here; he's back in Houston, Texas." Dr. McCray peeked into the mess compartment. "Becca, could you stay here with Jamal for a minute? I need to have Professor Witherspoon sign a couple of documents in my cabin."

"Yes, Dr. McCray," she automatically replied. He frowned at her and she shrugged sheepishly. "I'm sorry, sir, I know what you said, but I just can't see myself calling you by your first name."

He shrugged it off. "Take your time, Becca. We all have to get used to one another."

Rebecca saw a confused expression on the professor and Jamal. "It's a familiarity thing. I'll explain it to you later."

The oil scientist escorted the university professor up to his cabin, leaving Jamal and Rebecca to get acquainted. They stood inside the cafeteria, with its permanently-mounted tables and chairs. A muted monitor was showing the last bite of the undersea ruin story. Outside the mess compartment, they heard muffled voices of crewmen calling to one another as they prepared to get underway. The two feigned an awkward smile at each other, trying to decide what to talk about. Finally, Rebecca pointed out some photos of ships on the cafeteria bulkheads that told about the ship's name.

A small breeze blew some dust through a porthole and landed in Jamal's eye. He grimaced as he tried to wipe it off his eyelid.

"Oh, that must hurt." Rebecca reached into her pocket and pulled out a scarf. "So, why do you like history, Jamal? I never really paid much attention to it."

"Thank you." He spit into the cloth and wiped both eyes. Jamal spoke elegant English with a British/Farsi accent, and held the scarf in his hand as he expounded his ideas. "I believe if we understand the actions of the past, we will understand how to live better in the present. For example, Saladin was a great Muslim leader, who conquered the Crusaders from Europe. He gained control of important cities in 1187 such as Jerusalem and Ashkelon, but unlike the Europeans, encouraged the Jews, Christians, and Muslims to live in harmony."

Rebecca loved the sound of his voice and was intrigued with his viewpoint, but sensed his little speech was rote. "You mean *you* respect peace with Jews?"

Jamal looked annoyed. "Not all Muslims hate the Jews."

Her posture drooped. "Oh, I shouldn't have said that. I don't know what came over me. It's just that I thought the Middle East wanted to rid themselves of the Jews in Israel."

"Do they not need a place to live?" he said, waving her handkerchief in the air.

"Yes, I guess they do. It's just…you are more congenial to Israelis than most of the other Muslims I've met, that's all." Rebecca was gratified by his kindness. She grew up only hearing stories of Muslims hating Jews when she accompanied her father to Egypt as a Christian missionary.

Jamal accepted her analysis with a shrug, 'Do unto others' was quoted long before Jesus was born," he added.

"Really? I didn't know that."

80

"Yes, if you had a Bible, I could show you." He absentmindedly stuck her handkerchief into his back pocket.

Rebecca reached into her backpack and pulled out a small, well worn, leather-bound book. "Do you remember the verse?"

"It is in the Old Testament section…the book of Leviticus, chapter 19," he pointed out.

Rebecca flipped through the pages in her search. Soon she stopped and shook her head when she found it. "I can't believe it. I have never have seen this before. …*you shall love your neighbor as yourself; I am the Lord.*" She was impressed with her new colleague's knowledge. "I didn't know you read the Bible, Jamal." Rebecca wished she could have taken the last sentence back.

One of his eyebrows rose. "You do not know me to even say that. Just because I read the Qur'an, does not mean that is all I read. That is twice you have assumed too much, Rebecca. Let me add that I am in my post graduate work, for a doctorate in history."

"I didn't mean…it's just that…oh, never mind." Rebecca who always was sure of herself in theological discussions suddenly felt clumsy. "Thank you for setting me straight," she added, as gracefully as possible.

The door to the cafeteria squeaked opened and the two turned in unison to see Tony walk in. "So this is the new guy, huh?"

Rebecca stuffed the Bible in her pack to address her shipmate. "Yes, Tony, this is Jamal. He came aboard with Professor Witherspoon."

Tony gave a quick nod to Jamal and then winked to Rebecca. "I'll tell ya right now, mister, she's the prettiest one on board."

She rolled her eyes and sighed deeply. "Thank you, Tony." Rebecca briefly turned to Jamal to diffuse the flattering remark about her beauty. "Of course, Jamal, there *are* only two women on board."

Tony put his hands on his hips. "Now don't be trashin' Mrs. Ganjavi. She's a sweetheart too."

Rebecca knew sarcasm when she heard it. "Is there some other reason you came up here, other than to shower me and Mrs. Ganjavi with compliments?"

"Of course, darlin'. J. Bob, I mean, Doc, said I should show the new guy to his cabin. He's bunkin' with that other Doc. Later, Doc McCray wants you two to meet with the staff in the conference room at 1700."

Rebecca smiled kindly to her guest. "OK then, I guess we will talk later, Jamal."

"It was a pleasure meeting you, Rebecca," Jamal said, bowing his head.

"You can call me Becca."

"Yes, I could, but Rebecca is such a beautiful name; I would hate not to hear its fullness."

She was caught off guard with the compliment and blushed. "OK…if you want to."

Tony rolled his eyes. "Come on, Mr. Jamal, let's go. I'll show ya to your cabin."

"I'll catch up to you later, Jamal," she assured.

Jamal picked up his and the professor's suitcase and followed Tony to a cabin on the third level. Jamal found two bunks and set the professor's suitcase down and tossed his onto the bunk closest to the window. Tony briefly showed Jamal the amenities, then left the room. Jamal checked his watch for time and a compass for the direction to Mecca.

Rebecca had given Jamal some time to settle in and felt an urge to talk with him again. She was in a good mood and found herself singing an old childhood song. She knocked on Jamal's cabin door and he quickly answered.

Jamal smiled when he opened the door. "You have a lovely voice, Rebecca."

"Thanks." She glanced in the room to see his prayer mat on the floor.

"May I help you?"

"Actually, I thought since you will have to familiarize yourself with the ship, I could show you around."

"That is very kind of you, Rebecca. I will be right with you."

Rebecca stood at the door while Jamal went in to roll up his mat. "It's funny to hear an Iranian speak English with a British accent," she chuckled.

"Maybe I have been spending too much time with Professor Witherspoon. Does it bother you?"

"No. It sounds…cute." She turned around and cringed as she replayed her comment in her mind. *I can't believe I said cute! I am a professional for goodness sakes!*

Jamal smiled as he closed the door to follow her. She gave a tour of the vessel, from stem to stern and bilge to pilot house. Eventually, they ended up on the main deck, leaning against the tow winch used for underwater vehicles. They were both hypnotized by the afternoon sun sparkling through the foam and spray, stirred up by a test being conducted on the ship's propellers before leaving port.

Jamal followed up on their conversation in the cafeteria. "It was unusual to see a Christian carry a Bible. You must be dedicated. I try to pray five times a day. What about you?"

"No, just whenever the Spirit leads me." She paused to think. "But morning is my favorite time."

"The Christians I have met only pick up Bibles on Sunday and get drunk and act disrespectful on the other days. When Christians have wild parties, the police say nothing, but if a Muslim has a party with alcohol, the police take them to jail." Rebecca was quiet and pensive, concerned about Christians around the world continuing to set bad examples.

"It looks like both of us have been misled by our experiences."

Her uneasiness was visible, so Jamal changed the subject. "I heard you singing. What kind of music do you like?…Bob Marley?"

Rebecca laughed. "Doesn't he sing reggae?"

"Yes, he is very popular in Tehran."

"Well, I usually listen to music that is uplifting—without filthy lyrics. Uh, I'm sure Bob Marley is fine." She thought he sang only political songs. "I thought western music was frowned upon in Iran."

Jamal squirmed a little. "Things are changing in Iran. People want more freedoms, and the mullahs are loosening their grip on newer music."

"That's good. I hate it when even my parents tell me what to listen to," Rebecca said.

Jamal pulled out a small bag from his front pocket. "Would you like some ajeel?" He held it out for her to try.

"What is ajeel?"

"Try it," he encouraged. "He reached into the bag, grabbed a handful of the nuts and dried fruit mixture, and then tossed it into his mouth.

Rebecca gingerly reached in for a small sample, trying to be polite. She mimicked him by tossing some in her mouth and a familiarity crept up her face. "Oh, this is like trail mix."

"Trail mix?" he asked.

"That's what we call something similar to this in America." Rebecca looked at her watch. "Oh, it's almost five o'clock, that's 1700 in nautical jargon. We should get up to the conference room, everybody will be there."

"Everybody means anybody?" he asked, whimsically.

She caught on. "Anybody is OK, too. Even nobodies."

"Are we nobodies?"

"No, we are somebodies," she announced with pride.

"But we will be dead-bodies if we don't get up to the meeting," he added. They realized the forthright silliness of their conversation and burst out laughing.

Rebecca pointed to Jamal's ajeel. "It must be your trail mix." He nodded in agreement with a pained grin.

Jamal and Rebecca left the main deck, climbed the ladder to the first level, and entered the conference room as the other staff members were filing in. A large table with chairs was in the center of the wood-paneled room and a library of books was strapped into shelves hung on the wall. After the pleasantries of introducing the professor and Jamal, Dr. McCray showed the professor a map of the survey site and spread it out on the table. While the others sat down, Rebecca helped pass out recent printouts of the slab inscriptions. With the slab now safely stored with the Azerbaijan National Academy of Science, Dr. Witherspoon would have to rely on the prints.

"Have you seen any artifacts like this in your travels?" Bob McCray asked Professor Witherspoon.

The professor adjusted his glasses and examined one photo after another, muttering to himself all the while. Soon he looked up at Jamal over his glasses. "The writings look *very* familiar, don't they, Jamal?" He handed a particular print to his Iranian student.

"Are these the same, sir?"

One side of Dr. Witherspoon's mouth curled up. "Quite. And possibly confirming the dating of this slab to be around 7,500 years ago."

"What are the same?" Rebecca asked the professor.

"There was Jamal's accidental find of a box, my pottery urns in the Tigris, and now the etchings on the slab you discovered. The new people group that I mentioned earlier and your ruins contain identical writings." The professor stood back to take in the new information. "I am amazed to see the coincidence of ubiquitous archaeological evidence revealed in such a short duration in three different locations. Any archaeologist would have been happy with one great find, but three in one year?" He shook his head with an incredulous countenance.

"Do you know what the words mean?" asked Dr. McCray.

"I believe I can translate a few of these words, but I would have to compare them with some of the data we have collected at the university."

Rebecca held some printouts from the seismic survey in her hand, waiting to give them to the professor. "Based on the location of the ruins, we can only assume that there must have been an underwater city here?"

The professor almost laughed. "An underwater city? You have been watching too many cinemas, my dear. Highly unlikely."

"Then what do you make of this?" She handed him three-dimensional scan of the area with the obelisk lying on the side of the zigguarat and some city walls clearly defined.

"Hmmm. This is fascinating, to say the least," the professor replied, examining the printout.

"So how could structures end up under the sea?" she asked.

Dr. Witherspoon scratched his cheek. "The most reasonable deduction is that (A) the waters were lower with the city on dry land, or (B) the city was once on ground higher than the current elevation."

"I guess aliens dropping it out of the sky is out of the question," mumbled Tony.

Dr. Witherspoon thought for a moment and his eyes lit up. "Wait. I just recalled a study done by a group of paleoclimatologists from San Francisco in 1998. They concluded that 8,200 years ago the world's climate was cooler by about eleven degrees for several hundred years. That would constitute a small ice-age right after the beginning of the Holocene Epoch, our latest warming period after the last great ice age."

"So how does that relate to an unknown city?" asked Rebecca.

"Kindly bear with me a moment, Miss Belmont," he said, holding up a finger, as if lecturing a class. "First of all, if there was an abrupt cold climate shift, it would have interrupted global warming and slowed the melting of the northern ice sheets. Secondly, there would be less feed water from the Cacasus and Elburz mountains to the west and south. Lastly, the arid conditions would increase evaporation in the sea itself. Thus, with a massive loss of water to the Caspian Sea, the results would translate into exposed land masses."

The staff in the room kept silent, intently focused on the professor's hypothesis. Dr. Witherspoon circled his hand flat across the map on the table. "Look here. The depth of the top third of the sea is less than twenty meters. In a sudden six-hundred-year cooling, relative to Earth's long life, it is a pittance to lose. Now, let us speculate that the Caspian Sea was smaller, and actually two separate lakes separated by a land bridge. These Gunishli Shallows along the Absheron ridge that Dr. McCray pointed out, is a logical location where a strip of dry ground would be 7,500 years ago. If this hypothesis is correct, then the waters of the sea would be low enough to expose dry land for an advanced culture to build a city. Maybe here," said the doctor, pointing to the survey site on the map. "Where you found the ruins. And according to these photos, I estimate it to be a large one, built by a thriving culture."

"So that is how the city was able to be built?" asked Rebecca.

"I was just daydreaming, my dear. It is highly unlikely that that much water would evaporate."

"But it is possible," she added.

"I have always enjoyed telling stories…and may have gotten carried away with this hypothesis. Therefore, this is the only fairy tale I could muster up for the moment."

"Fairy tale? In theory, bumblebees shouldn't be able to fly, because their weight is too heavy for their wing size. Your ideas sound more believable than that. Even the cab driver said that there was some sort of ancient cart ruts that went into the sea to… maybe a city?"

"Cart ruts?" asked the professor. He shook his head. "Please don't get me started on another rabbit trail. I appreciate your confidence in me, Miss Belmont, and I am unclear of these cart ruts you speak of, but I am a man of science. This is just *one* idea. I am not prone to devote myself to the first idea in my mind. My preference is to brainstorm with other scientists awhile and then develop an idea to get carried away with," he said with a wink.

"Let's forget the time period for a moment. You can't deny there was at least a village or small city of some type can you?" she added with desperation. "Either way, this is definitely worth an in-depth study.

Dr. Witherspoon sighed and gave in to her persistence. "Yes, you're correct. Both of your comments seem true."

CHAPTER 9

AN ANCIENT CITY

Three phases of the moon had passed since the blond-haired giants attacked the city of Tuball, leaving death and destruction in their wake. Yet the marring of the city gates from the siege was the only sign left that invaders had infiltrated the great walls. The large brass loop atop of the sacred ziggurat was repaired from the last lightning strike and the final miscellaneous repairs of the interconnected stone dwellings were complete. Citizens had overcome their grief of lost loved ones and commerce was again at full strength.

Shem cracked open an eye when the morning light rays hit his face. He yawned. "Oooo! I fell asleep on the roof again!" He looked up at the sun. "Aahchoo!"

He stood up and stretched out his muscular arms to the air, then scratched his short, curly brown hair on his head with his fingertips. He had been used to mightily save the city and had barely a wound to show for his heroics. The citizens believed Shem's god showed favor upon him and some abandoned their faith in the gods El, Anat, Baal, and Mot, to worship the great invisible God. Shem was honored with many gifts, including the upper stone dwelling near the great outer walls of Tuball.

A steady breeze blew over a short stone wall at the edge of the flat roof where the young Sethite watched twelve men walk out from the city walls. He rested his elbows on the stone railing with his fists under his chin and examined the elders and learned men as they stepped carefully to avoid deep cracks separating the semi-solid ground.

Shem shook his head and called out. "Only God has control over the land and waters of the earth, not man!" He assumed their endeavor was foolish, since the ground wasn't good solid rock.

The men that Shem scrutinized were too far away to hear him. They were the great minds of the people who had erected the huge obelisk and other grand structures in the city. They were known as *masters* and *thinkers* and claimed it was possible to build upon the dried marshes to expand the city's boundaries. They stepped out over the dried marshes holding long wooden poles in their hands. Shem watched as they conversed with one another one moment, then drove the poles down into the ground the next moment. After pulling the rods back up, a thinker would examine the depth mark and make notes on a tablet. The others would gesture their ideas to him and then continue across the strip of land to repeat the process in another area.

Shem turned his attention to nearby fishermen in small reed boats and rafts, casting their nets in hopes of good fortune. Reflections of the rising sun shimmered off the tips of waves as they worked. Farther west, others were digging in the oyster beds near the edge of the sea where the Kura River entered. The dry season had been good to the tribesmen on the outskirts of Tuball. Even the wheat that his uncle Zakho had sold them had grown tall, with their golden tips bending gently in the wind. Other fruits and vegetables had also grown well in the arid land, assisted by the ingenious irrigation system developed by the city's Water-Master.

"Fish, fish, buy our fish! Bread! Fresh bread! Meat! We have meat!" All were the morning calls of the busy market that caught Shem's ears.

He walked to the other side of the roof to observe the merchants and artisans conducting business. The popular wheel toy, commonly used by children, was now being used on the sides of carts. Hauling loads was effortless when compared to the dragging of a wooden sledge. It wasn't long before the aroma of baked breads wafted up to him and he closed his eyes to absorb its effect.

"Shem! Shem!" someone called out from below. He opened his eyes, delighted to see a familiar dark-haired woman in a simple tunic dress and sash waving excitedly near a fruit stand.

Shem smiled, returned the wave, and then motioned for her to come up. It was Kara, the young mountain woman of the Seva tribe that he had become so fond of. Shem had called her his angel when she had saved his life in the mountains, and they had become very close over their time together. It was expected that Shem and Kara would be united once they received their parents' blessing. But their parents lived numerous days away from the city and Shem, swooned by the city's grand culture, had procrastinated on even planning the trip.

Shem watched Kara finish inspecting the quality of some items, tuck them in a pouch slung from her shoulder, and pay the vendor. She brushed her long black hair back and glanced up to him with her beautiful, yet mysterious, dark eyes. He quickly climbed down a wooden ladder from the roof and strode through the atrium of the grand home to open the door. By the time he opened the door to greet Kara, she was at the top step.

Kara held her hands behind her back and Shem eyed her suspiciously. "What do you hide from me, Kara?"

"Close your eyes and open your mouth," she ordered coyly. Shem obeyed.

The young Seva woman swung a bag of mulberries out from behind her and picked out the largest, dark-red berry she could find. She popped a big one onto Shem's tongue, and he instinctively chewed the juicy, sweet, and tangy fruit. He cocked his head, a smile crept up his face, and he opened his eyes. "Mmm! Good pick, Kara."

Never having visited the area before, Kara was enjoying the unfamiliar foods. She held up a berry for him to see, as if instructing a child. "This is a mulberry. Is this not the sweetest thing you have ever tasted?"

Shem reached out and embraced her, unconcerned they were in a public place. "I would not say it is the sweetest thing I have ever tasted."

Kara blushed, pushed the berry into his mouth, and removed herself from his grip. She checked to see if anyone in the market was looking. Vendors and buyers concentrated on making the best bargain, not on the likes of young love. "Shem, why do you do this to me?"

Shem swallowed the berry and wiped his mouth of the juice with his sleeve. "Do what?"

"Play with my feelings. Many others have accepted your god because of your great deeds, but I still have many questions."

"Does that mean we cannot be close?"

She frowned. "Was it not you who worried about my gods...that we should not be *too* close?" Kara provided a painful reminder of their differing faiths. "You know you cannot let your manhood drag you from your beliefs."

It was Shem's turn to become flushed. "It is a hard thing to re-member after I have tasted your lips, Kara." Since she had arrived in the city, they had been as tight as peas in a pod, and once his mind was set on something, it was difficult to think of anything else. Shem felt ashamed that he was being careless with his behavior, and that it took someone outside his faith to set him straight. "You are right," he replied, dejected. "Can I at least hold you?"

She stepped near to him on the stone stoop. "That is fine."

Shem wondered if he would ever tire of Kara's keen mind deep inside her light, oval face. He unpredictably grabbed her around the waist and tickled her. She dropped to her knees with a con-tagious laughter. "Stop it!" Kara shouted between breaths. "I will wet myself!" She tried to release herself from his attack, but he was persistent. She slapped his hands hard and Shem pulled back.

"Ouch! That hurt."

The strong-willed woman gathered herself and faced him sternly. "You are bad!"

Shem chuckled, then turned to another topic. "Oh, Kara, Bulla said he would introduce me to a special thinker who has wonders beyond belief. Come with me today." Shem had been given free access to any part of the city by Bulla the Grand Elder. And with his celebrity status for protecting the city he was willing to use it to satisfy his endless curiosity.

"I have been thinking about your people, Shem. Have you talked with your Uncle Zakho? You were to leave with him in half a moon."

Shem sighed. "I know…I have been learning many things and had forgotten of it. Does your promise to come with us still hold true?"

She nodded. "It is the right thing to do."

Shem looked over Kara's shoulder to see a portly, well-dressed man suddenly at the bottom of the steps. "We were just talking about you, Uncle!"

Zakho started a climb up the steps. "Of course you were, I am a valuable topic."

Shem rolled his eyes and shook his head. Zakho had curly brown hair and bright brown eyes that glistened when he spoke. That and his jovial nature made him a good trader. Shem's uncle reached the porch, tipped his head to Kara, and continued addressing Shem.

"Nephew! We must talk. I have heard some good news."

Shem was always amazed at how much vitality his hefty uncle had. Shem waved them into the eating area. "Come inside."

They went in and sat down on some cushions next to a raised stone slab. Zakho stretched out sideways on his elbows and scratched at his brown beard, while Shem sat upright with his legs crossed. Kara instinctively went over to the ash pit to start a fire and make some tea.

"I see you have new linens on. Is that what excites you, Uncle?" asked Shem, examining the embroidered sleeve on his robe. "No one from back home would even dream of having something as nice as the fine robe."

Zakho brushed a speck of dirt from his shoulder. "Hmm. I am proud of this one. It is very soft, from the finest wool, but that is not what I am here for." He leaned forward. "I have spoken with some traders who have returned from beyond the mountains to the south of the twin seas and discovered a new way back to your father's land."

Shem perked up. "Did they meet with my father?"

"Yes, but only a short while. The traders said it was a good path, and I convinced them to lead us back there—for the right price. It would take us through the mountains on a path that will save us many days. They say we must leave soon or the trail will be too difficult the closer we move toward the cold season."

It was hard for Shem to imagine cold mountain conditions while they sat in the middle of sweltering summer heat. His near death experience months earlier in the snow still hung fresh in his memory. Shem spoke with cautionary wisdom. "Some traders in the city told me of a safer trail that would take us back to Anbar. From there our steps would be easy."

Zakho laughed. "I cannot believe my ears! You want to take the longer, safer route?" Kara looked over with sympathy, but Zakho laughed it off. "Do not worry, Nephew. If we go over the southern pass soon, I am told there will be no snow."

Shem knew how his uncle became anxious and edgy when staying too long in one place, and hoped Zakho's desire for a new trade route didn't cloud his mind. Zakho and Shem had crossed the southwest mountains in the fall and gotten lost during an unusual snow storm. It was virtually impossible it would happen in the summer.

Shem rethought the logic of Zakho's words and let go of his apprehension. "You are right, Uncle; it is time. How many days can we save taking this new path?"

"They told me two full moons."

Kara brought a pot of black tea to them and poured some of the steaming brew into ceramic cups. Shem grasped the lip of the cup with his fingertips and sipped. After a few sips, he set the cup down on the table and tapped the side of the cup while he was in thought. He could feel Kara sitting quietly at the end of the table watching him as he considered Zakho's quicker route home. Shem glanced back at Kara, and she produced two dimples from a faint smile. Shem was comforted by their fondness for each other.

"Kara is coming with us, Uncle," Shem stated matter-of-factly.

Zakho shrugged. "Bring her. I am sure Noah will want to meet her," he replied with a smirk.

Shem detected a jab from Zakho that assumed his father may disapprove of Kara because of her beliefs. But Shem was certain that if his father spent time with Kara, he too would appreciate her beauty, knowledge, and wisdom.

"When should we leave, Uncle?"

"In a few days. It will be my honor to do the packing."

Shem smiled warmly. "It will be good to see Father and Mother again."

"I am sure they worry for you, Nephew," Zakho replied. "I would too, if I knew about the battle you had with the Leviathan, the cave bear, the snow cat, and such. God has mightily been watching over you, Nephew."

"Please do not tell my parents of those things, Uncle," Shem half-whined, not wishing to upset them.

"If you wish. So be it." The experienced trader abruptly slapped the table and rose to a stand. "Come now—let us not be slow as snails!" he barked. "We have many things to prepare!"

CHAPTER 10

THE JOURNEY HOME

The time had come to leave the city, and Shem convinced his traveling companions to meet early outside the main gate before sunrise. He had tired of the daily kowtowing that Tuballites threw themselves upon him for dispelling the northern barbarians. Shem wanted no part of a sendoff with much regalia. Once he, Kara, and Zakho were outside the gate, they met up with the two traders Zakho had mentioned. They were twins who wore cloaks that hid their faces.

Bulla, the new leader of the regional tribes, had followed the group outside the city walls to say his farewells. Shem had fought beside Bulla and befriended him without any desire for personal gain. The death of Bulla's father during the great battle for the city required Bulla to accept the position as Grand Elder. Like Shem, he showed disdain for the insincere flattery that many of his citizens bestowed upon him.

While the others waited several paces away, the war-hardened leader reached out and gripped his friend's wrist. The sturdy man was clothed in his military leather vest and heavy calf-high sandals. "I will miss you Shem, son of Noah. I trust you will return to the city."

Shem smiled. "I will return, my friend. My word is true."

Bulla hinted at a smile. "Then I will hold you to it."

Shem thought about Bulla's duties as the new Grand Elder. "My father once said that a man carries a burden when he has little, but a man carries an even greater burden when he has everything."

"Your father is a wise man, Shem. I must meet with him."

"I have that same hope, Bulla," said Shem.

While Shem and Bulla conversed, Zakho hummed a little tune while he conducted a last check on the donkey's load of jewels, spices, tools, and fruits. "I expect that this will be one of the best trades I will have."

"You have many things to trade with the tribes of the south, Master Zakho," said Kara, preoccupied with trying to eavesdrop on Shem and Bulla.

After ensuring his goods were in order, Zakho walked back to Kara. "Look how the Grand Elder favors my nephew for his great deeds...even letting Shem call him by name."

Kara admired the two strong men of heart. "It is not Shem's great deeds Bulla admires, but his friendship."

"It did not hurt that Shem was the only brave one left to help fight off the Oka with Bulla." Zakho briefly watched the two men carry on a serious discussion, then reached up and slapped the packs on the animals. "No matter. I will gladly bow to him and call him Grand Elder as long as he showers me with more gifts than I can carry."

Kara laughed. "You are a true trader, Master Zakho."

Soon Shem returned to Zakho and Kara. "Bulla is a good man and will lead his people well."

"There is none better," stated Zakho wisely. Zakho pulled on the donkey's leather leash. "Now, let us greet the day with strength, as we have many days ahead of us." He walked with the animals to catch up with the two guides, while the young couple straggled behind.

Shem recalled Kara's older brothers, Bura and Itsu, who lived in the city. Shem had only made a brief stop the day before to bid farewell, but he knew they would miss her. Although they were protective of Kara, he hoped the brothers knew she would be in good hands with Shem, as long as they were reunited in a few seasons.

"What of your brothers? How did they take your leave of them?" Shem asked.

Kara took Shem's hand. "In truth, I will miss them greatly. Bura said he and Itsu may return to our tribe before the cold season. They trust that the gods will protect me. It is good my brothers are together now. They may travel home after the Feast of Harvest. I have sent word to Mother and Father that we will see them before the next New Moon Festival."

Shem still winced at talk of her gods. He recalled the bad omen that Kara's tribe had mistakenly laid upon him for their misfortunes. "Will your people in the mountains accept me, Kara? We did not part as friends when I left."

"Why do you talk so? You and your god have saved the city from the evil northern tribe. My tribe *must* honor you now."

"I do not wish honor—only kindness, Kara."

Joining the conversation from a fair distance away, Zakho called back to Shem and Kara to get them moving. "They will not be able to honor anyone if we do not leave soon! Come!" They set aside their discussion to join Zakho and the two other traders.

Shem, Kara, and Zakho walked close to one another day and night, yet their guides stayed paces away and kept mostly to themselves. The two pathfinders were tall and mysterious brothers, both wearing long, sand-colored cloaks. No one knew where they were from, but by their pale skin and almond eyes, many suspected them from the east.

In three days, the party of five traveled along the western coast of the southern sea, and stepped carefully around a strange mud volcano that bubbled out a brown goo. They continued south, stopping briefly to visit and eat with fishing clans along the way.

At the southern shore of the sea, they reached the base of a steep mountain range, where the slopes rose sharply from a dry and arid base to snowy white peaks.

While Kara and Shem rested on a log by the sea, the two mysterious traders pointed out aspects of the new route to Zakho. He nodded in agreement as they advised him on the safe section through a valley between the white-capped mountains.

Kara was suspicious of the two quiet traders. As she mixed some herbs into the midday meal of fresh pike, she examined the guides. "They speak little to Zakho and never talk to me," she pouted. "Is it not hot here? And yet they still wear their long clothing."

Shem took a sip of tea and glanced back at the pair. "They must like the heat."

"I think they are hiding something. See how they hide their faces with hoods? And they keep many paces away from us when we walk the paths."

"I have not seen you like this, Kara. Are you wary of all traders?"

She shook her head. "No. But it is not right. Most of the men my father traded with were friendly and liked to talk of their great deeds. These men keep quiet and do not befriend us."

"Maybe so, Kara, but they are guiding us to my father's land. For this good deed, we should rid ourselves of bad thoughts toward them." She said nothing, only watched and listened closely to the men's words.

Shem wondered if she was correct. He knew Kara's mind was bright and piercing like the sun, and she would be wary for good reason.

Soon Zakho returned to the fire and fish. He slapped and rubbed his hands together. "I have talked with our guides. After the meal, we will take the valley of the white river. It will lead us over the mountains and one step closer to our homeland."

"Is that what your new friends say," she asked, with skepticism.

Zakho chuckled at her youthful presumptions, then picked up a wooden spoon and plate. "They know more about the other side of the mountains than we do about Tuball. Should we wander like sheep without a shepherd?"

"It depends upon the shepherd," she countered.

Shem steered the conversation around to kinder thoughts. "I think you are glad to be out of the city, Uncle."

Zakho scraped a portion of the fish mash onto his wooden plate. "You may be right, Nephew. But it also may be that you and I have much in common."

"How, Uncle?"

"New lands excite us both. It is in our blood."

Kara looked at Shem, then back at Zakho. "It must be true, as you come from the same clan."

Shem shrugged it off. "The only land I am thinking of now is the one in a valley next to the Tigris River."

Zakho wagged his spoon. "Not the secrets of Tuball?"

"Well...two things," Shem admitted sheepishly. "When I return to the city, I will visit the great thinker. He will tell me many things."

"So I have heard," groaned Zakho. "All things are great at your age, Nephew."

After their meal, the group was full in the belly and ready to blaze a trail next to the river that flowed down from the mountains. They started their climb, and went higher and higher, until the air was cooler. Before long, all but the twins were wearing an extra layer of clothing.

It took the group several days to cross over the many snowy ridges. Although the terrain was at times steep and dangerous, the mysterious traders tried to hold to a pace that Kara could manage. She never complained, but Shem noticed she had slipped and fallen hard on her shin and favored it as she walked.

Shem confided in Zakho. "Uncle, we must rest in one place for a time, Kara has hurt her leg."

Zakho observed how she grimaced whenever she took a step. "Hmmm. I will tell the brothers."

The traders acknowledged Zakho's concern and led the group to a flat area adjacent to the stream they were following. As they made camp, they noticed a small tributary feeding the main stream, creating an unusual mist. Shem squatted down to fill a flask with water when one of the traders took his staff and rapped the Sethite across the shoulder.

"This is not good here," he warned firmly, pointing to a dead fish floating sideways just out of reach.

The brook was fed from a boiling geothermal spring a few paces away, and Shem's hand would have been seriously burned if the guide had not stopped him from touching the water. Venturing down the main stream to a pool, the men discovered the waters were warm, yet safe. They concluded it may be a blessing from above for Kara to warm and heal herself. Therefore, while she rested in the pool, the men went upstream to get fresh water and catch fish.

After a few choice catches of mountain trout, Shem left the men early to check up on Kara's condition. To his surprise, Kara had just exited the pool naked and was reaching for her deerskin dress hanging on a tree. Shem instinctively ducked behind a large pine tree. After a moment, he checked briefly to see if she was dressed. She wasn't. Shem pulled back, but couldn't help but notice her shapely feminine curves. He also spotted a large bruise on her shin and was thankful they had stopped for her to recover.

As he leaned against the pine trunk, his mind wandered to what their life might be like in the future. Would they live near his father and plant crops? Would he end up trading like Zakho? How many sons would she bear him? Shem caught himself thinking too far ahead in his life and remembered that he would need to get his father's blessing before bonding with her. Feeling guilty of his voyeurism, Shem quietly regrouped with the men to give her time to dress.

One of the brothers saw Shem return and approached. As the man passed by Shem he pause a moment to speak. Rarely did the brothers speak. "This one is not for you."

"What is not for me?"

The man didn't even look at Shem, but only passed by to walk to the water's edge.

Shem watched the guide bend down to pick up the fish in a net. "If you speak of that fish, you can keep it." The guide said nothing.

The men returned to see Kara tossing twigs on a fire for the evening meal. The men held up the fish, then handed their catch to her so she could clean and cook them. After the meal, the men bathed in the warm pool to wash off their sweaty bodies and soothe their aching muscles. It had a medicinal effect and seemed to reinvigorate them.

Realizing its therapeutic capabilities, they stayed another day in hopes that their strength would be renewed and bring them safety over the final portion of the mountain range. With wrinkled skin and restored energy, the group packed up for the last leg of their journey. Without protest from the others, Shem dedicated the pool as a holy place to his god.

The weeks passed, and the travelers finally crossed over the mountains into familiar surroundings. They approached the precipice of a mountain ridge overlooking the Tigris River nestled in a fertile green valley, and gazed at its beauty. This was the last leg of their journey home and all were grateful.

As the party descended, Shem's thoughts took him back to childhood memories: wrestling with his brothers to test their strength, making his father proud when he made his first fire, and cutting his leg at three and burying his face in his mother's waist for comfort.

Soon they were upon the riverbend where the start of sculpted fields flowed in golden glory. Shem's pace quickened and his heart beat faster when he spotted his father in the distance standing near their home. The wayward young man was unconsciously jogging, leaving the others behind. Shem slowed when he neared their home, where he saw Noah displaying a broad grin.

"Shem! Come and greet your father," Noah called with out-stretched arms. Shem ran, and they clasped one another tightly. They held each other for a long moment while Zakho and Kara followed and arrived soon after. Noah stepped back to get a better look at his son. "Look how you have changed! Your hair is short and your shoulders are thick!"

Shem beamed pleasure. His father looked exactly as he did a year earlier, a tall majestic man with a silver beard and brilliant yellow-green eyes. "Much has happened in the city of Tuball, Father."

Noah 's voice softened. "And what of your inner path? Have you found it, my son?"

Shem's eyes welled up. "I have learned many things, Father," he breathed unevenly. Shem hadn't realized how much the absence from family affected him. He wiped his tears with his sleeve and looked into his father's piercing eyes.

Noah quickly patted the side of Shem's head. "We can swim the deep waters later, but now go to the house and greet your mother."

Shem nodded and sprinted to the mud-brick home. He flung the door open and went inside. Everyone outside grinned as they heard a joyous scream in the house from Noah's wife, Naamah.

Zakho greeted his brother Noah with a hug and introduced Kara. "Noah, this is Kara, son of Vard. She is from the northern mountain people known as the Seva."

Noah glanced at his brother with an unspoken question, then bowed slightly to greet her. "Our home is open to you, daughter of Vard. You must have food and drink. Follow Shem's steps to my home and my wife will care for you."

Kara bowed her head. "Thank you, Master Noah." She smiled, then walked on to the house.

Zakho pointed back several paces to the twins, who stood poised with their hands folded in front of them. "And you have met these traders. Many thanks are due for their skill in guiding us through the mountains." Noah respectfully bowed his head without a word, and the two men did likewise.

Zakho started to follow behind Kara, but Noah pulled him aside. "Brother?" he whispered tipping his head toward Kara.

"She and Shem are very close," he stated, nonchalantly.

"How close?" Noah asked, with apprehension in his voice.

Zakho wiped sweat from his forehead. "Do not worry, Brother. Shem has acted faithfully."

"That may be good, Brother, but he is not the one I worry about."

"Let us dwell on this later, Noah. My lips are dry and my feet are sore. I could settle for some ripened goat's milk."

Noah sighed. "Where are my manners? You are right, Brother. We will talk of this later. Come, rest yourself."

Noah led his brother into his cool mud-brick home and looked back for the secretive twins to follow, but they preferred to stay outside. Word spread quickly into the small community and soon other family members arrived from the fields. Shem's brothers, Japheth and Ham, his sisters, and his cousins packed into Noah's home to welcome Shem and the others. After an hour of joyous laughter and reminiscing, it was as if Shem had never left.[2]

[2] Noah (Noach-Hebrew & Nuh-Arabic), Shem, Japheth, Ham and Lamech are characters taken directly from the Bible. Some Jewish traditions assume that Naamah was Noah's wife, whereas the Dead Sea Scrolls mention his wife as Amzara. The author chose to have Noah marry Naamah after his first wife Amzara died. All other characters in the book are fictional.

CHAPTER 11

INFESTATION

Shortly after sunup, Shem's mother, Naamah, served him and the others a special meal of hardboiled dove eggs, fried spiced lamb, and boiled wheat with barberries. While they relished their meal, the youngest brother, Ham, made claims that he could beat Shem in a race to the hills. Shem scoffed at the idea and challenged him in an afternoon run. It wasn't long before wagering on the winner had begun. Through the meal, other family members boisterously carried on their conversation, while Noah stayed quiet and introspective. Without notice, Noah silently left the house to gather his thoughts.

Shem was bantering with Ham when he noticed his father walking alone away from the house. Suspecting something was amiss, Shem left the table and found his father strolling through a patch of wildflowers near the river.

"Father, you do not look well. Are you sick, or have the plantings been poor this year?"

"No, I am fine...so too is the harvest." Noah studied Shem closely. "It is you I worry for, Son."

Shem smiled with confidence. "Do not worry for me. I feel strong and have learned much since I have left."

"In truth, it is not as much about you than it is about the woman you brought with you that I worry about."

"Kara?"

"Yes, Kara. I sense much strength in her, which is good in a woman, but she is from the north and does not believe as we do. I am right on this, am I not?"

Shem was about to expound her virtues, but stopped short. Instead he hung his head, because he knew what Noah was about to say. "Father, in all ways she has my heart, except our god."

"That will not do, Son. You cannot infect yourself with her idols. You are young and full of great thoughts with her, but you cannot let this continue."

"What? Why? She may not be a Sethite in blood, but could she not be one in her heart?"

"That is between her and the Almighty. You know we must separate ourselves so that we do not learn to accept their gods."

"But I tremble with joy when I am with her, and I wish to spend my life with her."

An ugly frown flashed across Noah's forehead. "You have not joined with her have you?"

Shem pulled back. "No!" he was indignant.

The patriarch relaxed. "I had to ask. Once you *know* a woman, the path only goes forward."

"Father, it has already taken us forward. I am drawn to her. I cannot, and do not, want to let her go."

"Indeed, you listen with your heart—but be wary of its wonders. The heart can trick one with its soothing warmth." Shem looked intently at his father, not with anger, but with puzzlement.

Noah softened. "Shem, sit. It is time I tell you of my earlier days." Shem sat down crosslegged on a large dry patch of moss and Noah rested on a carved stump. "Before you were born, I was like you, wandering the trails like Zakho, reaching out to find new lands. But then I met a woman named Azarah. She was as beautiful as a flower on the outside and full of life on the inside. I was bonded with Azarah and we were as close as any two could be. Have I not mentioned her to you?" Shem shook his head in dismay.

Noah looked across the river and continued his story. "We decided to wander trails together and see all of God's wonders...far to the western sea and up beyond the northern mountains. My father, Lamech, warned me of getting close to the Cainites, but I ignored him. Azarah and I lived life carefree and without worries...until one day God took her from me."

Noah paused, dropped his head, and leaned forward on his walking stick. He pulled himself up and took a step, then stared at the smooth flowing river. Shem could sense a rare, strong emotion from his father as he tried to compose himself. Noah's eyes started to fill and his throat choked when he tried to speak.

"What happened to her, Father?" Shem whispered.

Noah cleared his throat and wiped his eyes. "It does not matter how she died, Son. What is important is that her death plagued me for many seasons, and I was angry at God for letting my innocent beauty die. For many years, I did not follow God's ways, and left everyone I knew to live high in the mountains. After many more years, I found myself alone, not only from Azarah and my family, but also from the Creator. But I believe he used her death to draw me closer to him. When my anger finally left me, I gave homage to the Creator and had peace once again. Then one day, I sat on a high point in the mountains far north, and God spoke to me. He granted me a vision of what was to come."

Shem moved closer and spoke respectfully. "What did he show you, Father?"

"He showed me many things—many wonderful things: such as how our children will grow many in numbers and will walk in righteousness...about how man can turn from good to evil, and many horrible things that I wish not to remember. It is not my time to tell you all I saw. But as the Creator takes away, so does he give back. And in losing Azarah, I gained your mother. Naamah has been a good and faithful wife, and as we have stayed faithful, peace has covered this family."

Shem nodded. "She has been a good mother."

"Son, do not think because your heart pulls you toward this woman that it is meant to be."

"Are you saying you will not give me your blessing, Father?"

"No. What I am saying is I am not willing to give you my blessing on this day."

"Have I not kept your teachings, and have I not been faithful?" Shem looked around the ground as if to find a solution, then spoke up with an answer. "If she accepts our ways, will you honor our bonding then?"

Noah partially smiled. "You truly want this woman as your wife?"

Shem straightened up and folded his arms across his chest. "Yes, Father."

"There are so many women of your own kind. Why are you so blinded and wish to choose one so different—" Noah stopped himself.

Shem smiled inside, knowing that after Noah just told of his love for Azarah, he should understand how Shem too must love Kara. He couldn't force Shem to simply reject the Cainite woman so easily.

Noah paused in thought and looked back at Kara laughing with Japheth and Ham outside the house. "Very well. If you can persuade her to accept our God and disown hers, I will bless the union between you two."

Shem grinned broadly, then jumped up from the ground to hug his father. "Thank you, Father. You will see, I will help her understand our God."

"I am sure you will try."

Noah put his arm around Shem's shoulder as they walked back to the house. When they neared the home, Ham had just finished losing a game of leg wrestling to Japheth. Kara smiled when Shem approached and went to stand by his side.

Noah rejoined Naamah, and together they watched as Shem, with a twinkle in his eye, took Kara's hand to show her the wheat fields. "I do not like one so young playing games with other gods. It is not safe, my wife."

"Has the Creator spoken to you, Husband?" she asked.

"Not as yet, but I ache for an answer."

Zakho had left Noah's land to visit their father, Lamech, who lived a few days to the west. The twins had told Zakho that they would be traveling northwest to Anbar market, so Zakho traveled alone. Shem promised his uncle that he and Kara would meet up with him at Lamach's after the harvest, then journey to Kara's home in the northern mountains.

It was mid morning, and Shem left Kara with Naamah to learn of the roles of a Sethite women, while he went to see his brothers in the fields. Japheth, tall and fair skinned, and Ham, stout and dark, were diverting the waters of the Tigris into the rows of grain. With the water bunching up at the edge of the field, Japheth instinctively kicked away large clumps of dirt so the water could flow freely through the rows. While inspecting the stalks of wheat, Japheth noticed one large grasshopper munching on a husk. Annoyed with the insect, the eldest brother deftly grabbed the insect and crushed it in his hands.

As Japheth walked back to the house for the midday meal, he reunited with Shem and displayed the insect. "Look at this grasshopper, Brother."

Shem flicked at the big insect in his older brother's calloused hand, to confirm it was dead. "That is the biggest one I have ever seen—it spans your hand, Japheth! You must show Father."

"I will. It is strange to see such a large grasshopper." Japheth smiled and elbowed his brother. "It is almost as strange your short hair."

Shem brushed his hand over his head. "It will grow back."

Japheth's smile disappeared. "Did you know that I was glad to see you leave many months ago, Shem? You did not work hard like Ham and I, and it was not fair to us. But now that you have returned, I am glad you are well."

Shem smiled. "It is good to see you too, Japheth. I did not know what a good brother you were to me until I was away."

"Ha! You were just wanting for mother's cooking." Japheth pushed his shorter brother affectionately. As they walked through the tall rows of grain, Japheth became pensive. "Do you think you will be a wanderer like Uncle Zakho?" he asked, half-inspecting the wheat as he walked.

"I do not know, Brother. Trading is not easy and could be lonely. Ask me after harvest."

Japheth nodded and stuck a piece of straw in his mouth. They continued to stroll through the golden fields, contrasted with the bright blue river on one side and tan mud-brick homes on the other. When the two brothers returned to the house, they sat down to lamb stew. Noah had already finished his meal and sat with some colored beads so as to calculate the yield of his crops.

Before Japheth ate, he showed Noah the insect. "Father, when I was watering the fields I saw this yellow grasshopper with spots. Are they not smaller and green?"

Noah's looked up from his counting and his face paled at the sight of the arthropod. "That is a locust! They are not like grasshoppers who live alone; they band together with hundreds of their kin and eat all that is in sight. Since before you were born, they have left us alone and the harvest has been good. It is sensible they wait for our best crop. We have not gained enough storage grain for another year, and they will strip not only the wheat and barley but everything down to our sandals."

Shem tried to console his father. "He found only this one, Father. Maybe it will not be as bad as you say. We fought off many large raiders of the city of Tuball with God's blessing. Why should we worry about one big grasshopper in the field?"

"That does not help us, Shem. God always teaches us through his handiwork, but that does not mean he will always protect us from evil. The pest that Japheth found shows us that others are not far behind." Noah stood and gazed out at the acres of beautiful golden crop. "Where did you find the locust, Japheth?"

"At the southern end of the fields."

"I do not know if it is the work of God or the Devil, but that is where we will do battle." Noah waved for Japheth and Shem to follow him.

"How can we battle them if they are from God, Father?" asked Shem.

"God may be testing us. Sometimes we do the same task for different reasons."

Noah studied the land and instructed his sons to plow a wide strip of earth from one end of the field to the other so that a collar of soil would separate a thin line of wheat from the rest of the crop. The men obeyed by dragging the plough wedge in a semicircle through the crops. At the end of a long day, they had accomplished the task by creating a swath of earth between the main portion of the field and a thin one. The men slept uneasily that night, fretting about what the next day would hold for them.

By morning, Noah inspected the fields only to find dozens of locusts creeping along the perimeter of their land. He knew they were only a small part of the swarm. Noah knew he had little time and instructed his sons to spread lamp oil among the buffer strip of wheat and stand ready. Noah made a small fire outside the fields and waited. By the afternoon, the sons saw what their father had feared. An eerie brown haze edged over the horizon and started to move toward the fields at about as fast as a man's run. Noah and his sons stood still, waiting to see what the invading cloud would do...whether it would turn away or attack their land.

A mild breeze blew toward them with the brown haze pulled with it. It grew larger and larger until it was nearly upon them. Noah estimated it was time to react and gave the order for his sons to burn the thin barrier of wheat. Each of the sons put his unlit torch into the fire and sprinted away to his assigned position. They threw their torches into the thin section of dry wheat and oil, which burst into flames immediately, sending up a cloud of heavy smoke. They felt the blazing heat from the fire and drew back into the edge of the field to watch.

Noah waved his hands outward. "This small part of our crop must be sacrificed to save the rest." He was somewhat dubious of his plan and watched for any moment to make a change.

The brown haze came into focus to reveal a swarm of insects at field's edge. The swarm was so thick and so numerous that even the sun had darkened. The marauding arthropods began their descent to forage, but the heavy smoke and fire forced them to abandon a landing.

Some insects penetrated the smoke and landed in the fire, while the remaining ones skipped up and over toward the east. Japheth and Ham gave a cheer when the locusts veered away. They jumped up and down and sent victorious curses at the pests.

"We have beaten them, Father! We have beaten them!"

They watched the swarm retreat a few kilometers to the east, when the breeze shifted. It suddenly blew from east to west and with it, the insects. The faces of the men sagged in despair as the finger-long insects descended once again toward the wheat for the next attack.

Japheth watched the movement of the insects. "Look how they move with the breeze! They follow the wind! God must want this! Why?" Japheth lamented.

Ham grabbed his brother Japheth and they ran into the fields to fend off the yellow thieves from swallowing up their hard labor and crucial food source. Shem ran to assist.

Noah took a few steps backward and watched in dismay. The calamity was sinking in, and the thought of stripped vegetation was the only thing he could envision. Noah's legs became weak. He dropped to his knees and held his hands up to the sky.

"Lord God of creation, we are your children. We have been faithful and honored you. Why do you send these dreadful creatures upon us? Please use your mighty hand to save us and we will glorify your name."

Noah gazed proudly at the young men as they took off their cloaks and frantically swung them at the voracious invaders. Like warriors on a battlefield, they ran and swung their cloaks in a circle, to dissuade them of a meal. Japheth, Shem, and Ham all worked together at swatting, stomping, and crushing the demons anyway they could. The insects came down by the millions, singing a cacophony of clicking and buzzing tones as they flew. Thicker and thicker the onslaught became, and it became difficult to breath without inhaling one or two. The young men's strong arms started to weaken from the endless swinging and smashing.

While Noah's sons fought on, his attention was drawn away. His mouth hung open in amazement. A second cloud, darker than the first, rose up from the east. "Another swarm?" Noah whispered. "What have we done to deserve this punishment?"

Ham staggered back when he too saw the second swarm. "Japheth, look!" he shouted and pointed to the sky.

Japheth dropped his cloak to his side and squinted to see through the flying insects. "What is it?" yelled Japheth, pulling off handfuls of locusts landing in his face and hair.

Shem trotted to the edge of the field where his father stood and pointed into the sky. "Father, do you see this other cloud! It is much bigger and louder than the first! We cannot stop another one!"

Noah examined the new swarm more closely, then took a few steps forward. "That is not a locust swarm. It is something else! It might be a dust storm!"

If it was indeed a storm, Noah knew the wheat would assuredly be destroyed. It seemed inevitable they would either lose their crop to pest or storm. Noah looked back to his home, grateful to see the women blocking the open windows and rushing inside for safety. Naamah had seen several storms before, and it was her duty to be a calming influence on the girls and young ones.

The dark cloud grew high and wide, blotting out the sun, turning day into dusk. Noah called off the battle against the locusts, and they froze in place, mesmerized and puzzled by the second mysterious event. The thunderous cloud grew bigger and louder, quickly descending onto the fields. The loud buzzing of the insects that penetrated their head was soon being drowned out by a rumbling roar of this new approaching cloud.

Fearing for their lives, the men raced toward the safety of the river. Watching the event from a new perspective they realized the second cloud was neither insects nor dust storm. To their astonishment, it was an immense flock of Collared Doves—a flock of millions!

"They are birds!" Shem shouted.

A deafening flapping of wings smothered the buzzing of insects as the doves pressed down upon the locusts. The birds methodically went to work snatching up the unaware locusts resting on the wheat. The insects started to abandon the wheat and fly off with the wind, but the chase was on.

The birds took to them like a thirsty man to water. The insects seemed to fly in a swirling pattern, trying to outsmart their predators, but it was useless; trying to make a meal of the crops, they turned into a meal themselves. Within minutes, the doves flew in circles, corralling the locusts until every last one of their victims was gone. Satisfied with their snack, the flock rose up in a fluttering torrent and dashed away to the north.

The four men stood motionless in the river water, mouths gaping, as the birds eventually disappeared over a distant ridge. The horrendous buzzing and flapping sounds were replaced with quiet water rippling around their legs and a distant lamb bleating near the house.

Noah scanned the main portion of their wheat crop—it was virtually intact. After a restful moment he addressed his sons. "Remember this day well, my sons. For God has shown how he watches over us."

"I have never seen doves in such a large group like that, Father," said Ham.

"Nor I," added Noah.

"And neither have I. But I knew God would protect us," Shem boasted.

"You are correct this time, Shem," Noah replied. "Come, my sons. We must thank the Most High for his blessings and plan quickly for the harvest before God changes his merciful mind."

CHAPTER 12

SABOTAGE

A mosquito had just landed on Harold Witherspoon's arm, poised and ready to bite. With one smooth motion, the professor smashed it, flicked it off, and reached for his English Breakfast tea. Bob McCray had collected his staff in the cafeteria to formally introduce Dr. Witherspoon and Jamal as an integral part of the expedition to survey the undersea ruins. The government of Azerbaijan would normally want a participant from the National Academy of Sciences, but to expedite the examination of the ruins and eliminate bureaucratic gymnastics, the credentials of Dr. Harold Witherspoon were a satisfactory substitute. McCray put him in charge of proprietary excavation techniques during removal of any of the artifacts. All other personnel were a supporting cast, expected to perform their usual duties as when they conduct a shallow hazard survey.

With most of the ship's personnel in the cafeteria, the last of the supplies were being brought aboard by local vendors. The long line of men carrying boxes on their shoulders up the gangplank and down to the lower decks was beginning to thin. Soon the last of the supplies were on board and the meeting in the cafeteria ended. The crew went back to their stations to prepare for departure.

The ship adjourned from the dock and was cutting through choppy Caspian waves at fifteen knots. The crew brought out the survey equipment to be used at the site, while Jamal and the professor received an informal lecture given by Tony on the operation of the Remote Operating Vehicle.

Jamal turned on his computer to enter some data only to find his rechargeable battery dying. He cursed in Farsi, then looked for help. "Professor, do you have any back-up batteries? My laptop does not hold a charge when I remove the plug."

"I didn't bring any spares with me, Jamal. Maybe someone on board could help you."

Rebecca was on her way to the conference room and passed by the men. "Hi, sweetheart!" Tony called out, gregariously.

Rebecca blew out a puff of air. "Hello, Tony." She slowed her stride and addressed Jamal. "Did you say you needed a battery?" Jamal nodded. "I think I saw some spare batteries in the DSOG equipment room, Jamal. Come on, I'll show you where they are before I meet up with Dr. McCray."

"Thank you, Rebecca," said Jamal. He set his computer down and waved to the professor and Tony. Tony put on a sour smile.

Rebecca avoided the noisy generator compartment and took Jamal through the main control station, down a passageway, and into the switchboard room. Once in the electrical switchboard room, Rebecca tried to lift the handle to the DSOG compartment where the batteries were stored. The door was stuck.

"Here, let me help," offered Jamal.

Rebecca stood aside to let him open it. She thought that this was where a man was useful. The door latch was tighter than usual. "Why is this so tight?" Jamal grunted without success.

"Let's both do it," suggested Rebecca. Together they pulled.

Barely had the door been opened when *Whoosh!* Jamal's eyes widened as the hatch flew open with all the might tons of sea water could muster. The force knocked the two backward, slamming them against a large electrical panel with hundreds of switches not far off the deck. Water poured into the compartment, along with floating boxes of equipment, food, and other debris.

"Ouch!" cried out Jamal, smacking his head against the metal panel. "We must close the door!" He swung the door partway, but the force of the water was too much for him.

Struggling against a shin-high current of water, Rebecca tried to regain her wits. With her back against the electrical switchboard, alarm bells rang out in her head. "Jamal! If the water was any higher, we might have been electrocuted!"

Jamal let go of the door and started for the door that they came in by. "Then let us leave this place!"

Rebecca reached for the intercom on the bulkhead. "Let me call topside first." She flipped a lever and a red light came on. "Captain! Dr. McCray! Anyone—we have an emergency! Water is flooding in the electrical room!" She flicked the lever a few times so as to hear something, but there was no answer to her distress call. "Helloooo!" She shouted into the device with her voice oscillating.

Still, there was no answer.

Jamal motioned with a panicked wave. "Come on, Rebecca, the water is rising and almost up to the electrical circuits! Let us leave here!"

She waded forward, but felt a tug on her leg. Scuba equipment, hoses, tanks, and other debris floated in and around their shins. As the water rose, something like a hose or rope had tangled itself around Rebecca's leg and under the electrical panel. Rebecca tried to free herself, but was forced back to the panel as the water gushed into the room.

"Oh, for goodness sakes! I am stuck on something!" Rebecca had little time to worry about danger and just reacted. "Turn off the switches to the outlets, Jamal, so we don't get shocked. Then I can get this thing off me without worrying about getting shocked. I think that big one to the right feeds the ones on the bottom."

Jamal nodded, and turned it off. "Now what?"

The lights in the room quickly darkened and the emergency light came on. Jamal stood mesmerized by the scores of switches on the panel.

"I think we hit the main breaker. Try the smaller ones."

He reached toward the bottom switches and began swatting them off with both hands, working his way up to the top. The smaller switches were at the bottom, medium ones chest high, and at eye level was the big one he had turned off. Jamal worked his way up to the top, while Rebecca reached down into the water trying to undo the entanglement. With the lights out, and no luck removing her entanglement, Rebecca started to panic.

"Turn the lights back on!" she shouted. "We need to see what we're doing in here and my leg is still caught. Umph! And I'm stuck against this stupid panel!"

Jamal finally located the compartment light and turned the switch back on. He realized the water level, although streaming out into the passageway, was almost up to the bottom of the panel. "What do you want me to do now? The water is rising." His voice was intense.

"I don't know!" she responded with exasperation. Rebecca started breathing rapidly.

"Well, I don't know either! I'm going to go for help."

Rebecca grabbed his wrist. "Wait." She calmed herself by taking steady deep breaths and regained her composure. "There is a hose wrapped around my leg. Help me get it loose, then we can wade out of here together—away from the panel."

Jamal nodded and dove under the knee high water to try to find the cause of the entanglement. Miscellaneous debris in the already murky water complicated his assignment. After about a minute, he came to the surface gasping for air. "I cannot see a thing!"

Rebecca looked around for a solution, then recalled the layout of the ship. "I believe there is an axe in the passage. If you can get it, I think you can cut through the hose."

Without hesitation, Jamal let the current drag him out into the passageway where indeed an axe stood like a sentry, waiting for its assigned task. Jamal tore it off the bulkhead and fought against the current. He made it back to Rebecca, who was steadfastly fighting to pull herself away from the panel. She was a strong woman but was no match for the grip of a reinforced rubber hose.

"OK now. I'll pull my leg up and you can cut it," she suggested. "—the hose, not my leg."

Jamal's face turned a lighter color. "As you wish." He swallowed and stared at the axe in his hands.

Rebecca was able to lift her tangled ankle up just enough reveal the hose line. With her hands interlocked under her knee, she pulled back, while Jamal pushed some floating scuba cylinders out of his way to get a clean path. He wasted no time in swinging the axe at the hose. However, when it sliced through the water it veered off and clanked against the metal panel. She held her breath, hoping he would strike accurately. Jamal swung the axe a second time, but this time hit the water and angled the sharp end downward toward her knee.

He dropped the axe to his side and wiped the water and sweat from his face.

"This will not work! I will cut off your leg off! Can't you pull your leg through it?"

Rebecca barely had enough strength to pull her leg up. She relaxed and her leg dropped back into the water and her body sprung back to the lower part of the panel. "NO!"

She thought for a moment and got an idea. "See that big switch at the top?" she indicated with a nod.

"Yes?"

"Turn it off. Maybe it will shut down the electrical bus-bar feeding these circuits."

Jamal was getting irritated. "If you say so, but we will lose our lights," he informed.

"Emergency lights are better than being electrocuted."

Jamal started to reach for the switch. "No! Wait!" Rebecca shouted. Jamal curtly pulled back his hand. He started to complain to her, but she was looking up at the ceiling with closed eyes.

She whispered loudly. "Lord Jesus! We could really use your help right now."

Jamal rubbed his forehead when he saw her praying to Jesus. Rebecca's eyes were shut and she was quiet for a full thirty seconds. He couldn't stand the delay. "Rebecca! What are you doing?"

She opened her eyes and faced Jamal firmly. "We have a problem. The main electrical bus feeds the switch. Even if you turn it off, power still comes *in* to the panel…and lots of it.

Jamal looked back at the intercom, annoyed. "Why has no one answered us?"

Rebecca shook her head and brushed her wet hair away from her face. "I don't know, but you were right the first time. You need to go for help."

Jamal groaned. "I should have done that earlier. But now it is too late; the water is already up to our waist. My life has been crazy in the last few weeks! I am an intellectual not a Red Crescent rescuer!" He looked down at the flooding passageway. "Help! Can anyone hear us? Help!" He looked back to Rebecca. "I am *not* going to leave you here to die alone."

Rebecca gave him a thankful smile. "In other circumstances, I would think your heroism was romantic, but don't worry, Jamal. I won't die," she assured. "Just go for help."

"I am not going to leave you, Rebecca Belmont. I mean it."

Rebecca thought for a moment, looking down at the axe by his side. "OK then…I have another idea. Open the knurled screws on the electrical panel and we'll be able to see inside."

Jamal set the axe aside, unscrewed the knobs on the panel face, and swung it around on its hinge. Inside were three copper bars running horizontally, one for each phase of the electrical 440-volt circuits.

Jamal stared inquisitively at them and moved closer to inspect them, but Rebecca cautioned him. "Don't get your face too close. Those are hot, Jamal; hot with electrons," she pointed out.

"What do you want me to do now?"

"Take your axe and hit in between the bus bars."

He was aghast. "What!? You said they were hot. With an electrical engineering degree, you tell me to hit the bars with a wet axe? I will die for sure!"

"No you won't. Electricity always follows the path of least resistance. That means if you cross the two bars, the flow of electricity will short between the two legs and not you. By doing that, it will overload the ship's generator and shut off the power to this panel."

By this time, the water was up to their chest and they had no time to debate the issue. Jamal grunted a reluctant compliance, holding tightly on the axe handle, and squinting out an aim toward the bus bars. He made a few short test swings with the axe in the air, then glanced over at Rebecca trying to lean as far away from the panel as possible. Jamal lined up the swing a last time, then cringed as he heaved the axe forward. The room brightened brilliantly, accompanied instantaneously by a loud *BOOM!* For a moment, the two were blinded by the flash and deafened by the explosion. When their eyes adjusted, the emergency light was back on and they saw dimly the axe welded between the bus-bars.

"*Peeuw*, that stinks," said Rebecca waving away the acrid electrical fumes floating out of the panel. "Good job, Jamal. Now we have a little time left to get me out of here."

"My ears!" said Jamal, wiggling his finger in his ear to dispel the ringing.

She calmly stretched out to retrieve some floating scuba equipment and handed it over to Jamal. "The ringing should go away soon. Here, Jamal, put on this mask so you can see underwater. I will adjust the regulator so you won't run out of air while you work to loosen my restraints." She tugged on the hoses attached to a cylinder and held it up above her head to make sure the adjustment was correct.

Jamal stared at the mouthpiece for a moment, looked at the rising water level and then back at his trapped companion. "I do not know how to use this thing," he replied with exasperation.

"Well, you're gonna learn quickly, because I can't stay here forever."

Jamal looked at the neck-high water creeping up to her chin. "OK! Show me how to do this," he answered, anxiously.

"Relax, Jamal, I know Jesus has a plan for us and it isn't to die in here."

By this time, he was frantic. "Stop it with your Jesus and show me!"

"OK. Take it easy," she replied coolly.

Rebecca quickly pointed out the basics of breathing with scuba gear, then Jamal strapped on the mask. She adjusted the regulator and gave him an OK sign. Jamal's breathing was erratic, but not so irregular that he couldn't perform his duty. Unclamping an underwater lamp from the bulkhead, Jamal followed the tangled hose under water to where it was wrapped around the frame of the electrical panel support bracket.

With only a moment under water, he shot back up to the surface. "I can't do it! I cannot see a thing!"

"Yes, you can," she replied calmly. "Try it again. When you are in murky water, just feel around to get a picture in your mind's eye. It will be easier that way."

"There must be another way to release you," he mumbled. He put the mouthpiece back in and dove back to the bottom, feeling his way to her ankle.

The water continued to rise. Rebecca's muscles tightened to their threshold as she struggled to keep her chin above the waterline by kicking with one leg. When the seawater rose above her chin, she closed her mouth and started breathing through her nose. As the minutes ticked by, the water started to creep over her nose, so she cupped her hand around her nostrils to create a makeshift snorkel.

Under the water, the intellectual figured out how to work the tangled line like unwrapping a ball of string. After what seemed endless moments of twisting and pulling and undoing the hose, Jamal noticed Rebecca's body relaxing. The tension on the line gave Jamal enough slack for him to loosen the knot and remove the hose from around her leg.

Successful at her release, Jamal jubilantly sprang up to the surface and ripped off his mask. His heart sank when she lay face down in the water. Her arms had floated to the surface and she lay motionless.

"Rebecca? Rebecca!" he shouted, as he lifted her face above the water. Her eyes were closed and she wasn't breathing.

There was only a foot of air between them and the ceiling with no way or time to revive her. Jamal instantly grabbed her shirt collar and pulled. With Rebecca in tow, he didn't waste any time swimming out to the passageway to the outer hatch. Before continuing, Jamal stared at the door at the end of the passageway, lit only by the amber emergency light halfway below the waterline. He realized that if he opened the door, it might flood another compartment. Changing direction, he quickly swam back to the DSOG equipment compartment, maintaining Rebecca's head above water.

Finding an overhead hatch, Jamal hoisted his limp companion and himself up the remaining rung of the ladder toward a ceiling access. With one hand, Jamal twirled the round handle until the hatch popped up and the air whooshed up around them. He struggled to pull the heavy weight of Rebecca's unresponsive body up to the main deck and clear of the opening.

He slammed the hatch and locked it, then turned Rebecca onto her stomach. Jamal reached from around her back and under her belly, clasping his hands together. He then jerked her up forcefully, to dispel any water in her system. Water spilled out of her mouth and onto the deck. Turning her over on her back, he contemplated how to give her CPR. He nervously pressed a few times to her chest, then opened her mouth to breath new air into her lungs. With no response, he turned her over to push out more water.

Jamal looked around and was about to call for help when Rebecca coughed a few times. Jamal dropped down and kneeled next to her prone position, then brushed her hair from her face.

Rebecca groaned then slowly got on her hands and knees. "Oh, my head aches."

"You are alive," he whispered, with tear-filled eyes.

The water-logged young woman cleared her throat a few times, spit out some phlegm, and then plopped down on her side. She wiped her mouth of seawater and brimmed with confidence. "Of course I'm alive. I told you it would be OK, didn't I?"

Jamal hoped that Rebecca couldn't see the silent tears of joy trickling down his wet cheeks. The two drenched and exhausted escapees sat on the deck, trying to regain their strength. Out of nowhere, Dr. McCray approached them with Tony tagging behind.

"I was told you went down to the DSOG compartment. I hope one of you wasn't responsible for the power failure, because we were right in the middle of a computer software simulation." He paused. "You guys are soaking wet!"

Unaware of their ordeal, Tony only shook his head. "I bet you didn't get that battery, either."

Rebecca and Jamal looked up with exasperation.

CHAPTER 13

RETURN FOR REPAIRS

R ebecca sat on the deck and squinted up at her boss as the sun beamed over his shoulder. "Didn't you hear us calling on the intercom?" she asked in an accusatory tone.

Dr. McCray looked bewildered. "What are you talking about, Becca? I was in the middle of a conference when the power went off, then on, then off again…the intercom was dead silent." He looked at Tony, who shrugged a "don't-look-at me" expression.

Suddenly, the ship pitched downward. She looked up to see Captain Kovacheski in the pilot house. She assumed he had cut the engines on the *Bering* to determine why the electrical power shifted to emergency status. In seconds, the chief engineer Chuck Gohn and the ship's electrician ran past her to the lower level ladder leading down to the switchgear room.

McCray stood to follow the chief engineer. "We'll talk about this later. I need to find out—."

Rebecca interrupted. "Wait! I need to explain something!" The ship coasted to a crawl and Rebecca and Jamal staggered to their feet, still groggy from their ordeal. "There is a flood in the compartments just below us!" Rebecca bent over and coughed out some more seawater. "We have to stop it right away or you can forget about not only your computer simulation, but the ship too." Rebecca looked up to see two Azeri deckhands who had stopped their work and approached with curiosity while sharing a smoke.

"A flood?" Dr. McCray's eyes widened. "Down here?" he asked, pointing to the hatch on the deck.

"Yeah, down there!"

McCray dropped to one knee to grip the hatch handle on the deck and quickly spun it open. A burst of air whooshed past him. Water had climbed most of the way up the ladder. The workers leaned over McCray's shoulder to catch a glimpse, but he slammed the hatch down before it could rise any farther. He called out to the chief engineer. "Chuck! We have a problem!" McCray turned to Rebecca and Jamal. "Are you guys going to be all right?"

"Yeah, we're fine," said Rebecca. Jamal nodded.

Seconds later, Chuck ran out from the lower level. "Hey, you guys! The switchgear room and the DSOG compartment are flooded!"

"We know!" shouted McCray. "Chuck, just fix it. I'll call the office in Baku so they can be aware of our situation."

Chuck spouted orders in Russian to the idle Azeri workers. The men jumped back, nodded vigorously, and sprinted out of sight.

The diesel engines were still operable for propulsion, but with the main switchboard down, shipboard operations were seriously compromised. In another moment, a wailing emergency siren blared throughout the ship and the robust chief engineer returned with the two Azeri deckhands back to where Jamal and Rebecca still stood dripping wet. The men packed a large gas-powered pump and grunted as they set it down near the hatch. With their cigarettes still skillfully hanging on their lips, the Azeri workmen attached hoses on both ends of the pump. The engineer set his foot on the pump's housing, yanked the noisy gas-powered engine to life, and signaled the men to open the hatch.

With the hatch open, the men scrambled over to lower the hose into the water. Soon, at a great velocity, the pump was pouring a mixture of seawater and miscellaneous debris over the side of the ship. Chuck watched to see if the water level in the lower compartment would drop faster than the water coming in. He gave a thumbs-up and Rebecca returned a sigh of relief.

Chuck kept a watchful eye on the progress, and slowly but surely, the water receded from the compartment. It was just before sunset, when the crew had sealed the leak and allowed the ship's electrician to concentrate on the electrical switchgear. He removed the welded axe from the main distribution panel and vigorously blew the circuits dry with compressed air. Once the electrician felt confident it was safe, he donned rubber gloves, energized the main disconnect, and then strategically turned on the appropriate breakers one at a time.

Main power had returned and the ship's operating systems were virtually back to normal. With danger at bay, Jamal and Rebecca soon found themselves draped in large towels and sitting in Dr. McCray's stateroom. Curiosity brought Professor Witherspoon in with them.

After handing his guests some coffee, McCray got down to business. "Would you two like to tell me what happened below?"

Rebecca and Jamal took turns retracing the events as they happened. In the course of their play-by-play explanation, Bob McCray's head bobbed back and forth as if watching a tennis match. Toward the end of the inquiry, the chief engineer arrived at the cabin and rapped on the door. Dr. McCray saw him through the door's porthole and waved him in.

Chuck entered the room holding up a twisted piece of brass with his thick fingers. "I think I found out why the compartment flooded." He shut the door and handed his boss the shattered object. "The water in the compartment isn't drained out completely yet, but we found a relief valve, or what used to be a relief valve, wedged up on the overhead light. With the pipe wide open, the seawater must of come rushing in. And valves don't break open by themselves, so it had to be knocked off. And the reason Becca couldn't get ahold of us?" Chuck answered his own question. "The intercom junction feeding the DSOG storage and switchgear compartments was disconnected. To make sure all circuits are functional, I'm having the electrician check them all, one by one."

"So it's sabotage," Dr. McCray summarized.

"Looks like it," Chuck agreed.

"What is going on here? We are on a simple survey expedition. Why would someone do this?" Dr. Witherspoon and the others were silent in thought.

"I don't know, J. Bob," Chuck replied.

McCray patted the engineer's shoulder. "Thanks, Chuck, for your remarkable sleuthing—as usual. If you find anything else, let me know."

The engineer waved a casual salute and went back to check on the clean-up. McCray turned the crumpled metal over in his hand.

Rebecca was concerned that even if they could continue their voyage, the saboteur may still be aboard. *But if he or she is still aboard, who could it be?* She caught the eyes of McCray and knew he was thinking the same thing.

"Do you have any ideas who might do this?" she asked McCray.

"No. This is all very odd." Rebecca and Jamal snuggled into their towels. "Why don't you two get some rest. We'll discuss this with the staff and make a decision on how to proceed later. Are you going to be all right, Rebecca? I would understand perfectly if you didn't want to continue on this project."

"No, I'm fine."

"Well, I want you to get a check-up when we get back to shore."

She sloughed off the concern. "I'm fine."

"Becca, according to your story, Jamal had to revive you. That requires more than a dry towel."

Rebecca wiped her nose with the towel. "OK, OK. Whatever you say."

"How do you feel, Jamal?" asked the professor.

"Tired. Please do not worry for me, sir. All will be well in the morning."

"You're a good man. Glad to have you aboard."

Rebecca and Jamal rose from their chairs and McCray opened the door for them. "Without your quick thinking, things could have been much worse. Good job."

After McCray closed the door, Dr. Witherspoon faced McCray seriously. "If you feel it necessary to discontinue the expedition, Jamal and I can always return to Tehran."

"Not if I can help it, Harold," he replied stoically. "I want the expedition to continue, and I really could use you."

The professor smiled. "Then I will stay."

The two escapees left McCray's stateroom and walked beside the railing on the main deck. Jamal was halfway down the passageway when he stopped Rebecca. He looked both directions then spoke softly and confidentially.

"Rebecca, there *was* an incident at the university not long ago. When I was visiting friends in Armenia, I found a box with a parchment inside. Dr. Witherspoon had deciphered most of the ancient language on the parchment when someone anonymously accused him of removing the box illegally. As a result, the professor was put in jail. A thief stole the box and parchment just when we were going to make an announcement to the press of its importance. Do you think I should tell Dr. McCray of this?"

"What does your box have to do with these ruins in the Caspian?"

"There are so many strange occurrences, and it seems that ever since I found that box, nothing but bad luck has followed me."

Rebecca consoled him. "Now don't get superstitious on me. I'm sure there is a logical explanation for all of this."

"But it is hard not to consider, no?...and I miss that box," he muttered under his breath.

Rebecca changed the subject to mention something that she hoped would cheer him up. "Jamal, I don't want to sound dramatic, but thank you for saving my life."

Jamal paused. At five feet nine inches, her bright green eyes were level to his dark brown ones. "You know, you have a great smile on you, Rebecca Belmont, a calm head in the middle of danger, and...nice lips," he added slyly.

She blushed. "Wha...? Hey, don't embarrass me when I'm trying to compliment you." She pushed him affectionately. He steadied himself and then continued down the passageway.

"Jamal?" she asked, as they approached his quarters.

"Yes?"

"Were you afraid of dying?"

"Yes!" he replied with disbelief. "And you were not?"

She shrugged. "I guess I didn't have time."

Jamal shook his head and stood in front of his cabin to unlock the door. "You are a strange American woman. It is too bad you are a Christian or I think we may have had a chance together." Jamal twisted the knob on his cabin door and opened it. "See you tomorrow."

"Um...Good night?" she waved uneasily, unsure what he meant.

He waved back, then shut the door. As the door closed, Rebecca stood there speechless. *Why did Jamal say that?* She touched her lips, wondering what happened between them on deck. Rebecca went back to her cabin and took a quick shower. *Why would I be less desirable because I am a Christian?* She dressed in her favorite floral pajamas and lay down in her bunk fully awake. *I've got to admit, he is intelligent, and loyal, and self-sacrificing.... Oh! Stop it Becca! Jamal is right; how on earth could I even entertain the thought of dating a Muslim man? We are worlds apart—it's ridiculous!*

129

The *Bering* had anchored for the night to allow the late shift an opportunity to scrutinize the watertight integrity of the ship and ensure proper electrical and mechanical operations. The next morning, the senior staff sat down for a meeting on the ship's damage. With the vessel now stable, and no need of a tug to tow them back, the men unanimously agreed that they return to port for a thorough investigation. Although Dr. McCray accepted the fact that safety takes top priority, he was still disgruntled at being so close to such an historic site, yet so far from such a prestigious assignment.

When the others left the meeting, Dr. Witherspoon approached Bob McCray. "Robert, I know how this must disappoint you. Throughout my years conducting excavations, there were many missed opportunities. Nevertheless, I have always recovered from difficulties grandly, and I predict so shall you."

"Thanks, Harold, but that's not quite the pep talk I was hoping for."

"Hold on, my friend, there is something else. While you were busy with damage control, I was examining your Guneshli Shallows photo of the stone tablet and spotted something that may be of interest."

"Such as," he replied blandly.

"Such as, evidence from my work in Iraq and your undersea ruins here." The professor had McCray's attention.

"I believe the Guneshli writings are identical to the ones I found near the Tigris."

"So the cultures are the same?"

Witherspoon elaborated. "Yes and/or no; we need to conduct more research. Additionally, I noticed something fascinating within your pottery photos. Some of these more sophisticated pottery containers at the ruins have a distinctive stamped seal. These seals were pressed into the mud-covered top to serve as a mark of ownership. I have seen identical markings in photos of seals from Hassuna, an ancient town located near Mosul, Iraq. It would mean that either your newly discovered city used the same seal design, or that the Tigris culture brought these specific seal designs to this city."

McCray was tired and rubbed his forehead. "What does that mean?"

The expert linguist leaned forward. "I hate to use the word 'hunch,' and I need corroborating evidence to confirm this, but I think there is a strong possibility that a large influx of the population from Northern Mesopotamia could have ventured to the Caspian area. I have already suspected a written language connection, but it is essential I send for some data from Tehran University. If we return to the undersea ruins to retrieve samples of the pottery, we could conduct a comparative analysis to confirm whether my hypothesis is valid." The professor couldn't read Bob McCray's nondescript poker face. "There may be a silver lining on this dark cloud. Shall we give it another go, Robert?"

"So you think there is a connection between your dig in Iraq and these underwater ruins?"

"Yes, quite."

McCray sighed. "I guess probable good news is better than no news at all. OK, I'm on board with that, Harold. Call your associate and make it happen. However, if we have any other setbacks, I may cancel this whole project. My background is in science, but I also have to consider company profitability."

"I wouldn't expect anything less," comforted Witherspoon. "Walk with me to the radio room, I will explain more."

Bob McCray listened as the professor expounded on his and Jamal's deciphering project and the eventual theft. It seemed that there had been more spectacular archaeology discoveries in one year than the professor had seen in the last twenty, and even if McCray was discouraged with the progress, he felt that the professor wasn't going to let this opportunity disappear. When they reached the radio room, Witherspoon wasted no time calling the archaeology department at Tehran University. McCray stood by, pretending not to listen.

He soon connected with his secretary in his office at the university. "Hello, Mary? Is that you? There is a bit of static. Can you hear me? Good, good. How are you doing, my dear?" He glanced at McCray with a sad expression. "Hmmm. You don't sound too chipper, my dear. It will pass."

McCray could sense the professor wasn't cheering her up.

Witherspoon nodded to the receiver. "I see; you reorganized the archives...I'm sure you have done a splendid job. However, I believe I could use you in a different capacity. How would you like to take a trip to Baku?" He turned to McCray with a big smile and a nod.

The professor briefly highlighted the situation to Mary. He instructed her to go to his house and make a copy from the original computer disk with the deciphered writings, and copies of selected Hassuna pottery photos. To ensure the information arrived safely, Dr. Witherspoon asked her to bring it to him in Baku personally. The professor hung up the phone and looked pleased with himself.

McCray couldn't help but catch some of the professor's enthusiasm. "So Harold, is she coming?"

Witherspoon's eyes twinkled. "I think I detected a glimmer of excitement in her voice. Mary said she would arrive in Baku in two days."

McCray patted the back of Harold Witherspoon. "Well you sound pretty confident about all of this. I hope we don't have any more snags to contend with. I could use a drink. Do you like scotch?"

"Like it? I have a good portion in my blood," replied Witherspoon.

"Good. Then you can tell me more of your archaeological adventures."

CHAPTER 14

THEOLOGY 101

Before the *Bering* pulled back into port, a dispatch of the alleged sabotage was sent to the head of Terra oil in Azerbaijan and the local authorities. With Terra's influence on the Azerbaijan economy looming over the region, the Baku police immediately conducted an investigation when the *Bering* docked. All personnel were suspect, screened and ordered to submit to a vigorous fingerprinting and background check. Once cleared of suspicion, each person then received an authorized pass to come and go.

The following morning was a cool one, and, with local tradesmen starting repairs on the damaged compartments, Rebecca found a chance to get in some exercise. Dressed in a sweatshirt and pants, she warmed up with a brisk walk around the ship. As Rebecca passed by Jamal's cabin, she heard him chanting: "Ilaha illa Allah. Muhammed rasol Allah." It was the familiar Shanada, the creed that says, "There is no god but Allah, Muhammad is the messenger of Allah." Rebecca wondered how much inspiration Muslims get from the tradition, or if they get bored with doing the same old routine. She listened a moment, then walked on.

At the top of the gangplank, she showed her new I.D. to the policeman and he waved her on. Standing on the pier, Rebecca adjusted her headphones and set her MP3 player to her favorite songs. She started a slow jog, watching seabirds flying in circles and cawing noisily. A rhythm between Rebecca's breathing and running pace soon set in while she gazed out into Baku bay. She was amused at the contrast of well-kept boats and ships floating in the foreground of a series of degrading oil platforms strewn across the horizon.

Rebecca looked at her watch and made a turn back to the Bering. Her mind wandered back to Jamal's dedication to his faith. Since learning he was accepting of other faiths, she hoped that he would be open to theological questions. And as an evangelical Christian, she felt it a necessary duty to express her views for the benefit of his salvation.

Upon completing a sweaty run around the pier, the young scientist took a relaxing shower, and afterwards made her way up to the radio room. Rebecca had sent a message to her parents earlier, in hopes of connecting with a familial voice. She reached for the door handle just as it opened and there stood Jamal, with a silly grin on his face, waving a photograph in front of her.

"Rebecca—good news! My sister just had a baby boy!" Appearing in the photo was a cute, chubby baby, scrunching its face from the camera's flash.

Rebecca admired it. "He is sooo cute."

Once she approved of it, Jamal slipped the photo in his shirt pocket and patted it. "So, are we ready to go swimming again? You Americans always say that one should get right back on the horse after it bucks you off, eh?" Rebecca tried to hit his arm smartly, but he pulled back to miss her swing and laughed from a safe distance.

She wagged her finger at him. "I'll get you when you least expect it." He laughed. "Hey, Jamal, do you know if my parents called? I left a message yesterday on their voice mail about our…little incident."

"No, I have not heard of any calls from America, but you can check inside the radio room," he advised, walking back to her.

"Hmmm, knowing them, they're probably on another mission trip." When he was close enough, she punched his arm, laughed, and brought her fists up ready for a fight.

Jamal rubbed his aching bicep. "You win. I will not battle a woman. They can be vicious. Although, speaking of struggles, I must ask you something, Rebecca. Were you not scared during the flood…even a little?" Jamal asked, holding up his index finger an inch from his thumb.

Rebecca dropped her fists and put them in her pockets. "The more I think of it, the more…let's not talk about it." She paused before venturing into unknown territory. "By the way, I have seen how dedicated you are to your prayer times. May I ask you a theological question, Jamal?"

"Sure. We can talk on my way to the R.O.V. That computer engineer, Rick Klocke, wanted me to download a test program I wrote for him. He liked what I showed him and he said it may be more helpful than the preconfigured program included with the hardware."

"Download a program? Are you a historian or a computer programmer?"

Jamal thought for a moment "I would have to say…I *love* history, but my hobby is computer programming."

As they ambled through the passageway, Rebecca broached the question that had been nagging her. "Jamal, do you believe God will accept you into heaven?" Her brows scrunched together and she tried on a weak smile.

"Yes," he replied without hesitation. His eyes lit up. "Oh, are you are thinking about death…about paradise?"

"I guess you can say that. Can you tell me why you will go to heaven?"

Jamal wasn't bashful at all and almost strutted as he spoke. "In Surah 4:57 of the Qur'an, it is stated that those who believe and do deeds of righteousness, shall be admitted to gardens, with rivers flowing beneath."

"What are these 'deeds of righteousness'?"

"Those who are balanced heavily with good deeds will be successful."

She stopped walking. "You mean like a teeter-totter? As long as you do more good deeds, you will weigh heavy on God's mercy?"

He stopped and tilted his head with intrigue. "Yes. That is right. Do you have an interest in Islam?"

She walked again, concentrated on his answers, and ignored his question. "Hmmm. But how do you know how much 51% is?"

Jamal became introspective for a second, then shrugged. "It does not matter. I am faithful and good, and can tell the difference. I have not had sex out of marriage, or hurt anyone, and I give to the poor. As you see—my deeds are overwhelming—much more than 51%." Jamal stopped at the R.O.V.'s control panel and set down his laptop to transfer the data.

Rebecca stood above him. "But that is based on *your* view of things. Let's take sex for example: in the Bible, Jesus says even if you think about a woman with lust, you have committed adultery. So you see—"

Jamal interrupted without looking up. "Ah, but your book on Jesus has been corrupted. My people have the true writings." He pressed a few buttons on the keyboard to start the download.

"What? *You* have the true writings?"

He looked up at Rebecca dismayed. "Yes, the Qur'an was given by Allah to correct the misunderstandings of the Old and New Testaments."

Rebecca was flummoxed. "But if the Torah, the Psalms of David, and the Bible are the 'Word of Allah,' how could Allah allow them to be corrupted?"

Jamal wrinkled his face. "You are twisting my words. I do not understand all of Allah's motives."

Rebecca persisted. "Jamal, I don't want to get into interpretation of the scriptures. My point is that trust in the correct writings is useless without a relationship with God. I believe we cannot cover our sins with good deeds, because we cannot trust our sinful self.

We can't even trust if we are reading the sacred scriptures as we should. We can only trust a perfect God to remove our sins."

Jamal was flustered and unprepared. "I thought you were interested in my religion, not here to challenge it. I do not think we should talk on these things right now." He turned off the control panel, removed the patch cords, and excused himself abruptly.

"Is there a better time we could…talk." Rebecca called out to his back as he climbed the ladder to the next deck. He gave no answer and disappeared around the corner. She slumped against the R.O.V.'s hull. "I am so stupid!" she chastised herself. "Now I know why I didn't go into the ministry."

At lunchtime, Rebecca found herself one of the last to go through the chow line of the plump Mrs. Mehsati Ganjavi. She wore a blue headscarf, and had rosy cheeks and a body that easily filled out her white smock. The stout cook plopped some rice and lamb pilaff on her plate and, sensing something was amiss, peered at the weary Californian.

"Man problems?" she asked in English with a heavy Azeri accent.

Rebecca came to life. "Huh? How did you know?"

"It is always man problems," she spouted knowingly.

Mrs. Ganjavi was the only other woman on board, so Rebecca felt an affinity to open up. "It's nothing really. I just wanted to know if he would convert to Christianity."

"Who?"

Rebecca glanced behind to make sure no one was listening, then set her tray on the counter. "Jamal. Jamal Ramezani."

She tipped her head to the side. "He a nice young man."

"Yes, but he is Muslim. I heard that some Muslim families disown those who convert to Christianity."

"I have heard that too." Mrs. Ganjavi didn't mention that she was Muslim also. "So why you think he would leave Islam?"

Rebecca unconsciously picked up some rice grains and chewed them one by one. "I don't know why. I am just being a responsible Christian—to preach the Word of God."

"Good for you. But why you want *him* to convert and not all the other men on this ship?"

"I don't know. Maybe because…he is religious…and would be open to topics about God."

"Hmmm. And maybe, you like him. Yes?"

A crewman came up behind and Mrs. Ganjavi dropped a couple of scoops of food on his plate. Rebecca smiled warmly and let him pass. After ensuring they were alone, Rebecca continued.

"I can't believe, of all the men I have avoided on this ship, the one I like is a Muslim. To be honest with you, I swore to myself that I would stay away from men after my wedding was cancelled."

Mrs. Ganjavi was all ears. But Rebecca wasn't ready to reveal her whole personal past. "So why am I doing this to myself?"

"Maybe you like what you cannot have. It is safer that way, eh?"

Rebecca realized that Mrs. Ganjavi was more that just a cook. "You may be right," she conceded.

"Do you want what God wants or what you want?"

"Both?" Rebecca replied with uneasy hope.

The rotund cook laughed. "You Americans; you want it all. Do not worry so much—what will be, will be."

"Please don't tell anyone about this," Rebecca said painfully.

Mrs. Ganjavi went back to tending to the food. "Why should I? It is none of my business."

The following day, Jamal had finished going over some documents with Professor Witherspoon, only to bump into Rebecca in the passageway. He had hoped to avoid further remarks by Rebecca criticizing his religion, but believed that things may go better today. They stood awkwardly in the passage, like on the first day they met.

Rebecca broke the silence between them. "I hope I didn't offend you, Jamal—when I asked those questions of your faith."

Jamal crossed his arms. "No, not at all."

Rebecca grinned. "Really? Well, have you considered some of what I said?"

"Um, yes."

She laughed. "Well? Tell me."

"It was very interesting information." Jamal had never been in a debate with a Christian before and he didn't like it. He thought it was best to focus on their work.

"Interesting?"

"Yes," said Jamal, slowly inching his way along the bulkhead, trying to avoid an interrogation.

"Just interesting? That's all you have to say? Because you left very quickly yesterday."

Jamal wiped some perspiration off his forehead with his sleeve. "For now, yes. Excuse me," he said with a nod then passed around her. *Why does she bring up these strange questions? Can we not find mutual ground in our discussions?*

Rebecca scratched her head. "OK...we're still friends though?"

"Yes, do not be silly," he replied, not pausing a step.

Jamal started to turn the corner and glanced back. He breathed easier when he saw she was gone, and vowed from then on to steer clear of religious topics with her. After his evening prayers, Jamal was invigorated. He calculated that when Rebecca brought up a topic remotely related to spirituality, he would intentionally divert it in a subtle way.

The next day, Jamal's plan worked; when Rebecca mentioned her church, Jamal mentioned some historical cathedrals in Europe, and when she mentioned a Bible study she was involved with, he steered the conversation to his university study group. Unfortunately, throughout the next couple of days, he noticed a change in Rebecca. She began to refer to him only as a colleague, ending the playful banter they had when they first met. The warmth that Rebecca once had toward him now subsided. It was as if a comforting blanket was taken away from him. He didn't like it. Yet, dedication to the plan did require some sacrifice.

Later in the day, Jamal was standing at the aft end of the ship gazing out to the horizon, mindlessly winding up a computer patch cord around his hand and elbow. He had just finished conducting a test between his laptop and the ship's aft computer terminal, and was ready to get some lunch. Without notice, Tony appeared.

He rested his foot on the tow winch drum and leaned on his raised knee. "Howdy, Raz."

Jamal was preoccupied, but nodded politely. "It is Ramezani."

"Yeah, I know. I just like the shortened version." Tony looked out at the sea then back to Jamal. "You Muslims do a lot of prayin', don't ya?"

Jamal paused for a moment. The night before, he had seen Tony come back to the ship with a couple of Azeri shipmates, drunk and stumbling. He wondered why someone like Tony would suddenly demonstrate such an interest in spirituality. "I am not sure what you mean. It is our way of life and an honor. Do you know nothing of Islam?"

"Frankly, no. But it's not hard to hear ya chantin' every day. Maybe you can give me some pointers on it some time."

Jamal stopped for a moment to verify Tony's statement. "Some pointers? You mean you are interested in Islam?"

"Sure! I'm always game for new things."

Jamal's spirit lifted. "I would be glad to, my friend."

Tony leaned closer. "Ya know, I heard you two talkin' back there on deck the other day—you and Becca—and thought I'd add my two cents."

Jamal closed his eyes and groaned. "I do not need anymore Christians to argue with." He picked up his laptop and patch cord, then started to walk away.

"Now hold on, just because I was brought up with religion doesn't mean I'm wavin' the flag."

"Then what do you want to tell me?"

"I'm not spiritual or any of that, but I do know you two got along a lot better when you didn't discuss it."

Jamal stopped and turned around. "That is what I think too. I try to stay away from discussing theology, but she is very assertive. She does not understand how Allah weighs the sins of men—it is all in balance."

Tony looked up in he'd eaten. "Yeah, that makes a lot of sense. Nobody's perfect, so just do the best you can."

Jamal was encouraged. "Exactly!" *Maybe I have thought wrong of this Texan infidel.*

"Ya know, my daddy said more than once that 'good deeds can no more cover bad sins, than good caramel covers a bad apple.' It always made me feel like I had a bad seed and nothin' I did was good enough. He used that one on me one too many times and I swore to forget the whole damn thing. But I think I like your balance idea."

Jamal set his laptop down on the winch housing and turned a little pale. "...good caramel covers a bad apple," Jamal mumbled under his breath. "Is that what I'm doing with my life?"

Tony pulled back like he'd eaten a sour lemon. "No! Not you. My old man said that about me."

Jamal suddenly understood what Rebecca was trying to get through to him. *The smallest sin is too much for Allah to be near. If Tony's father was correct, then all the good deeds I ever do would never be good enough to be in the presence of a perfect god.* Jamal suddenly felt sick. *But would not Allah be merciful and overlook my sins? Or is even the smallest of my evil deeds too much for God to accept?* Jamal excused himself and started back to his cabin to absorb this paradigm.

Rethinking Islam's version of balances only made him nervous and unsettled. After returning to his cabin, Jamal turned on his computer and emailed his older brother in Tehran for advice. While Jamal sipped tea, he read the return email from his brother. Jamal's questions were met with brotherly concern by stating that Jamal should stay away from western women. As a post graduate, Jamal had learned never to be satisfied with one diagnosis. Therefore, he decided to go to the one person he always admired.

Jamal climbed the ladder to the conference room, where he knew Dr. Witherspoon was examining some photos of the newly discovered slab. Jamal gave a couple knocks.

"Come in!"

The student was relieved to find his mentor alone and shut the door. "May I speak with you, sir?"

Dr. Witherspoon was comparing the slab photos with some photos of artifacts he discovered while in a dig at the Tigris. Not answering Jamal, the professor addressed his student as if he were a sounding board. "When we get to the ruins, I will be anxious to compare some of the artifacts with the Tigris findings. If the languages from both cultures are the same, we should be able to decipher the parchments much easier."

"Oh?" Jamal replied politely.

The elder academic's eyes twinkled. "I am also intrigued with the possibility of an upper Mesopotamia Diaspora…." Professor Witherspoon regained some etiquette when he noticed Jamal was only listening out of respect. "Please, sit. How can I help you, son?"

This was the first time Jamal had ever brought up the topic of religion and got quickly to the point. "You are a Christian, yes?"

"I was brought up in the Anglican Church, yes. Why do you ask?"

"Rebecca has told me all my good deeds are useless and that God will not allow me into paradise. Do you agree with her?"

Dr. Witherspoon rolled his eyes. "Becca is what is known as a fundamentalist. They are very conservative in their thinking. They take the Bible literally. It is perfectly understandable for her to base her opinions on what many others consider a metaphor for good and evil. Do not pay too much attention to her. God is a big god; he knows a man with a good heart. I would suggest that you focus your mind on our tasks at hand and do not preoccupy yourself with it. Believe me, greater men than we have asked such questions, and still the debates continue."

The professor is right. I should not carry such a burden. Rebecca is, after all, only an American. God knows my heart. He will understand. "You make much sense, sir." Jamal got up to excuse himself.

The professor's eyebrows rose and he waved a pencil in the air. "By the way, I have sent for Mary. She should arrive this afternoon."

Jamal's disposition waned. "You will not need me?"

"Do not worry, son, I am not replacing you. I need that data we worked on in the last few months, and in her condition she needs purpose."

Jamal relaxed. "It will be good to see Mary again. Thank you for your time, sir."

After leaving the room, Jamal walked to the port side of the ship and looked across the bay. He still couldn't shake Rebecca from his mind. He enjoyed being around her, but avoiding her would only exacerbate their working relationship. Therefore, he concluded they must have an honest talk together.

CHAPTER 15

BAKU HIGHLIGHTS

At daybreak, Rebecca locked the door to her cabin and was going to check in with Dr. McCray when she heard footsteps behind her.

"Rebecca?"

She turned around, expressionless. It was Jamal. For days, Jamal had all but ignored her and she had gotten the hint not to pester him anymore. "Yes?"

"I need to speak with you."

Before Jamal could continue, he was stopped by the sound of someone coughing. It was Tony, with a suspicious smile. "Excuse me." He intentionally walked between the two.

"Hi, Tony," Rebecca said nonchalantly.

Jamal acknowledged the muscular man with a nod. The two men eyed one another for a split second, and then something caught Jamal's eye.

Rebecca turned to where Jamal was looking and caught sight of a familiar woman stepping from the gangway and onto the ship. The woman wore a black headscarf and a matching long-sleeved, knee high manteau coat over her pants. As she stepped on deck, Dr. Witherspoon greeted her.

Jamal recognized her immediately and shouted. "Mary! Salam!" He waved and strode over to her. Rebecca followed Jamal. "Later, Tony." She said over her shoulder.

Mary waved to Jamal, then set her suitcase down and put her hand to her chest. "It is good to see you, Jamal."

Jamal conducted introductions. "Rebecca, this is Mary Van-Wilpe, she works with the professor and at the university." He turned to Mary. "And this is Rebecca Belmont. She works with Dr. McCray conducting oil surveys."

Rebecca nodded and smiled cordially. "It's nice to meet you, Mary."

Mary put her hand on her chest and returned a smile. "And it is nice to meet you, Rebecca."

"Mary has been the best administrator I have had the pleasure to work with," praised Dr. Witherspoon. "Jamal, would you take her baggage? Robert McCray suggested Mary should be staying in Miss Belmont's room. I assume that's all right with you, my dear?"

Rebecca's face lightened. "Sure. It will be good to be with another woman for once." Jamal picked up her luggage. "Come on, Jamal, I'll unlock the door for you." She led the way, while Jamal carried Mary's bags. After climbing up a deck, Rebecca glanced back and noticed that Mary and the professor had stopped, so she tried to resume the earlier conversation. This was her chance to find out what was on his mind. "What were you going to say to me, Jamal?"

Jamal stopped, looked back at the professor and Mary several yards behind, then back to Rebecca. "Maybe this is not a good time to discuss this. Would it be all right if we talked about this later?"

Just tell me! Is it about me...us...what? Men can be such a pain in the butt! Rebecca's eyes said no, but what came out was: "OK, no problem."

Mary pulled on Dr. Witherspoon's arm. "Professor?" She spoke in a hushed tone.

The professor stopped. "Are you letting Jamal and Rebecca go ahead to ensure some privacy, my dear?"

"Yes, Doctor. I think you may want to see this." She handed him a letter. "Johan sent it to me from Lake Sevan."

"Your deceased husband?"

She nodded an affirmation. "Yes."

The professor recalled the lake. "Isn't that the place where Jamal found the puzzle box?"

"Yes, that is why I wanted you to read this."

"Well, let's see what your long-lost husband has to say." Dr. Witherspoon eagerly opened the letter and read it to himself.

My Dear Mary,

If you are receiving this letter, you know that something has happened to me. I know it has been a long time, but you were the only one I that I could completely trust. The field of archaeology is smaller than you might think and those who wish to take advantage of it are even smaller. I think I was followed by some men at Armenia's National History Museum because of an ancient box that I found in the mountains above Lake Sevan.

I have kept a safe deposit box under your name at the Yerevan INECO bank. You can have everything in it. You deserve at least that from me. I never told you, but I'm sure you knew that in the past I used you to get to artifacts at the university. For that, I am truly sorry and ask your forgiveness.

Love, Johan

"I am so sorry for you, Mary. You have been through many disappointments lately. If you need to go straight away to Yerevan, I will understand."

"Did you not notice the point about the box?"

Dr. Witherspoon stared at the letter. "Oh, the box! Johan had possession of the box also?"

"Yes. I thought you might take an interest in that fact."

"Hmm. Something does not fit here, Mary. Jamal said he found it in the water. Somewhere between your husband and Jamal, Erol ended up with the box. Now that is coincidental…or is it?" He set aside his propensity to solve puzzles and looked up at Mary with sympathy. "Does it hurt you to read this?"

Mary was poised. "It has been years since I have seen Johan. He has hidden so much from me; I do not see why I should hurt now."

"Hmmm. Quite," replied the professor, unsure if he should dig deeper.

"Once again I have let a man use me to get to your work— think I was only fooling myself," she stated emotionless. "I just want to forget the past and move forward, Professor. Thank you for letting me come with you."

"You did bring the information I asked for?" She nodded. "Then I should be thanking you. I am sure you will find the time away from Tehran refreshing. Come, let us get you to your cabin."

The professor extended his hand for her to go ahead of him up to Rebecca's door. Jamal had dropped off Mary's bags, and Rebecca waited inside to help her settle in.

Meanwhile, the police had concluded that everyone onboard was clear of any sabotage and could resume their duties without being scrutinized. It was assumed that the perpetrator of the flood had escaped before the ship sailed, but new precautions were in place to screen shipyard workers. Terra management gave the *Bering*'s staff authorization to proceed with research on the ruins. It had taken a couple of days, but the crew had worked around the clock to get the vessel cleaned up and back in top condition. For a much needed break from the extended hours, Bob McCray gave the crew a day off before leaving port.

Most of the staff decided to spend the day around the old town section of Baku referred to as *Ichari Shahar,* which means "inner city." They checked out a few bathhouses and art galleries, and shopped in the Fountain Square where many tourists and locals congregated. The aromas of sweets like pakhlava (baklava), shakarbura and goghal enticed them to snack. At lunch, the men purchased beef donner kabobs and vodka from a street vendor in Fountain Square. Rebecca settled on fruit juice and minced lamb meat with rice wrapped in grape leaves, known as dolma.

After lunch, the group wandered along the narrow alleyways with overhanging balconies and passed by men playing dominoes near medieval style walls. The air was punctuated with sounds of Muslim prayer or traditional modal music merged with jazz known as *mugham* jazz. Eventually, they arrived at the historic key-shaped Maiden's Tower.

Rebecca gazed upward. "I think the cab driver told me about this tower."

Dr. McCray looked at the brochure he had picked up in Fountain Square. "It says here that the origin of the thick stone tower is mysterious, built as early as 800 B.C. and as late as the 12th century A.D. That's quite a range."

"You'd think they could narrow it down a century or two."

McCray continued reading. "Being near water, it was generally accepted as a defensive position and a lighthouse, but other researchers theorize that it was a Zoroastrian temple."

Rebecca remembered what the cab driver told her when she arrived in Baku. "I heard that it got its name from the legend of a girl, who threw herself off the tower because she couldn't marry her true love."

"No kiddin'," said Tony. "That's a cryin' shame. You wouldn't do something stupid like that, would ya darling?"

"No, Tony, I would let the man do it for me. You could be the first."

Tony laughed. "Are you trying to sweet talk me into it?"

"Uggh!" She pushed him forward. "Come on, we're wasting time."

By the end of the day, the American part of the crew found themselves loaded down with quality Azerbaijani carpets, jewelry, and small wood carvings.

The Iranian entourage consisted of Harold Witherspoon, Mary, and Jamal, who had spent their day in the Azerbaijan National Academy of Science inspecting the recent ancient slab Terra had donated. Later, they scrutinized the local architecture. When evening arrived, the three headed for the Terrace Disco to meet up with the rest of the crew of the *Bering*. The Tehran trio sat at one table, while Rebecca and the other staff members sat down at another.

Dr. Witherspoon soon began a debate with Captain Vladimir Kovacheski on essential esoteric calculations and devices of measurement, and it didn't take long for Tony to convince Chuck, Rebecca, and Jamal to play a game of pool. Left alone, Mary removed her headscarf and shook her hair free from the confines of cultural expectations and listened to a combination of American and Azerbaijani music blaring out to an empty dance floor.

Bob McCray's mind was back on the ship, sorting out last minute details for the next deployment, but was distracted by Mary. She was directly in his line of view, rocking her head and tapping her fingers on the table to the beat of the music. He had only met her briefly, but felt a compunction to assist her.

After a half-hour of watching Mary stare out to the dance floor, McCray couldn't stand it any longer and stepped over to her table. "Come on." He held out his hand toward her. "You've been wanting to dance since we arrived."

Mary's jaw paused open while she found her voice. "But...I cannot dance. It is not permitted."

"By who? The mullahs in Iran? You took off your scarf, so you can't be that dedicated."

"Umm." She glanced at the professor who was gulping down theoretical concepts faster than his warm Irish beer.

"Come on, you don't need his permission." Slowly she stood and took McCray's hand. "You have danced before, haven't you?" McCray asked.

"Yes...a few times," she confirmed.

"Well, I can only do a country swing, so try to follow my lead."

Soon the two were on the dance floor mixing with a few newly arriving couples. Mary was stilted and mechanical, but soon relaxed in her partner's arms. At the end of the song, a grin crept up her face, like a little girl who had been spun on a merry-go-round. When the next song started, she again took McCray's hands, this time swinging and turning to the beat with ease. Even the stoic Bob McCray gave a hint of a smile when he dipped her at strategic moments to hear her squeal with glee.

Rebecca had been successfully racking up points at the pool table with her teammate Tony. Jamal and Chuck were suffering an embarrassing defeat by making such moves as sinking the 8-ball prematurely or hitting the cue ball off the table. Tony kept putting away the beers, which somehow helped his game. Rebecca was pleased with his ability and gave him "high-fives" whenever they made a tremendous shot.

Rebecca also cheered her opponent Jamal as he juggled a few of Tony's empty beer bottles. "Where did you learn to do that?"

Jamal shrugged. "It is a trick I learned in an Iranian gym, called the *House of Strength*."

Tony moved around the table several times trying to set up his shot and the others waited patiently. It was a strategic point that would win two out of three games. Jamal moved closer to Rebecca and spoke quietly to her.

"Could I talk to you a moment, Rebecca?"

Rebecca focused her attention on Jamal just as Tony made the last shot to win the game. The moment was gone.

Tony tossed the cue on the table, tipped his hat, and offered his hand to Rebecca. "Come on, sweetheart; let me show you how a Texan dances. We deserve to have a victory dance."

Feeling an obligation to her partner, she followed him to the dance floor. Tony tried to impress her with a Texas Two-Step, but she subversively watched to see if Jamal was looking. Tony's remarkable pool playing was overshadowed by his terrible dancing—his beer and vodka binge had finally taken their toll.

During the second painful song, and a two-step on Rebecca's foot, she beckoned with her eyes for Jamal to save her from her ordeal, but hesitated. *Maybe he is unaccustomed and ethically discouraged to dance with a single woman in public. I would think that this would be an exception to the rule.* Finally, after pleading glances for help from her, Jamal reluctantly ventured over.

He finally tapped on Tony's shoulder and asked to dance with Rebecca.

Rebecca quickly released herself from Tony and put her arms around Jamal's neck.

Tony did not take it lightly. "Well look who's here; Jamal. I would say that you're about as welcome as a skunk at a lawn party."

"Is it not customary to tap on the man's shoulder to dance with a woman?"

"No, you heard wrong, partner. Becca's an American, she belongs with an American man!" he slurred loudly, shoved Jamal's shoulder, and pulled Rebecca away. The muscular Texan then crossed his arms to confront Jamal, silently daring him to make a move. Jamal stood calmly, and looked toward Rebecca for support.

Tony blocked Jamal's view. "You don't need a woman to bale you out."

As the two men stared at one another, Rebecca hit her Texan shipmate on the arm. "Tony, what's with you? He wasn't doing anything wrong!"

Tony ignored and stepped closer to Jamal.

Getting a whiff of his alcohol breath, Jamal finally stated the obvious. "You are drunk."

"So what if I am." He pushed against Jamal's chest.

The graduate student kept his hands out to his side to avoid a fight. "Tony, I am not taking her from you, I only thought you might like a rest. Did you not say you wanted Rebecca and me to 'get along'?"

"HA! That's a laaffff," he slurred, then slapped his knee. "I was hopin' you two would argue again so you'd split up for good—"

Tony cuffed his hand to his mouth, then tried to backtrack. "Oops! Forget what I just said."

"I can hardly do that, my friend."

Tony mimicked his British accent. "I can *hardly* do that, my friend. HA!"

"You have little worth as a man in your state of mind," Jamal stated arrogantly, trying to step around his aggressor and reach for Rebecca.

"Oh, no, you don't." Tony grabbed Jamal's left wrist. Within a split second, the Texan locked onto the Iranian with one hand, spun him around , and with the other hand pinned Jamal headfirst onto the table. Even inebriated, Tony's experience with hometown brawls gave him the advantage.

"Stop it, Tony!" Rebecca shouted. She scanned the club to see if someone else would help, then weighed alternatives to stop him—such as kicking her drunken partner in the knee or another part of the anatomy. The other patrons did nothing to help, and a few people even started making wagers on the scuffle.

With his cheek smashed flat against the wooden table, Jamal painfully made his demands through half his mouth. "You have proved your strength. Now let me go!"

The sounds of disco music and conversations were suddenly quiet as the strong Texan's prowess became the center of attention. Tony turned around wearing a smug victorious grin, but the staff sat stiffly with disappointing frowns.

It was obvious that this really wasn't an equal fight, so Tony released the Iranian and wiped his face with his sleeve. "You're lucky I gotta take a pee." He glanced pompously at the others, then headed for the toilet.

The club patrons resumed their activities, sorely disappointed in a worthwhile fight. Rebecca consoled Jamal with sympathy. "Are you all right?"

"Yes. I am quite all right." Jamal straightened his clothes and massaged his arms. *Please* do not tell me you came to rescue me."

Rebecca peered at the side of Jamal's face, which was red and imprinted with the table's wood grain. She assumed his pride was bruised as well. "No, of course not. I just wanted to know if you were hurt."

Jamal tested his injury. "I am fine. You have nothing to worry about."

"You need an ice pack on your face or you will have a serious bruise." She reached up to inspect the wound, but Jamal turned his head before she could touch him.

"I will do that," he replied abruptly. He dropped his shoulders and walked toward the bar for ice.

Rebecca sat down with her peers at the staff table and watched Jamal talk to the bartender. She was sure he harbored more than a bruise to his head. It was twice that Jamal had tried to talk to her. Now that she had seen his integrity wounded, would their friendship be severed for good?

Moments later, Jamal returned to his table with some ice in a rag to his head.

Bob McCray saw the events that took place and escorted Mary back to the table where Jamal and the professor sat. She thanked McCray for the dance, and then he excused himself to visit the men's room. His face was stern and glowing as he headed for the restroom.

Pushing open the door, McCray saw Tony wobbling in front of a urinal. "Tony, that was uncalled for! If you were my kid, I'd tan your hide!" he snarled.

Tony glanced back through red eyes. "But I ain't your kid, J. Bob, so don't sweat it."

McCray stood a few steps back, with his hands solidly on his hips. "Listen, buddy, if you pull another stunt like that on guests of mine, it'll be the last time you work for me."

Tony looked as if someone accused him of killing a kitten. "What? Are you shinin' me? I was just foolin' around. We've had worse fights in nursery school back in Texas." Tony finished relieving himself, zipped his pants, and faced his supervisor.

McCray poked his finger on Tony's chest. "We are not in Texas! This is the Near East. There's lot of dangerous hostility around here, and I don't want to see it started by us—capiche?"

Tony relinquished by holding up his hands. "You're the boss."

"Yes, I am! Now…wash your hands, before you spread hepatitis, too." McCray barked. He shook his head in disgust and stormed out of the room.

Bob McCray caught Mary watching him when he returned to the other table with his staff. McCray gave her an expressionless nod. Harold Witherspoon turned to his assistant to gently question her. "It is none of my business, Mary, but is dancing acceptable for you?"

Mary brought her gaze back to the professor. She picked up her drink, sipped on the straw primly, and smiled. "Yes. When in Azerbaijan, do as the Azeris do," she replied between sips.

"I assume that you enjoyed yourself?"

"Yes, I certainly did."

Dr. Witherspoon grew a coy smile. "Indeed."

CHAPTER 16

UNDERWAY

Rebecca was still mulling over the events the next morning on her usual early morning run. After her run, she stretched out on the pier and started up the gangplank just as the morning Muslim call to prayer sang out across the harbor. She arrived at her cabin and opened the door to take a shower. Mary was sitting at the edge of her bunk inspecting a pair of Rebecca's Levi jeans, but was startled and set the pants down. Rebecca noticed Mary checking out the pants.

"Hi, Mary."

Mary acted squeamish. "I only brought two things from home," she admitted. "These clothes are very nice."

Rebecca tried to be a good hostess. "If you need any clothes, you can wear mine. I may be a little taller, but otherwise it looks like we're about the same size." Rebecca reached for a cloth to wipe the sweat from her face. "I heard the call to prayer. I'm going to take a shower. So if you need to pray, I won't disturb you."

"Thank you," she said, politely.

Despite Rebecca's consideration, Mary made no effort to follow the Muslim prayer tradition. She walked over to look through the porthole and set her chin on the sill. Vendors were selling breakfast food to workers going to the shipyards while seagulls swooped down onto leftovers.

Rebecca finished her shower, dried her hair, and slipped into her usual jeans and T-shirt, all while Mary gazed through the round glass window. Rebecca then opened her Bible to continue with the next verse for the day.

Mary glanced over to Rebecca, then strolled over beside her. "Do most Americans read the Bible in the morning?" asked Mary.

Rebecca winced. "Unfortunately, no."

"Then why do you do it?"

"I guess it's just a part of me...sort of like a Muslim's habit of daily prayer."

Mary's face reddened. "I do not follow that habit. I guess I am not faithful enough. To tell you the truth, I would rather be an American. I have a weakness for western culture. You can worship whatever you want, and wear whatever you want, and do whatever you want...without someone judging and watching you."

Rebecca snickered. "Oh, I am watched all right, but usually by a bunch of sexually active men."

Mary smiled and her eyes seemed to go to another place. "Robert McCray was very kind to me," Mary replied.

Rebecca was caught off guard. "Dr. McCray?"

"Yes, he danced with me. The last time I have danced was at my wedding. "

She eyed Mary, surprised about her openness to western culture, and Dr. McCray. "Hmm. I guess during the scuffle I missed that."

"English and American men are kinder to women. I want to be a strong woman like you."

"Believe me, Mary, it's not all it's cracked up to be in the U.S. Be thankful that the mullahs want to protect you." Mary looked down silently and solemnly. "It can't be that bad in Iran. Jamal said they have your best interest in mind. Don't they?"

Mary became pensive and looked back out the porthole. "Yes, but I do not belong there...I never have. If the government had not taken care of my daughter—she is blind and in a special school—then I would have found a way to leave."

"Why?"

"I can only blame myself. I have made terrible choices lately. The only person who cares for me is the professor." Mary's brown eyes began to well up with tears, but she quickly gained composure and cleared her throat to change the subject. "When you have a moment, could you take me to the conference room? I have forgotten how to get there and I have a meeting at nine o'clock."

The scientist in Rebecca wanted to know what terrible choices Mary had made, but the woman in Rebecca sensed her new roommate wasn't ready. "Sure, no problem," she assured. "After I finish here, we can get something to eat, then I'll take you to the conference room. By the way, maybe we can go shopping for some American clothes sometime."

"You do not have to do that."

"It's no problem."

"It would be too much trouble for you, Rebecca."

"Really, it's no big deal; and call me Becca."

"If you insist. That would be very kind of you, Becca."

Rebecca walked back over to her locker and sifted through her clothes. "In the meantime, would you like to see what my limited wardrobe has to offer?"

"Thank you, but I could not. You only have enough for yourself," Mary replied.

"Now let's not go through that again," Rebecca insisted. "I can always buy more," she chortled.

Mary gave in. "If it would make you happy, I would be happy."

Rebecca laughed and showed Mary more of her belongings. It didn't take long for her Iranian roommate to abandon her head scarf, put on a sensible blouse, and borrow some snug-fitting blue jeans. The pants only needed the cuffs at bottom to be rolled up once. After fitting Mary, they ate a light breakfast at the cafeteria, and the ladies made their way to the conference room. Mary carried a thick leather briefcase with her.

Rebecca saw Tony popping some dried apricots in his mouth when he spotted them. She tried to steer clear of him but it was too late.

"Hey, Becca! We kicked some serious butt out on that pool table last night, didn't we!" he chuckled, then gave her a buddy slap across her buttocks.

She was incensed and pointed a rigid forefinger in his face. "Tony! You are such a jerk! First of all, don't ever slap my butt again; secondly, how can you not remember what happened last night?"

"But that was just a friendly pat on your—" With her arms crossed, Rebecca glared at him while tapping her foot on the deck. Tony backed off. "OK, I won't do it again." He leaned against the guardrail and rubbed his head. "Things did get a little fuzzy after our pool game, and I'm nursin' a mighty strong headache... so I guess I did miss a few things."

"Let me refresh your memory: You were rude and violent with Jamal, made a spectacle of yourself, and drank way too much. Which is another reason I believe drinking is overrated: 'it only gives birth to foolish behavior,' my father always said."

Tony laughed. "So what else is new?" He tried to avoid Rebecca's inquisition and scanned Mary's body. The dark-haired woman had a slim waist like Rebecca, but she was almost two sizes larger in the bust and derriere. "By the way, Ma'am, your new duds are really doin' you justice."

Mary turned beet red and looked toward Rebecca.

Rebecca groaned. "Oh, for goodness sakes, Tony! You're hopeless!"

"You sound like my fourth grade teacher," said the Texan.

Rebecca faced her new friend. "This is what I was talking about, Mary; men can barely contain themselves. Now, if you will excuse us, Mr. Hansen, we have an appointment." Rebecca put her arm protectively around Mary and led her away. Tony whistled at her harsh scolding and shook his head.

With Mary close behind, Rebecca entered the conference room and noticed that Jamal's bruise had turned a dark blue. She knew that it must have been a humbling experience to be pinned down in a tussle with a woman watching on in pity. However, she was less worried about the dent in his manhood and more about what he wanted to tell her.

Rebecca tried to catch Jamal's eyes, but his attention was focused on Mary's new wardrobe. Dr. Witherspoon also took ample notice. They absorbed Mary's revealing figure and long dark hair, concerned that she hadn't adhered to traditional Iranian dressing. Fortunately for the moment, Mary had kept her cosmetics to a minimum. Jamal frowned at her appearance and considered scolding her, but instead deferred to the professor's seniority.

The professor peered at her over his glasses. "So last night when you said 'when in Azerbaijan, do as the Azeris do' is this too what you were talking about?"

Mary wore an impish smile. "I guess it is." Before they could reply, she reached into her briefcase. "Now here are some of the prints you asked for, Doctor."

Dr. Witherspoon shrugged his shoulders at Jamal and without a word moved on to the science at hand. Mary laid out the archaeology data next to the photos taken from the Gunishli Shallows, and instantly Jamal and the professor's minds were distracted by the prints. The two men became intrigued with the similarities between the archaeology photos of the undersea ruins and the pottery fragments from the Hassuna site. Rebecca and Mary stood idly by to listen to the men mutter ideas.

The professor held up two particular prints. "Do you see the checker motif pattern, Jamal? Other than the pictograph in the center of the Gunishli photo, the seals from both societies are the spitting image of one another. If we could only get the other half of that slab from the sea, we just might be able to clear up whether or not there was a diaspora."

Rebecca felt obligated to enter their discussion. "Wasn't the Diaspora when the Jews were dispersed to Babylon around 600 B.C. by King Nebuchadnezzar?"

"Or, it could mean any people group that had been displaced from its traditional homeland," Witherspoon clarified. "Don't be misled by more recent popularized information. Look at this photo, for example..." He pulled out a familiar symbol from the batch of photographs.

"That's a Nazi swastika!" she exclaimed.

"Exactly my point. You thought it came from the Nazis, while many others believe the Hindu people were the originators. But in reality, this symbol was used in many cultures. This particular swastika surrounded by these fish-like patterns was found on the interior of a plate from the Samarra period in Mesopotamia."

"So how old is that?" Rebecca asked.

The professor pursed his lips and wobbled his hand. "I estimate about 5,000 to 5,800 B.C."

"That's over 7,000 years ago! Strict Creationists believe that, based on the records of the Bible, man wasn't even around before 6,000 years ago."

"Oh, are we entering into chronology as per sacred writings? I always believed that the Bible was to be used as a guide to spiritual growth, not as a history book."

"Why not both?"

"Because, my dear, the evidence does not support both."

"How so?"

The professor adjusted his glasses and shifted into teacher mode. "Pardon my generalizations, but I must assume that you haven't had the prerequisites to Archaeology 101. There are unearthed excavations of an ancient village of Catal Hayuk in Turkey that dates as far back as 9,000 years. Or, maybe you are more familiar with the famous city of Jericho in Israel, which was also founded about the same time. Does this not indicate the immediate conflict in your assumption of an early earth?"

"Well, maybe the dating techniques are wrong," she countered. "Unless a person nowadays had a time machine, it is only a theory to claim that an ancient people existed at such and such a date."

The professor scowled at her. "That is your response? Young lady, great scientists for decades have honed the art of radiocarbon dating techniques. Your comment is hardly a sensible answer."

Jamal stepped in to intervene on Rebecca's behalf. "Actually, sir, carbon dating tests have been shown to be uneven and relative because the rate of radiocarbon production is not constant. Hasn't dendrochronology proven this? And if so, Rebecca may have a point."

Rebecca gave a smile of gratitude for his support, but Jamal didn't reciprocate.

"Jamal, you are referring to the recent popular use of analyzing tree rings, which have really only provided minor adjustments in previous records," reminded the professor. Don't throw out the whole system because of a few discrepancies."

"But when past assumptions are proven wrong, does it not cast a shadow on scientific techniques, sir? On the other hand, Rebecca," he said, turning to point out her misunderstanding of ancient time intervals, "dating conducted by many Creationists may have over-looked critical evidence in the Bible. For example, it seems unlikely that Genesis was ever meant to be genealogically complete, if we inspect some verses in the Old Testament." Jamal scratched his head. "You don't have your Bible with you, do you?"

"There is one on the shelf," Rebecca pointed out. She walked over to the shelf, slid it out of its slot, and handed it to him.

Jamal flipped through the Old Testament and put his finger in one spot while searching for another. "Here they are." He flashed the verses to her. "In Ezra 7:3, Azariah was considered the son of Meraioth, but in 1 Chronicles 6:6-9 you will see six generations listed between the two names. The difficulty is with the words 'begat' or 'son of.' It is apparent that they do not always mean the immediate 'son of' as one would assume, but rather 'descendant of.' And 'father of' sometimes implies 'ancestor of.'"

"Hmm. I see history *is* your first love," noted Rebecca, trying to gain some sort of positive response from him. Jamal still didn't reciprocate.

Dr. Witherspoon relented. "You have some valid points, my boy, against both our arguments. Geologists and paleontologists work in earlier time frames, which may seem to contradict archaeologists like myself, but my associations with biblical scholars have largely been polite enough to overlook these issues. Therefore, for the sake of propriety, I will try to concentrate my scientific dating techniques within the context of archaeological differentiation, if Rebecca concedes that the Bible not be considered an exact time-line of history."

Rebecca tried to show she was above the fray. "I was only pointing out what other experts believed. I didn't say I agreed with them. I guess I just like playing the Devil's advocate."

The professor raised a bushy eyebrow. "Hmmm... You're a sly one, young lady. One part of me says not to let you off the hook that easy. But we do have some critical data to sift through here and little time to carry on our discussion. So if you will allow us to continue with our work, I will be happy to set aside a time for an extended debate on this topic." He smiled. "Is that fair?"

Rebecca softened. "Thank you, Professor, I appreciate your offer. I really didn't mean to open up a can of controversial worms." She paused and looked up in thought. "But now that I think about it, timelines probably wouldn't be as important to God as his intention of a sacred link between a father and son. Ya know what I mean?" The others agreed and nodded pensively. "With that said, I'll leave you two to concentrate on your work and take Mary with me."

Harold Witherspoon detected her competitiveness. "Hold on, Becca. I suppose as a child you wouldn't leave the carnival until your father had won a stuffed toy for you to take home, either."

Rebecca crossed her arms with a smirk on her tanned face. "Actually, yes. How did you know?"

The professor tapped the fingertips of each hand together. "As Sherlock Holmes would say: 'Elementary, my dear Watson.'" He then waved her off. "It doesn't matter anyway. You are correct to assume that I need some time alone with Jamal to digest these photos."

"Good. We'll be back in an hour," said Rebecca.

With little time available, the women quickly left the room and the ship to buy some additional clothes for Mary. They merrily trotted down to the pier and fortunately found a store with western fashions. After Mary had made her purchase, she turned to Rebecca and happily raised the package up like a trophy, beaming from ear to ear. However, over Rebecca's left shoulder and outside the store window, something caught Mary's eye, something or someone very familiar. Her face lost all color and the joy left her heart. "Erol!" she whispered harshly.

Rebecca glanced around, saw nothing, and then turned back to Mary. "Are you all right?"

Mary ran to the window and looked in both directions. The street was bustling with locals and tourists alike and she craned her neck to find what she saw. She shook her head and the color in her cheeks returned. "It is nothing," she replied, exhaling with relief.

"What is nothing? You look like you saw a ghost."

"I may have...or it just may be my imaginings. It is nothing." Mary looked again up and down the pier then composed herself. "Should we not hurry?"

Rebecca looked at her watch. "Oh my gosh! We only have a few minutes!"

They quickly tucked the packages under their arms, ran down an alley, and crossed traffic on the pier. Shore power was just being disconnected from the ship. The American gracefully leapt up the angled gangplank with her breathless, yet grateful, Iranian friend in tow. Rebecca flashed her I.D. like a cop, swaggered aboard like she owned the place, and escorted Mary back to their cabin.

Right behind the women walked the newest member to board the ship. He was a fit man with bright blue eyes, who looked and dressed like Stalin—square black mustache, buttoned raised-collar, long sleeved jacket. The government had assigned an official from Azerbaijan's National Academy of Sciences to observe the expedition. The man made his way to the pilot house and introduced himself to the captain. He and Captain Kovecheski didn't take long to reminisce about old Soviet war stories. The captain excused himself to ring up Dr. McCray and informed him everyone was aboard.

McCray gave the word to cast off, and within the hour, the *Bering* left its birth and cruised out of the windy Baku Harbor into open waters. The ship headed to its destination on the warm cloudless day. It passed a series of dilapidated oil platforms, which were destined for dismantling. Like many oil rigs on the peninsula, the derricks at sea were rusty old monoliths, built in the late 1800's, and now skeletons of a never ending metal forest.

Hours later, the *Bering* had left the colorful oil slicks in the bay and neared the intended coordinates of the survey site. The captain called down to Rebecca's cabin to let her know. She eagerly jogged up to the computer room to monitor the seafloor. She called up to the pilot house to slow down and soon the research vessel dropped its speed to a crawl. Rebecca alerted Dr. McCray that they were almost on-site, then continued to check the monitor for the ruins. The atmosphere on the ship became electric. Like a Swiss watch, the team of men moved smoothly and efficiently to prepare for the recovery of the stone slab's other half.

At mid afternoon, John Hanak took two of his scuba divers and headed to the bottom of the seafloor to secure a line around the large chunk of stone. They carefully tied a net-like diamond hitch knot around the precious artifact, then signaled topside to engage the winch. Within minutes, the large stone tablet was safely aboard. The slab was inscribed with a combination of pictographs, drawings of stylized people and animals, decorative motifs, and a primitive alphabet.

Dr. McCray and the staff surrounded the artifact, waiting for Dr. Witherspoon to examine it. When Dr. Witherspoon and Jamal arrived, they meticulously cleaned then dutifully recorded the chiseled inscriptions. With this section of stone tablet on board, they now had both pieces of the original stone tablet, which would give a more complete understanding of the text.

The professor opened up his briefcase and removed some printouts. He compared the inscriptions on the stone tablet with the Tigris and Lake Sevan writings. Professor Witherspoon grinned broadly, confident they had a match.

Dr. McCray bent down to watch the professor jot down critical information. "I would guess by the size of your smile we hit pay dirt."

"You have assumed correctly, Robert. However, we still need to analyze and decipher the etchings."

"Take all the time you need, Harold. If you find anything important, give me a yell so I can contact my boss."

"I doubt you will have to wait long, my friend."

McCray smiled and patted the professor on the back, stood to leave, and then turned around. "By the way, Harold, Rebecca and I will lay out a preliminary grid to inspect the ruins. I trust you, my chief engineer Chuck Gohn, and I will be the first to board the submersible for an up close look tomorrow?"

The professor saluted with his pencil. "Fabulous! It's a date!"

Jamal snapped some pictures with a digital camera and returned with his mentor to the conference room. The professor carefully opened the restricted dictionary burned onto the computer disk that he and Jamal had spent months deciphering, and worked through the night translating the ancient writings.

Somewhere in the wee hours of the morning, Jamal had succumbed to sleep with his head buried in his crossed arms on packets of paper spread over the table. In contrast, Dr. Witherspoon had endless energy and was still jotting down crucial notes.

By the time the eastern sun was shining through the porthole, the professor had achieved great strides in understanding the obscure language. The professor set his pencil down and stood back to re-read what he had completed.

"Jamal!" the educator exclaimed. "My assumption was correct!"

The weary student jerked up with a start, sending papers flying off the table. "Uh,…mazerat mikhaam?" he responded instinctively in Farsi.

Dr. Witherspoon excitedly held out his list of strange alphabet symbols with decoded English on the side. "No need to be sorry, son. Look here; there *was* a mass migration, as I hypothesized."

Jamal blinked a couple times before examining the professor's notes. Witherspoon leaned back in his chair as if a great weight had been lifted from him. He tapped the eraser end of a pencil to his teeth a few times. "As best as I can summarize: amidst some notations about making sacrifices to their gods, it seems that there was a drought or some kind of danger which forced a 'people of the south' to find refuge in the city. And leading these people was a man named Shem, the same as the signature on the parchment you found in your puzzle box. I would feel more confident about this if I could retrieve more evidence from the ruins. I need more to support my assumption of a diaspora."

Jamal tried to catch up to what his mentor had learned. "If these people are indeed the ones from northern Mesopotamia, why would a whole people group be so desperate as to uproot from their homeland and cross hundreds of miles over treacherous mountains to a foreign city?"

"That, my boy, is what I would like to know."

CHAPTER 17

NEWS OF DESTRUCTION

Kara rested her elbows on the window's stone ledge, her hands cupping her chin, and listened to a morning dove coo. She gazed across the fertile land, beyond the river, and up to the distant mountains. It was a long march for Kara to take from the city to this foreign land with an unfamiliar tribe. While she enjoyed remaining in one place for awhile, she hoped that they would journey back soon to the mountains of her homeland.

The dove flew to the window and pecked the stone for seeds. Kara held her hand open; to her enjoyment, the dove stepped on her palm.

"Hello, my beautiful friend." She glanced around with a smile, hoping someone could see her. Kara stroked its head and the bird closed its eyes. "Were you sent from above to comfort me?"

A man's voice outside broke the quiet and instinctively the bird flew out of her hand. Not far away from the house, two men grunted from their hard work with large urns.

"Ugh! You filled it too high," complained the young man.

Kara turned her attention from the bird to one of Noah's workers. He had pulled one of three heavy, red-glazed urns from the outdoor oven. The other worker had overfilled a large ceramic vessel and spilled some onto the ground. After it was filled, they wedged some beeswax over the opening and covered the top with mud. Finally, they pressed a stone cylinder with an engraved pattern of Noah's mark onto the mud, then carried the urn to the storehouse.

Kara looked around in hopes that the bird would return. She went back to her straw bed and opened the puzzle box her father had given her on the day of womanhood. After a series of slides of the wood strips, the lid was unlocked. She opened the lid to see the steel bladed knife her brother gave her and a past note from Shem. She stroked the fur lining and smelled the cedar inside, which brought forth the scent of home.

Kara had never been away from her family this long and wondered how difficult it would be to leave her parents forever if needed. Ever since Kara found Shem unconscious in the mountain snow, she was drawn to him, and yearned the day they would be bonded. She was confident that her tribe would accept Shem, but was unsure if Noah would accept her. After Noah had expressed his dislike for the northern tribesmen, it left her uneasy.

The door opened and Shem stood with a grin. "You have not left the house? Come meet my other kin."

Kara shut and set aside her box. "If it will make you happy."

"Do you not wish to meet them?"

Kara didn't want to put a damper on his enthusiasm. Her mind was still far away. "If you do, I do too." Shem took her hand and proudly introduced her, praising her kindness and intelligence.

After the evening meal, Shem coaxed Kara to play a tune on her flute for his family. She agreed and produced a wooden flute her father made for her. As she played, they tapped their feet and clapped their hands. Kara soon began to warm to their enthusiastic support. Kara was finishing the last of three special tunes when she noticed Shem glancing out the window. In the afternoon light, the silhouette of two men stood in the distance. Shem waited for her to finish, then walked to the thick cedar door and opened it.

While Naamah and the women praised Kara's talent, the men stepped outside to study the strangers. Naamah instinctively pulled out some food and drink. The rest of the family walked outside and stood in front of the house, squinting to see who the visitors were. Kara had never seen the men before, but soon Noah answered her unspoken question.

"It is my brother Tabas and a younger man. I have not seen my brother in many seasons. How odd that he comes here so near to harvest time. They should be working my father's land."

Soon the two men were at the front of the door. The older man was shorter and more robust than Noah. The younger man was husky and hairy, a couple years younger than Shem. Noah approached Tabas and they embraced and held each other for a moment. It was plain to her that they cared much for each other.

Noah held out his shorter brother to get a better view. "Little brother, how grand it is to see you! Not only have I been gifted by your arrival, but so too has my son has returned," he pointed to Shem, who stepped toward them.

Shem bowed to Tabas, then gave his younger cousin a grin and a wrist shake.

Tabas looked back to his brother. "It does my heart much good to see you too, Noah. Do you remember my son, Shinar?" asked Tabas, slapping the back of the sturdy young man. Shinar bowed to the respected man and Noah ruffled his bushy head.

"I see you carry a spear, Son. No doubt you will be as good as your father," Noah encouraged.

Shinar lifted his spear and pointed north. "Some day I will explore the lands Shem has."

Shem chuckled. "And someday I may grow hair on my chin like you do. Both may take a few seasons."

Noah readdressed his brother. "Tabas, this is truly a blessing to see both of you. Come into my home where you can rest, eat, and talk."

When Tabas entered, Naamah wrapped her arms around her husband's brother in a long squeeze, then instinctively broke away to serve him and his son something to eat and drink. Kara tried to help, but was told there were enough hands in the food. Naamah laid out some lamb mash and flatbread in a large wooden bowl and provided mugs of fresh goat's milk. Kara was not introduced, so she stood back and watched closely at how the lowland family drew close to one another.

After sharing past memories and the health of the extended family members, Tabas' disposition veered toward the serious. "Not all is well though. Evil has swept our land," he informed, gripping tightly to his wooden cup.

Noah's smile vanished. "Oh?"

"It's the locusts," blurted out Shinar.

Tabas stared into his cup. "Yes… the locusts." After a pause, he looked carefully at Noah. "How have your crops fared, Brother?"

Noah and the others gave a knowing glance to one another. "We have done well, by the mercy of God. But I fear, you have not."

Tabas held back tears. "We lost all of our crops…every tip of wheat and barely." There was a stunned silence. "That is why we are here."

Noah rested his hand on his brother's shoulder. "We will give you whatever you need."

Tabas patted Noah's hand. "Thank you, Brother, but you could not provide enough to feed the house of our father, or the houses of our kin."

"Then how can we help?"

"By giving us the aid of your son, Shem."

Shem looked puzzled and Noah was taken aback. "Shem? How can he help you?"

Tabas paused, took a long drink of his tea, and then wiped his dense beard. "After the pestilence, all our kin came to ask Father's advice. He listened to our grievances and it was agreed by all that we would find safe haven elsewhere."

"Where would that be, Brother. Here?" asked Noah.

"No, the city of Tuball."

Shem's jaw dropped. "How did you learn of Tuball?" he asked.

"Brother Zakho told us about it. You and he know the trails to it and you could guide us there. Zakho says the city people respect you. And if they respect you, it is our hope that they would respect us too." He looked back to his brother. "Noah, if you provide a small amount of your crop to Father, Mother, and the weak can stay behind, while the fit of us can walk to the city."

Shem eagerly turned to Noah. "I could take them, Father. There is much to eat in the city."

Noah's worry turned to displeasure. "You would mix with the Cainites too, Tabas?"

"Only for a few seasons, Noah. Enough time for the land to heal itself," he reassured.

"So it is coming to pass," Noah said, looking upward momentarily. All eyes were on the spiritual leader as his gaze dropped and he started to pace. "This does not bode well for us." After a long uneasy moment, Noah suddenly stopped and faced Tabas. "Their gods are as filthy rags!"

It was a rare thing to see Noah in anger. Kara shrunk back against the wall with her flute at her side. Shem's compassionate eyes met hers. All stayed quiet except Tabas.

Tabas stood and held his hands out. "It is either that or lose many of our kin to starvation!" countered Tabas.

"I would rather die with honor, than to live with *them*!"

"You are as stubborn as an ass, Noah!"

Shem leaped in between his elders. "Father, it has been done before, by me and Uncle Zakho. It can be done again. The Creator kept me safe, and I have seen many Cainites now worshiping our God. I am willing to do this for them. Please, Father."

"Listen to the youth, Brother. He knows," said Tabas.

Noah restrained his anger by taking a deep breath. "Let me think on this." He moved toward the door, scanning nothing in particular on the floor. "Yes, I must think on this. Naamah, I will not eat tonight." Noah opened the door and strode briskly up to his favorite grassy knoll.

After Noah left, Tabas tried to apologize for the confrontation, yet began to plead his case to Japheth and the others.

While the debate on mixing with foreign tribes occupied the men, Kara slipped outside and huddled next to a stack of wheat. As kind as Shem's family was to one another, she wished she wasn't an outsider. *If Noah so distrusts tribes of my kinsmen, why would he allow me to be with Shem?* She felt helpless. Kara had heard wise words from the masters in the city talk of bringing all the tribes of the many lands into one, as a bundle of twigs. Separate they were weak but together they could be strong. Kara saw the Sethites as a kind people but misguided, and now wondered if they ever would be able to allow themselves to be part of a family of tribes.

That evening, a bonfire was lit to thank God for his blessings of food and safety, and to petition help for Lamech's family. As Noah's immediate family and nearby cousins gathered to hear of news from the west, it wasn't long before Tabas had begun to loosen his tongue about Zakho and Shem's adventures.

"Cousin Shem," he called out across the fire. "Tell us some tales of the beasts you fought or of the giant men far north or the—" Shem stood up quickly and interrupted Tabas with a glare.

Shem had avoided expounding on his exploits to the north; he thought it would only worry his mother and father when he traveled north again. But since Zakho had divulged their exploits, Shem realized he would soon have to divulge the adventure to his family.

"If you know so much, I will let *you* tell them, Uncle." Shem turned and walked out of the circle of fire, beyond the edge of light.

Kara followed and sat down next to Shem. "I think he is proud of you."

Shem shook his head. "Tabas is only proud to hunt and talk of the kill."

"Is that so wrong?"

"It is when he risks the lives of others to find adventure."

"You think he does this only for himself?" Kara tried to peek into Shem's eyes. Shem repeatedly poked a stick into the ground. "Shem, is this about your uncle or something else?"

Shem stopped and faced Kara. "Did you not see my father? I have learned that when he gets angered it is for good reason. Father may be right; I am only one when I wander, but to ask all the Sethites to wander may invite danger."

Tabas could be heard in the distance, repeating the stories Zakho told him of Leviathan, the bears, and the Great Battle in Tuball. Everyone oohed and aahed at the great deeds Shem had accomplished, and soon recognized Shem in a new light...as that of protector. Noah had come down from his meditation on the hill and listened intently to the stories.

After awhile, Shem had had enough and stormed back to the fire to stop Tabas from tempting others with high adventures, but Shem's younger brother Ham spoke first. "I want to go to Tuball, like you Shem!" he exclaimed suddenly. Shem threw up his hands and shook his head, worried that these wild stories would be taken out of context.

Noah reached out to his son with a tired plea. "What of your work here, Son?"

"Others can do the work. You do not need me. Shem left for the great city. Can not I?"

"Is what we have here less than that of the city, young Ham?"

"Yes! Did you not hear the tales, Father?"

"I heard. Your brother was protected by the Almighty's vast hand from terrible dangers. You wish to risk your life too?"

"Yes! We live in dirt—they live in a great city!"

Shem locked onto Noah's painful eyes, knowing and understanding his thoughts. Shem knew his father's concern was about mixing with Cainites, but Shem sensed that there was more. As Ham zestfully poured out envious words of the city, Noah's disposition settled.

"If you must, you must." Noah sighed then turned to his eldest son. "And what of you, Japheth? Do you wish to go?"

"My place is with you, Father," he replied without a flinch.

Noah breathed easier. There was a pregnant silence around the campfire; only the crackling pitch from burning cedar could be heard. "Then it is settled. Shem will lead the tribe."

Tabas was skeptical. "You agree, Noah?"

Noah addressed the many clansmen. "My brother is right. It would be better for Sethites to be away with an enemy alive, than at home starving." The others nodded in agreement. "But there is something else…I am coming along."

The faces around the fire turned pale. Everyone knew that Noah was the mainstay of the community. They looked at one another then back at the patriarch.

Tabas approached Noah. "Brother, you do not need to go. You are needed here. Shem will guide them."

"No. I see now that this is the Creator's plan. I must finish what I have started."

The clansmen murmured questions to one another. Tabas came closer. "What are you saying, Brother. Finish what?" he whispered.

"You will learn soon enough, Tabas." Noah turned around. "As for my own land, I will give it to my father, Lamech. He will stay here where the food is plenty. It makes no sense to drag food to a barren field when ours is plentiful. It is the right thing to do. We will carry as much as the donkeys and ourselves can be burdened with. I will not be coming back."

The joyous moment turned into one of puzzlement. Shem wondered why Noah would change his mind and travel with them into Cainite territory. But he expected that Noah would give the answers at the right time.

After the fire died down, the kinsmen returned to their homes, and Shem dowsed the fire with water, he overheard his brother Japheth speak with Noah.

"Father, you asked me to stay with you, and yet now say you will leave?"

Noah put his hands on Japheth's shoulders. "I wanted to see your faithfulness to me, Son. I am proud and can rely on you. You must stay to watch over the harvest while I am gone."

"But you do not need to go, Father. Let Shem lead Tabas on his misguided journey to the Cainites."

"Japheth, it is my time to leave. As for Tabas and the others, they must follow their own way. Let us hope that they will let God direct their steps."

"I worry about the burdens you carry. There is more deep inside you that you do not say, Father. Please tell me."

Noah faced his eldest son. "Worry not for what a man does not say. His actions speak for him. I will tell you all at the proper moment."

CHAPTER 18

BIRTH OF A DIASPORA

Noah's father, Lamech, removed another portion of the depleting grain from the underground storehouse, then returned to his home for the evening meal. Later, he sat outside his large mud-brick home on a bundle of straw, pulled off his head wrap, and stared out into the barren fields. The land received its fertile soil from the Khabur River, a tributary of the Euphrates. But now, staring back at him, were rows and rows of naked wheat stems without tips. The patriarch of the western clans rested his bald head in his strong, weathered hands and wept.

Lamech's grandniece, Lily, was sweeping the stone floor inside his home and heard his cry. She set the straw broom aside and came to his aid. "Are you ill, Great Uncle? May I get you some water?"

He wiped his tears with his sleeve. "Do not bother, child. It does not matter. What does any of our hard work matter? Our God has provided us with so much fertile land to grow plantings, but look at our wheat, and look at our barley—all gone. Our yield was only fair last year and next year was to be the year to rest the land. This does not bode well for us; not at all."

Lily reached out with a tender heart. "It will be all right, Great Uncle. Look, we still have our goats and sheep." She tried to be as optimistic as possible given the obvious crop devastations.

Lamech frowned and touched his finger to his lips. "Do not speak too loudly, or they also may be lost." Lily lowered her head. He patted her hand and softened his voice. "But many thanks for your kind words, child. You are such a treasure to me."

Child? I am more than a child! she thought.

Lamech had been so preoccupied with the fields that he hadn't observed that the once cute little girl had suddenly turned into a lovely young woman. Her face was radiant, framed within golden-brown hair, and she had sprouted in height and strength. At thirteen years, Lily was beginning to show promise as a stable and reliable wife.

While Lily sat to console Lamech, they looked up to see a line of people cross over the small barren hill next to the Khabur River. The people carried packs with a few heavily loaded donkeys in tow. Before Lamach could ask who they were, a young goat herder jogged up from the near side of the river to announce the group's arrival. Visitors were scarce and always sparked an enthusiastic anticipation.

"Master Lamech! Tabas has returned with Noah and his family!"

"My son, Noah?"

Lily brightened at the message. "And Shem?"

"Yes, yes," he replied to both questions.

"Tabas must have given him the message, but I did not expect Noah to come. I pray God's good hand is on them. Tell my wife to kill and prepare a lamb," Lamech ordered. The boy nodded and quickly went on his way. "Lily, get some berries and dates and water. They will be worn of their travels through these hot days." She was gone before he could finish his statement.

Lily laid out the food on a low stone table inside, then exited the house to see the arrival of Noah's entourage. Shem was walking next to Noah. It had been many months since she had spoken with Shem. She recalled with admiration the night when he sat with her and gazed up at the heavens to point out his favorite lights. She remembered Shem's skill at throwing the spear during the harvest celebration. Even though he had lost by a technicality, she considered him more than generous to the winner. Their encounter was brief, but Shem had made a lasting impression on her.

Word of the visitors' arrival had spread quickly to other kin in the outlying community and an informal invitation was sent out. When Noah reached the house, Lamech reached out to embrace his son tightly. Noah's wife and the others were also greeted warmly with embraces. It had been years since the families had seen one another and the moment was cause for celebration. Soon, extended family from around the area had gathered to celebrate their arrival too.

By evening there was song and merriment with plenty of fresh meat to go around. Bitenosh had made sure Noah's family was well fed with lamb, onions, lentils, olives, and bread with honey. Cousins provided entertainment with traditional songs accompanied by cymbals, flutes, drums, and rudimentary string instruments. While Lamech got reacquainted with his son Noah, Lily made particularly sure she was attentive to Shem's every need.

Shem sat between Kara and Shinar during the meal. Shem questioned his cousin and discovered that the locusts had affected all the surrounding lands as well as Lamech's. Shinar readily answered any questions they had, but was more interested in what Shem had to say about his travels to distant lands.

As Lily provided another plate of lamb to Shem, he couldn't help but be preoccupied by her appearance. He spoke to Shinar and nodded to Lily. "Cousin, I remember Lily as a spindly young girl with round cheeks the last time I visited. Now, she has grown from a tender bud to a blossoming flower."

Shinar observed Lily brush the long hair away from her face, which in the firelight enhanced her emerging beauty. He smiled. "Father says that we make a good pair."

Shem looked back at Shinar. "Uncle Tabas may be right. I see how Grandfather favors her over the other women. May God honor the match, Cousin."

Shinar blushed. "Your words mean much to me, Shem."

Lily eventually made her way back and presented a wooden platter of food to Shem and the others. "Many thanks, Lily, for your kind service to us. Grandfather says only good things of you."

The young woman smiled bashfully and instinctively readdressed Shem's attention to the food. "Here, have some more lamb," she offered.

"You feed me too much. Save some for the others." Lily bowed and started to leave but Shem caught her arm. Lily blushed at his touch. "Have you met Kara, Lily?"

Lily had not even noticed her sitting next to Shem. "No."

"Kara has come from the far north." Kara smiled up at Lily.

"Greetings, and good health to you," said Lily. "Are you a trader's daughter?"

"No, I am a woodsman's daughter," replied Kara. "Your cooking is very good."

Lily grinned. "Many thanks." She quickly turned back to Shem. "Will you stay longer this time, Shem? I...we missed you."

Shem thought for a moment. "There are many things for Father and Grandfather to discuss. I cannot say."

"I hope it takes many days," she replied. Lily bowed then left to serve the others.

Kara caught Shem's gaze on Lily. "Do you like this young woman?"

"Lily?" he replied with surprise. "She is kind...and very helpful." Shem caught on to her meaning. "I think Shinar is to be a match for her." Shem lowered his voice. "Why? Do you think she likes me?"

Kara rolled her eyes. "Who does not see that she likes you."

Shem peered at Kara closer. "Does Lily wear her fondness for me so clearly?" he asked quietly.

"Yes, Shem," she informed, as only a wise seventeen-year-old could.

"But she and Shinar…" Shem watched Lily opposite the fire tending to guests. She glanced back to see Shem, so he waved politely. Lily grinned substantially, and for the first time Shem noticed a cute dimple in her cheek. He then turned to Shinar and saw him smile and wave to Lily too.

Shem chuckled. "It is not for me that she is fond of, Kara. It is Shinar."

Kara looked at Lily, then folded her arms and bit her lip in thought. The Seva woman sat politely in the presence of the Sethite tribe and spoke little through the evening. Despite the wonderful cooking, Kara told Shem her stomach carried an uneasy feeling and she wished to rest. Shem escorted her back to her room, where the Bitenosh daughters slept. Shem kissed her forehead, and Kara lay down on a bed of straw atop a wooden platform in the corner of the room.

The following day, Kara squatted at the river and washed her face and head. Her mind had worked steadily until the early hours of the morning, leaving her little time to sleep. She wondered if she would ever fit in. Would she be accepted with her gods and could she accept them with just one? And who was this young woman named Lily?

Kara heard some rustling through the grass and turned to see Shem. "Greetings, my beauty," he announced cheerfully.

Clumps of dark wet hair cascaded down from her face over her shoulders and breasts. Shem glanced around to see if they were alone. They hadn't had a moment together since before arriving at Noah's land. Shem brushed back her hair and cupped her face in his hands, then slowly and carefully kissed her travel parched lips. Kara responded by pressing him closer to her.

After a long embrace, she ebbed away and took his hand. "Let us sit, Shem." She led him to two large stones by the water. Kara stared at a leaf floating by but said nothing.

Shem eyed her. "What is it, Kara?"

"Shem, is your heart with me?"

"You know it is, Kara. Why?"

"I have made a decision." There was a long moment before she spoke and then she looked into his eyes. "I think it is time I take your God as my own."

Shem was stunned with joy. "You speak the truth?"

Kara nodded. "Yes, Shem."

"Why now?"

"Because if I do not take your God, I may lose you."

"Lose me to what?"

"I just do not want to lose you."

Shem wrapped his arms around her. "How can you lose what you already have, Kara?" They held one another an extended moment, then he released her. "Now my father will have to bless us. Let us go tell him." Shem pulled her up to her feet and they walked hand in hand back to Lamech's home.

Lily had returned from the river with an urn balanced on her head, and poured the urn into a water barrel at Lamech's home. She set her jug down and stretched her arms up to get the kinks out of her neck.

Lamech immersed a gourd into the water barrel. "Thank you, Lily." She smiled and bowed slightly.

Noah and Lamech leaned against the house and gazed out into the barren fields, wrestling with survival issues impacting the tribe. Lamech had warmed to Tobas' idea to move to Tuball but Noah claimed a reticence to associate with Cainites. Noah broke the debate to point out two large, long-horned aurochs chewing grass at the edge of the stripped fields. One of the large, hairy bulls tied to a post shook its head to clear itself of the annoying flies.

"It seems unfair that you have lost your grain and yet still have those two big animals to plow the ground with. How did you get those wild beasts to obey, Father?" asked Noah.

Lamech took a drink from his gourd and passed it to his son. "We brought them up from newborns whose mother had died. They can do the work of ten men." He shook his head and put his hands on his waist. "What do we do with them now?"

Noah drank from the gourd. "Make a good meal of them?" he suggested with a snicker.

Lamech was startled for a moment, then laughed and slapped his son's shoulder. "You are somber so often. It is good to see you act like the rest of us for once." The patriarch looked past Noah. "I think your joke is catching. Here comes your son wearing a smile as bright as the sun."

Lily had picked up her urn, but turned when she heard Shem was near. When she caught sight of the two holding hands, her face turned pale. Lily pretended not to notice them and hid behind the corner of the house to eavesdrop.

Shem and Kara were a stone's throw away from Lamech's mud-brick dwelling. "Father!" Shem shouted.

Shem beamed with joy. He pulled the young mountain woman up the steps. "Kara has accepted our God as hers!" he announced gleefully. He parked himself in front of Noah with his arm around Kara's shoulder. "You do not forget your words to me, do you?"

Noah couldn't help but smile. "If you need my blessing…it is given."

"They are to be bonded?" whispered Lily in shock.

"Thank the Almighty!" Shem shouted. In an unusual show of affection, he picked up Kara by the waist and twirled her around. Lamech laughed at their excitement and congratulated them.

Before Shem could get carried away, Noah muffled the enthusiasm slightly. "I will accept her as my daughter, but my blessing must be linked by the blessing of *her* tribe."

Shem paused, then scoffed. "They will…they must. We are meant to be as a cord."

182

At those words, Lily secretly turned away with tears streaming down her cheeks. She ran, weeping quietly with blurred vision, headlong into Bitenosh. The old woman had been stretching a lamb's skin near where her daughters coiled strips of clay to form bowls. Bitenosh was thrown against the animal skins, which loosened the wooden framework, causing her to land on several pottery bowls. The girls had just finished smoothing the sides of the pottery and were letting them air-dry before being fired in the oven. Bitenosh fell onto her side and bruised her hip.

"Ouch!" Bitenosh cried out as she lay in the midst of newly made pottery. "Lily!" The old woman was promptly helped up by her daughters from amongst the broken shards. Bitenosh started to scold the girl when she noticed her grandniece's tears. "Lily? Are you hurt?" she asked, in her aged crackling voice.

"No, I am fine," she replied hastily. "I am sorry. No good ever comes to me," she whined. Lily quickly wiped her eyes and sped off somewhere into the barren wheat fields. The older women watched her run away, left to wonder what had caused her pain.

CHAPTER 19

EXODUS

After Shem and Kara left to spread the word of their betrothal, Noah resumed his conversation with Lamech. They caught sight of Lily running across the field.

Noah nudged his father. "It seems as though the good news is out. Lily must be running to tell others."

Lamech's smiled quickly vanished. "Tabas tells me that you have decided to go wandering with the others. Is this true?"

Noah sighed. "Yes, Father."

"I would never have guessed you would mix with them."

"I must. It is time."

Lamech frowned. "Time?"

"Yes, God has saved my land as a sign that he is all-powerful. After seeing your crops destroyed by the locusts it has confirmed for me that this is the time for my duty to him. My land is now in your hands. I will not be returning to it."

Lamech scoffed at the idea. "You do not mean it, Son. You will return."

Noah, with his piercing eyes, glared painfully at his father. "You do not know the burden I have!" he lamented in a loud whisper. "These are the signs I have been expecting!"

Lamech backed up. "Signs for what?"

Noah said nothing of his previous visions, which foretold of the recent insect pestilence; and nothing of how God revealed that these events were only the beginning of more ominous events to come. Noah wished he could tell all he knew to one other person, but kept silent. It was his burden to keep and his burden alone.

Noah shook his head and summed it up. "Death!" Noah turned away.

"Whose death?"

Noah closed his eyes and dropped his head. "Many. My visions are muddled. I cannot explain them now."

"I am your father. You can tell me."

Noah shook his head. "No, I cannot. I wish not to talk on this any longer. Please take my land. You and Mother will be safe there."

Lamech shrugged. "If you lead our people, should not your brother Zakho be the one to help on your wanderings? Your path will be straighter with an experienced man as a guide."

"I agree that Zakho would be of good use on the trails. But Shem has great standing at the city of Tuball. Still, you make sense, Father; the trails would be easier with my brother at my side." Noah panned the distant horizon. "But...where is he, Father?"

Lamech stared out at the distant lands, his arms on his hips. "No doubt he is trading in the south to buy something of value. I will send word to him of our plans. The elders not far from here should be notified too."

As they were speaking, a messenger strode up to the house. The young runner told Lamech that the elders of the outlying areas requested him to join them in the sacred meeting house to discuss solutions to the recent crop devastation. The locusts had spread their destruction not only on Lamech's land, but to everyone in the region.

Lamech picked up his walking stick that leaned against the wall. "It seems it is time for me to tell our brothers of your plans, Noah. Tell Bitenosh, I will return on the next sun. You and Tabas can gather the clans for the journey north."

Noah nodded agreement and watched as his father left for the meeting. Oh, how he ached to tell someone of his visions.

Lamech followed the river several kilometers downstream to the sacred meeting place and arrived late in the afternoon. He approached the round, thatch roof house that was tucked in a bend where the river ran slow. From a distance, he could hear the elders of the outlying villages grumble about their devoured grain. Zakho saw his father approaching the meetinghouse and went to greet him. Zakho had returned from the Euphrates trading route in the south and had just finished mentioning a few of his exploits to the elders. Zakho led Lamech inside for the elders to greet him. Lamech was the last of the fifteen bearded elders to enter the meeting place, but being the oldest he was still first among them. Zakho led him to a floor mat of honor, next to Ozias.

Ozias was a gray, and a robust, man respected for his savvy business negotiations. Losing an eye in a child mishap didn't infringe on his skill to stare down a belligerent opponent if necessary. Lamech would normally lead the meeting, but deferred to his younger cousin. On mats in a circle were fifteen bearded elders sitting cross-legged, each representing their own village.

Zakho then stood to the side so they could continue their squabble about dwindling resources from the scourge of the locusts. Fear of survival had been on the minds of the elders, and this moment offered a chance to voice themselves. The Sethites had honed the art of cross-cultivating wheat and barley into a highly nutritional food and had become dependent upon it as their main source of food. They had replaced the arduous effort of hunting for domesticated herds of goat and lamb; hunting became used primarily for young men coming of age.

As the elders grumbled about their misfortunes with one another, Lamech whispered some pertinent information to Ozias while he munched on roasted gazelle rib. Ozias nodded to his older

186

cousin, then raised a thick hand to get the elders' attention. The others respectfully quieted.

Time was of the essence and Ozias didn't waste a moment. "Lamech tells me that his kin will be leaving this land and that they will go north to live among the Cainites. They head for Tuball, the great city that Zakho has told us about."

"Live with the Cainites?" asked Mordu, with disgust.

Zakho stood back, not wishing to argue with men of ignorance.

Mordu was a lean, tough, self-righteous man, designated the spiritual guide of the southwestern clans and trusted to keep tradition. "They are evil and would ruin us!" he stated with intensity. The other elders began to murmur nervously with one another.

Ozias remained cool and raised his hand as he spoke. "True enough. But it does not change the fact that they have decided to leave. We have groaned about our afflictions long enough and must decide on whether to stay here and make do, or leave with the others?"

Mordu fixed his open mouth toward Ozias. "Are you ill? Did you not hear me? We cannot mix with the Cainite filth!" he contended.

"Can we stay?" replied Ozias, firmly. "The foul smut damaged most of last year's crop and the insects have ruined all of this year's." The black, fungal disease that ruined most of the chaff and seeds for planting was still fresh in the minds of the elders. "There is something else you should know." He paused and glanced back to Lamech, who nodded for Ozias to continue. "Noah has chosen to leave also." Ozias sat back, stroked his silver beard, and let the unlikely scenario sink in.

The others were too shocked to say a word but glanced nervously at one another. The men gaped at the mention of such a holy Sethite man even considering the idea. They said nothing, but Zakho knew their minds searched for a reason why he would join with wicked northerners.

Ozias expressed some alternatives. "Lamech tells me that Noah's land was not touched by the pests. Is that not true, Cousin?" He faced his elder. Lamech nodded and Ozias readdressed the elders. "So if Noah plans to leave, it must mean that it is safer to mix with the Cainites than to stay on his own land."

Zakho started dozing off, but Mordu redirected a question at him. "What say you, Zakho? You have lived with the Cainites. Should we leave?"

Zakho twitched to attention. He had not had a good night sleep and could hardly keep his eyes open, but attempted to answer them despite his repose. "Men of honor, I will take you there if you wish or give favored blessings if you stay. The women of the city are beautiful and the food is plenty. But it is not my task to tell you what you should do."

Mordu frowned at the answer. "Noah is your brother, Zakho. Why would he mingle with godless people?"

Zakho sighed. He knew that Mordu expected him to discredit Noah somehow, but he would not take the bait. "I have stopped trying to know my brother's mind. Noah follows a strange and narrow path."

Mordu looked around at Lamech with pleading eyes, but the elder patriarch only shrugged.

"Though Noah is my son, sadly he does not share all of his thinking and prophecies from God with me. I and my wife are too old to travel to such a place, but do not let that keep you from doing what is right for your families."

Zakho saw Mordu sweat. It was well understood by any Sethite that they would not survive without abundant stores for the cold season, which meant hunting was the only alternative, and most of the good hunters were close to Ozias. Zakho knew Mordu had other reasons and would find it hard to concede.

Mordu brought forth another option. "We still have food stored up. If we spread out to hunt gazelle and wild pig, and slaughter our goats and sheep, we could make it until next harvest. God has protected us in difficult times before."

Ozias tried to show sympathy with Mordu. "But the wild animals are few during the cold season, and killing our animals will leave us with nothing. Last year three babies died from illness.

With less food upon us, I do not wish to see twice that number next year. We must have a better plan, my Cousin." Ozias opened his hand toward Zakho. "It may be that God has provided a wise trader as a gift to us."

Zakho was impressed. Finally, the clans looked favorably upon him…as a leader, and not just a wanderer traipsing across foreign lands for profit.

Ozias put his arm on Zakho's shoulder. "He could lead us. We must not overlook that." Ozias looked into the faces of his kindred elders. "The Creator gives and takes. This may be his way of forcing us on a path to a better life. Should we ignore it?"

Most of the men uttered a solid, "Noooo."

Ozias restated the positives. "If Zakho guides us, we will have less to worry about. He has wandered the trails for many years and knows them well. I say we follow Zakho to the city if our young ones are to survive the cold season. It will only be for one planting season, and it may help the ground heal. Even so, I will not hold it against anyone if they wish to stay." The elders looked to Mordu for a challenge, but he sat silent. Ozias used his staff to push himself to a stand. "If you wish to go with me, set your staff in the circle." Ozias set his down first.

One by one the others followed suit. A few other followers of Mordu waited until he made a move. With the flap of useless skin lying limply over Ozias's empty eye socket, he fixed his other brown eye solidly on his undecided cousin.

Zakho knew that Mordu was left to decide on losing the little he had, leaving the only home he had known, or believe in the stories Zakho had spoken of. Health and wealth within the city of Tuball was a hard story to put out of ones mind.

Slowly and reluctantly, Mordu nodded and eventually set his in too. Mordu's supporters followed after.

Ozias smiled at the unanimous vote. "Then let us not delay. Gather your kinsmen and what you can carry, for our path takes us to the north." Ozias reached over and thumped his staff to the ground, indicating the meeting was over. He moved closer to Zakho and whispered in confidence. "I am pleased the others agreed, for I would not be right to leave without them."

"How did you know I would say yes to guide you?" asked Zakho.

Ozias chuckled. "I didn't."

Zakho shook his head with a smile. "We must leave soon or the mountains will be too difficult to cross. I must contact Torak, the great hunter. He will be of much use in killing game for our many people."

"He is but three days from here. You must hurry," Ozias said.

Ozias turned to Lamech. "Cousin Lamech, I sensed the choice was not shared well by all of us. I fear I will spend many nights by the fire repeating how moving to the Great City is a good thing."

"That is wise," said Lamech. "One must keep an eye on the fruit so the whole group does not spoil. Mordu is one that seems to have lost his sweetness," he said in a low tone. Lamech straightened up and put his hand on Zakho's and Ozias' shoulders. "Noah and Tabas are preparing our clans as we speak. If we do not see you when the moon is full, we must be on our way."

"We will be there," said Ozias.

When Lamech arrived back at his land, Noah had preparations for the trek north well underway. Men worked feverishly to herd most of the livestock into temporary pens, but with nearly a hundred people to provide for and with such a long distance to cover, disputes arose as to what portions per person of wheat or barley to bring. Additionally, not being able to bring all their goods, they had to weigh out the present needs with future losses of personal belongings.

Shem intervened; it was evident that they needed an analytical mind to clear up the muddled arguments. He knew that the men would not take solutions from a young man easily and never from a young woman—yet Kara tabulated numbers like breathing air.

Shem convinced Noah to allow Kara to help them. She quickly counted the number of the clansmen, conducted an intuitive evaluation of each person's size, input the length of time to reach the city as determined by Enod, the star gazer, and then calculated the total amount of grain needed as a tribe.

With the leaders present, Kara stood next to Shem and wrote out the computation results on a reed papyrus. Shem then glanced over for the answers and relayed the solutions to the clan leaders. The men knew nothing of her scribbles and so it was assumed that Shem was the one with the keen mind. The clan leaders then took the information and passed it on to their people so they could bring the allotted grain, livestock, and other necessary supplies.

Shem was proud of how Lamech's clans had readied themselves. And not too soon, Ozias and several hundred of the southern tribesmen, their wives, and children arrived. They had been creative and loaded most of their household goods on travois carriers strapped to goats and donkeys. The carriers consisted of poles lashed to each side of the animal and down to the ground with a sling in between. As the animal trotted along, the other ends of the poles drug along the ground.

Fifteen clans of the south had traveled up the Khabur River with only minor challenges, but Shem knew it was like a pleasant walk compared to crossing over hundreds of miles of mountainous terrain. Zakho still had not appeared, and Shem was uneasy with the thought that he may have to lead the Sethites alone. Shem decided to lead the people on the route to the Anbar market that he had taken with his Uncle Zakho a year earlier. After that, they would have to find an experienced trader who would guide them through the mountains.

Lamech brought together the elders of all the clans for a meeting. The meeting produced a hierarchical structure for leadership while they traveled. Noah was to be at the head, Ozias the leader of the southern clans, and Tabas the head of the northern clans. After two more days, preparations were more than complete, people were restless, and Zakho still hadn't shown himself.

The sun crawled over the eastern trees on a warm, misty morning and Noah pulled the Sethite tribe together for a blessing. He stood on a small knoll overlooking the many clans within the tribe. Goats and sheep were bleating in makeshift corrals while the people stood quietly for Noah to pray for the safety of his people.

Noah raised his hands and shouted up to the sky. "Maker of all things, watch over us as we take one of many hard steps on a difficult path! Smile upon us as we begin again in a new land, and protect our hearts as we move among the Cainites and their strange ways! And Father, Creator, Provider, keep close and feed those who stay behind! So be it!" The crowd echoed with a "so-be-it." Noah lowered his hands and faced the crowd. "Come now. Let us be on our way."

Shem led the way, with Tabas and Ozias to his side and the many clanspeople behind. Tools, shelter materials, and food were packed on the goat and donkey travois carriers, or in sledges attached behind the auroch bulls. The sledges were more like small houses with wooden runners. Spirits were high, and unsubstantiated rumors of guaranteed health and wealth in the city abounded.

Noah turned to give his mother a hug. "Stay well, Mother." He then looked into his father's eyes. "You will be here when Zakho arrives?"

Lamech nodded. "Yes."

"And you will tell him when and where we went?"

"Yes, Son, I will tell Zakho all he needs to know. It is painful for me to see you go, and it will hurt to till the land you worked."

"You will have Japheth there with you, Father. He is a good, young man. Tell him I will send word next season."

Lily and a few others had made the decision to stay behind and accompany the elderly to Noah's land on the Tigris. As the massive group of Sethites started northward, Lamech and the few others waved goodbye to over seven hundred of their kinsmen heading north into the mysterious Cainite territory. Noah rejoined the tribe, but turned one last time to see his parents.

Lamech put his arm around Bitenosh. "The faster you leave, the faster you will return, Son. And I will care for your land as if it were my own." Lamech laughed. "...better than my own."

Noah smiled and waved goodbye, but said nothing about returning.

The day had passed with no sign of Zakho. Lamech sat with Bitenosh on the stony porch, calmly waiting for their son. The commotion had subsided and only a distant dust cloud marked their existence. It was eerily quiet, with a few goats bleating somewhere in the distance, and a handful of workers. Lily walked despondently by Lamech and his wife with an urn of water, but she did not go unnoticed.

Bitenosh was tired of her moping around. "You wander as if you lost a spotless lamb, Lily. What ails you?"

"Nothing." She poured the water into a larger container next to the house wall.

"Why did you not go with the others? You would be happier with those of your own age."

Lily covered the lid on the water container. "You need me to help with chores. I would only be sad to leave."

"You are sad to be here with us. Ever since that day when you bumped into me, you have been keeping to yourself. I do not hold that against you, child, for I know you did not mean to hit me."

Bitenosh peered closer to her grandniece. "Is there something else, child?" she asked gently.

Lily averted her eyes to the ground.

Lamech perked up. "Was that not the day when Shem and Kara received their blessing from Noah to...Oh! I see now! How did we not notice this before, my wife? Lily has taken to Shem. Lily took much effort to care for Shem's needs at the banquet."

Lily turned pink and stared down at the water container.

Bitenosh scolded Lamech. "Leave her be, Husband." With nothing else to concern herself with, the plump old woman resumed her questions with interest. "Is this true, Lily?"

Her face turned from pink to red. "No! I hate him!" Lily shouted, then abruptly ran off to the river.

Lamech and Bitenosh reeled back as if they had been splashed by ice water. What was this behavior? Did she truly have an interest in Shem? She was their favorite grandniece. They had always believed that their grandson Shinar would someday marry her. He was a strong, dependable hunter who took after his father, Tabas.

Lamech was going to suggest they talk to her when he heard an *Ah-EE* and turned around to see Zakho pulling hard on his domesticated ass. Behind Zakho was the tall, strong Torak and his two younger brothers. The two got up and met them at the edge of a barren field.

Lamech gripped Zakho's arm. "Son, the tribe has left without you. Do you still wish to follow them?"

"When did they leave?" Zakho asked.

"Two days ago," he replied with apprehension.

Zakho chuckled with an experienced confidence. "Worry not, Father. Torak, his brothers, and I will have little trouble meeting up with them." Zakho thought back to the meeting of the elders. "Did all of the elders and their clans leave together?"

"Yes, even Mordu."

"He may be trouble," noted Zakho.

Lamech nodded. "Yes. Can you blame him? He lost a son at the hands of the Caintes. That will be a painful walk for him." Lamech looked down to where Lily was squatting near the river's edge. "I know you can stay for only a short time, but I think there may be someone else that needs to go with you."

Zakho looked to where Lily was splashing water on her face. "The girl?" Zakho grimaced. "She will only slow us down."

"Lily would do anything for me and your mother, but she is wasting away with us ancient ones," said Lamech. "She will thrive with the young. You will not to have wait for her...she is as strong as some men."

Zakho sighed. "As you wish, Father."

Bitenosh took note of Zakho's weariness. "You must rest yourself, Son. Come, I have food for you and your friends." The men followed her obediently into her kitchen to eat the evening meal.

They ate well and slept well, and in the morning it became a bittersweet moment. Lamech and Bitenosh enjoyed the presence of their youngest son, who chose to make trades across many lands rather than grow roots at home. It was a painful hello and goodbye, but at least Lily was obedient enough to accompany Zakho.

CHAPTER 20

A Mother's Instinct

After bidding goodbye to his parents, Zakho and his small group walked north at a fast pace. Zakho was dubious about taking the unenthusiastic young woman, but she had strong legs and left no doubt that she could keep up with the men. As a bonus, she could cook for them.

They passed a herd of tan, long-eared onagers, who were bigger cousins to his donkey, Boko. Zakho estimated they could have carried the Sethite's entire load if they weren't so wild to manage. He glanced back at Lily, who was looking only at the ground. Like the onager, he hoped she wouldn't be hard to manage.

Two days passed, and Zakho felt confident they would be able to meet up with the Sethite tribe very soon. He was fortunate to have Torak, who killed game on the run as easy as picking out food from the storehouse. Torak stood eleven hands high, broad at the shoulders and narrow at the waist. His long face wasn't keen to look at, but he was fast, strong, and very clever. The bronze spear he had won at the last harvest festival never left his side and no one dared to take it.

On the evening before arriving in Anbar, Torak lay on his back next to Zakho. They had just finished eating a wild pig and watched the campfire flicker.

Torak's voice was as deep as he was tall. "You know the trails well, Zakho. You will be of great help for the tribe when we meet up with them."

Zakho picked some meat from his teeth with a bone knife. "Many thanks, Torak. And it is good to have such a grand hunter as yourself with me. I never even think of food anymore."

"Ha! By the size of your belly, you think of it plenty." After a pause to stare into the fire, Torak spoke again. "I heard you speak of Mordu with Lamech. I met the Cainite who killed Mordu's son."

Zakho's interest was raised. "Oh?"

"If he had not been with twenty of his brothers, I would have evened out the death. Mordu has never forgotten it and since believed that it is unwise to mix with the Cainites."

"Most Sethites feel the same way, Torak."

"Mordu may cause trouble," said Torak, poking the fire with a stick.

Zakho sighed. "He talks as if the Cainites will spread their false gods on us like disease, but I think he worries more about being taken as a slave. Tales of Cainites sacrificing men to their gods abound. I do not know if any of it is true. I have seen none of it myself. When we meet up with Noah, all will be well. The Tuballites are like any other people."

"How much longer before we reach Anbar?"

Zakho smiled broadly. "At our pace, the next sunset."

He glanced over to see Lily still melancholy, weaving a small straw pad for which to set hot stew on. Zakho had only seen the girl a few times and never paid attention to her. He prayed she would not be troublesome.

He leaned close to Torak. "Father told me she is fond of Shem. It did not go well for her when she found out he was to be bonded with Kara."

Torak shrugged. "It may be hard for her to forget Shem, but she is young and has her whole life ahead of her. Maybe one of my brothers will take her as a wife."

"Maybe so, Torak." Zakho took one last drink of his blackberry tea. "She cooks well and keeps up with our steps. They would be lucky to have such a faithful beauty, and she would be lucky to have worthy men such as them. Look, the fire is dying, let us sleep well so as to make much ground in the morning."

Torak set his fleece out on the ground next to his brothers. Zakho kept an eye on Lily. She poured water on the fire and stirred it up. *Maybe Torak was right. Lily does seem like she would make a competent wife.*

At daybreak Zakho squatted by the fire, blowing and stirring up embers from the night before while the others washed themselves and retrieved water from a stream not far away. He was anxious for them to hurry back so they could be on their way. Suddenly, there was a rustling in the bushes and Boko stirred from where he was tied to a tree. Zakho stood up and looked around.

"What is it, Boko?" he asked tentatively.

To his surprise, three little lion cubs broke out from the safety of the forest into the camp. They were fearless young creatures walking awkwardly in a comical sequence, the biggest in front to the smallest in rear. The little cubs were tan with white under their chin and on their chest, and dark-spotted foreheads. As the young cats strayed into the campsite, they pounced on toads, insects, and other smaller creatures.

When Zakho saw them he chuckled at the cubs, then laughed heartily when the second one jumped on the back of the first. Oblivious of the human being in their midst they tumbled and rolled only a few paces away. Zakho couldn't help himself and went over to pick one up. He chose the last cub who sat licking himself. When Zakho raised him up to get a closer look, the little lion growled with his tiny gravel-like voice.

"What brings you three so far north?" Zakho asked the feline, holding it under its arms with its legs dangling.

Lily, Torak, and his brothers returned from the stream and, unlike Zakho, didn't see the humor in wild animals wandering the camp. "That is not a wise thing to do, Cousin," warned Torak.

Zakho turned to Torak with a shining grin. "Look at this one. He reminds me of the cat I found at the city of Tuball, only fatter and with a bad singing voice." He chuckled as the cub creaked out a low meow.

198

"May I pet the animal?" Lily asked, then walked toward them.

Torak set his water jug down. "I would stay away from these young ones. The mother could not be far—"

Before he could finish his warning, Boko started braying and pulled against his tether, and a large lioness leaped out from the bushes with an angry roar. Zakho stumbled back, with hardly enough time to push Lily out of the way and cover his face. The big cat pounced on him and clamped her jaw on his shoulder, tore Zakho's muscles, and shook him as if he were a play toy. Zakho screamed from the pain, instinctively hit the big cat's head with his fist, and rolled over to escape his torment. The lioness let go of his shoulder momentarily, but was not about to let him escape so easily. She lurched forward as he crawled, and clutched his leg with her great claws. Zakho's leg was in a tug of war with the cat, who had bit down hard to squeeze blood and tears out of him.

Lily lay on the ground, wide eyed, motionless, and stunned speechless. Torak was astounded but reacted instantly. He ran to his belongings, took up his spear, and heaved it at the animal. The spearhead hit directly into its hindquarters and the lioness let out a howling cry. The cat released her victim and turned to remove the spear by trying to grasp it with her fangs. Zakho lay helpless on the ground, groaning from his injuries. The big cat went for the spear like a dog chasing its tail until she finally clasped onto the shaft. Torak had run to get another spear to finish off the animal, but it was too late. The lioness had already pulled out the spear, limped to the forest's edge, and gave one final defiant snarl at Torak before exiting the camp with the cubs.

While the other two hunters ensured that the lion was gone, Torak ran over to see Zakho's upper chest and thigh ripped apart. Zakho lay on the ground disoriented, searching his mind for a reason of what had just taken place. A large amount of blood was oozing out of his fine linen tunic and trousers.

Torak shouted orders to the younger men. "Get my pouch!"

The young men rushed to retrieve it and handed it to Torak. He took out a thin bone and fine sinew from his bag and without explanation started sewing up a loose flap of skin on Zakho's bleeding chest. Zakho moaned in agony, his face seemed whiter with the bright red blood splashed about his body. Zakho hardly noticed the experienced hunter as he sewed up any major wounds that leaked fluids out of the upper torso. Torak then ripped away the leg fabric to examine the wound. The injuries consisted of claw scratches from his knee to his ankle and deep fang punctures around his thigh. Torak wasted no time in finding strips of leather for which to wrap the injured leg from thigh to ankle.

Lily kneeled down next to the man who had saved her from the attack. Zakho's eyes blinked wildly, his head bobbing around as if looking for answers, until he eventually passed out.

Lily put her ear to his mouth. "His breathing is weak and he has lost much blood from his body. Do you think God will take him?" she asked.

Torak finished wrapping Zakho's leg "Our cousin is a strong man. It is hard to say," Torak replied warily. "I will not let him go so easily. We must give him back blood that the lion took away."

Lily picked up Zakho's head and rested it in her lap, stroking his brown hair back to comfort him. Torak instructed his younger brothers to watch out for other beasts while he went to kill another animal. He downed a wild pig within the hour and drained its blood into a gourd. When Zakho gained consciousness, they tried to force him to drink the pig blood. He drank little of the liquid, yet dizzily talked about past days wandering through distant lands and how he had always been wise to keep away from danger. Zakho repeatedly asked himself why he picked up the cub, eventually murmuring unintelligible comments until he fell asleep again.

At first light, Zakho woke up with excruciating pain, but was surprisingly clear-headed and determined to rejoin the Sethite tribe. Seeing his color had returned, Torak agreed. Zakho ordered the others to help him up and hurry to Anbar market so they could meet up with the northern Sethites before they headed off without them. Zakho insisted on walking by himself, but only a few miles out of camp proved him incapable.

When the small group stopped to rest, Torak sighed. "Zakho, you cannot travel like this."

"We must," Zakho replied. He winced as he lowered himself to a soft piece of ground. One of the younger men tried to help but he would have none of it.

"You are stubborn and have been on your own too long. I am surprised you have not been killed before," said Torak.

Zakho used his staff to try and pull himself up with one arm. "I am too stubborn to die." With a grunt, he started up then sat back down. "Blight that lion! What was it doing so far north?"

Torak stood over him, hands on his hips. "We need to carry you. It will go better that way."

"No, I will walk."

"You want us to hurry to join the tribe, but you slow us down."

Zakho grimaced when he shifted his body, then nodded. "So be it. But only until I get my strength back."

Torak had his brothers build a stretcher out of two pine seedlings and cover it with an animal skin. They laid Zakho in it and carried him over the rocky trail while Lily walked with Boko. Whenever they took a break, the odd man off would relieve a stretcher bearer. And so they continued their routine all the way to Anbar.

Zakho started to worry that this setback might separate them from the tribe completely. It was a vast unknown area that would make it difficult for most men to navigate, even for a hunter like Torak. Zakho guaranteed Torak and his brothers an adventure in hunting and a chance to see the great city. But this was not quite what he had in mind.

Two days after the mauling, the group of four entered the hard dirt streets of Anbar in the afternoon. The trading town had recently constructed a large square in the center of the town with some rectangular-shaped monumental buildings. Bartering was now in full swing, the clanging of metal echoed across the street, and traders called out for buyers of their goats, while domesticated dogs chased and barked after anything that moved. Zakho had only been away for a year, but the town had changed so much that he had difficulty recognizing it. Fortunately, Zakho's old friend, Duman, chief of the local clan, spotted Torak carrying Zakho and welcomed them.

"Greetings, my friends," Duman said, approaching them with an open palm. The big chief wore his usual fur leggings, leather belt, linen shirt, and beads around his neck and left ear.

"Greetings," replied Torak, setting the stretcher down.

"Zakho? I thought that was you." Duman ignored the fact that Zakho was pallid and weak. "Are you so important that people carry you like a grand elder?"

Zakho made no introductions and dispensed with his usuall idle talk. "Duman. Get your wife, the one who heals, to patch me up. We are to join my tribe," he spoke weakly.

The chief peered closer. "You do not look well, my friend. Did you know that your tribe of Sethites passed through here two suns ago? I thought they were an army that had come to kill us."

"They have left?" Zakho gave a sneer of disappointment at missing them and grunted from his painful injuries.

"Come, let us not talk here. We will fix you at my house."

Duman brought Zakho into his rock-built home and called for his wife. She assessed the damage and quickly set to work with herbs and concoctions for healing the wounds. The stench of gangrene's gaseous poison had worked its way into the tissue and all knew the smell was not a good sign. The faces of those in the room indicated Zakho's condition did not bode well. Duman let his wife work her spells, while the rest of the group ate a meal and slept in his large home that night.

The next morning Torak and his brothers took a walk through the active cacophony of trading while Duman's wife worked on Zakho's wounds. Lily sat and studied closely her methods of healing and the herbs she used. Later in the day, Torak returned to the home and found the rotund chief sitting next to Zakho, who was alert and sitting with his back against the wall.

Zakho was still fighting off a fever and he wiped off beads of sweat from his forehead. He looked up to see Torak addressing the chief.

Torak bowed to the chief. "How is he?"

Duman nodded toward his wife, who was inspecting the leather bandages she put on the day before. Zakho tried to put on a good smile. "Torak, come here."

Torak tried being jovial. "You must not be well my cousin. All you do is lie on your back in the comfort of this fine home and eat all their food." Zakho had not even touched the dish of peas, lentils, and lamb. "What are we to do with you?"

"I will be up in no time," replied Zakho softly. "Soon I will be making deals with Duman once again."

Duman smiled, then informed Torak of the progress. "My wife started the maggots on his leg at sunrise, to eat at the evil within. Once they do their work, we will wash them and the rot out."

Torak watched the woman clean out the brown, foul-smelling puss. "Do you think you will be able to leave, Zakho?"

Zakho perked up. "Oh, we will leave," he assured. "I wanted to meet Noah here three days ago but better later than not at all."

Zakho noticed that Torak was scrutinizing the healing methods of the Cainites. "If you still cannot walk, we might be able to make a sling between donkeys and carry you," said Torak.

"Do not fuss over me. All will be well. I have had wounds this bad before," Zakho falsely admitted. "I swear that before long, we and the tribe will all be joined together and on our way to the city of Tuball. You must promise not to leave my side, Torak."

"I promise, Cousin." Torak patted Zakho's shoulder, then signaled the chief to step outside. Duman followed. "How bad are his wounds?"

Duman stood motionless. "Deep and broad."

"Should we stay here until he heals or take him as he is?" asked Torak.

"Walk with me," said Duman. The men strolled away from the home along a stream. "My wife is a good healer, but if I were of your people, I would not wait. The black evil may be too strong for our medicine. You should take him to be with his brothers before he moves on to the afterworld."

"We do not have a guide. How will we find them?" asked Torak. "I have never been north and do not know the land."

"You saw the great numbers in your tribe. Anyone you meet along the way would tell you their path. Besides," he said with a sly smile, "how could you not miss this?" Duman stopped walking and pointed to the ground before them. There were deep grooves and footsteps as if a herd of auroch had stampeded through. "Even the simplest-minded wanderer could follow tracks as obvious as this."

CHAPTER 21

REVISIT OF THE RUINS

The *Bering* lay anchored in the Gunishli shallows with an anxious survey team ready to continue a more extensive excavation of the undersea ruins. Rebecca and Dr. McCray had just printed out a schedule of equipment deployment for the day but were waiting for the professor to provide details on how they would proceed. A photo of the stone slab was wired to Houston and ultimately to the C.E.O. of Terra Petroleum Industries in England. If the professor confirmed his hypothesis, a news bulletin would be released to the public.

As Dr. McCray and Rebecca were finishing up their meeting, she recalled her many scuba dives off the coast of California and wondered what it would be like in the Caspian. "Bob, do you think I could take a dive to inspect the ruins before the submersible is launched?"

McCray was speechless for a moment and his jaw hung open. "I can't believe it."

She became defensive. "It will only be a short dive."

"No, no. Sure, go ahead. We have plenty of scuba gear for you to use. What surprised me is that you called me Bob. I didn't think you'd ever call me by my first name."

"Oh, I see. I guess when I found out you asked Mary to dance, I realized you weren't such an ogre after all. So I thought I would try *Bob* on for size."

"An ogre, eh?"

"Yeah, that was very kind of you to ask her to dance—she being away from her country for the first time."

"Don't read too much into it, Becca. Mary wanted to dance, and I had nothing better to do."

"OK, if you say so," she conceded with curious skepticism.

"I'm serious," he replied, with the most sober face he could muster.

Rebecca gave a smirk. "Well, to tell you the truth, the only reason I'm calling you Bob is that I had a dog named Bob when I was a kid, and calling you that gives me the perfect way to remember him."

He scoffed. "I really don't care if that's true." He abruptly looked down to study some notes on his desk. "By the way, Houston sent back the interpretations of the data, and I'm concerned about this bright spot here."

"I guess that means we're done with your love life?"

"Yeah, I guess we are." He showed Rebecca a three-dimensional print of the survey site. "It looks like there are gases just below the ruins. What do you think?"

She scrutinized the photo for a moment. "Hmmm, I see what you mean. It could be a nice pocket to drill in, but I don't think there is any way on God's blue earth that environmentalists would let us drill on this site."

"We might be able to drill around it. I'm sure we can get creative to extract what we need. In any event, we may want to evaluate this further."

Rebecca didn't want to waste time critiquing data, but instead focused on finding a buddy to swim with. "Can we look into it when I get back from my dive?"

"Sure, knock youself out." He waved her out. "Go on. Have your fun."

She left the cabin and grabbed a piece of toast and an apple from the cafeteria before going back to her cabin to find the authorized list of divers. On her way, she decided to make a detour to see how the professor and Jamal were progressing on the ancient inscriptions. With a piece of toast in her mouth, Rebecca rapped on the door of the compartment and poked her head in. Professor Witherspoon was pointing out to Jamal the validity of two blended societies based on the recent findings.

She pulled the slice of multigrain out of her mouth and entered. "Good morning," she said, still munching. Jamal looked haggard. "Did you get any sleep last night?"

Jamal glanced up. "Yes, a full hour." He rubbed his eyes. "But, as you can see, the professor runs on hopes and dreams and doesn't need any sleep."

She chuckled. "Well, I just wanted to let you know I'm headed down to the underwater site this morning. Anything new to share?"

The professor beamed like a child with a toy. "Funny you should ask, my dear, we have made plenty of headway. There is no doubt that the cultures were integrated. The icons from the Hassuna pottery seals match perfectly to the images on the slab taken from the Caspian Sea." He brought out the snapshots of the undersea pictographs and started to compare them with the photos Mary had brought from the university. "As you can see..." Rebecca checked her watch to make sure she had time to listen, "I'm sure you have to attend to some other business. Let me just say we are making good progress."

"Good! Glad to hear it," Rebecca said.

Dr. Witherspoon raised his hand. "May I tag along with you on your scuba dive? I want to confirm something at the ruins."

"You scuba dive, Professor?"

"Don't look so surprised, some of my finest successes were at the sea floor. The earthenware at Alexandria was a stellar find to say the least, for example. So do not leave without me."

"OK then, that'll be just what the doctor ordered." She saluted. "But we have to be quick, because Dr. McCray wants to take you down in the submersible after lunch." Rebecca knew in the last couple of days Jamal had wanted to tell her something and she was still eager to find out what it was. "You coming too, Jamal?"

"You are asking me to scuba dive?"

Rebecca's face scrunched. "Oh, yeah, you don't know how." *Oh my goodness, I probably made him feel worse after being manhandled by Tony. And I know he's angry that I asked pointed questions about his faith. I am such a dope!* She brightened. "Well, it looks like I am going to have to give you some lessons," she found herself saying.

Jamal perked up. "I would love to examine the undersea articles firsthand. You would give me lessons now?"

"Um, no. But after I get back, I promise."

He sank back into his chair and shooed them away with his hand. "Take your time and have a good dive. I will be watching on the cameras from above." He sighed. "I think I need another hour or three of sleep anyway."

"I'll teach you how to scuba dive in no time when I get back. I promise." She waved weakly to Jamal, then stepped outside the cabin, leaned against the bulkhead, and closed her eyes. *I said I promise twice! What am I trying to prove with him? Maybe he just doesn't like me. Then why am I trying to make him like me? Oh, if I would just focus on my work, we could move on!*

The professor stood at the door. "We won't be long, my boy. We can go over my ideas this afternoon."

The professor closed the door. "Rebecca, I'll meet up with you at the scuba prep area after I pick up something from the cafeteria. I need a little fuel."

"OK. I'll meet you there in a few minutes."

Rebecca went to the aft end of the ship and started sorting out scuba equipment. The professor returned with a small can of pomegranate juice. She picked up what looked like a smashed gas can sprouting hose lines and held it out to the elder diver.

Dr. Witherspoon swallowed the last of the juice and set the can aside. "What is this?"

She put on a serious expression. "You *are* familiar with more than just the open circuit scuba systems, aren't you? Here is the latest rebreather."

He adjusted his glasses. "I guess it has been awhile for me."

"I'm sure you know how it is able to reuse the oxygen left unused in each exhaled breath while simultaneously removing the CO_2 by a chemical trap. The U.S. Navy swears by it. We can study the ruins for hours and there aren't any bubbles to get in our way."

He squirmed a bit. While he examined the equipment, Rebecca giggled. "I'm just kidding, Professor. You would need some training, before you use it." She pointed to the scuba equipment a few yards away. "I'm sure you would feel more comfortable with those." Dr. Witherspoon physically relaxed when he saw the standard scuba gear and cylinders.

"Hey, Becca!" Yakov shouted down from the radio room porthole. "Your mother is on the line. Can you talk to her?"

Rebecca excused herself and made a beeline up the ladders to the compartment where Yakov held out the phone to her. "Mom?" she asked into the receiver.

"Hi, honey. We got your message that you called. Is everything all right?"

At first Rebecca was soothed to hear her mother's voice, but she quickly fidgeted when she remembered that they had not returned her call. "Where have you guys been, Mom?"

"Oh, I'm sorry, dear. Your father tried to pass a gallstone and it was so large he passed out. I thought he had a heart attack, so I took him to the hospital, where they said his gallbladder had so many stones it looked like a bag of marbles. The doctors convinced us to remove the gallbladder and we agreed."

Upon hearing the bad news, Rebecca found a chair to steady herself. "Is Dad OK?"

"The operation went well, until they found out that he had a tumor in his stomach. It was small and praise God we caught it before it spread. The doctors suggested he stay for observation and a few tests, so we did. After a couple days, he was doing very well and the doctors didn't find any other evidence of cancer. Your father was doing great, but since we were close to your uncle in Phoenix we stayed there a week to catch up with family and let him recuperate. So that is why we haven't been home and missed your call, honey. How about you; is everything going as expected in your new job?"

Rebecca's near-death experience flashed through her mind. "Yeah, everything is great, Mom...just wanted to say hi. I'm glad dad is doing fine." Rebecca looked through the porthole to see Dr. Witherspoon suited up and waiting for her. "I have to go, Mom. I'll call you when I get back to Baku—love you."

"I love you too, Becky. You're always in my prayers."

Rebecca hung up the phone and started back down to the main deck. Although she felt her father's pain, it seemed to her that every time something dramatic happened in her life, her dad would outdo her. Rebecca tried to dismiss her own issues and be thankful for her father's life. When she returned to the scuba prep area, Dr. Witherspoon was strapping a bag for samples on his weight belt. Rebecca quickly slipped into her wet suit and donned her rebreather, weight belt, mask with wireless com-link, and fins, and then picked up a flashlight.

Rebecca and Dr. Witherspoon stepped down to the dive platform near the water to check their gear one last time. Tony and McCray appeared above them sipping coffee. As they leaned on the rail to watch the pair dive in, McCray spoke up.

"Oh, Becca," he called down. "After your dive with the professor, don't forget you will be coordinating the survey procedures on board when I take out the submersible."

"OK," she assured. "We won't be long...um, Bob."

McCray let out some air and shook his head with a smile. "It's really tough for her to say that, isn't it, Tony?" He took another sip of his coffee and broke into an unhurried smile.

Tony agreed. "She's tough all right."

Rebecca squinted at them, holding back a retort. She, instead, reached down to rinse out her mask. "Chauvinists," she muttered under her breath. Rebecca adjusted her mask and fell backward into the sea. The professor waved goodbye to the crew and also made a back roll entry into the water.

With Rebecca and the professor pursuing their undersea excursion, Dr. McCray prepared to make use of the submersible. He had just opened the hanger door to finish making some last-minute checks on the vehicle when an Azeri seaman pointed out another ship on the horizon. McCray picked up some binoculars and spotted the familiar ExxonMobil logo on the side of the ship. He knew Exxon had their own ability to interpret massive volumes of seismic data and were good competitive geoscientists in analyzing data and optimizing hydrocarbon recoveries.

"There's our competition," McCray announced into the air.

The Stalin-looking scientific observer "on loan" from the Azerbaijan science community quietly walked up next to McCray. "May I use your binoculars, Doctor?"

McCray was mildly startled by his stealthy approach. "Oh, I haven't had the opportunity to be formally introduced to the new representative of the government. And, forgive me, I forget your name."

"Dr. Gusseinov, Mohammad Gusseinov." He produced a confident smile and extended his hand.

Dr. McCray shook his hand and passed the binoculars to him. "It's a pleasure, sir."

The observer put the binoculars to his eyes and adjusted the focus to scan the ship. "What are they doing out here?

McCray shaded the sun from his eyes. "I suspect that Exxon is conducting some surveys of their own. I am sure you're aware that they have had some dismal results lately, such as the Oguz well, which they finally closed down. They no doubt will be successful elsewhere. Isn't Terra the only company authorized to be in this area?" he asked the Azeri scientist.

Dr. Gusseinov nodded with the binoculars still held close to his eyes. "Yes, yes, but what is that smaller vessel not far from the larger ship?"

McCray took back the binoculars. "Hmmm. I don't know. It look's like a small military vessel...a gunboat of some kind."

McCray slowly lowered the glasses. "And it's headed this way—in a hurry."

The observer spread his thick mustache slowly. "What would a military vessel be doing here?"

"Maybe they just want to ensure we have the correct concession papers. I would assume it's the neverending disagreement on how to divide the sea among the Caspian's bordering countries. You've got Iran and Turkmenistan wishing to divide the Caspian into five roughly equal shares, while Russia, Azerbaijan and Kazakhstan are in favor of dividing the sea along the country's shoreline. It would be nice to get a solid agreement on the littoral boundaries some day." He eyed the gunboat carefully and sighed. "I hope they don't give us any trouble."

Mohammad Gusseinov stroked his chin. "Caution tells me they may not be friendly. To keep the survey site safe, you may want to move the *Bering* a few hundred yards away," he suggested. "I have heard that Turkmenistan is as paranoid as North Korea and a military vessel usually means trouble."

McCray nodded. "Good idea, Mohammad. Come on up to the pilot house with me. I may need you."

Once in the pilot house, McCray gave orders to Captain Kovacheski to slowly back the ship up westward.

"What about your divers?" asked Kovacheski as the ship moved slowly away from the survey site.

"We'll be back to pick them up soon after we have a chat with the Turkmen," assured McCray.

The gunboat had slowed to about three hundred meters off the port side like a shark ready to lunge at its prey. It sent a message to the radio room, which was patched up to the pilot house. "Research vessel! You are ordered by the government of Turkmenistan to hold your position and be boarded!"

McCray's caution turned to annoyance at their blunt and brazen orders. He took the microphone to respond to their demand. "This is a research vessel leased by Terra Petroleum with permission from the government of Azerbaijan. Boarding is highly unnecessary." The *Bering* continued to move slowly forward.

All remained quiet for a moment, then a flash of light appeared from the smaller boat, followed by a *boom*! Shortly after the blast a large splash of water gushed up a few yards in front of the *Bering*. McCray and the crew were a little rattled by the shot over the bow. The *Bering*'s crew stood motionless for a long moment, unsure what was going to happen next and they certainly weren't capable of taking a retaliatory response. The men at the prow of the ship evacuated the area and ran to find cover. The captain reversed the engines for a dead stop.

McCray was indignant. "Those idiots actually fired on us!"

A reply came through the speaker "That was a warning. Do not move."

McCray's blood pressure shot up. "This is outrageous! We're just conducting research! I'm not just going to sit here and take this!"

"Shall we put in a distress call to the Azeri Navy?" asked Captain Kovacheski.

Mohammad Gusseinov intervened. "I doubt they could reach us in time, Captain. I believe it would be unwise to take the Turkmen threat lightly."

McCray contained himself, then paced in thought. "We should at least let the office in Baku know what's going on. Vladimir, radio Baku while I talk to our visitors. I want to know what the Turkmen have to say for themselves."

As the thirty-meter patrol boat idled abreast to the *Bering*, it flaunted an ominous 33mm cannon in front and a 12.7mm machine gun aft. McCray noticed a dozen men on board, but was sure the vessel could hold twice that. Some of the *Bering*'s crew held onto wrenches and other heavy objects to defend themselves. Not wanting to escalate matters, McCray ordered his men to be cooperative. The soldiers threw a line to be secured to the larger vessel, and after ensuring a solid link between the two boats, an officer and four soldiers with AK-47s jumped aboard the *Bering*. The militia efficiently spread out to inspect for any contraband or any other potential threats.

Dr. McCray put on a less-than-angry face and stepped forward with his hand out to be civil. The officer was lean, with dark wavy hair, and rested his hand on his holstered sidearm. Reluctantly, the officer shook McCray's hand.

"I am Dr. Robert McCray, the head of this expedition. What seems to be the problem?"

"We are required to conduct a search of your vessel because you have violated Turkmenistan waters, Doctor," he claimed.

"I don't know what you're talking about. According to my maps, we are perfectly legitimate," McCray asserted. "I am working in conjunction with the Azerbaijani authority to conduct research in this area. We are fully within our rights to be here."

"I did not come here to argue with you. Only to inspect your ship for contraband and escort you back to Turkmenbashi."

McCray's anger flared. "What? Escort us to Turkmenistan? We are conducting research, not terrorism!"

"I am sorry for the inconvenience, but I have my orders," he replied without any sympathy. "We must leave immediately."

McCray felt a flood of his past army experience start to dominate his emotions for control. "This is ridiculous. You do not have the right to do this!"

"My authority as a Turkmenistan officer and my superior weapons, say I do." A sinister grin slid up his cheeks and the soldiers hanging on the military boat's rails laughed.

Bob McCray quickly scanned the armed men surrounding them. McCray remembered the recent fiascos of border disputes in the Caspian and didn't want to become another statistic. He took a deep breath and succumbed to the Turkmen official. "Could you at least talk to the Azeri government before hauling us off?"

"My orders do not include the Azeri government." The officer then put out his hand toward Dr. McCray as if he were a child. "Come now. I suggest you stay calm and let us do our job. If we find nothing contradicting our laws, you have nothing to fear." He motioned for four of his soldiers to spread out and conduct their inspection.

Jamal had heard the warning shot from the military vessel and opened his cabin door a crack to see armed military men poking around the ship. He looked around to see where the professor and Rebecca were, but saw Chuck, the portly engineer, directing an Azeri workman to secure the military vessel.

Chuck looked back at Jamal. "You better stay inside, bud. We don't want to cause any problems with the Turkmenistan Navy."

"Did Rebecca make it back on board?" Jamal asked.

Chuck scratched his head. "Last time I saw her, she and the professor went diving for the ruins. I don't think they made it back aboard."

A soldier turned the corner and pointed his rifle at the Iranian. "Move!" he shouted in native Turkmen. Jamal stepped aside and the man went into the cabin. The soldier opened closet doors, checked drawers, and threw papers around recklessly. The soldier eventually found a laptop computer humming quietly and noticed some ancient writing on the screen. He immediately closed the lid and picked it up. Jamal objected and grabbed the computer, but before he could take it, the soldier lifted up the butt end of his rifle and struck Jamal on the head. He fell down hard and was left with a bruise and imprint of a rifle butt on his forehead.

The Turkmen soon returned one-by-one from their appointed tasks to report back to their leader. The soldier who barged into Jamal's cabin held up a laptop computer and nodded to his superior. The officer tipped his head sideways, indicating he wanted the subordinate to return to the military vessel. He then turned back to Dr. McCray. "You see, my men have found only a few things of minor importance. So the rest of your concerns should be incidental. I am sure there will only be formalities when we get to port."

"Are we still going with you?"

"Yes, you must follow us. When we reach port, we will straighten this all out."

McCray blew out a frustrated puff of air. "I have two people underwater, right now. Surely we cannot leave them behind."

"Can you see them from here, with your monitoring equipment?" the officer asked.

McCray suddenly remembered that they had moved the ship. "Um…no. But we may be able to signal them. The officer looked at McCray keenly, leaned back against the ship's railing, pulled out a pack of Marlboro cigarettes, and lit up one. He then pompously waved for McCray to proceed. The officer watched as McCray used the ultrasonic wireless underwater communicator to contact Rebecca and the professor, but there was only static.

McCray tried to explain. "They may be out of range for some reason. We have to send divers down to get them."

"I do not believe you." He blew out a puff of smoke. "But in the spirit of cooperation, I will give you twenty minutes to get them anyway."

McCray sent his best diver, John Hanak, down and within twenty minutes he was back without them. "Did you see them anywhere?" asked McCray. Hanak shook his head with disappointment.

McCray confided to the officer, "I must be honest. We have moved away from the site and need to get back to the correct coordinates."

The officer put the cigarette out on the railing and nodded to the other men that it was time to go.

"You are lying," the Turkmen declared, firmly yet calmly. "I did not believe you the first time and will not be taken as a fool. Follow us or you will lose not only your phantom divers, but also your ship."

"I am telling you the truth!" McCray shouted, worried about the survival of Rebecca and Dr. Witherspoon.

"It does not matter. We leave *now!*" The officer raised his arm and swung it into a circle to signal his men. "Some of my men will stay here to ensure you obey." Several men returned and stood at attention.

"At least let me notify the authorities in Baku so they can pick up my divers," McCray implored.

"I cannot allow any further transmissions." The officer ordered his men to stand guard at the pilot house and port and starboard of the main deck. "My men will be in charge of your communications from now on. Your divers can catch the next ferry to Baku. It should be along anytime," he laughed sardonically.

Dr. McCray followed after the officer and continued to emphasize the need to rescue Rebecca and the professor. The officer walked calmly back to his gunboat, placating McCray with incidental nods as if he were listening. Seeing he was getting nowhere, McCray spotted the rubber raft hanging on the side of the aft end of the ship and ran to it. He released a latch that held the raft and the rubber boat dropped instantly to the water with a splash. McCray pumped his fist in a show of triumph. Before he could be gratified at his ingenuity, McCray watched helplessly as the raft slowly floated away from the *Bering*, while the Turkmen soldiers used it as target practice. McCray froze where he stood.

Meanwhile, Jamal had been knocked dizzy for a few minutes and found himself being helped up by Chuck. "Are you all right, bud?"

"Yes," Jamal said, rubbing his head. "But he took my computer!"

Jamal heard some gunshots, ran out of his cabin, and watched as the Turkmen ship revved up its engines. He saw the rubber raft that Dr. McCray released, riddled with holes, and knew it was too late.

Jamal walked up to McCray, who stood staring down at the deflating raft. "Dr. McCray? Rebecca and the professor have not made it back and the soldiers took my computer."

McCray looked up at the sky, then closed his eyes trying to contain his frustration. "You don't think I know that?"

"But we must do something! At least call the authorities in Baku and they can send help."

"Thanks for the advice. Listen, Jamal, I'm trying my best, given the circumstances. As much as I would like to call in the cavalry to rescue Harold and Becca, there are guards posted on this ship to make sure we behave. The safety of my crew comes first. You'll learn that you can't fight every battle that comes your way."

Captain Kovacheski strode up to McCray with a worried expression.

"Did you get a message off to Baku?" McCray asked.

The captain shook his head. "No. There was only static on the line. Maybe they have a scrambler on their ship."

He glanced at Jamal. "Does that answer your question?"

Jamal looked over to the Turkmen boat with narrowed eyes. "I will not let them get away with this."

McCray ran his hand over his head, scratched his neck absent-mindedly, stood for a moment with his hands on his hips, then spat on the deck. "Good for you. Go get 'em." He glanced at the captain. "It looks like I've let us down. I'll be in my cabin." McCray stomped off and kicked a dent in a garbage can in his way.

CHAPTER 22

ABANDONED

Rebecca and Harold Witherspoon glided effortlessly along the seafloor taking pictures of the fallen slabs of stone. Most of the northern section of the area was strewn with rectangular debris stacked next to one another like a crumpled-up jigsaw puzzle. Heavy sections of the ancient wall's base still stood, lonely and encircled by a sea of stone rubble. The two divers closed in on a large triangular structure that dwarfed the surrounding ruins. Even with seaweed and sediment covering the monolith, one could plainly see the shape of an ancient ziggurat. Mesmerized by such a grand formation still solidly in place, they encircled the structure and eventually found an opening half way up the ziggurat.

As they swam slowly up to the opening, Rebecca checked her watch to find they had been diving for twenty-five minutes. Dr. Witherspoon could stay down only a fraction of her time below. She swam through an archway in a few meters, while the professor examined the etching on the outside of the opening. The passage had darkened and for safety's sake Rebecca went back to nudge him to follow her. As they swam forward, Rebecca turned on her wide-beam flashlight to discover that the corridor turned left and led up an underwater stairway.

Taking several strokes over the flooded steps, Rebecca saw the end of the water above her and moved up slowly into a pocket of air. She climbed out of the water and started to take off her fins to continue up the steps. The professor, just behind her, reached out and squeezed her leg for her to stay close. Rebecca relented to her elder and stopped, but she couldn't help but slip off her full-face breathing mask to see if the air was breathable.

She sniffed at the air a little and grinned. "Look, Professor, we don't need our gear!"

Seeing she was breathing normally, Dr. Witherspoon removed his mask and mouthpiece to test the air. "This is a pleasant surprise; stale but acceptable."

"Did you see how neatly that fallen section of wall was on the seafloor?" Rebecca asked, as she removed her rebreather from her shoulders. "It looked as if a giant had pushed it right over."

"It was rather impressive, I must say."

"So what do you think this room is, Professor? And why did you stop me? I'm dying to see what is around the corner up there."

"It is more likely to be a corridor to a larger room. As much as I would like to accompany you on an expeditionary tour, I have learned to be cautious. Before we attempt to investigate any further, we must contact the ship. I only have about twenty minutes of air left, and I could have sworn that I heard some rumbling. Earthquakes are not unusual in this region, but it sounded different somehow."

Rebecca imagined what it would be like if these ancient stones fell upon them. "I guess you're right. Too bad, because my rebreather won't run out for a couple days. How about we go back, bring a few others back down with us, and you can get another twelve liter cylinder." She adjusted the tiny microphone in her mask and tried to contact the ship, but there was only static. She shrugged. "Huh. Nothing. I think the thick stone structure is blocking the signal. We might as well swim back to the surface."

Dr. Witherspoon set his feet in the water and held his face mask. "Two days of diving?"

Rebecca raised her eyebrows. "Oh, yeah. And no bubbles! I'm telling you, Professor; you need to make the change from open to close-circuit scuba."

The professor nodded, put on his mask, and started back into the water. Rebecca followed him and soon they were making their way back to the surface. Rebecca popped her head out of the water to signal to the ship, but it wasn't there. She turned around to see if it had moved…but only water was near her. She took off her mask to get a clearer view and saw the *Bering* and a smaller ship about a mile away moving eastward.

"What? Hey!" she shouted and waved frantically. "Where are you going! We're still here!"

Dr. Witherspoon surfaced with a grin. "This far exceeds any of my best dig days," he announced to Rebecca, lifting the mask to his forehead.

"I don't think you would say that if you just saw what I saw." She pointed to the east. "Our ship is over there, and moving farther away."

His joy turned to disbelief. "Why are they leaving? I don't understand."

"Neither do I." Rebecca stared at the ship, trying to make sense of its departure. "They must be conducting a test of some sort." She watched as the ship got smaller. "But they wouldn't leave without telling us."

"Try communicating with them now that we're on the surface."

Rebecca spoke into the microphone. "Hello, *Bering*, this is Rebecca Belmont. Do you read me?" Only static spilled out. "*Bering*, *Bering*, do you read me?!" she yelled. Again only static was heard. She was astonished. "Unbelievable!"

Dr. Witherspoon spied something on the water a short swim away. "Look over there…it looks like a life raft."

"A sorry looking one," she added, seeing the deflated sides. "You don't think it's here for us, do you?"

"Possibly. There has to be some relationship between it and the ship's departure."

"Well, unless it has a motor, it won't be of use to us anyway." Rebecca looked around. "Actually, I would be happy just to crawl onto it. So what do we do now, Professor?"

The elder diver treaded water, scrutinizing the horizon for a moment. "The only thing we can do, my dear…wait."

They waited an hour, then two. Neither of them hardly spoke a word. After two hours of treading water Rebecca finally complained to the Caspian sky. "This has been the worst job I have ever had!"

The afternoon sun reflected a deep red collar along the bottom of some ominous-looking cloud. In a few hours, they would be in darkness.

"We must assume they may not be back for a while," said the professor." It is time to consider survival tactics."

"Do you have survival training?"

"I specialize in archaeology…I was hoping you had some expertise."

Rebecca hit the water repeatedly with her fists. "This is just great! I…I.." She whined a little, treaded water with one hand and covered her eyes with the other, then spoke between sobs. "I almost drowned on ship, I turned Jamal against me, my boss hates me, and Bill left me! And now I'm going to drown again!" Rebecca started to go into a full fledge cry. Before breaking down altogether, she took a deep breath and closed her eyes to think clearly. *I've got to be strong, I've got to be strong, I've got to be strong. Oh, for goodness sakes, I'm going nuts! I can't do anything right. Lord Jesus, please don't let us die out here.*

When she opened her eyes the professor had treaded close to her, waiting until she composed herself. "It is important we stay calm, Becca."

Rebecca cleared a knot in her throat. "I don't know if I can do this any longer. I'm done with this job!"

"Shhh, don't talk like that. You are a fine, strong, intelligent young woman. If we do not lose our composure, all will pan out. Besides, Robert thinks the world of you."

Rebecca straightened up. "Dr. McCray?"

"Quite. He told me so."

She didn't believe the professor. "But he puts me down whenever he has the chance. He asked *me* if I wanted to leave after the flood, but wanted *Jamal* to stay on. Can you believe that? What a chauvinist!"

Dr. Witherspoon laughed. "He may be old fashioned about women, but that certainly has nothing to do with respect for you."

"Come on. Really?"

"Yes, really."

"It doesn't make sense."

"He confided in me that he admired not only your cognitive abilities, but your potential as a leader. Robert did not give me particulars."

"Well, in that case, other than being stranded in the middle of the largest inland body of water, I've got that going for me."

Harold chuckled. "That's the spirit."

Rebecca took a deep breath and calmed herself. "What about food, Professor? All I have is an energy bar with me. It won't be enough for the both of us if we're out here for a couple days, and I really wouldn't want to wash it down with this salty water."

"Hmmm. Yes, water. We're swimming in it and we can't drink a drop." The professor shook his head. "Even though the Caspian is less than a third as salty as the ocean, it would take a piece of desalination equipment to make it suitable to drink, not to mention a filter to rid the water of any contamination from oil spills. We also need to concern ourselves with the sea surface; the wind is picking up and the waves will no doubt become a nuisance."

"Harold Witherspoon, if you can't say something nice, don't say it at all," Rebecca scolded and shook her finger at him as if he were a child. She somehow managed to crack a smile, seeing that it couldn't get much worse.

The professor laughed. "You can be a very funny woman, despite your circumstances."

"I'm not funny, I'm just giving up on reality."

223

Small waves lapped up and around the two swimmers' shoulders as they treaded water. Rebecca scanned the vast waters for assistance and remembered the raft drifting a hundred meters away. "Wait a minute. What about that raft? There has to be sea rations on it."

"Something just occurred to me. Are there sharks in the Caspian Sea?"

"Not that I know of. I'm getting the rations." Rebecca swam rapidly to it while the professor stayed behind.

Dr. Witherspoon looked at his watch, at the setting sun, and then across the horizon. "This is not good, old boy."

She grabbed the sinking raft and dug through the side pockets. "Hey, look!" she shouted, waving a packet in the air. "Food and other goodies! Thank God!"

"Very good, Becca! The water is starting to get rough! Now come back—I think I have an idea!"

"Yeah, OK!" Rebecca slowly towed the deflated raft with supplies back to the professor.

When she arrived, he suggested a temporary solution to their dilemma. "Is it possible, Ms. Belmont, that we can go below and stay within that air pocket of the structure we found? We can rest for the night and preserve our energy."

"Sounds good, but if they come back, how will they know where we are?"

"Hmmm. We could turn on the life preserver locator light, then tie a line from it and to the entrance to the sunken structure. When they return, they can follow it down to our underwater flat. In the morning, we will return to the surface."

"Good idea, Professor." She treaded water a bit and looked intently at the seasoned diver. "I'm glad you came with me. I would really hate to be out here alone."

"You aren't the only one, my dear."

Rebecca cocked her head and stretched her neck as long as possible. "Did you hear that, Professor?"

"Hear what?"

"Boat engines." She swam in a circle and squinted, then shook her head. "Forget it. Sometimes you just want to hear what you want to hear."

The professor turned on the vest's survival locator light and tied on a seventy-five-foot retaining line, while Rebecca let out the remaining air in the raft. They adjusted their masks and dove back down to the structure with their supplies.

It wasn't ten minutes later when a large ferry traveling from Baku to Turkmenbashi cruised nearby the underwater site.

Harold Witherspoon secured the tethered line from the life-jacket around a heavy stone at the archway. Rebecca dragged the raft up the steps and to the landing. They removed their gear and searched through the supplies by flashlight to examine them. There were two flares, a plastic tarp, a life raft repair kit, a signal mirror, a police whistle, a knife, a CO_2 bottle for emergency inflation, an inflation pump, a magnetic compass, a dye marker, glow sticks, a flashlight, MRE food rations, a fishing kit, and even a small seawater desalting pump.

While contemplating what they might be able to do with the supplies, Rebecca pointed out the emergency food rations that were provided. The professor eyed the spaghetti with meat sauce meal, and she went for the barbecue pork and rice. She broke open a glow stick, turned off the flashlight to save batteries, and said a quick prayer of thanksgiving before eating.

"These really aren't that bad," she remarked with a burp. "How's your dinner?"

Dr. Witherspoon nodded with approval. "Given the circum-stances…outstanding." He smiled and inspected the young woman as she licked the remainder of her packet. "You know, Becca, I have a daughter about your age."

Rebecca leaned back against the wall with her meal. "Oh, does she live with you in Tehran?"

"No. I assume she is somewhere in Europe."

"It sounds like you haven't talked to her in awhile."

"Frankly, no. I am sure she is doing well in her studies. She is working on her doctorate in anthropology. It would be delightful if she worked with me some day." He paused and stared off into distant memories. "In times like these, we think of the ones we love, eh?"

Rebecca's eyes watered. "Yeah."

"If I'm not being too nosy, who is Bill?"

"One of those who we think of in times like this." Rebecca dabbed at her eyes and Dr. Witherspoon waited for further information. "He was my fiancé who just wasn't ready for marriage…and I was. Or I thought I was." She looked to the ceiling with a lump in her throat. "It was the day before our wedding and he told me…or I should say he told the best man to tell me that…he—I just don't understand why he would do that?"

The professor shrugged. " I can't offer any advice, due to the lack of information on the man."

Rebecca didn't absorb his statement. "Any normal human being would have mentioned something earlier; much earlier…before…." She breathed erratically and started to tear up again. "I thought we were perfect together. We went to college together and we had so many plans. Why?" She wiped her eyes and glanced at the professor. "Looks like I have a lot of pent up emotions, doesn't it? I'm sorry."

The professor reached over to pat her hand. "Don't be, Becca. Based on my own experience, it is better to sever a relationship prior to marriage than to live many years drifting apart and ending it then."

She cocked her head. "Are you divorced from your wife?"

He nodded. "My dear Becca, your heart is young and it will mend. Emotions heal quicker when dealt with early rather than later." The professor took a deep breath. "I should be sorry I brought up painful memories for you."

She smiled and relaxed a little. "No, this is good. I have stuffed my feelings about this for too long. If I had been married to him, I never would have broken it off. You are right though. He wanted me to be a stay-at-home mom and be less adventurous. I should have known it wasn't going to work out then. Ha! If he could only see me now, he'd probably have a heart attack."

Rebecca set aside her food and mindlessly wound up the crank on the side of a self-generated flashlight for about a minute.

The professor took off his glasses and cleaned them with a handkerchief. "What are you doing with that?"

Rebecca stood up and focused the light down the corridor. "It's one of those wind-up flashlights. Although it gives us only ten minutes of light, it has the advantage of never wearing out batteries. Excuse me." She started away from the landing.

"Where are you going?" asked the professor.

"You know where. You coming?"

Dr. Witherspoon picked up the amber glowstick and followed her.

Thoughts of water bursting through a seam in the wall crossed her mind, but she continued down the long passageway. They fanned out their lights across the walls, and walked slowly and carefully. The passage was made up of huge blocks of granite on the walls and ceiling and basalt on the floor. The ceiling expanded three times in height for many paces until they came to a dead end.

To the left of them were two tall, clean, sturdy doors standing majestically as if they had just been closed. Each door had two thick knurled handles, knee to head high and was embossed with ornate gold plating and colored jewels. Within each door were panels of intricate engravings of unusual stylized pictures and writings. Rebecca and Dr. Witherspoon stood speechless for a long moment while they marveled at the ancient entrance.

CHAPTER 23

RESCUE

J amal was awestruck by not only the Turkmen's theft, but their callous indifference to leaving two people abandoned in the Caspian Sea. He walked back to the aft end of the ship and watched as the rubber raft floated in the wake of the ship. Mary slowly crept up the ladders to be next to Jamal. Mary was accustomed to the routine of the university schedule, not a chaotic militaristic dispute.

She touched his arm. "What is happening, Jamal?"

Jamal pounded his fist on the rail. "The Turkmen have taken control of the vessel, and we are leaving the professor and Rebecca stranded! That is what is happening!"

"I am sure Dr. McCray knows this and will do something," she assured.

"I don't think Dr. McCray has much control of anything at the moment, Mary."

Jamal turned around to see Tony tensed up with a wrench in his hand, like a shoreworker ready for a brawl. Several guards were posted around the ship and it didn't set well with the crew. Jamal walked over to the Texan and signaled him into an alcove.

Tony followed. "You look like you got somethin' on your mind, partner," he tipped his baseball cap to Mary, "Ma'am. Two months ago some guy stole my wallet in Turkmenbashi. So if it's about the Turkmen, I'm in."

Jamal lowered his voice. "Although I would like to retaliate against the soldiers, I am more concerned about Rebecca and the professor. We can't leave them stranded in the water."

"You got that right, Raz."

"It is Razemani," corrected Jamal.

"Yeah, yeah, whatever. But we need a plan."

"I think I've got one, but we need to let Dr. McCray know about it."

Jamal presented his ideas, Tony gave some input, and together they developed a plan. Afterwards, Tony, Jamal, and Mary marched up to Dr. McCray's cabin. Tony rapped on the door with two slow taps, followed by three fast, and then two more slow ones.

McCray answered their knock with a raised eyebrow. "Come on in." He then looked to see if they had been followed and shut the door. "OK, what's this about?"

Tony only produced a devilish smile, an eybrow raised.

"Don't tell me—you want to go on a rescue mission?" They nodded in unison. McCray sighed. "Listen, I appreciate your concern, but I don't want to be responsible for another missing crewmember from this ship."

Jamal spoke up. "You do not need to be concerned. I am not a member of your crew."

"Oh, really. For a while there, I thought we were a team. Now you're an independent contractor."

"He won't be going alone," inserted Tony.

"You too?"

"Somebody has to watch over Raz."

"It is Razemani...or Jamal," said Jamal.

Tony shouldered a hug around Jamal like they were school buddies. "Sure, sure, Raz."

"I see. And I suppose you want to go too, Mary?"

She shook her head no, then grinned. "I am going to be the diversion."

McCray rolled his eyes. "This is not an army ranger's mission, people. This is deadly serious, and someone could get hurt." He found a chair to sit in and proceeded to rub his eyes, then waved them away. "Go back to your cabins and we'll work this out when we get to Turkmenistan."

"We cannot leave them out in the water, Dr. McCray," Jamal pleaded.

McCray straightened in his chair. "Listen!" his voice cracked. "I've lost men before, when I was in the army, and I don't want to see it happen here." He abruptly swiveled around in his chair and looked out the porthole, his arms crossed. There was a moment of silence.

"Doc, we already have," Tony reminded.

Jamal was serious about his intentions, but would not move until they had permission from McCray. "Please, sir."

McCray turned around. "You know, even though I expect my crew to follow my commands, I appreciate it when they take their own initiative to accomplish a task." McCray gave in. "I've never been one to follow strict orders, especially by some foreign gangsters, so I guess I shouldn't expect you to either. I just hope we're not making a mistake."

"We?" asked Jamal.

McCray took a deep breath. "So what's this diversion plan?"

Moments later, Mary was standing at the port side of the ship, where an inflatable, Hypalon tube, dive boat was hanging. She glanced up at the boat number to ensure it was the correct one. The keel had an aluminum strip protector and a large diesel motor for speeds up to thirty knots. Mary had borrowed Rebecca's dinner dress with a low neckline and high hemline, and being well endowed in the breasts and hips helped the dress accentuate her feminine mystique. She straightened the dress and seductively walked by one of the soldiers standing guard. As Mary passed by, she dropped her purse, and slowly bent down to pick it up. When the soldier predictably lurched down to pick it up for her, she initiated a conversation with the man and coaxed him to walk with her around the corner.

With the soldier taking the bait, Tony and Jamal quickly ran over to the winch and stood ready to lower the boat. To mask the sound of the winch, they waited until Bob McCray turned on some loud jazz music. Soon, Earl King, singing, "come on let the good times roll," blared throughout the ship's speaker system. The plan worked without a hitch. Tony and Jamal tossed some gear onto the floorboards of the boat and when it was in the water climbed down a rope ladder off the side of the ship.

Meanwhile, the soldier with Mary expected to let his own good times role, evident by his aggressive groping and fondling of her. At first, Mary was enjoying the roll she was playing, but when she tried to back away he ripped her dress at her breast. She abandoned the ripped fabric he held to leave the scene, but he grabbed her arm. Mary tried to push the man back but he would have none of it and slapped her hard enough that she fell down trembling. As the man started pushing up her dress, someone coughed behind them.

Before the soldier could turn completely around, a large wrench connected with the attacker's head. The soldier dropped like a limp rag. Mary whimpered and cowered in the corner, then glanced up to see Bob McCray.

"I wanted to ensure our plan didn't get out of hand. And by the looks of it, I arrived just in time." McCray extended his hands out to her and she accepted them with the embarrassment of a torn and revealing dress.

McCray looked down at the unconscious soldier. "That ought to keep him out of trouble for a while." He put his arm around her to comfort her. "Everything will be fine, Mary. You did great."

She covered her breasts with shaky hands. "Thank you."

Without notice, Dr. Gusseinov appeared. He saw the soldier lying on the deck with a large wrench beside him and Dr. McCray consoling Mary. "May I be of assistance?"

McCray looked guilty…and proud of it. "I assume you won't tell our Turkmen friends about this?"

"What do I care about an uncoordinated soldier that bumps his head into airborne wrenches?"

McCray chuckled. "Thanks, Mr. Gusseinov. I appreciate that. If you will excuse us, I was just taking Mary back to her room."

Mary cocked her head and looked closer at Gusseinov's bright blue eyes. "I know you. Without your beard you look like…" her eyes grew big. "You are not a scientist. You are Mohammad Jalil! You almost fooled me. What are you doing here in this disguise?" Mohammad pressed his forefinger to his lips to silence her.

McCray looked at Mary. "You know him?"

"Yes, from Tehran."

McCray focused on Mohammad. "If you're not Dr. Gusseinov, we need to talk."

Suddenly the grinding start of the rescue boat's 250 horsepower outboard engine echoed off the *Bering's* hull. McCray and the others ran around to the side of the ship to see if all was good. Jamal and Tony had unclipped the lines from the winch and shot away at full throttle. Tony was victoriously waving his cowboy hat in the air.

Another soldier from the starboard side of the ship ran to the railing and shot a burst of rounds from his Kalashnikov rifle at the boat. The bullets sprayed into the water but missed the small craft as it sped off. The soldier then ran up to the pilot house to where another soldier stood guard next to the captain. He got on the phone to inform his superior on the Turkmenistan ship of the escape.

Dr. McCray ran up to the pilot house after the soldier. He yelled back as he ran. "Take Mary back to her room, Gusseinov, or whatever your name really is?"

"It's still Mohammad," Jalil said.

The young Turkmen, who, upon finishing his conversation with the officer on the military vessel, saw McCray enter the pilot house, thrust the handset to him. McCray put the receiver to his ear.

"Dr. McCray?" The officer's voice was calm yet firm.

"Yes."

"My man tells me your people have left without permission. I am not pleased with my guards and I am not pleased with you."

McCray could sense a threat coming. "We couldn't just leave our people stranded out there."

"I will only say this once more. Do not attempt anything else like this again or I will do more to you than just escort your vessel to shore."

"What do you mean by that—" McCray started to ask, but the officer hung up.

McCray looked over at Captain Kovacheski with a crooked smile. "I hope he doesn't get too upset when he finds out that one of his soldiers may have a concussion." McCray knew that this was the only rescue attempt they could make. He set the handset down, then picked up his binoculars and followed the small rescue boat as it bounced over the waves. "They better know what they're doing."

Tony and Jamal whisked their way on the water as fast as the rescue boat could take them. The motor's whine changed pitch whenever they skipped over the waves. Jamal gazed into a hand-held Global Positioning System device, while Tony peered across the sea with one hand on the steering wheel and the other on the throttle at the stand-up console.

Jamal felt the Texan watching the back of his head for close to an hour, but said nothing.

Tony spoke over the engine's noise. "Hey, Raz."

Jamal was tired of correcting Tony's nickname to him. He glanced over his shoulder with an unsettled acknowledgment. "Yes?"

"Sorry about the other night. I had a few too many."

Jamal had tried to forget about Tony's drunken abuse ever since it occurred. He looked closer at the Texan and believed his

233

apology was genuine. "It is forgotten." He swiped hand over hand, then turned back to look over the prow toward their destination. Neither spoke another word about it.

Seaspray splashed onto the GPS device and Jamal reached into his pocket to get a cloth to wipe it off. He pulled out Rebecca's scarf she had let him use the first day they had met. Jamal held it to his face to smell her perfume. A lump in his throat formed and he quickly put the small scarf back in his pocket.

After racing out to sea for two hours, they passed near the ExxonMobil ship they had seen earlier in the morning. Jamal knew they were close to the dive site and checked the GPS again. He sliced across his neck with his hand as a signal for Tony to cut the throttle. The Texan smartly slowed the engine to an idle so they could examine their position.

Jamal smiled and pointed to the GPS device. "I think we're near the coordinates."

Tony gave a thumbs-up and reached down to get the underwater communication equipment. "Great. Let's hope they are still there. The weather seems to be changing." He pointed to the thickening clouds. "And we don't have enough gas to search the whole Caspian."

Jamal looked over his partner's shoulder with a worried frown. "Tony. We are not alone." A larger vessel had been following them and was approaching fast. "Who do you think it is?"

"My guess is—not the good guys. Dollars to doughnuts, they're here for the same reason. "

Jamal looked a few meters away to see the floating lifejacket with a flashing light. "Look a lifejacket! 'Bering' is printed on it, so the professor and Rebecca must have left it as a signal." Jamal yanked the lifejacket out of the water and broke the attached line to the seafloor.

"Looks like it was tethered to the bottom," Tony said. "They might be in the water below us. Hide the lifejacket, Jamal." Jamal threw it behind the console.

The military boat approached quickly, then idled up to their small craft. It was a sixteen-meter long craft with Turkmenistan markings, fitted with a light machine gun on the side.

Tony groaned. "Oh, for the love of Pete! Don't these dopes have anything better to do than harass innocent rescuers?"

The official in the front smiled broadly, evidently seeing the lifejacket flashing. Three other soldiers leaned against the aft rail of the ship, while two other men came from below deck. One was tall and dark, in a smart looking suit, and wore a gold chain around his wrist. Another, short, stocky man, who seemed like a bodyguard or bouncer, was a half step behind. As the taller leaned on the rail, Jamal thought he knew the man.

"Hello, my friends," the man said in English with an Armenian accent. "Did you need some assistance?"

Tony tipped back his cowboy hat and leaned forward against the console. "No, we're mighty fine on our own, mister. But thanks for the invite."

Erol gave a steely gaze. "Do not patronize me, my friend. We know what you are doing here. So I suggest you leave before something terrible happens."

"Don't call me friend unless you know my mama, bud," said Tony.

It finally dawned on Jamal who the man was, and he unleashed his fury. "You are Erol Chenian! You stole my box!"

The man stayed calm. "You are half-right. My name *is* Erol. However, my associate and I did not steal *your* box. It belongs to the country of Armenia; I took back what rightfully belonged to Armenia."

"And can we assume that your *patriotic duty* was well compensated for?" replied the young Iranian.

Erol smiled. "We all have to make a living."

"So it seems y'all know what we're here for," Tony said. "But why are you here, mister? Just to tag along?"

"Research, of course. Isn't that why you are here?"

"What do you mean?" asked Tony. "We were just taking in the scenery."

"Do you think me a fool? We saw you pull that lifejacket out of the water. I assume it is a marker."

"Now if you two will kindly move on, my divers have a schedule to keep."

"I've got a better idea, bud. The four of us here like our own company. So why don't you move it along?"

"I only see two of you. Where are the other two?" asked Erol.

"They're right here. Smith and Wesson," the Texan replied, lifting his shirt to show a pearl-handled, 44 magnum revolver. Jamal's jaw dropped. He should have expected that a cowboy would carry something like that.

The shorter thug angrily spoke to Erol in Armenian. The slick-looking Erol put up a hand. "My comrade wants to kill and be done with you. Maybe this will change your mind." He then nodded his head to the soldiers and they walked to the rail with their rifles resting against their shoulders.

Jamal knew Erol was capable of following through on his threat. "Please, sir. The truth of the matter is that we have only come to search for our friends, who have been stranded out here since yesterday. If you let us find them, we would be willing to allow you to dive freely." Unlike Tony, Jamal did not have aspirations of engaging in a gunfight.

Erol looked down to him with condescension. "You are not in the position to tell us what to do. Where are your friends?"

"We think they are down below. But with the weather turning, we need to dive and make sure."

Indeed the weather had gotten worse and an easterly gust forced the men to hang onto something to stand upright. The clouds darkened into blood-red pillows resting over the pale-gray sea. Erol straightened the cuffs on his sleeve, then turned briefly to speak to his comrade and the soldiers so that Jamal and Tony couldn't hear. The two soldiers promptly aimed their sights on the small craft.

The wind gathered strength, forcing Erol to raise his voice with his offer. "This is your last chance. I would suggest you leave immediately, as I do not have the time to argue with you. We will care for your friends if we see them."

Jamal was unconvinced that Erol would care for Rebecca and the professor. However, he was certain that Erol would follow through with his threat and told Tony to turn the boat around. Tony revved the motor up, then drove the rescue boat away. Jamal leaned close to Tony and once again began to strategize. Directly in front of their boat, the clouds above opened up in a very peculiar way. It caught his breath to see what looked like the tornado from The Wizard of Oz.

CHAPTER 24

THE TORNADIC
WATERSPOUT

Erol and the other men on the military craft looked up to observe a distinct vortex dipping down from ominous red clouds. The wind had gained momentum and droplets of water spiraled downward until they created a sinewy column that hit the surface of the sea and completed the evolution of a water tornado. Only a few boat lengths away, the misty, boiling spray churned outside of the column, while seawater got sucked upward into the center of its eyewall. Under other circumstances, the large waterspout's deadly mass poised in front of a calm blue backdrop would have been an awesome and intriguing event to observe…but not on this day.

Jamal shook Tony's arm. "Turn to the right! Hurry!"

Tony reacted instantly by pushing the boat full throttle and cranking the steering wheel to the right. The boat surged forward, with the newly formed funnel only a few hundred yards to their side. For several minutes, they sat in their boat mesmerized by nature's creation. After the formation of the funnel, the bottom third suddenly became translucent and virtually disappeared. Eventually, the middle of the column vanished.

The Turkmen pilot revved up the engines to get clear, but all was for not. The tornadic waterspout had unsuspectingly rematerialized beside them, rotating its savage spray vortex across the sea like a lasso until it ensnared the larger craft. Within an instant, the vessel was pulled around and up into the column of water with the crew hanging on for their lives. The boat traveled twenty-five meters upward, with frightened men yanked from its hull one by one into the waterspout's vortex.

The boat was soon discarded back to the sea, helpless and fractured in large sections, only to be caught up in a newly-formed whirlpool. The storm spun a bubbly wake that swirled outward like a pinwheel, making boat and men captive in the endless effervescent waves. The men tried desperately to stay alive by clinging to anything afloat. Erol had found safety by climbing on a large storage chest when his husky comrade dog-paddled toward him.

"Get away, Berk!" shouted Erol. "This cannot hold the both of us."

The stocky man tried pulling himself aboard the chest. "I cannot swim well!"

"We'll both drown!" Erol kicked his associate in the shoulder and Berk fell backward into the water.

Berk treaded water, then swam back. "I thought..." he coughed up some water, "we were friends!" He tried to climb up on the chest.

Erol kicked again. "I told you to get away! You should know by now that I do not give second chances!" This time he hit Berk in the face with a force that dazed him enough to send him down under the waves. Ten years of association were gone in an instant as Erol watched his partner disappear forever.

Tony and Jamal had their own set of troubles. When the tornado touched down, they were moving at full speed, but the huge spiraling wave spread out quickly. It heaved against their small craft with enough force to pitch up the aft end in a vertical position and twirled it around like a toy top. The two were instantly cast into the turbulent waters, left to fend for themselves while their boat twisted and bounced over the waves. The boat performed several nose-to-end flip aerobatics, until it landed solidly upside down.

With a renewed attempt for survival, they swam through the waves toward the boat. With each stroke, they continued to be hammered by an endless barrage of waves. It was apparent that their optimistic plans of rescuing others had unexpectedly turned so perilous that their own survival was now in jeopardy.

<hr/>

The ancient corridor was quiet and serene. Rebecca watched as Dr. Witherspoon shifted into analytical mode to scrutinize the inscriptions on the massive doors. He put the flashlight under his arm and took out a pad and pencil to make some notes. After several minutes of examining some of the etchings herself, Rebecca broke the silence.

"These markings are the same as the ones from the stone slab, aren't they?" she asked.

The professor scanned across the writings. "Yes, it seems so." He didn't look away from the inscriptions.

Rebecca listened to the professor mumble and debate with himself about the meaning of the writings, then stood back to the opposite wall. She shook her head at the immensity of the door. She knew nothing of ancient glyphs, but decided to address her elder with the obvious.

"You want to open it? Or is that a dumb question, Professor?"

Dr. Witherspoon stepped back and played down the discovery. "I don't know. This doesn't seem like anything to write home about. If we leave now, we might catch the ferry to Baku."

"Ha ha, very funny, Professor. I didn't think you had it in you." She scratched her cheek and rethought his comment. "Is there really a ferry operating in the Caspian Sea?"

"Actually, I believe there is, my dear. However, I hear that the ferries are large vessels that only run when there is enough cargo, such as rail cars and such, to transport between Azerbaijan and

Turkmenistan. In this part of the world, 'scheduled' is used in the very loosest of terms. It could be days."

Rebecca was disappointed and refocused on the professor's interest. "Well, forget that idea. So, what do you think is behind the doors?"

He shrugged his shoulders. "It could be a treasure trove of antiquities or an empty room."

"I could go for that."

"Or, possibly a chamber full of seawater."

"Seawater? Nevermind. Maybe we should just leave well enough alone."

"Hold on, Becca. Don't get hasty." The professor lay down on the floor and flashed his light through a crack under the door. The light traveled a fair distance. "Good news, there isn't water in there." He then sniffed the air. "It seems to be safe to open. Why don't we give it a try and open them?"

"What were you smelling down there?"

"The air in the next room. From experience, I have learned to be leery of the atmosphere in caves. Sometimes methane or other deadly gases could be there. If you get a headache or feel dizzy, it's not a good sign. Fortunately, we can safely rely on our scuba gear for air if that happens."

They set their lights down and together pulled on one of the huge door handles. Rebecca put one foot on the opposite door and grunted with her partner as they strained to open it. The heavy wood dragged along the ground, sliding open a finger-width before stopping. The doctor and Rebecca realigned themselves to achieve more leverage, then pulled and groaned once more. Without success, they released their grip and leaned back against the door to catch their breath.

"It doesn't look like we can open the doors by ourselves," Rebecca said, wiping her forehead.

The professor leaned his head back with his eyes closed, still worn out from his previous sleepless night. "Why don't we get some shut-eye. We can try to open them again in the morning."

Rebecca looked at her watch. "Well, it's only 5:30, how about I check the surface to see if anyone has spotted our signal?"

He waved her on. "If it will make you feel better, Becca, be my guest. I'm taking a nap."

They walked down the corridor and back to the raft, where the professor sat down to rest. Rebecca stepped down the steps to the water and gathered up her gear. She noticed a thin cord floating in the water and reached down to pick it up. "Hey, Professor, how well did you tie the line to the life jacket?"

Dr. Witherspoon got up and looked down at Rebecca pulling a long line from the water in the glowstick's yellow light. "I know quite well how to tie a knot, Becca. Our survival depends on it."

She pulled and pulled until she held up the end of a frayed line. "Well, it's not attached now."

The professor came down and heaved a heavy sigh as he examined the cord. "This line wasn't cut, but broken, which means my square knot didn't fail." His admiring smile turned sour. "I hope the floatation device didn't float away. If it did, our signal could be miles away by now."

"I agree…another reason for me to return to the surface." She adjusted her mask to her head and put on her flippers. "I'll be back," she quoted with a familiar Austrian accent.

Rebecca dove into the water, swam down the sunken stairway, through the ziggurat archway and across the seabed a few meters, then noticed that the bright blue water had turned grey. She cautiously swam upward and caught sight of a rifle sinking down, and shortly thereafter a cascade of canned goods, tools, and other shipboard supplies. Rebecca looked up to see a boiling mess of bubbles and correctly assumed the weather had taken a turn for the worse. Upon reaching the surface, the fierce localized storm beat against her with both wind and waves.

Rebecca treaded water a safe distance from the large whirlpool. It spun horrifically around, drawing in large pieces of a capsized vessel, while a few men close to its vortex struggled to stay afloat. She contemplated helping them but knew it would only endanger herself. Rebecca looked around behind her and saw a cowboy hat, then noticed a smaller capsized craft bobbing up and down on jagged swells. Upon closer inspection, she realized Tony and Jamal were struggling to hang on to the small boat's inflatable tube grablines. She swam briskly over the choppy water to discover what had happened.

Jamal saw her first and with one hand gripped on the boat's grabline, waved her over with the other hand.

Tony yelled through the wind. "Darlin'? Is that you?" She signaled an *OK* sign.

Rebecca came to the side of the boat and removed her full-face mask. "Did you two come out here to rescue me?" she shouted through the windy spray.

The waves smashed the swimmers against the side of the boat. "Yes, that was our intent! But as you can see it did not work out as planned," admitted Jamal, wiping his face. "This strange waterspout came out from nowhere!"

"It's much safer down below," she informed.

Tony kept one eye on the waterspout. "That's a no-brainer, sweetheart, but we ain't got gills or scuba gear like you do."

"Where we're going, you won't need it." The whistling wind died to a lower decibel for a moment. "How long can you hold your breath, you guys?"

"Four minutes—five tops," Tony guessed.

Jamal was impressed. "Really? I doubt I can hold it one minute."

The wind and spray surged again. "I think Tony can make it. I'll be back for you in a little bit, Jamal!" she shouted back.

"Where are we going?" Tony asked.

"You'll see." She adjusted her mask. "Just follow me and hang on to my weight belt!"

Tony didn't have to be asked twice to grasp her waist. Rebecca dove underwater using her strong legs and fins to propel her and him downward. She made a straight line toward the ziggurat, and brought him around its base, through the arch, and up into the air chamber. When Tony reached the steps he burst out of the water and inhaled deeply, then crawled up a few steps.

Tony laughed, plainly proud of himself. "Woowee! If we had to go another minute, I'd be a goner." This was highly unlikely, since the strong Texan swam like a fish ever since he was a child, and this unpredictable dive was only a game to him.

The professor's nap was interrupted when Tony splashed out of the water. Dr. Witherspoon raised himself to sit on the upper stone step, then clasped his hands with his elbows resting on his knees. "I didn't expect to see *you* here, my boy. Are the others here to rescue us?"

Tony held a couple fingers to his right nostril and blew out some mucous. After doing the same to the other nostril, he sat down on a step. "Not exactly, old timer."

Before Tony could answer, Rebecca grabbed Dr. Witherspoon's scuba equipment. "I'm going to need this, Professor. Tony will explain." Without a chance to rebut, the athletic woman was back in the water. When she appeared again at the surface, the waterspout and whirlpool were gone. The cool rain had cut off the warm humid air and eliminated their source of power. Nevertheless, a whipping spray and choppy sea still continued to batter Jamal, who struggled intently to hang on to the boat.

She lifted her mask to her forehead. "It looks like my promise to give you diving lessons starts now! Here, strap this on!" Jamal said nothing and let her help him slip on the scuba tanks. "This is your mouthpiece; just breath through it naturally and don't panic. Got it?" He nodded slowly, but his worried eyes showed otherwise.

Rebecca understood his concern, but due to the circumstances couldn't teach scuba diving basics. "Just be calm!"

Jamal winced. "Calm?"

She didn't even believe her own advice. "There is a safe shelter for us with a pocket of air. Do your best and hang on to my waist belt when we go down. I need you to trust me and not panic."

"Do not ask me again to not panic or I think I may!" Jamal pointed to the other men who struggled to stay afloat. "What about them?"

"We'll deal with them later. You can close your eyes if you want to. You don't need to see. But you *have* to breathe through the mouthpiece. Ready?"

He nodded again, inserted the mouthpiece, and started breathing. They lowered themselves beneath the torrent and down into muffled sounds below. Jamal's ears began to feel the pressure as they descended several meters but he held onto Rebecca and concentrated on his breathing. He had little interest in the ancient ruins at the moment, though he nervously watched all that was around him. With little effort, she pulled him down and through the archway, where the stairway light filtered down from the passage above. As they climbed up into the air chamber, Tony helped them up and out.

Jamal popped up with a grin. "I did it! It wasn't as bad as I thought it would be." He looked up at his mentor smiling. "Did you see me, Professor? I think I did well."

Dr. Witherspoon nodded and smiled. "Good show, my boy."

Tony helped Jamal take off the scuba gear. "If you say so, Raz," he said with a yawn.

After resting a moment, Rebecca readjusted her equipment to leave again. "I've got to go back and help the others," she announced abruptly. Tony, Jamal, and the professor quietly looked at one another with trepidation.

"You may want to rethink that idea, my dear," suggested Witherspoon.

She looked at the others and felt like she had just walked in after missing a major news story. "What? What's wrong?"

The professor looked at the younger men. "Tell her, Tony."

Tony quickly explained who the men were, and how the men had threatened to kill them. Rebecca banged her head lightly against the stone wall when she realized this wasn't going as expected.

"Urrr!" She composed herself and resumed checking her instruments. "Well, we can't just leave them up there."

"Why not?" asked Tony. "They were gonna shoot us and leave!"

Jamal grimaced. "They threatened us in their boats, Tony. I do not think they would or could shoot us anymore."

"You have had your head in the books too long, partner. They would have killed us if that storm hadn't started, and they may do somethin' stupid down here. I say leave 'em be."

"Oh. So one bad turn deserves another?" Rebecca asked.

Tony puffed up. "Yes! When our lives depend on it!"

Jamal became introspective. "He may be correct, Becca. He is a thief and took advantage of Mary back in Tehran. What good will it serve us to save them, just so they can take advantage of us later?"

"Not to mention that this will be your third trip to the surface. You must consider some barotrauma effects," advised the professor.

"Don't worry about me, Professor. I've been ascending nice and slow to avoid the bends. It wouldn't matter anyway, because I wouldn't abandon anyone up in that storm—even if they are Turks with bad dispositions!" she stated emphatically to the men.

"Well, you're not bringing 'em down here!" Tony shouted even louder. "And they're Turkmen, not Turks; Turks are from Turkey!"

She faced him arrogantly with her hands on her hips. "Listen, if you don't like my little place down here, you can always leave. Whether they're Turks or Turkmen, I'm helping them."

Tony was exasperated and turned around with his hands in the air. "You think these are lost kittens or…a child in an airport? Woman, you're a dern fool!"

Rebecca's eyes blazed. "Coming from you, Tony, that's a compliment." She sat down to put her feet in the water. "My father once said that doing the right thing at the wrong time beats out the wrong thing at the right time, any day." She reached over and grabbed the diving knife she had taken from the raft, adjusted her mask, dove back in the water, and swam out of sight.

As Rebecca stopped about every five meters to off-gas excess nitrogen, she considered Tony's caution, but dismissed it as unnecessary paranoia. "Love conquers all" she kept repeating to herself. Several minutes later, she poked her head out of the water, briefly, to assess the situation. Any trace of color in the sky was replaced with a gray, cloudy, windy downpour. Two men clung tightly to some small buoys and one was on a big chest as the wind whipped at them. Another man lay face down in the sea, bobbing and rolling helplessly over the swells; one less man she had to worry about.

Rebecca treaded water for a moment and prayed. *Lord God, what now? Am I saving these three men only to endanger the others? For once, I really don't want these jerks to die without knowing the kindness of a Christian.* The spray from the sea swirled and beat upon her and a wave crashed over her. She came back to the surface to see the men weakening. *If I'm going to do this good Samaritan stuff, could you at least protect me?* Rebecca studied the situation once more, then swam a Californian freestyle toward the men.

CHAPTER 25

LIMBO

A glow stick was anchored on the wall to illuminate the area at the top of the landing where the deflated raft lay with its emergency items. Jamal huddled at the lowest steps with his arms wrapped tightly around his legs, staring into the water. Tony rose from the steps and ventured to the top of the landing. He looked over the shoulder of the professor, who was scribbling some notes on an erasable diver's plate.

"Hmm. Looks greek to me," said Tony examining the strange lettering on the pad.

The professor set down his writing pad and turned around. His voice became stern. "Robert McCray told me of Becca's valor in saving a child at an airport. The way you said it to her made it seem as though she was self-aggrandizing. It was uncouth and uncalled for, my boy."

Tony dropped his head for a second. "Yeah, I may have overdone it a bit. But they're killers, Doc! I had to say something!"

"Next time say something else," added Jamal.

Tony rolled his eyes. "OK, I'll work on it." Tony slapped the rock wall of the ancient passageway, then changed the subject. "You've got a nice little home away from home here, Doc."

The professor nodded his head and sat back down to scribble some more. "I would have to agree."

"Thousands of years old and still full of breathable air." Tony nodded his head. He looked around the corner where the corridor was dark. "So where does this go, Doc?"

Dr. Witherspoon looked up at the Texan. "Hmm? Ah, yes, down there. It ends where there is a spectacular set of large doors."

"How far down?"

The professor picked up his flashlight and turned it on, then put a spot of light on a wall about fifteen meters away. "That far."

Tony spat on the floor. "That's it? That's all the farther it goes? Dang, we're as good as being in limbo."

Jamal, wet and cold, began to shiver, unconcerned with digressions on the ancient tunnel. He looked up at his friends in the dim light. "That funnel cloud was horrible! How did it appear so quickly?"

Tony sat back down and leaned against the wall. "Ya know, October is when storms usually start showin' up, but a midsummer water tornado…I never heard of that. We're pretty lucky to have such a handy place to wait it out."

The professor sighed. "And to think just an hour earlier, Rebecca and I thought being here was our demise."

A splash at the water's edge erupted and Jamal jumped back to allow Rebecca to climb up. She exited the sea, stood to the side, and removed her rebreather. Behind her came the military officer, who took in a deep breath as he exited the water. He seemed not the least bit shaken as he combed his hair back with his fingers. A muscular soldier followed next, and like his superior officer seemed unaffected by the dive. Lastly, Erol came out of the water, shoeless and exhausted. He flopped down at the stairs coughing and hacking the sea from his lungs.

Rebecca flipped off her mask and shook her hair to dry. She addressed the professor and pointed toward the men with her thumb. "I told them to go one by one, but they all wanted to dive together."

After the last of the men were out of the water, Tony took a few steps down and pointed an accusatory finger at them. "I don't know why Becca saved your sorry hides, but if it was me you'd still be up there."

Rebecca scowled at him. "Oh, for cryin' out loud, Tony! Knock it off! They're human beings. Besides, they promised to behave themselves."

Erol coughed out some water, then looked up from his prone position to address the savage Texan. "The woman is correct. I have pledged a truce until help comes for us." He rid himself of the silk tie that dug into his neck.

"And when help comes, all bets are off?" Tony suggested, poised with his chest out, his white knuckled fists ready at his side.

Erol raised a hand. "No," he coughed up some more water. "I promise."

"Don't hand me that bull. Jamal already filled me in on how you misled that little lady, Mary. Your promises ain't worth a plugged nickel around here, mister. I'm watchin' you." Tony spat on the stone floor near Erol then walked back up to the landing.

Erol coughed a few more times and said nothing further.

"So what do we do now?" asked Jamal, between shivers.

"As I said to Rebecca earlier, we wait," said Witherspoon. "There are food packets in the rubber raft. I suggest after what you all have been through, you could use some rest."

"Can we start a fire?" asked Jamal, half serious.

Tony chuckled. "Sure. We'll take bets on whether you would die of smoke inhalation first or the lack of oxygen. But I get dibs on the scuba gear."

No one laughed. No one felt like doing much of anything but recovering. The men removed their wet clothing down to their briefs and found the hi-tech heat blankets from the supply pile to cover themselves. Tony wasn't the least bit cold and began rummaging through the food packets. Rebecca, perfectly comfortable in her wet suit, noticed Jamal had made his way down the corridor. He sat alone huddled in a corner with his dripping clothes still on. She opened a foil blanket, walked down the passageway, and wrapped it around her friend's shoulders.

Jamal just looked at his watch, then sulked. "I missed prayers."

Rebecca raised an eybrow as she put a rubber band around her hair to make a ponytail. "Don't tell me you haven't missed prayers before, Jamal."

He sighed and pondered a moment. "I have never been to Mecca either. With my bad fortune, I never will."

"Eh, Mecca isn't the greatest place to be." she stated nonchalantly.

Jamal looked envious and confused. "You have been to Mecca?"

"Sure. I grew up there." Jamal squinted up at her in the poor light, then started to repudiate her statement. She cut him off before he got upset. "Mecca, California, USA," she clarified.

Jamal started to groan, but a small snicker came out. He turned and looked at the opposing wall in thought.

Rebecca knew something else bothered him. "Is that the real reason you are depressed?"

Jamal shook his head and stared at the floor. "Things have not turned out the way I thought they would have. I had hoped to save you and the professor, not the other way around."

"I don't think your manhood was destroyed because things didn't go as planned. I thought you were brave to come back for us," she affirmed. "Don't forget that you saved my life by hauling me out of the electrical room."

Jamal shrugged off the compliment. "Thank you, Rebecca. I should be thankful we are both alive." He looked up to her. "We are even, now that you have saved my life."

Rebecca scowled at the suggestion. "There is no *even* in saving one's life." Sensing Jamal wanted to be alone, she started to walk away from him, but he reached up to stop her.

"Wait. There is something I have wanted to tell you," Jamal said, in a hushed tone. She stood still. The words didn't come to him easily. "These last several days, I have been avoiding you."

Finally, he's going to tell me! Rebecca glanced back at the others to make sure they weren't listening. Holding her amber glow stick between them, she whispered. "I thought you might have been. Why?" She squatted down.

He gazed into her green eyes. "To be truthful, you have made me uncomfortable with your theological questions…I needed time to think about your comments and not be pushed. You are a very pushy woman. It is well known in my country that Americans like to push people around."

"Pushy?" She shoved him over on his side. "There! That's pushy."

Jamal chuckled as he repositioned himself. "You know what I am talking about. Paradise and what is beyond our lives."

Rebecca was relieved to know they could be friends again. "I only wanted to know you better, that's all…but I understand. I am rather direct sometimes. Thank you for being honest." She extended out her hand for him to shake. "How about I try not to be so…pushy. OK? Friends?"

Jamal took her hand gently and patted it. "Friends? We are more than friends, no? After all, we almost drowned together. And…" He pulled out her scarf. "I wouldn't have kept this if I didn't think so. Can I keep this?"

They kept their gaze on each other's eyes, and she let him continue to hold her hand. *He is so charming and such a nice guy, but he is also so Muslim. Maybe Mrs. Ganjavi was right, I wanted him because I couldn't have him. Maybe because he is so different than Bill.* Anger started to rise up when she thought of how Bill cut off their wedding so abruptly—no warning—no explanation. *What a jerk! Come on, Becca, focus. Forgive and let go.* She released her hand from Jamal. "OK, Mister More-Than-A-Friend. Of course you can keep it. But we still need to stay alive down here. So don't think I won't give out anymore advice," she warned playfully.

"How could I expect anything less?"

Rebecca smiled. "I need to check up on our other guests. So I'll talk to you later?"

Jamal turned serious. "Rebecca, beware of Erol. Remember when I told you someone stole my box in Tehran?"

"Oh, yeah, what about it?"

"Erol was the one. Mary saw him with it at the hotel before he left Tehran."

"Why didn't you go to the police?"

"Mary was afraid that they would arrest her for getting involved with him."

"Hmm, I see." Rebecca shrugged her shoulders. "Well, I'm not worried about an art thief."

"That is not all. Moments before you came to our aid at the surface, I saw him kill his own man to survive."

"You're kidding! That must have been one of the men I saw floating in the water," reflected Rebecca. "Wait a minute! Mary looked like she saw a ghost and mentioned that name when I went shopping with her."

"That means he was in Baku during the time of the flooding in the electrical room. Rebecca, be careful."

"Don't worry, Jamal. I'll be careful...and so should we all."

She got up and walked back to the group of men, mulling over strategies to gain their trust. Tony now sat back against the wall, shirtless, with his arms and legs crossed, watchfully keeping an eye on the other men. Erol and the soldiers were fastidiously wringing out their shirts and pants, with the high-tech material wrapped around their shoulders.

"I see you've found the foil blankets," she remarked with praise.

"Yes," said Erol. "They are surprisingly warm. But not much to look at."

Rebecca picked up a food packet and pretended to be examining the supplies. "While we're down here, we'll need to work together, so I hope we can cooperate." The others nodded without saying a word. "As the professor said, after what we've been through, you probably could use some rest. After a good night's sleep, I'll check the weather again at the surface and then we can figure out a game plan to get out of here. I might get lucky and see a rescue ship."

Rebecca noticed Erol and the older soldier give one another a knowing look. Rebecca found a spot away from the men, sat down, rolled the survival tarp into the shape of a pillow, and adjusted it behind her head. Tony gave her a wink, as if to say he would watch the other men for any devious behavior. She closed her eyes and huddled in a ball with her hands in her armpits. "Goodnight, guys."

In the last glow of the light, the men mumbled goodnight and tried to shift into comfortable sleeping positions. The professor sat down opposite the great doors next to Jamal, leaned back against the stone wall, and examined the ancient script from the light of the glowstick that lay on the floor. Dr. Witherspoon mulled over the ancient writings and scribbled some more notes onto his waterproof diving pad until he eventually fell asleep.

Hours later, Dr. Witherspoon's natural alarm clock woke him up to find the passageway pitch black. He pressed the light on his watch…it was 6:05 am. He saw that Jamal had slid down with his head laying on the cold flat stones. Dr. Witherspoon let the others slumber while he took his flashlight and reconvened his analysis of the writings.

Rebecca woke to hear the professor's unintelligible mumblings and noticed the flashlight's beam moving across the doors.

She stretched out for a minute, then stepped quietly down to where the professor stared at the door. "Did you sleep at all?" she whispered.

He glanced over. "Oh course, my dear. I only need a few hours." He turned his attention back to the writings, flashing a spot of light to a certain area of inscriptions. "I have determined that these doors are an entrance to a temple of sorts."

She admired the curiosity in the archaeologist. "You really want to get in there, don't you?" she said, elbowing him.

He smiled, like a boy in a candy store. "We have the time," he replied frankly.

"Well, what about me going to the surface to see if there is a rescue boat? I would think that is the more immediate concern, eh?"

"Oh, yes, the rescue. By all means, Becca." He didn't sound convincing.

Rebecca knew he wanted into the temple more than he wanted to be rescued. She barely held back her smile. "I'm sure we can find the time to check out what's on the other side...even if there is a boat waiting for us. If they haven't shown up, I'll cut out a section of the raft and inflate it with the CO2 bottle as a signal for them."

"Splendid idea, my dear. You do that."

While they had been talking, Erol had scooted down to within earshot, with the foil blanket wrapped around his shoulders. He had been eavesdropping and spoke up from his seated position. "It could be a treasure room," he suggested.

The professor looked over his glasses. "Oh, our guest is up."

"I didn't mean to intrude, but they may have collected gold and other valuables," Erol suggested.

"Or not," the professor replied, knowing common men expect to see gold and silver stacked head-high. "I have been in this business a long time; finding a treasure is rare."

"If there is treasure, we could split it evenly between us and no one would have to know."

Rebecca rolled her eyes at the professor. "Great," she whispered. "Just what we need with us—a greedy mercenary." She turned to Erol sternly. "I would know. Besides, survival is first, all else is secondary...OK?"

Rebecca looked over to see a sparkling gold crucifix dangling from his neck. "Nice cross."

The professor looked over at Erol's jewelry. "It looks Byzantine—eighth century maybe."

"I'm surprised a guy like you would wear something reverent like that. You know it's not a lucky rabbit's foot," she noted with cynicism.

Dr. Witherspoon stepped closer with his flashlight. "I think I have seen that somewhere before."

Erol's face dimmed. "You do not know what this means to me." He held it up, kissed it, and then tucked it inside the blanket.

"This was my father's, and he was given it by his father. It is very precious and I will not have you ridicule me."

Rebecca wasn't sure if he was truthful, but decided to play it safe if they were to spend time together. "I'm sorry if I offended you. I'll try to be more civil." Erol nodded a silent thanks.

As the others started stirring, Rebecca walked over to pass out food and drink packets, and started up conversations. She surreptitiously tried to find out the intentions of the soldiers while they put their moist clothes back on, but they were vague and willing only to talk about family or crack racial jokes about their northern neighbors, the Uzbeks. The higher ranking Turkmen soldier was tall, lean, and seemed friendly, but he was like a brick wall when it came to revealing military directives. The other man didn't seem very bright and Rebecca felt that later she might be able to pry him away from his superior so she could glean some confidential information.

Rebecca cut out a good tube section of the raft, then took it and the repair kit down to the water's edge. "I'm going to check the surface again," said Rebecca. "Behave yourselves, boys." She put her feet in the water, donned her gear, and plunged into the water. She swam to the surface to find a strangely calm sea. Not a soul was around. She blew up the yellow makeshift buoy with the CO_2 cartridge and set it afloat. She tied a line to it and went back down to the ziggurat to secure the buoy. When she popped out of the water by the steps, the men were just finishing their breakfast.

She took a sip of bottled water and leaned back against the wall. "We may want to have someone up on the surface. The storm has passed, but it may be awhile before someone spots our buoy," said Rebecca.

Tony nodded. "I don't think Doc will want to go. He keeps mumbling and smiling at his precious inscriptions."

In the middle of their conversation, Erol interrupted. "I cannot believe it!" he exclaimed, igniting his lighter. "It is still wet, yet lights."

Tony shook his head. "Thank God for small favors."

Erol held out the golden lighter and turned the flame on and off. When he put the lighter back in his pocket, he took out a soggy pack of Ararat cigarettes, which he carefully set aside to dry. He sat back against the wall and looked out into space.

"I could use a glass of oghi right now," Erol declared about the Armenian drink distilled from grapes and flavored with anise.

At the other end of the passage, Harold Witherspoon was only half-listening. He had been intent on resolving the language puzzle. "Look!" he pointed with his flashlight. He scanned across the door panels. "There was quite an adventure getting to this…temple." He waved them to come over. "I believe I have ascertained what happened. Would you like to hear my assessment?"

"Go ahead, Professor," Tony said, indifferently gnawing on an instant doughnut. "We're all ears."

The professor waited for everyone to surround him, as if he was preparing to lecture a class, then held the flashlight up to the door panels. When their attention was focused, he followed the inscriptions up and down and across and proceeded to narrate his version of the events that had transpired thousands of years earlier.

CHAPTER 26

THE ARARAT VALLEY

Noah stood many miles away from Anbar, watching and waiting for his brother Zakho to catch up with the tribe. "Do you see him?"

"No! Not yet!" Shem called down from his perch in a fifty-foot fir.

Noah turned his back to the southern route. "Come down, Son. We have rested the tribe long enough and must move on."

With the approaching cold season, the Sethites couldn't stay idle in one place. They had traded some goats and sheep for flint, copper axes, and other tools when they were in Anbar. Additionally, Noah enlisted the help of two guides who said they could take the seven hundred tribesmen as far as the mountain Ararat. The guides were the same twins that had led Shem back to his home earlier in the summer. The men were still as mysterious as ever, speaking little and keeping mostly to themselves.

While Noah talked with the elders of the clans, Shem looked one more time to see if his Uncle Zakho was coming. Shem suddenly felt a heavy burden of responsibility for his people. The journey would be quite a challenge to safely herd hundreds of people and animals over rough terrain. The guides would only bring them over the summit. It would be up to Shem to lead them to the city.

Noah gave the signal and soon the tribe was on its way north again. The Sethites crossed several ragged ridges and down steep ravines, being keenly aware not to lose sight of streams and other sources of water. It didn't take long for the people to grumble about the difficulties of egging on their beasts of burden up rocky trails and never being able to settle in one place too long.

Eventually, they happened upon the great mountain river, Murat, flowing through an open valley. There was a plentiful supply of fruit from blackberries and apricots, and meat from mountain goats. It was apparent these guides knew the trails as well as any fieldhand knew his fields, leading the people skillfully through unknown and mountainous territory. The guides permitted the tribe to rest a day and give the herded animals a chance for adequate feeding.

Shem spotted smoke from a hillside home and noticed a young boy nearby playing an eagle-bone flute. Although this was a different trail than the one he and Zakho had traveled, Shem continued to fret nonetheless. He approached Tabas with his concerns, so the husky warrior sent his hunters to scout the area. The hunters returned with news that the local mountain people were more fearful of the large numbers of foreigners.

Since his last journey through the mountains proved hazardous, Shem still wanted reassurance. So he talked to the guides. "Others live in this valley. You must know of these people," Shem presumed. "Will there be trouble?"

The twins glanced up with little interest. "They are the least of your concerns," said one guide. "There will be plenty of hardships for you in the days ahead."

Shem was not comforted. Yet as the guide predicted, after several days of walking, there was not one adverse incident from mountain people. The Sethites moved easily up the fertile valley, eating all that the land provided. A spectacular peak of the Ararat Mountain became visible high over the hills and became the topic of the day. It was a sacred mountain that many surrounding mountain clans held in the highest respect, going near it only for ceremonial duties.

After they left the Murat river valley, the altitude increased and several men and women complained of headaches and difficult breathing. The twins guaranteed the symptoms would not last and pushed the Sethites at a slow, methodical pace. Through narrow, rocky paths, they weaved their way up a series of hills that eventually gave way to a large barren plateau.

Mt. Ararat was the halfway mark, and it was now in full view. It was a huge, symmetrical, composite volcano with a wide cone and a wisp of smoke drifting up from the peak. The Sethites feared that only God himself could rest on the white-tipped giant, so out of respect they made their way on the north mountain pass with quiet reverence. Once they had reached the summit, great relief spread through the tribe, knowing that the city of Tuball was downhill from there.

The people were pleased to look down upon a green valley where a river known as the Aras[3] flowed. It was in this place that the Sethites decided to make camp and rest for several days before making the final descent. Shem hoped that this wait would also give his Uncle Zakho a chance to reunite with them.

When the tribe reached the river, Tabas spotted a herd of Red deer on the other side of the river that could easily supply the tribe with fresh food. He quickly organized his hunters to kill game and assess any potential threats. Ozias and the other elders organized the living areas by clan, while the women started fires for meal preparation. By mid-afternoon of the late summer day, the valley was arrayed in white and gray tent cloths that stretched out across the pale yellow grass.

Kara finally found a moment to herself and pulled out two small figurines of the gods El and Anat from her travel pack. She set them

---

[3] This actual river has other names: Araks (Armenian), Arax (Azerbaijani), or Araz (Persian).

on her special box to thank the gods for bringing them safely to this land. Kara knew of the sacred valley and of Ararat; her tribe called it the mountain of pain. Old stories were told of red hot liquid that covered a long-gone village at the mountain's feet. She bowed and said a few words in prayer, asking for additional protection on the trip and guidance into living with the Sethites.

Noah was outside her tent speaking to one of the elders when he saw her worshiping through a slit in the tent flap. The patriarch dismissed the elder and strode over to the tent entrance. With his face turning red, he firmly grasped the edge of the flap and took a deep breath before charging inside. He stood with his eyes closed for a long moment then stopped himself.

The young Seva tribeswoman awoke from her meditation with a shiver. She turned around, walked cautiously up to the entrance of her tent and stepped out, but no one was there. She saw the back of Noah and other Sethites busily focusing on their tasks at hand. Feeling as though she had been watched, Kara went back into her tent and wrapped the idols in a small cloth and hid them.

Noah went to look for Shem and Ham. He found them providing kindling for some elderly widows. He bowed to the women, then addressed his boys. "Sons, it is time I show you something."

Shem saw something wrong in his father's disposition. "What is it, Father?" he asked.

"We must walk to the base of the sacred mountain. Let the others tend to their needs while I speak with you two."

Shem and Ham obeyed without question and followed their father to the northeast side of Mt. Ararat. Upon leaving the grasses, they crossed over a patch of lava rock at the base of the mountain. Shem eyed the summit, where smoke seemed to puff at a greater rate than he had first seen.

Shem looked up at the peak with worried eyes. "So what is this you wish to show us, Father?" Shem finally asked.

"You will see, my son."

"Can you not tell us now?"

"Just as I follow God and wait in his time, so too must you do the same. You are still so anxious. Have you not learned patience in your travels?"

Shem slumped slightly. "Yes, Father. I thought it would only save time." He noticed Ham had found it safer not to question his father but stayed silent.

"We have much time. Worry not for that, Shem. Concern yourself with the things closest to you, such as your woman." Noah paused. "Did she renounce her gods?" he asked, nonchalantly.

Shem thought back to her words of commitment that she had accepted the one true God, but couldn't remember them exactly. "Kara? Um, yes."

"Good." Noah said nothing more. But in Shem's mind Noah said much more. He knew when his father opened up and dropped a statement like that it meant that he should think on it.

When the sun was high, Noah stopped his sons at a spacious area on the other side of the lava flow. Shem looked down to see rock after rock stacked next to one another like a big puzzle to form what seemed like a large oval stone pond. It was evidently not a natural phenomenon, but rather two days' work of many men or maybe many days' work for one.

Noah answered their unspoken question. "I laid these stones here many years ago." He gazed down at the field of stone.

"What is this place?" asked Shem. "Will you build a large house here?"

"No." Noah seemed to consider his words carefully. "God has revealed another purpose for me."

"What purpose, Father?"

"I am to build a great boat," he replied, expressionless.

Shem did not question why he wanted to build a boat. Shem was occupied more with the location of building it. "Would it not be better down by the river?" he said pointing back to the Aras waterway.

"This boat is not to be built to catch fish."

Shem was confused. He scanned the plateau hemmed in by the surrounding peaks. "Then what?" Shem frowned, tired of his

Father's omissions. *Why does he not tell me? Why does he toy with me? Is he teaching me something? Does Father not know I have always been faithful?*

Noah smiled as if reading his mind. "Do not be so restless, Son. In time, you will be ready. God has great plans for you. Often words from God sound confusing, even silly. But I have learned to obey them. It becomes a small burden to do what he asks, a large burden when I do not, so I follow him…and you must do what I ask."

Ham had listened to the conversation silently while jabbing his walking stick into the earth between two stones. "I will do anything you ask, Father," said Ham.

Shem rolled his eyes at his brother. "And I would not?" They were taught from very young that it was important to listen and to respect any elder's words, so obeying was never an issue.

Noah continued. "When our people live in the city they could be as a flame in a cave, providing light to a dark world. But…we could as easily take on the Cainites' wicked ways. Do not think that because you have lived with them a season that you will stay clean for a lifetime," he advised. "Soiled clothes do not stink to the man that has worn them for many days."

Shem was sure Noah would be a great model for others to follow. "Why do you tell us of this, Father? Will you not guide and teach our people at the city?"

Before Noah could respond, Ham looked beyond his father to where the tents spread out. "Father, something is happening in the clans."

Noah squinted to the tiny figures below. "What is it you see, Son?" he asked.

The farsighted Ham shaded his eyes. "Our people are gathering near the river. We should go to them. There may be trouble."

Noah nodded and the three made their way back to camp to investigate.

From far away, Shem saw the husky body of Tabas and many men in a wide line with their spears held up ready to protect the Sethites from a small group of men. As Shem drew closer, he noticed something familiar, yet unforgettable. The man in the lead was Sevag, the chieftan's son of the Seva tribe that Kara belonged to. Sevag was a large man with a bushy beard hanging on a flat face and who carried his favorite ornately engraved wooden club over his shoulder.

Tabas tilted his bone-tipped spear forward. "Stay where you are," he stated firmly.

"We do not wish harm to your people," said Sevag. He bowed his head to reveal a torn right ear.

Tabas kept a healthy caution for men with spears and clubs, while he tried to gain some insight from their facial expressions. The men raised the spears in their hands up over their heads to indicate a peaceful meeting. Sevag lowered the big end of his club to the ground, turned his gaze from Tabas, and smiled when he spotted Kara weaving through the crowd.

Kara stood next to Tabas with a somber expression. "Hello, Sevag." Sevag was still as big and awkward as she remembered.

He bowed his head to her. "Kara, I am pleased to see you." When he brought his gaze back to her, there was glee in his eyes.

Tabas put his spear down to his side and faced Kara. "You know these men?"

"Yes, Tabas, they are of my tribe that lives around Lake Sevan, not far over those mountains," she said, pointing to the north. "Sevag is the son of our chief."

A strong, lean man pushed from behind the other men and stood before Kara. He looked so much like her brother Bura, tall with brown wavy hair, that she almost wept. It was her brother's best friend, Pashi. She loosened up as he reached out and squeezed her briefly. Pashi had always been the practical joker who was almost glued to her brother in friendship.

Shem waded through the crowd to see the visitors. Pashi looked up to see Shem and released himself from Kara to shake Shem's wrist. "So it is true! You are alive."

Shem smiled out of one side of his mouth. "It seems so, my friend."

"Tales have been told that you worked with the gods to defeat the enemy of the city."

"I only worship the one Creator God, Pashi," Shem reminded.

"And may you and your God keep me as a friend."

Shem smiled, then looked to the big brute, Sevag, and nodded cordially. Shem tried not to show his dislike of the man. He knew Sevag would have killed him if he had stayed with their tribe through the last cold season. Shem never forgot it and secretly hoped that the big man would die a premature death.

Sevag's countenance diminished the moment Shem appeared. The last known account of Shem was that a mountain lion had eaten him. This would have served Sevag well, knowing Shem was dead and no longer competition for Kara. Tales of Shem's great deeds to save the city of Tuball from invaders spread through the land, but Sevag disputed them as only rumors. This moment proved otherwise and that did not sit well with him. The mutual dislike between the two men had to be postponed for the time while the Sethites could explain to Sevag what they were doing in the territory.

Shem was happy to be in a position of strength for once. "Sevag, this is my father, Noah,"

Noah came forward and planted his staff to his side, and Sevag bowed his head respectfully. "You are the son of a chief?"

"Yes, master Noah."

"I hope he is well." Noah got to the point. "I am sure your tribe is wary of such a number of people as us. Do not be concerned, for our tribe is resting in the valley before heading to Tuball." He spoke calmly, with his bright green eyes fixed level with Sevag's gaze, which unnerved the big man. "I assure you that we will not venture to your land. We pose you no threat."

The chieftan's son seemed to be satisfied. "Thank you, Master Noah, for your words. I will tell my father he needs not worry of your people...as long as they do not wander." Sevag glanced at Kara. "Were you also returning Kara to her family?" Sevag added.

Shem hoped that Noah would hold to his promise.

Noah didn't even flinch. "That was not my plan, but I am sure Kara would be happy to see them." Sevag grinned, exposing a mouthful of crooked teeth.

Kara glanced at Sevag, then took hold of Shem's arm. "Thank you, Master Noah, Shem and I would be pleased to get my parents' blessing." Sevag saw her and Shem together and his grin disappeared.

Pashi's jaw dropped, then he slapped Shem's shoulder. "You two are to be bonded?"

Shem smiled bashfully. "If it is acceptable by Kara's father."

"Anat will be glad about that," Pashi said, nudging Shem. The Sethites had no idea Anat was the Cainite's fertility god and that she was Pashi's favorite.

Noah put one hand on Shem's shoulder and the other on Kara's. "I do not see why they could not go with you Sevag. If Shem returned before the next moon it would not affect our travels to the city."

Sevag became flush for an instant and tensed up. He looked around at the many foreigners, at Shem, and then back to Noah. Shem grinned at the sight of Sevag's discontent.

"Then it will be as you say," Sevag agreed.

"Good, you will stay for the evening meal," Noah informed. He turned to address the crowd that had formed. "Now let us show our new friends some kindness."

That evening the Sethites treated the hunters to a celebration of friendship with food, song, and dance. Pashi entertained a large group by balancing his spear on his nose while walking across a log. Shem and Kara sat and laughed at his antics.

Pashi then recounted his latest adventure with a mountain lion. With lively antics, he chronicled how he had been chased up an alder tree with the big male cat close behind. Pashi told how he skillfully climbed to the top of the tree and leaned his body to bend the treetop downward. The animal crept up the tree behind his prey, steadying himself with his sharp claws, even as Pashi brought the treetop downward. When Pashi was within jumping distance of the ground, he leapt from the tree, releasing it with a spring. The big cat was catapulted backward, only to land in front of Sevag and the others, spears poised. Deciding it had had enough, the animal dashed off into the woods for a less troublesome meal. Pashi's attentive crowd clapped at his story and took to him quickly, dispelling any notion of him as a threat.

The celebration continued into the evening with the dancing of young women around the fire. They were young and lively women who had not yet come of age, yet were skilled in leaping and twisting with the beat of the drums. Shem peered over at Sevag randomly, curious of the big man's intentions. The performance seemed to take Sevag's mind off his troubles for the moment, but Shem knew it wouldn't last.

CHAPTER 27

A SAD ARRIVAL

The following morning, Shem was packing some warm clothing into a travel bag before he left with the Seva group. He looked up to see his father with a staff walking toward him.

Noah motioned with his hand. "Walk with me, my son."

Shem followed his father till they were out of hearing range of the Seva people. "What is it, Father?"

"The guides tell me that they must leave in three more sunrises as the days are becoming shorter. I have convinced the twins to keep on awhile longer till we reach the lowlands. I fear you will not be back before we leave."

Shem was unaffected. "Why do you worry, Father? I will get the blessing from Kara's father and return before you leave."

Noah shook his head with a smile. "You are still so young. You are to receive a blessing from your second father, not a fast message from a runner. Spend a day or two with them, then go east and meet us in the lowlands."

"That is wise," said Shem, considering it a practical idea to save time.

Noah gripped Shem's forearm and glanced toward the Seva warriors. "Be as a fox with these men. I do not trust them."

"Nor do I…except maybe Pashi."

"Very well then. I will see you on the eastern side of those mountains," said Noah, pointing to the right of where Lake Sevan lay.

Naamah walked up with Kara and gave Shem a lamb pie. She and Noah hugged Shem and Kara, wished them good fortune, and waved goodbye. Shem and the others donned their traveling pouches and doused their fire. Soon the group was on its way. Shem turned around and waved. He spotted one of the guides standing stoically in the crowd, shaking his head slowly back and forth. Shem turned around. He was sure the guide was looking straight at him. *Was he looking at me? Does he think ill of what I am doing? Should I ask him what concern he has?* Shem looked back over his shoulder and the guide was gone. Shem shook it off and focused on the path ahead.

An unexpected surprise greeted the Sethites just a day after Shem and the Seva tribesmen left. The tribe was preparing for the final leg of the trek to Tuball, mending clothing, stocking up meat, and gathering local herbs, as part of their daily routine. Over the sounds of bleating goats and sheep came the outcry of a young Sethite lookout who had rushed down from the western pass by Mt. Ararat to the camp.

Noah had been scrutinizing the features of the mysterious mountain and caught sight of the youth, who seemed to be going nowhere. He recognized the boy as the grandson of Ozias.

"They are coming! They are coming!" the ten-year-old boy yelled as he ran. "They are coming!" he shouted again and again as he ran between the goatskin tents scattered near the river.

The boy stopped in front of Noah and slumped to his knees from exhaustion. He breathed so hard he could scarcely get the words out.

"Who is coming?" asked Noah, seeing the urgency in the boy's voice. A crowd had gathered and was anxious to hear the news. Tabas, his son Shinar, and a few men stood ready with their spears, in case there were invaders or beasts.

The boy caught his breath and seemed to forget what he was about to say. He squirmed and looked to the sky in thought because he hadn't made time to study the people closely. "Um….ah…I do not know." The people laughed hysterically and the boy dropped his head in embarrassment.

Noah took the boy by the hand and pulled him aside. "Show me where you saw them." The boy pointed to the large hill to the west of Mt. Ararat. It was the summit passage that the tribe passed through a week earlier. Before Noah could say a word, Shinar had started running to the summit.

Tabas called out to him. "Son! Wait for us."

"I will be fine, Father!" he called back, racing off without waiting for an answer. "I will meet you at the pass!"

Tabas turned to Noah. "My son told me he has been bored with stretching out deer skin. He wishes for thrills and cannot stand still."

"He is too much like you, Brother," said Noah.

"Yes, and I do not like it." He waved a hand for two other hunters to follow them.

"Shall we see what the fuss is about, Brother?" asked Tabas.

Noah nodded, then the two strode up the hill together.

Shinar sped off alone and soon reached the pass, where he saw a band of people standing still. Next to them were two donkeys, who carried sling apparati on their backs, eating grass. It looked as though the group was uncertain as to the route they should take. Shinar waved to get their attention, then sprinted to greet them. There was a tall man and two others to his side. Recognizing the tall hunter as Torak, the great hunter, Shinar ran straight to him first.

"Torak! It is me Shinar!" he shouted several paces away. When they met, Shinar shook the tall man's wrist vigorously. "I saw you at the last harvest festival. Do you remember me?"

A grin crept up Torak's cheeks. "By the Almighty, it is Tabas's son. I did not know you from the many hairs on your chin." Shinar grinned at the compliment.

Torak introduced his brothers. "Zakho is with us too. We set him down over there." He pointed to a flat, shady spot. "Lily is with him."

"Lily? Was she not staying with grandfather Lamech?" asked Shinar.

"Things change," replied Torak. "Come." Torak led Shinar to Zakho.

Zakho was laying flat on his back. Lily brushed back her long auburn hair as she gave water to Zakho. She stood up when her cousin neared. Shinar nodded bashfully and Lily nodded kindly in return. Her eyes glanced cordially to him, then back to Zakho.

"It is good to see you, Lily," Shinar said. Then he turned to Zakho. "Uncle?" Shinar knelt down beside him.

Zakho looked up. "It is good to see you, Nephew."

Shinar became pale. "What happened to you, Uncle?" The once sturdy wanderer who ventured distant lands was thin with sallow cheeks.

"Nothing that a little rest won't take care of." His voice was weak and raspy.

"A lion bit him," offered Lily.

Zakho sluffed it off. "Ah, only a scratch. Where is your camp, Nephew?"

"Not far; down by a cool river. I will lead you there." Shinar glanced, with worried eyes, at the others.

"Well!" Zakho bristled to the other men, then coughed a few times. "Let us be off! Walk beside me, Nephew."

Torak's brothers picked up the stretcher once again. Torak led the group and Lily picked up the rear.

As Zakho was carried, Shinar recounted the events after departing Anbar, and how Noah enlisted the aid of some guides and crossed over the mountains without incident.

Halfway down from the summit, Noah, Tabas, and his hunters joined them with cheer and consolation. But Noah was unnerved to see his younger brother in such a terrible condition. The occasion was bittersweet, a reunion of kinsmen intertwined with the looming threat of death. When they reached the main camp, Noah immediately called for the Healer.

The healer arrived, pulled back some of Zakho's clothing, and waved a hand in front of his nose. The foul smell of the watery discharge from Zakho's blackened skin spelled trouble. The healer took one look at Zakho's swelling injury, put his hand on Zakho's forehead, and gave a disparaging glance toward Noah. "I am surprised wolves did not attack. They follow a smell such as this," informed the healer.

Torak thrust his spear into the ground. "We killed one that got too close...and ate it."

"Someone used the maggots," the healer noted. "They worked well...but not well enough." The leg was almost completely black and two toes had dropped off. "The blackness has spread too far."

Noah knew Zakho's life was at its end. "It is good to have you with us, Brother. I would hate to have you die without us."

"Die? Who says that? I just need a little rest," Zakho said, wheezing. He could hardly hold his dizzy head up.

"I wish Shem was here," said Noah. "He would like to see you."

"He is not? I almost miss the endless questions from the youth," Zakho laughed, then coughed several times, spitting up blood.

Zakho gripped onto Noah's sleeve. "You are a good brother, Noah."

"You are as well, Zakho. Come, you will stay with me tonight."

Noah signaled for the men to take Zakho to his tent and looked worriedly at Torak, who averted his eyes. Noah could sense that Torak felt responsible for Zakho's outcome. In the coming days,

Noah would reassure Torak that it wasn't his fault. But in the present time, Noah stayed up and listened to Zakho through the night. Zakho's time was near and so Noah brought up stories of old and good times as children.

Zakho drifted in and out of consciousness through the night, until early morning when he was clear headed. The weakened wanderer reached out to Noah with a smile. "I will see you on the other side, Brother." Zakho slowly closed his eyes and stopped breathing.

Noah put his brother's hand on his stomach and stood to gaze at him a moment. Noah left the tent before sunrise to walk alone.

When the news of Zakho's death was known, wailing from the women spilled throughout the camp. Up against time, Noah had Zakho's body prepared with scented herbs and oils. He was then taken up to a spot at the base of the mountain. There, in a rocky grave, the great wanderer faced the northern mountains and was laid to rest in his best linens and precious jewelry. Noah stood stoically quiet while Tabas said intimate words about his life and speculated that future generations would proudly speak Zakho's name. After that, all others except Noah returned to their tents. He kneeled at the grave and scratched the soil mindlessly, letting two large tears trickle down his cheeks.

Zakho was liked by all who had met him and now he lay dead in the middle of nowhere. Maybe this was just where a wanderer should be—with all of his kin near him, doing what he had done most of his life—wander into foreign lands.

Noah had made up his mind not to enter the city of Tuball, but had told no one until now. He asked his wife, Naamah, and a few others to stay behind and prepare for the cold season. For their home, they were to utilize a cave at the base of Mt. Ararat that he had discovered years ago. The rest of the tribe had packed up their supplies, and with the Aras River to their side, the tribe pushed forward to the city.

Led by the guides, they walked in the shadow of the mighty mountain till they found a lush spot to camp. It looked to everyone that following the river would be the obvious route; but by the next day, the twins approached Noah and told him of their plans to take them around to the east of Lake Sevan through a rarely used path.

Noah was skeptical. "The mountains are difficult. Should we not keep to the river?"

"No. The Aras will take too long. We will save five days moving up through here." He pointed to a range of brown ridges.

Noah looked as though he had eaten a piece of rotten meat. "But we need to replenish water and food for all my people."

The guides gave no indication of worry. "Water will not be your concern. It will be quicker this way, and since the snow is gone, the path will be safe. Have your people fill all of the wares that can hold water."

The patriarch was flustered at the idea of abandoning a well-worn route. But as a man of faith, he knew he had to trust them and acquiesced. "As you wish." Noah told the elders to pass on the information.

The hundreds of Sethites filled their gourds, skins, and urns, and then moved away from the river. Across the valley, they headed up to a wall of foreboding mountains that looked to be their doom. The guides knew the people could not scale difficult ascents and directed them on a secret path that proved reasonable.

At one point, they crossed through the range and it opened up to a wide open space where it seemed only white-tipped peaks stood before them. Before the tribesmen could grumble, the guides brought the people around to a large stream. There they replenished themselves with fresh water. The stream meandered through a valley that was broad for a half-day then narrowed through steep terrain.

The following day, the tribe eventually abandoned the stream, crossed through a forest, and ultimately landed in a grassy field. The grassland sat on a wide plateau and was as dry as the late summer could make it. This was where the tribe would stay for another two days until Shem arrived.

The guides pointed out to Noah which direction he must go to reach the end of the Aras River. From there, the Aras would flow into the Kura River and it would then only be three days more before they reached the city. The guides had kept their promise and then some. The Sethites had prepared to give thanks and gifts to them for their help on the following day, but before Noah could give them a proper blessing and goodbye, they had disappeared.

CHAPTER 28

LAKE SEVAN

The Seva hunters walked in a column of twos on the path to Lake Sevan, with Shem and Kara in the rear walking arm touching arm. Every time Sevag looked back at them, his hatred would rise up a notch. He thought of their decision to be bonded and wondered how the gods could disgrace him like this. Kara should be his and Shem should be dead. The year before, Sevag had seen proof of the blood where a mountain cat had killed Shem. He had reported to his father that it was fact…so how did Shem survive? Now Sevag will look like a fool when they return together. The chieftain's son resigned himself to be patient and wait for the right time to gain back his honor—by ridding Shem of life. Sevag relished the idea of smashing Shem's head.

Sevag kept a calm exterior and disclosed only amicable regard to Shem; inside, he emphatically convinced himself Kara was to be *his* woman. Sevag had prayed to the gods about it and in his dreams seen her by his side. He was the son of a chief. It was meant to be.

Sevag searched for an opportunity to help Shem find an unfortunate accident along the way…maybe lure him to the edge of a cliff for a fall, or lead him into a bear's den to be mauled. However, with Kara so close to Shem, nothing presented itself a viable condition. To make things worse for Sevag, Kara treated him, the son of a chief, as a common tribesman.

Finally, at a resting point halfway to the lake, Shem left the group momentarily to fill the water flasks.

Sevag signaled the other men to leave so he could speak with Kara alone. "Kara, I need to have words with you."

Kara was focused on retying her sandal with a deer tendon when she suddenly realized the others were gone. "What is so valued that you wait for the others to leave, Sevag?"

Many times before, Sevag had averted his eyes from her gaze, but this moment proved different. "It is the stranger Shem. Do you think it is right to bond with a stranger to our tribe?"

"He is not a stranger to me."

"But he is an outsider to the tribe," he replied with disdain.

"Others have bonded with outsiders in past seasons. Why should I not?"

"It is not good. The gods will not like it."

Kara yawned. "The Shaman has stated no law against it. Are we not taught from our youth to learn and befriend outsiders? What of you, Sevag? Have *you* not found a woman in the tribe who you can call your own?"

He knew Kara was only trying to be civil to him. She never gave him a chance to be trusted. *Is she now asking me questions to distract me? Or does she take interest in me?* "Yes, I think I have," he answered without revealing a name.

Kara turned away to retrieve a water flask from her traveling pouch. "What happened to your ear, Sevag? It is half gone."

"Mountain cat."

She kept her back to him. "I am sorry for you."

"Do not be. I now have the cat's pelt."

Sevag kept his gaze on her and examined the curves of her body. Kara didn't face him and he suspected she knew it was her name that he would speak. Sevag waited a moment for her to drink, then stepped into her personal space. He took the leather flask from her mouth and peered into her dark eyes.

"Why do you avoid my questions? It is not right you are with him," he whispered and stroked her cheek with the back of his large hand.

Kara closed her eyes and tensed up. "Why do you keep saying that? You are not a matchmaker." She grew nervous. Kara had never feared him before, but she had never seen him so determined.

Sevag smiled inside with cunning. He had always been awkward and clumsy in her presence, but his new disposition unsettled her. Sevag remembered her weak spot. "It is not right between you two, for Shem does not believe in our gods, Kara. Did he denounce his god for ours?" he added for good measure.

She lowered her head and Sevag grinned in his triumph. She said nothing, which meant everything. Sevag lifted her chin up and forced her to look him in the eyes.

"Your face speaks for itself. You know I am right. *You* belong on *my* arm."

Before Kara could reply, voices and crackling twigs broke the tension. The Seva men were returning, so Sevag released her, then stood up to admire the once bold and prideful woman, defenseless before him.

"We will talk later."

Sevag went to talk with the men, while Kara sat on the ground with her head down. Even when Shem returned, Kara spoke little to Shem. Sevag cherished his victory over her. He was the chieftan's son and she was to be his.

The group continued their trek through the night and the next day, and Sevag steered clear of Kara so she could stew in his statements. Early after the morning meal, the hunting party skirted the western marshes and rounded the northern shore where the expert fisherman, Razdan, and his family lived. The local people greeted Sevag with a bow of respect, then noticed Kara.

278

They greeted her warmly and peppered her and Shem with questions about the lands they had seen. Sevag let them have their moment and then hushed the crowd when he had had enough. "Kara and Shem have traveled far and must be tired. We must get her back to her family."

Shem was wary of Sevag. "Rest your legs, Sevag. Kara and I know the way from here."

"But I heard of a crazed mountain cat. You will need protection," said Sevag.

Pashi stepped in. "They will not need to concern themselves of the animal. I will guide them as far as my home," he suggested.

Sevag gave a pompous nod. "So be it."

Kara thanked the people for their kindness. Pashi led Shem and Kara on the northwestern trail above the lake while some of the fishermen's children followed for a few miles. When the three reached Pashi's home, he bid Kara and Shem goodbye and they ventured on alone.

Shem noticed that Kara had been very quiet for several miles. "You have not spoken but a whisper to me for half a sun. Are you ill, Kara?" Shem asked.

"No." She tried to avoid his concerned gaze.

"Do you have the moon's anger?"

"What?" she squinted at him in wonder.

"I have seen how women sometimes get angry or distant when the moon is full," he informed with earnest conjecture. "When women bleed they—."

"I know what you mean, Shem." She rolled her eyes. "No, it is not that. Maybe it is not knowing if my mother and father will approve of our bond."

"That is what you worry about? Hmmm. That is something *I* would worry of, not you." Shem shrugged his shoulders. "As father would say, 'Let us not worry about today's bear eating tomorrow's honey.'" He put his arm around her and squeezed her. Kara leaned her head on his shoulder and sighed.

Shem began to consider Kara's comments on meeting her parents. He put on a strong face for her but inside he had his own apprehensive thoughts about their return. Kara's father, Vard, was a good and fair man, but her mother, Komo, was suspicious of Shem from the first day he entered their home.

The familiar trail seemed to calm Kara. It was late in the day, dry and warm with a few deciduous trees starting to change from green to yellow, and the surrounding boulders and pines were old friends. When they neared the big log house, they stopped to see an older boy submerging a jug into a large barrel of water.

Kara whispered to Shem. "It is my youngest brother, Domo." The sun's rays filtered through the trees on his face. "Domo?" Kara said with a smile.

The dark-haired boy of eleven years shielded the sun with his hand and froze for a moment. He squinted from the sun, but then his eyes grew wide in excitement. "Father! Mother! Kara is back!" he suddenly yelled.

Domo dropped the jug into the barrel and ran to hug his sister. Shem grinned when he saw Kara and Domo greet one another with a joyous embrace. Only a moment passed and her mother, father, and little sister came through the door. Soon all four were around Kara trying to get their hugs in. Komo wept tears of joy to see her daughter safely home.

Albeit a happy occasion, Shem was nervous about how he would ask for Vard's and Komo's blessing. Komo had disliked him from the start and preferred Kara to unite with Sevag. Therefore, asking to be united with Kara seemed virtually impossible. After speaking his thanks to the gods, Vard broke away first to receive Shem.

Shem bowed his head as the stout woodsman neared. "Greetings, Master Vard."

Vard smiled grandly and reached out to shake Shem's wrist. Shem clasped it. "Greetings, my young friend. I am awed to see you still alive and am grateful to you for bringing my daughter back safely."

Shem shrugged off the compliment but was pleased at the reception. Vard had always been considerate to Shem in the past; it was Komo's response he worried about. Komo soon broke away from Kara, brushed her tears and hair back, and then walked toward Shem with determination. He took a step back and held his breath.

Komo kneeled before him with her head down in reverence to him. "Honored one, will you forgive me for the many times I thought and spoke badly of you." She kept her head bowed and gripped Shem's ankles.

Shem was dumbfounded. This was not the response he expected from her. Shem hoped that he would be welcomed by her, but this was strange and uncomfortable. "I...forgive you." He covered his face to shield his blushing. "Please rise, Mistress Komo." Kara's mother brushed off her knees and gave a quick bow to him. He quickly helped her up. "Why do you bow to me?" he asked.

She didn't even hesitate. "You are the favored one," she stated matter-of-factly.

Shem looked at the others for a clue and then back at Komo. "What do you mean favored?"

"Your great deeds!" she answered with a laugh. Shem stood dumbly. "...at the city of Tuball. Come, you must have something to eat." She motioned for Shem to follow, then put her arm around Kara's shoulder. "Daughter, you too, I have your favorite food prepared—roasted marmot." Ushered by her mother, Kara glanced back at Shem with a smile and shrugged her shoulders.

Shem was indubitably perplexed by Kara's new and improved mother who invited him in so graciously. Vard smiled and shook his head as he watched his wife talk to Shem as if he were a dignitary. Vard then shut the door to the house and they all sat down to eat the evening meal. What happened next astounded Shem even further.

"Shem," Komo said, setting a bowl full of stewed roots before him. "Would you like to say some words over the food. I have been told it is your people's custom."

Shem would have choked if he had taken a bite. Instead he nodded, but was still leery of his new position. Shem closed his eyes to pray. "Creator of the heavens and the earth, we thank you for this food and those who prepared it. May we have strength to do your will." Shem looked up and the others got the cue to pass bowls of food to each other as if it were a normal prayer of theirs.

After the meal, the family sat by the fire and listened to Kara and Shem tell of their adventures to the city of Tuball, back to Noah's land, and ultimately to Lake Sevan. When it was time to sleep, Vard laid out some straw in the workshop so Shem could bed down. Kara went back up to the loft with her younger sister and brother, while Komo and Vard slept in their own room. Shem looked out through an open window and thanked his God for such a pleasant evening…one he would never have dreamt of.

As day broke, the Vard family had finished their morning meal without Shem. They remembered how he was a late riser. Kara and her mother left a bowl of stew for when he rose. With the others out of the room, Kara asked her mother to sit with her by the fire.

"I ached for our family when I was away. It is good to be back," Kara said to Komo.

"It does my heart good to see you well, Daughter."

Kara threw a stick in the fire. "Mother, I am worried about the gods."

Komo was puzzled. "Why do you worry about them? They watch over you."

"It is not me. It is Shem. He does not believe in our gods. Will that not be hard to bear?"

Komo leaned forward. "His god must be very strong to defeat the Oka with fire from the sky, no?"

Kara nodded, still staring into the fire. "Shem will ask Father to let me be his wife. I will have to accept his god."

"Shem is a good man. You must accept his ways if you are to be his woman."

Kara looked up with a start. "Accept his god?" Kara's mouth gaped open for a moment. "Mother, I do not even know you. You, of all tribeswomen, who taught me of the ways of the mountain gods. El, Anat, Baal, and Mot will be angered."

"Shem has proven otherwise, my daughter. I thought ill of him from the first day I laid eyes on him. I thought he had brought the curse of the storms with him, but the Shaman has changed my thinking." Komo lowered her voice. "He says that Shem's god may be more powerful than ours. I will never let go of El and the others, but we may want to pray to the Sethite god too. It would be a safe thing to do, no?"

Kara nodded pensively. "Yes, I do not see why I cannot believe in our gods *and* his creator god too. Thank you, Mother, this has removed such a burden on me." She reached out to give Komo a hug. Kara then pulled back to look her mother in the eyes. "Then you approve of him?"

Komo patted the face of her beautiful and determined daughter. "How could I not? Now go wake him before his food gets cold."

Kara kissed her mother's forehead, picked up a cup of hot mint tea, and sauntered over to the workshop. Shem partially opened an eye to a creaking door, where Kara stood with the cup of tea.

"Wake up, Shem, we have eaten and there is little left."

Shem adjusted himself so that he lay with his elbow down and his cheek on his palm. "Kara, do you know that your mother put her arm around me last night? She is sick, Kara."

Kara giggled, then glanced back in the direction of the cook oven. "Shhh! She will hear you."

"Why is she so kind to me? She wanted me dead only two seasons ago."

"Do not ask why, Shem. Be thankful." She set the cup down by him.

Shem sat up on the straw bed and took a drink. "We need to ask for your father's blessing while I am still in their favor."

Kara chuckled. "My mother even granted it good to pray to your god."

"I must still be asleep. Do not wake me or this amazing dream may end."

"I cannot believe it myself, Shem. Let us do this while you are in their favor. After your meal, talk with Father when he starts his woodwork."

Shem jumped up and nudged the door to shield Komo's view, then gently kissed Kara. She held his face as their lips touched tenderly. Shem ebbed back and smiled impishly. "See, I told you, Kara. You had nothing to worry about."

"Uggh! Me?" Kara whined, then slapped his shoulder. "You were the one to sweat over mother's thoughts of you. Go eat, you…you…man!" Shem grabbed her and tickled her. Kara tried to suppress her laughter.

Komo was cleaning some wooden plates when Shem exited the workshop with Kara giggling. Vard opened the front door and set down a chunk of oak that he was to work on. Katcha was watching from above.

"I saw Kara and Shem touch mouths!" she asserted with a titter.

Vard rolled his eyes. "Katcha, is it not time for you to fetch some water at the stream and fill the barrel?"

The brown-haired girl gave him a sour look and slowly climbed down from the loft. "I will go. But if you talk, tell me what is said."

Vard patted her backside. "Go on, little one. And tell Domo I said to help you."

After Katcha left, Vard turned to Shem who had just sat down to eat. "I will be in my workshop if you need to speak with me."

Kara smiled keenly at Shem. "I will be outside with mother if you need to tell me something." Komo went ahead and Kara closed the door behind her to leave Shem with her father.

Shem felt as though he had been a pig that had been prepared for cooking. He felt that this moment, to ask for Kara's hand, was the moment he had been waiting for. He thought that once Komo favored the union, his upset stomach would settle, but it hadn't. He had never been afraid of beasts or warriors, but permission to take a woman was something else. This decision would be the one that would impact him for the rest of his life. As he stared into his empty cup, he suddenly gained confidence. He swallowed the last bite of stew, then walked over to the woodshop.

Vard didn't look up from his work when Shem entered.

"Did you want something, Shem?" he hid a smile and continued to smooth a piece of wood with a rough piece of hide.

"Yes, Master Vard. It is about Kara and I."

Vard stopped and turned around. "Oh?" He acted surprised.

"We wish to be," Shem paused, then took a deep breath. "We wish to be bonded."

Vard grinned. "You have my blessing...and my wife's."

Shem breathed easy. "I did not think this would be so hard."

Vard came closer and whispered. "It would have been much harder if my wife did not change her mind about you. She thought Sevag should be the one for her daughter. But that was before you helped throw out the Oka invaders from the city."

Shem nodded. "I think that was the only good thing to come from the Oka."

Vard put his hand on Shem's shoulder. "Do your customs expect the ritual for your union soon?"

"I had not thought on that," pondered Shem. "My father said I must receive your blessing first."

"No matter," said Vard. "Now that you are promised to one another, the bonding ritual is up to you."

"My thanks for your words, Master Vard, for I must return to my tribe to lead them to the city first. My father is a holy man and I wish that he seal the two of us. It may be another season, but I will send word to you and Mistress Komo about the ritual."

"Very well, Son. Now let us come out of my workshop to tell the others."

Shem and Vard announced the news to the others and that evening there was a joyous celebration of song and dance in the Vard household. In the ensuing days, word spread to the members of the Seva tribe and ultimately to Sevag. The promise between Kara and Shem had finally been established. But not all were happy.

Shem watched the sun set two more days and realized it was time for Kara and him to return to the Sethites. Komo packed up some food for the journey. Kara pulled Shem aside before leaving.

"Shem, I heard from Pashi that Sevag does not approve of our bond."

"What do I care? I do not need his blessing."

Kara leaned closer. "I worry for us. He spoke to me when we were alone on the trail and said I belonged to him."

Shem frowned. "Why did you not tell me of this?"

"I thought that once Father and Mother blessed our union, he would give up."

"Giving up does not sound like Sevag." Shem patted her cheek. "Do not worry, Kara. We will be on our way and will be able to leave him and his jealousy behind."

Later in the morning, the young couple waved goodbye to the Vard household, promising to meet back in two seasons. They followed the ridge above Lake Sevan on a trail that Shem had walked several months earlier. At sunset, they made camp in an open field, high above the lake, with millions of brightly lit stars filling the sky. Shem and Kara snuggled close and she pointed out her favorite grouping of stars.

"I like the way those are in the shape of an urn." Kara tucked her head under his arm. "Which of the heavenly fires do you like, Shem?"

He pointed out the Ursa Major constellation. "Those over there." He traced out the shape with his finger toward the heavens. "They make a dipping spoon."

For an instant, Shem remembered how he had said the same thing to Lily about this time a year ago. Lily was a good servant. She would make a good wife for Shinar.

Kara rolled over and sat up to make lines in the ground with a stick, by the light of the fire. "Why do you make scratches, Kara?"

"Some thoughts came to me. I believe that if your tribe traveled east around the mountains this way," she said, scraping a curved line around some small pebbles, "and we cross over along this ridge, we will meet up with them in two days where the Aras meets the

Kura rivers." She tilted her head to look at her calculations and then back up to Shem.

He was so proud to have such a clever woman. Kara was bright and beautiful with her long black hair and dark eyes. They gazed at one another with young love for a moment, then kissed. She wrapped her arms around him and soon he felt every part of her body very close. Her kiss was sweet and tender and he wanted it to last. Shem's heart beat rapidly. He pulled her closer to caress her body.

Suddenly, in Shem's mind, he saw his father standing with his arms crossed and wearing a stern frown. He watched as Noah moved forward—a twig cracked with a loud snap. Shem pulled away from Kara abruptly.

"What was that?" said Kara, turning around.

"You heard it too? I thought it was in my mind."

"Is there an animal out there?"

Shem stood and looked around, but saw nothing. Shem became sullen and somber. "It was the spirit of my father."

Kara gave him a shove. "You are playing with me. Come, we are here alone, and soon to be bonded." She kissed his cheek.

Shem kissed her back, but stopped. He realized his flesh was taking over and couldn't get his father's image out of his mind. "Wait." He turned around and searched the brush around the area to confirm that they were indeed alone. For an instant, Shem would have wagered that he saw a shadow move back into the woods, but otherwise found nothing. "This will be hard for me Kara." He squatted down by her side.

"What Shem?"

"Keeping us apart until our union."

"We are to be together. Why do you wish to keep us apart, now that we are to be joined as man and woman?"

"We must wait for my father's seal upon us."

Kara smiled with admiration. "You are a good man, Shem. Unlike the Seva men in my tribe, you can master your urges."

The next morning Shem awoke with Kara's head on his shoulder. He smiled and brushed her hair. She woke up and automatically went to fix the morning meal. Later, the two bid goodbye to the Lake Sevan basin and descended the eastern slopes of the mountains. After one last look back, they continued eastward on an unforgettable journey that would keep them longer than expected.

CHAPTER 29

FIRE

A day had passed, and Kara and Shem crossed an open plateau where he estimated the tribe would have to cross. They walked a kilometer when they saw the Sethite people encamped at the foot of a cliff. Hundreds of people were sprawled across the basin in and around their tents. The two young betrothed ran down to the tribe and were graciously received back into the fold. With Shem and Kara now accounted for, the tribe could continue the descent into the plains. Shem approached Noah, who had been leaning on his staff gazing across the valley.

"Father, it is good to see you."

Noah smiled. "I trust all is well with your father's blessing, Kara?"

She grinned. "Yes, Master Noah. My father and mother have honored our bond."

Shem looked around. "Where is, Mother, Father?"

Noah turned and pointed in the direction of Mt. Ararat. "I left her and a few others in the Aras River valley by the sacred mountain. I have entrusted your sisters to Tabas."

Shem frowned. "I know my sisters will do well. They are young and healthy, but Mother….I do not remember a time when she wasn't by your side."

"Worry not, Son. I will return to the valley. It will be up to you to lead the people to the city without me."

"By myself? Why can I not lead the tribe with you or Uncle Zakho? He is here now is he not?"

Noah dropped his head. "Your uncle has gone to be with the Most High."

Shem's mouth dropped open. "He is dead?" Noah nodded. Shem looked around in a panic. "But…he…How could he die? I saw him less than a moon ago."

Noah put his hand on Shem's shoulder. "A lion clawed him gravely. I thank the Almighty that he allowed me to see my brother one more time." Shem just shook his head, trying to understand how his favorite uncle could be gone. "He asked about you, Son. I believe his best times wandering were with you." Shem teared up. "He did not even mind your endless questions."

Shem gave a short laugh and wiped his eyes with his wrist. "He taught me much. I will miss him much."

"So shall we all. But we need to move on in our hearts…and with our bodies. That is why I need you to take the tribe onward."

Shem was surprised and nervous. "They do not respect me, Father. My age betrays me."

"They will learn to look within a man, and not on his outward appearance," Noah replied pensively. He patted his son's shoulder. "Do not worry; I have talked with my brother Tabas and the others. You are only a guide, not their master."

Shem thought of how wonderful it would have been to have his family in the city with him. They could have shared in the wonders and glory of the city and spent their lives as a part of the bundled tribes. This was not going as Shem had planned.

"Why can we not all live in the city?" Shem moaned.

Noah wore a painful smile. "We will be together during the next warm season, but your first concern is getting our tribe to the city."

Shem kicked a dirt clod with his sandal.

"I also must tell you all what God has revealed to me…when you return to the Aras River valley."

That information alone piqued Shem's interest. Knowledge of words from the Creator of the Heavens always outweighed any interest in fanciful toys or adventures.

"And you will not tell me now?" Shem dared to ask.

Noah smiled. "You know my answer to that. In time, my son, in time. Come, let us enjoy our time together."

Throughout the next day, Shem held sorrow in his heart for the man who taught him the skills of wandering. He spoke little, thinking back on their days with one another, wandering to new lands. Those days were now behind, and he now had no way to tell his uncle how much he loved him.

The Sethite tribe was in good spirits. They ended a long day of walking by camping in a soft, grassy field of grain that bent gently in the breeze. Beyond the grassy plains, they would meet up with the Aras River and follow it to the Kura River. From there, Tuball was only a few days away.

That night, Shem lay on a large sheepskin looking at the stars with Kara at his side. He relished the sounds of song and flutes filtering across the camp. Thunder rumbled to the northwest and when he turned to its source, lightning flashed across the sky. Children whined and whimpered and huddled close to their mothers for protection. For Shem, it was an awesome spectacle. The air made his hairs stand on end, and he watched the event until he fell asleep.

The lightning strikes and thunder lasted throughout much of the night, followed by a dry wind, which blew through the camp. By morning, two scouts returned to report that a large fire was spreading in their direction. To ensure their safety, Noah forced the tribe to break camp early and pursue their trek to the west. Hours later, the Sethites were still in open fields, hoping to find a safe haven. Noah looked to the rear to see the fire dropping quickly down the mountains. The flames jumped from tree to tree to bush like an animal pouncing on its helpless prey.

"Shem!" Noah called out to his son in the front of the clans.

Shem looked back and ran to his father's side. "What is it, Father?"

"The fire is a fast one."

Shem examined how extensive the fire was growing. It was a few kilometers back but gaining ground. "We must move faster. The smoke and fire are almost upon us."

Noah nodded in agreement and they passed the message onto the tribespeople.

The wind had picked up, and soon fire and smoke would spread to the edge of the grasses. At the rate the fire was approaching, Shem calculated that it would be upon them before they could reach safety. Noah had the same idea and instructed the elders to prod their clans to a rocky hill two kilometers east. As they labored through the grasses, the smoke hit them first. It was only a hazy smoke and not yet thick.

Nevertheless, Shem heard the worried cries of his people and passed the word that they should cover their faces with hand cloths. The strong had no problem, but soon the weak coughed and struggled to find a breath in the hazy breeze.

Noah stopped to catch his breath and again waved Shem over. "It is time for you to take the tribe and leave me."

Shem was aghast. "I cannot leave you now, Father!"

"I am many times the age of anyone here. I cannot move like I once did. It is time for us to depart."

"I will get some of the stronger men to help you." Shem looked around for the biggest men he could find.

Noah squeezed his son's arm. "I said you do not need me to lead. I will be fine on my own."

"I will not leave you here, Father! You will die!"

Noah was calm. "All will be well with me." He took off his cloak and soaked it in a large urn of water hanging on one side of the donkey.

Shem looked at the fire gaining ground, then at the many tribesmen covering their faces from the cloudy air. "Is this truly as you wish, Father?"

"Yes. The wind is in our favor. I do not have time to argue. Leave me your flint." He knew Shem would never abandon him without a direct order. "Now hurry! You must obey me! Go!"

Shem hugged his father tightly and handed the flint to him. He was still confused as to why his father would sacrifice himself so quickly; Noah could be carried or even ride a donkey. It didn't make sense. But as requested, Shem coaxed the others to move quickly away from the fire. Leaving their spiritual leader standing alone in hip-high wild grass, they muttered to one another, worried that this was not a good omen.

The smoke drifted left of the tribe as they climbed the rocky hill, but Shem's mind was preoccupied by his father's predicament. Once the tribe reached the top, they stopped to see if their patriarch was alive. Smoke and fire surrounded where Noah stood. Cries and moans for their leader spread quickly.

Kara came beside Shem. "I do not know why your father stayed behind."

Shem peered down to get a glimpse of his father through the smoke. "He said he was too old to move fast." He turned and pointed to the east. "The river is not far from here, and we will be safe on the other side." Shem choked up. "All except my father." Shem only shook his head in grief and disbelief. He tried to locate his father, but the haze was too thick.

❈

The smoky air was getting thicker and the fire nearer. Noah bent down and carved out some ground with his staff, then started a small fire of his own. He soon stood up and watched patiently until the tribe was well downwind and then lit the end of his staff wrapped with cloth. He took the torch and dragged it along the ground for many paces, then watched as the manmade fire burned just behind his kinsmen. Noah waited until the grass in front of him had been burned completely, then stepped into the blackened area to stomp out the remains of some embers. Although the smaller fire was farther in front, the larger forest fire had crept up close behind him. Noah coughed incessantly from the smoke until he couldn't stand it any longer. He then laid down on the blackened soil and covered himself with the moistened cloak.

⸎

Shem didn't move from the summit of the hill. He wanted some sign that his father was alive or dead so he could know whether or not to bury his body. The view was spectacularly awful. The fire had extended from north to south for as far as the eye could see. Flames covered the valley from south to north, with the thickening smoke filtering the afternoon sun to a blood red.

With the breeze bending the foliage forward, the fire was as a brilliant carpet passing across the land. Shem and the others stood still...waiting in anticipation. The line of the fire passed around where Noah once stood, then left behind a blackened signature. Shem peered closer to see his body on the charred land lying still. His throat tightened at the thought of his father's death when something on the ground moved. In short order, the patriarch stood up, removed his cloak, and shook off the embers that had landed on him. The outside of the cloak was sooty and charred, but the inside was light and untouched.

The Sethites on the hill let out a cheer to see their leader un-scathed by the fire. Noah heard the cheers and waved up to them. He then casually wrapped his cloak around himself, picked up his staff, stepped across the dark, naked earth, and walked westward.

Shem watched his father with relief and amazement. He knew that doubting his father was a useless venture and more importantly it showed a lack of trust. Shem breathed easy until he looked down the hill at the approaching fire. It had changed direction again and was climbing toward them. The son of Noah was assigned to guide the tribe to safety and he intended to succeed. His people were nearly at the brink of exhaustion, yet he knew he had to push them forward.

Shem didn't have to coax the tribe to move toward the river; Tabas and Ozias had already urgently pressed the clans onward.

The hundreds of kinsmen were tired from the trek up the hill and wanted to rest, but they still had a few miles before meeting up with the river.

After a kilometer of running, Shem looked behind to see the fire cresting the ridge behind them, giving little time to spare. When he caught up to his kin, they had slowed down when they entered the thick woods near the river.

"Hurry! The fire will be upon us soon!" Shem yelled. "Keep moving!" The tribe slowed to a crawl. "What is wrong! Move!"

A bottleneck formed as the huge group lined up to follow a narrow path. Torak and his brothers took it upon themselves to slash through the limbs and undergrowth, but the going was slow. The wind propelled the blaze nearer to the woods, and a smoky haze once again weaved its way ahead of the fire toward the people.

To speed up the columns, Tabas ordered more men to split up to slash the undergrowth. It worked; the people were moving at a good trot. Moments later, the tribe could hear the sounds of the river ahead. The fire finally reached the woods and began to climb the trunks and up to the trees' canopies. The timber crackled and popped as the flames leaped up the branches and danced out into the sky.

"We will die!" clansmen wailed. "The Almighty God wishes us dead!"

"I will kill you myself if you do not move faster!" shouted Tabas, seeing the river only several paces away.

The woods were finally cleared to the river and the tribesmen streamed into the river. Many stopped to drink of its waters and clear their eyes of the smoke.

Tabas was crazed with his mission. "What is wrong with you people! I will beat you senseless if you do not move to the other side!"

Shem admired the newfound leadership that Tabas assumed for Shem knew that he was still too young to lead such a mass of clansmen. As the sun set in the west, the wind suddenly shifted and died. This did not deter Tabas from prodding his tribesmen on. The river current was slow and allowed them ample time to cross. One by one, the Sethites trudged to eastern banks through the knee-deep water to the other side. Once on the opposite bank, the people dropped down to the ground in thanks.

Shem looked back at the waning fire, then ahead at the opposing peacefulness. "We have been spared," Shem remarked to Tabas.

"God has been good to us. It also helps to carry a big stick," Tabas added with half a smile. "We should rest here for the night. I will keep a few men up to watch for other dangers we may be unaware of."

"Very good. Thank you, Uncle," Shem said. "I trust you will tell the elders."

Tabas nodded, then left to inform the elders to pitch their tents.

The tribe warily set up camp with the fire still burning on the other side of the river. The wind reversed direction, which gave great calm to the people. It was twilight and the tribe was exhausted from the day's ordeal. They unanimously abandoned any meal preparations for dried food, then laid down to get some sleep.

Shem was lying near the bank of the river when he saw one of the guides running toward him with a spear in hand. The twin kept his face hidden in his hood as he ran. Shem stood his ground, all the while the guide raised his spear on the approach. Shem tried to move to the side, but the man threw the spear too fast and it pierced his arm.

Shem woke up, jumped back, and reached down to remove the spear, but there was no spear…it was a burning ember. To his side was his spear a foot away undisturbed and no sign of the guide. He rubbed his eyes.

Shem sat up and threw some dirt on the ember, his heart still pumping fast. *What did this dream mean?* He looked down to make sure Kara was safe. She slept soundly, curled tight in a ball.

Shem picked up his spear, jogged down to the water, and splashed the soothing coolness across his burn. In the hours before sunrise, the wind had shifted again. Flames had rekindled themselves and lit up the sky, reaching high above the trees' canopies, and pushing embers across the river. The yellow light reflected off the calm flow of the river with a captivating eerie beauty. Shem watched as a few of the embers arched in the air over the river and landed in the Sethite camp site. The treetops above had just started to burn. He wondered why the lookout had not sounded the alarm.

Shem turned to the left of the riverbank to see that the lookout had fallen asleep on a large rock. He threw his spear into the sandy soil in disgust, then strode several paces to reprimand the lookout for neglecting his duties.

"Cousin, get up!" Shem shouted, backhanding the man against the head. The man lay still. Shem looked closer in the firelight at the man's head, and saw that it had been smashed and blood was oozing out.

Shem gasped at the man's demise and jumped back. He wanted to notify Tabas when he saw the silhouette of a large man with a heavy club and a torn ear. The man stepped up the bank. "Sevag!" Shem spit out with distaste. "You killed him!"

Shem looked back to where he had left his spear and his heart sank. He glanced over at the clubbed lookout, then bent down to remove the spear from his dead hands. He held it expertly in his right hand, confident that the big man's club was no match at this distance. Sevag stepped closer to let the firelight shine on his face. Shem's eyes narrowed, spear ready.

Sevag seemed possessed, donning an evil grin. "I thought I would have to follow you all the way to Tuball before I could kill you." He laughed sardonically. "Do not fear, Mot will gladly take you to the netherworld. It is where you belong. Even Kara's mother wishes her daughter to be mine. It is as it should be." He raised his club and rested it to his shoulder.

"You know Kara's father has given his blessing to us. Even if you could kill me, Kara would never have you!"

"Pray to your god, Sevag!" Shem raised his weapon when, from behind him, a cloth wrapped around his mouth and someone yanked the spear from his hands. Two other men had grabbed and held Shem's arms to negate any offensive struggle.

"We will see. We will see." He gave out a wicked laugh. "It was good you did not lay with Kara in the mountains. It would have spoiled her."

Shem's eyes narrowed. *So it was Sevag that was there the night I was with Kara.*

"And now I will have much pleasure to be rid of you. It is your time to pray, son of Noah."

Many thoughts flew through Shem's head as he struggled to free himself. *What of Kara? What of my people ready to be burned in their sleep? Why was the Creator taking me away so soon? Did I not have a purpose that my father talked of?*

Shem attempted to get some footing and push off the rock but it was no use. He knew that Sevag could crush a man's skull in one blow. Sevag moved toward his victim with his club raised and a wild crazed expression. Shem watched helplessly as the silhouette of the rudimentary weapon seemed to drop in slow motion at him…as if in a dream. But this time it wasn't a dream. Shem struggled with all his strength to move, yet there was nothing he could do but pray for a quick death. As the club fell, the blow hit Shem squarely in the forehead and his body collapsed.

Kara had not been able to sleep. She put her hand out to where Shem was supposed to lay. Kara looked around, then got up and walked to the river's edge. She saw a large man with a club. In an instant she knew it was Sevag, with his oversized head and torn right ear. She crept close along the bushes and was alarmed to see Shem held by two other men. To Shem's right was the dead lookout. She knew Sevag wanted Shem dead and that this was his chance to follow through. Kara nearly tripped over the spear Shem had left behind and picked it up.

Kara heard Sevag speaking to Shem and crept up quietly to hear. As Sevag swung his club back, she knew she had to react quickly. From behind the big man, she stepped out from the shadows of the bushes with her spear in hand. When Sevag brought his club up over his shoulder to gain momentum, she instinctively thrust the spear into his ribcage.

Sevag gasped, and his muscle recoiled, slowing down the swing of the club. The club still landed squarely on Shem, but not with his normal force. Sevag turned his head and she stood, in the flickering firelight, to let him see her face before he died.

"You will never have me, Sevag!" Kara spewed.

She had struck just below the armpit and deep into his chest. His face displayed surprise and anguish. Sevag tried to speak, but her spear went straight to his heart. Dropping to his knees, his eyes closed, and his lifeless body fell forward into the dirt.

The two other men had no quarrel with Kara and knew that without the guidance of the chief's son, it was time to make haste. Kara walked over to Sevag to ensure he would not waken and kicked at his head. He did not stir. She looked to where the other men left Shem alone. Her heart pounded at the sight of Shem's motionless body sprawled flat on the ground. Kara squatted down and turned his head toward her, fearing the worst. She put her ear by his mouth and could hear him breathing.

"Thank the gods!" she whispered with her eyes dripping tears. "Thank the gods!"

Kara returned to waken the tall hunter, Torak. He awoke when Kara cracked a twig near him. "Who is there?" He automatically reached for his spear. "Oh, you are Shem's woman. Why do you creep near me?"

"You were the closest," Kara replied. "The fire has spread to the treetops and the guards have been killed."

"What?" He jumped to his feet.

"I will tell all later, but we must wake your people."

Torak nodded and sprang into action. He grabbed a ram's horn that hung on a tree branch and blew it loudly. The people slowly began to stir from their sleep and complained about another rush to move. As the melancholy bellow of a ram's horn sounded, the elders ran to the source of the alarm.

"We need to get the people back to the river. The fire is upon us!" Torak said, pointing upward. Tabas and the elders needed no coaching and sped back to alert their clans.

The newly-formed flames filtered down and around the camp, fanned by a morning wind. There was barely enough time to get to the water and many were awestruck by the fires. They stood like stones, gawking at the flames falling around them.

"Move! Move!" Torak shouted. "Leave your things and come to the water!" he exclaimed.

Small fires were dropping unpredictably onto the tents, igniting them in rapid succession. The donkeys and other animals were nowhere to be seen, yet a few people stood still, mesmerized by the flames.

"Hurry! Hurry! Hurry!" Torak shouted again and again. He ran out and picked up slow children, two at a time, and deposited them at the river's edge.

Men, women, and children quickly splashed into the water, with elders encouraging them to make their way to the middle. As they waded out into the water reflecting the firelight, complaints of recent events spilled easily from their lips. The fire had now flared up on both sides of the river and they were caught in between.

Kara cradled Shem in her arms as the hundreds of people streamed out of the woods. Torak thought everyone had escaped, but as he peered closer through the trees, he saw a small group of people poised like statues. He quickly waded through the water, ran up the shore, and started through the brush. A large flaming branch crashed in front of him, blocking his path.

He covered his face with his arm and addressed those frozen in fear. "Get out! You must leave now!" Torak yelled.

They didn't move a twitch. It was too late anyway, because the brush around blazed brightly and swallowed them whole. Torak tried to find a way around the fire but couldn't shield himself from the heat and flames. He started to run in and save the fearful, but it was obvious that they were lost. He dragged himself back to the river and sat down at the bank.

Tabas waded over to him. "Are you hurt, Cousin?"

Torak stood dumbfound at the needless death. "Why did they not leave?"

Tabas shook his head. "I have heard of people turning to stone when a wood's fire comes…possessed by its evil." He turned to address the Sethites. "My Sethite kin! Let us follow the river to safety! The city is our only hope now! Come!"

A few strong men carried Shem, while Kara stayed by his side. Then with Tabas and the other hunters guarding the front and rear, the rest of the Sethites scrambled along the eastern bank of the river to safety. The group walked in the river shallows until they found an opening where the fire had not crossed. Whimpers and cries from the women and young said it all. The only thing they brought was what they could carry, all else was destroyed in the fire. The animals had run off and there was little food and weapons to kill with, and it was still three days until they expected to reach the city.

* * *

Two days later, Shem awoke, laying peacefully in a grove of trees near a green meadow. Kara was stroking his head and singing a melody. She swooned in relief when he opened his eyes. At first Shem tried to get up, but he became dizzy and fell back.

"Did this not happen before?" he asked, tilting his head toward her beautiful face. Her long black hair cascaded down her shoulders, her dark eyes greeting him. "I was ill and you saved me."

Kara chuckled. "Yes, but this time you almost were killed like a pig and roasted in a fire."

"How am I here? Sevag killed me," Shem whispered.

"Not before I stuck him with your spear. He will not be any more trouble for us. It must be that I exist to care for you."

"The tribe is safe?"

"Yes...only a few perished in the heat. We lost nearly all of our wares, but we did find the animals that ran off. Soldiers from Baku found us wandering and helped feed us. And see over there," Kara said, pointing east. "Before long, we shall be safe in the city."

Shem tilted his head and noticed the walls of Tuball, standing grandly in the brown late summer field. His tribesmen were marching in a line out from the meadow and up to the city gates. He smiled at their success to reach the city. Now they could rest.

However, their rest was not without a grand entrance. The people of Tuball welcomed the Sethites as their own. Kargi, the spirit master, had lit the sacred candles on each side of the doors leading into the ziggurat temple and the stone master set to work documenting the arrival of the great Sethite people from the south. By day's end, Shem had truly bridged two cultures into one, adding another strong link to the bundled tribes of Tuball.

CHAPTER 30

THE SANCTUARY

Tony had been playing *Mumbly-Peg,* flipping Rebecca's dive knife symmetrically around the food packets. He threw the knife sideways and it stuck in the door. The professor stared at the knife like he had eaten a persimmon, yanked it out of the wood, and felt the hole that the knife made.

Tony took back the knife from the professor. "That's quite a story, Doc. Now how 'bout we open the doors and see what's inside?"

"You may not appreciate my tales of ancient history, but I have summarized only one panel on the left door. There is much more here," Dr. Witherspoon said. "For example—"

Rebecca interrupted the professor's analysis. "Hold on for a minute, Professor. I have a question."

"Yes, Becca?"

"I know you mentioned that a large tribe of people endured hardships crossing over mountains to the safety of the city of Tuball...." She thought back to her Sunday school class. "I'm sorry, but I can't get that boat you mentioned out of my mind. That wasn't *the* ark was it?"

"I have to admit that I took poetic license in my story, my dear," the professor replied smugly. He scanned over the hieroglyphics and associated writings again. "It only says that Shem was the son of Noah, but it does not mention a boat in these writings." He looked up and skimmed the second panel for more information. "I see no further indication of Noah here either."

"Yes, but if Shem had a father named Noah, then there must have been an ark?" she assumed.

The professor pushed his glasses up his nose. "Don't confuse your deduction with solution. There may be a fundamental error of thinking that explains a phenomenon. It could also mean that a man named Shem had a father named Noah who might have been a boat builder, and, voilà, a myth was born."

Rebecca stared at him. "I assume you think Noah and the ark are only myths. So why should we believe in your theory about a diaspora happening?"

"It would be more correct if you phrased it 'my hypothesis'—the theory comes after testing the hypothesis—and no you shouldn't believe it outright. But my observations and physical evidence from the dig site at Hasada, together with what I have been reading, add a further layer of credibility to my hypothesis. Listen, Becca, even if the flood myth was true and someone found an ark on Mount Ararat, these writings wouldn't necessarily correlate to it unless we had connected proof between the two."

"OK, whatever. You're the expert." She crossed her arms and shifted her weight to the other leg.

He looked over his glasses at her. "Now you're just being stubborn. If the facts don't fit into your worldview, will you be devastated?"

"I think it works both ways, sir. Sometimes faith is true before science proves it. Didn't Jews and Christians believe that David was a king of the Israelites before archaeology eventually proved it true?"

"Ha! Touché, Becca." He rubbed his chin and squinted at her. "You remind me of a bulldog I once had. If he grabbed onto a towel I was holding, he would never let it go."

By this time, the others had lost interest and began walking away. They mumbled agreement with Tony and wanted to see what was inside. Rebecca heard their grumbling and worried that if a treasure actually did exist, there may be trouble with her guests. Should Dr. Witherspoon delay opening the doors or acquiesce to their desires? She now peered at the professor with wide, worried eyes and rolled her hand to get him moving.

The professor raised his arms with an undaunted smile. "I surrender. By all means, let us open the doors, especially since Tony may end up chipping them away with his knife."

Rebecca silently mouthed, "Thank you!"

Tony, Erol, and the brawny young soldier gripped the right door and yanked on it hard. It creaked as it moved a couple of centimeters, then stopped. They tried the second door but it didn't budge at all. The men went back to the first door and tried a third time. With all their might and all their grunts, the only results were minor creaks from the wood.

The professor waved them off. "Barmy! You brutes may pull the handle right off. We must be careful not to damage them."

Rebecca sighed. "The professor and I tried to open it earlier. I was sure a few more muscles would have moved it."

"Let me look at this a moment." Dr. Witherspoon shone a light around the edge of the doors to inspect the panels for a latch of some kind. "The large bronze hinges don't even look rusted, and there doesn't seem to be a bar or latch in the center," noted the professor, squinting through the slit between the doors. He stood back and scratched his head.

Rebecca got on her hands and knees, slipped her fingers under the door, and ran them across the floor. "Oh for goodness sakes! There's a stone wedged underneath. How did we miss this the first time, Professor?" She took her knife back from Tony, dug a bit, and scraped it loose from the door on the right.

After she got up, Tony reached for the handle and pulled the door. It creaked open easily, gained momentum, and swung around to hit the wall with a thud. The second door was locked from the inside with a bolt to the floor, which they left alone. As the group entered, they stepped cautiously and pointed their lights inside to see if there was any danger. The air in the room was warmer than the corridor by several degrees and Jamal's tense muscles relaxed.

The room was a rectangular space the size of a basketball gym with square columns that reached up to the ceiling to support immense wooden crossbeams. Dr. Witherspoon pointed his light to the opposite end of the room, where a ten-meter-high stone statue of a robed man stood with his right hand outstretched as if giving a blessing. His solemn face showed thick eyebrows atop mysterious dark eyes, and he wore a cone-shaped crown on his head.

Tony snickered at the funnel-shaped crown. "Looks like somebody fell into a pile of roadside cone markers."

Dr. Witherspoon walked closer and scrutinized the sculpture. "It's the supreme god El," he whispered. Two majestic statues stood on each side of the god El. "On the left is his daughter, Anat, goddess of fertility and war." He shined his light on a pregnant woman with a spear in hand. "On the right is his son Baal, god of storms and agriculture," the professor said as he focused on a man with a ring on his arm, which was raised up and holding a small cloud in his hand. Below El's feet was another statue lying on its side as if slinking to its prey. "And this must be El's son, Mot, the god of death." The professor stood back and shook his head. "But these are Canaanite gods. Why would they be here in the Caspian Sea?"

Rebecca walked over to another large statue in the corner of the room…it was faceless. "Who is this?"

The professor examined it from head to toe. The body was stylized with sharp angles, and the face was smooth; no eyes, mouth, nose…just flat. "I have no idea."

Rebecca was fascinated by the statues. "How old do you think these are, Professor?"

"If they are as old as the writings, most likely pre-canaanite—approximately 7,500 years old."

Rebecca turned her attention to the floor, the walls, and then the ceiling. "With tons of water above us, you'd think there would be at least a drop of moisture in here."

He peered closely at each of the statues. "That is a remarkable mystery, to be sure."

Erol examined the spear that the goddess Anat was holding. "Is this gold?"

Dr. Witherspoon turned his light on the spear briefly. "Ah...no. I believe it's bronze, but the amalgam with copper gives it a gold color." Erol gave a slight pout of disappointment.

Tony walked to the side of the room with his wind-up flashlight and pointed a beam of light on three semicircular indentations two meters apart. The three hand-wide, bow-shaped grooves were chiseled in a stone panel twice the size of the stones set in the wall. Above the grooves were symbols: the first symbol was what looked like a barley plant, the second was wheat, and the last symbol was of a flame.

Tony turned around. "Hey, Doc, what are these?"

Dr. Whitherspoon walked over and examined the depressions. "Hmmm. Interesting." He reached his hand into the slot and felt a metal bar at his fingertips. The archaeologist carefully removed his hand and opted to scrutinize the lettering above each of the slots.

Without asking, Tony reached into the slot and inadvertently pushed up on the bar to release the latch. The professor tried to stop him but it was too late. The square stone suddenly loosened and opened sideways on a hinge, which was followed by a gush of cereal grain that forced the door outward. Tony and the professor stepped back and watched as grain spilled out onto the floor until a large mound had formed around their feet.

The professor reached down and sifted the grain through his fingers. He looked up to the Texan. "That was not a wise thing to do, Tony. Anything could have been behind that stone access."

Tony looked back with a smirk. "It's just grain of some type. What's the problem?"

The professor examined the outer coating of the almond-shaped grain, called *aleurone*. "It looks like barley." He looked back up to the inscription above the access panel. "That confirms the word for barley. Now let me explain why you shouldn't have opened the door, Tony."

Erol had disregarded the professor's warning and went over to release the next one, before he finished correcting Tony.

The professor glanced over at the second access panel. "I said wait!"

Rebecca cringed. It could only mean that their lives could be in jeopardy. As the grain poured out, the professor jumped back, but nothing happened. She breathed a sigh of relief.

Erol started for the third door, but the professor grabbed his hand. "Oh, no, you don't! As much as we would all like to see what is in there, I strongly recommend we hold off." Erol stopped and stepped back.

"Why, Doc?" asked Tony.

Rebecca scolded Tony. "Because he said so!"

Tony scowled. "OK, Mom. Ya want me to go clean my room now too?"

The professor stepped between them. "As I was saying…we may have been lucky with the first two, but it was purely irrational. If there is something deadly or it triggers something unforeseen, we aren't in a position to protect ourselves."

"I agree," said Rebecca. "There may be tons of water behind that door, for all we know."

"Well, what do you suggest?" asked Erol. "There could also be something important in there."

Witherspoon held up a hand. "Let's not get ahead of ourselves. We should wait and bring down some surveying equipment to determine the safety of the space."

"What are you trying to hide?" asked Erol suspiciously.

The professor staggered back as if his dissertation on Near East artifacts was blacklisted. "I am not trying to hide anything. It's the prudent thing to do."

"But the first two doors were harmless," Erol argued. "This one may hold gold."

"Uggh! Gold and riches, gold and riches! Don't let that fog up your mind." The professor shined his light on the first and second symbols. "Do you see the grain inscription above these two storage rooms?" He bent down to gather a handful of seeds, then walked over to the second pile and did the same. "This grain is wheat, and those are barley." He shined his light on the third inscription. "Now, look closely at that symbol. It is of a flame, which could mean many things—fire, gas, anything! Our luck has been with us on the first two, but I am not going to risk testing this third one out without proper scientific equipment." Dr. Witherspoon stood with his back to the door and his arms crossed.

Erol's eyebrows closed in. "You are not a king here. We should take a vote."

Dr. Witherspoon scowled. "This is not a democracy. I have had more experience with archaeology alone than all of you combined."

"You are afraid of something!" he accused.

"Yes! Dying! We can't just go off thinking tickety-boo, let's open any ol' thing!"

Erol let the professor's words pass in one ear and out the other. "Then why are you afraid to take a vote?"

Witherspoon took off his glasses, rubbed his eyes, and gave a frustrated sigh. "If it will make you feel better, vote."

Erol addressed the others in the room. "All those in favor of opening the last door, raise your hand." Erol and the two soldiers raised theirs; Tony, Jamal and Rebecca didn't make a move.

Dr. Witherspoon smiled. "As you can see, the majority has decided against you." He raised his arms into the air victoriously and looked toward the ceiling. "Thank the heavens!" As he lowered his hands, the professor redirected his flashlight around the sanctuary. "Now if you wish to root out some other treasure, be my guest. But do not open it without telling me." His voice was stern.

Erol glared at his new adversary and grabbed the flashlight from the professor. "You can't talk to me like that," he grumbled. With a wicked smile, he pushed the professor away hard. The academic hit his head on the stone wall and was knocked silly.

"Hey—" Rebecca started.

Erol signaled the soldiers with shifting eyes and a tip of his head. The younger one quickly leaped onto Rebecca to retrieve the knife.

She struggled. "Let go of me!"

Tony went forward, swung his wind-up flashlight, and broke it against the young Turkmen's head. It had little effect. The more experienced soldier was on Tony like glue and put a judo grip to the Texan's neck. He followed it with a powerful elbow to Tony's head and he dropped like a rock. The soldier quickly muscled Tony into a full nelson to restrain him.

Jamal ran over to the statue of Anat and removed the spear. He returned to save Rebecca as she tussled with the soldier. He stood within jabbing range and tried to find an opening so as not to hit Rebecca in the process. She held tightly onto the knife and rolled over on her stomach to keep the weapon out of her opponent's hands. The soldier rolled her over onto her back. Facing her, he straddled above her on his knees, trying to undo her grip on the knife.

She clenched her teeth and gripped the knife with his hands wrapped around hers. "Get off! Stop it!"

Jamal found his opening and went to stab the young soldier, but the other soldier stuck out his foot. Jamal tripped and fell on his elbows, the spear tumbling against the stone wall.

The younger Turkmen squeezed Rebecca's wrists with his massive hands until she eventually released the diver's knife. He pulled it away, then slapped her across the face. She didn't scream out, but gave him a dirty look and touched her cheek.

Jamal let out a raging yell, picked up the spear, and surged at the big soldier. Erol flashed the light into Jamal's eyes, giving the soldier the opportunity to sidestep Jamal. This time the brawny young soldier tripped Jamal. He dropped the spear and again fell down on his elbows and belly. Tony was pinned to the ground—helpless. Jamal once again grabbed the spear from the floor and got to his feet poised to strike.

Before Jamal could attack, Erol flashed a light on Rebecca. There in the spotlight was the brawny man with a knife against her throat. Jamal groaned softly, dropped his head, stuck the spear on the floor, and leaned against it.

Erol laughed sardonically. "It seems as though the votes have not fully been counted, Professor."

Dr. Witherspoon was on his knees feeling around for his glasses. "It seems so," he grumbled.

"You promised not to fight!" Rebecca screamed. The knife edge pressed to her neck and she gasped.

"*I* promised not to attack you, but my friends did not," Erol elucidated.

Tony still had his face on the hard tile floor. "I knew we should have left you up there."

Erol chuckled. "What is it you Americans say? Oh, yes, God helps those who help themselves. So now it is time to help myself…to the treasure." He seemed to be relishing the moment. "Get the spear, friend, so we can get on with business."

The soldier pushed Rebecca away and grabbed Jamal's weapon.

Jamal let go of the spear and dabbed at his skinned elbow. "Allah will not take lightly to your arrogance."

"Yeah," agreed Tony, his head still pinned to the cold stone. "And here's another American saying: 'What goes around comes around.'"

"I tire of these useless comments."

"Shall we kill them?" asked the older soldier.

"That will not be necessary. Take them outside the sanctuary."

The older soldier released Tony, then corralled the *Bering* crew together. "Wait!" said Erol. They all stood still while Erol flashed his light on Rebecca's neck. "It looks like you're bleeding. Here, take my handkerchief."

Rebecca was bewildered. "Um…thanks?"

The professor adjusted his glasses and noticed the cross that had slipped out of Erol's shirt. "I just remembered where I saw your crucifix. It looks just like the one stolen from the Vatican a few years ago."

"What? It is?" Rebecca said, holding the cloth to her wound. "I knew you were lying."

"So I borrowed it for a while. Just as I will borrow some time to inspect the last door, and borrow the contents when I open it."

"I wouldn't do that if I were you," advised the professor.

"Enough!" Erol signaled with his head. "I hate being lectured! Lock them out of the sanctuary, so we can do this in peace. A warning to all of you: Do not try to stop me or someone may be hurt. I do not give second warnings."

The big soldier jabbed the bronze spear at Tony, and he and the others were escorted out into the corridor. With Tony, Jamal, the professor, and Rebecca out of the room, the Turkmen locked the door with the crossbar. Erol reached for the access door but stopped short of opening it.

In the darkness, Tony's voice echoed in the corridor. "I don't want to say I told you so, but—"

Rebecca groaned. "Don't say it, Tony. Just, don't say it."

CHAPTER 31

ADDING INSULT TO INJURY

E rol walked over to the carved-out markings and stuck his hand into the groove. He reached up to feel the metal latch, but stopped. He slowly removed his hand from the slot and turned to his cohorts. "What if the professor is right? What if there is water or a deadly gas behind this door?"

The older soldier spoke up. "If the teacher is right, we may die."

Erol stared at the access for a moment, then laughed. "I have another idea. Follow me."

Without the aid of their flashlights, Rebecca and the men couldn't see their own hand in front of their face. Jamal felt his way down the pitch-black passageway until he found the supplies. He tore open the last glowstick and held up a pathetic red one that provided only a little illumination. "What do we do now?" The four felt silly huddled so close together, nose to nose with the glowstick casting a red glow onto their faces.

"Well, we can't bust the door in. So I say we wait for them to leave the sanctuary, then jump 'em," suggested Tony.

"Jump 'em?" Rebecca snarled. "Are you nuts? They're *soldiers;* they train for this kind of thing."

"If you had listened to me in the first place, Darlin', we wouldn't—"

Jamal interrupted. "Let's not go over her past mistakes, Tony. It's not going to help anything."

The professor agreed. "Rebecca and Jamal are both correct. We can't win a fight with armed soldiers, and it certainly isn't useful if we fight amongst ourselves. Our only solution at this juncture is to take the scuba gear and leave immediately."

"What's the rush, Doc? They might find something valuable and take it," countered Tony. "Then all this recovery would be for nothin'."

"Let them have it," said Witherspoon. "They also might not survive to retrieve any valuables. And more importantly, *we* might not survive."

Rebecca looked at the professor and remembered what he said earlier about gases. "It's that flame symbol, isn't it? That's what you're thinking of…aren't you?"

The professor shrugged an admission of truth. "Yes, that's exactly what I was thinking."

Rebecca remembered something else. "You have good reason to think that way, Professor. Before we started our dive, Bob showed me a—"

"Did you say 'Bob'?" Tony smiled with surprise. "Do you mean Dr. McCray?"

"Tony, don't start. I'm working on it. By the way, what does the J stand for?"

The Texan barely held back a laugh. "Julian. Julian Robert Mc-Cray. His parents were hoping for a girl. A word of advice; don't use Julian and McCray in the same sentence."

She shook her head. "Anyway, he showed me a 3-D print of this area and there was a bright spot on it somewhere near this structure. Which means we could be standing right on top of large amounts of hydrocarbon gas reserves. If Erol opens that access door and it is full of gas, we all could be overcome by it."

"Which is why, logically, we should leave," said Dr. Witherspoon. "The four of us can share the scuba equipment and return to the surface." He shooed them forward. "Let's not waste another minute."

Suddenly the sanctuary door creaked opened and the four looked around to see Erol standing at the entrance. He flashed the light down at them and mumbled some things to the soldiers. The men walked down the passage without a word. The brawny soldier flashed the knife at Tony to back him up to the wall. Erol and his soldiers passed the group, turned the corner, and stepped down to the water's edge.

Rebecca watched from the landing. When the men began to pick up the professor's and her equipment that lay at the lower steps, she realized their plan to leave was about to be ruined. "Hey! What do you think you're doing? That's our gear!"

Erol flashed his light up to her while the soldiers slung the scuba gear over their shoulders. "I have decided to take the professor's suggestion and, as a precaution, open the access door with the proper equipment. I promise to return it when I'm finished." He laughed; his wicked laugh echoed down the corridor. The men walked back up the steps and passed around Rebecca and the others.

"Well ain't this just timely," spouted Tony.

"Mr. Erol?" Rebecca asked with a squint, her hand blocking the light in her face.

"Yes, Ms. Rebecca?"

"I'm still wondering something. Were you the one who was responsible for the flooding on our ship last week?"

Erol laughed, then laughed some more. He waved the soldiers to hurry with the scuba equipment, still chuckling. Without speaking, the three returned to the sanctuary.

Rebecca crossed her arms. "Well, I guess that answers my question."

Erol set his flashlight down in the sanctuary near the access with the flame icon. He turned to the younger soldier. "Help me with this."

The Turkmen helped Erol on with the professor's scuba gear, while the older soldier put on Rebecca's rebreather. The soldier then made some adjustments and checked the gauges for Erol.

The younger man stood watching. "What am I going to do?"

Erol looked at the young soldier with little regard. "If there is trouble, I will give you some of my air."

That seemed to satisfy the young man. Erol put his mouthpiece in and breathed. He looked back and the elder soldier gave the OK sign. Erol reached in the groove and felt the latch. He pushed it up and the door slid open. The three backed off and Erol shone his light inside the ancillary room. To their relief, there was no explosion and the chamber was not full of water.

The younger soldier grinned at Erol. "May I enter?"

Erol encouraged him to go by displaying the room with his hand. The young man took a couple of steps inside and Erol came right behind him with his flashlight. Once the three of them were inside, they stared at the artifacts that lined the shelves of the room. Many were bronze and silver statuettes, but many more sparkled with gold. They stood in reverent awe.

The young soldier became dizzy and leaned against the wall. Erol turned his head. "Are you feeling well?" he asked through his respirator.

The soldier didn't have a chance to answer. He collapsed on the floor. The other soldier went over to help, but Erol held him back. "Why do you stop me, Mr. Chenin? He may die."

"The moment you give him air is the moment you will pass out too. Do you want me to be the only one who gets the treasure?"

The soldier nodded and said a quick prayer over his compatriot.

Rebecca was just about to suggest a new plan, but Tony was looking up where Erol's flashlight flickered through the crack in the open door of the Sanctuary. He slowly stood up and stared at the sanctuary door. "Hey they left the door open!" he whispered loudly. He took a few stealthy steps up the corridor.

"Tony, where do you think you're going?" Rebecca challenged.

Tony glanced back. "After what you just told us, we haven't got a chance of surviving if we don't get our scuba gear back." He proceeded slowly to the sanctuary doors.

"Don't go after them, Tony." Dr. Witherspoon spoke with urgency. "We need to plan this out!"

Tony ignored him and picked up the pace. "It'll be too late for that. Don't worry about me. A man's gotta do what a man's gotta do," he quietly stated over his shoulder. Tony pulled open the sanctuary door, and went inside.

Rebecca was shaking her head when Jamal started after Tony. "You're not going too are you?"

"I have to."

"Please, Jamal, we don't need another cowboy acting stupid."

Jamal glanced back with a quick smile. "A man's got to do what a man's got to do."

"Oh for goodness sake! Jamal, please." She looked at the professor.

"I suggest we give them a long leash, my dear. We can't all be heroes."

Tony stepped lightly through the sanctuary and followed Erol's light from within the third access chamber. With the access door open, he stepped through as quietly as possible. Tony took few steps, then noticed the body of the younger soldier on the floor; Erol and the other soldier were gawking and fondling some gold idols stacked along the back wall. He didn't stop to analyze what happened to the unconscious man, but instead prepared himself.

"I'll tackle Erol, get the knife, and turn the tables on them," Tony mumbled to himself.

Erol turned around with a scuba respirator in his mouth and an oxygen tank around his shoulder. "If you would like to see our discovery, be my guest." His voice was muffled. Erol waved Tony to come forward.

Tony's muscles tensed. This was his chance, but he felt dizzy, "You son-of-a—."

Erol laughed and turned to the soldier. "It is good we took the professor's advice. This is the perfect solution to our dilemma. I think our friends are about to have a tragic accident, and of course they will not live to tell their story. Our big American friend here will be the first."

Tony staggered forward and reached out to pull off Erol's mask but his legs became wobbly. Erol kicked him in the chest, sending him backward to the entrance, where he crumpled down to the floor. Erol cackled at his superiority. But just when he had the best of the Texan, Jamal appeared behind Tony. Without a word, and without any ill-effects from the gas, Jamal pulled the Texan's heavy body quickly out of the sanctuary's treasure room.

Jamal's face was turning red as he yanked Tony's limp body over the threshold of the smaller room and through the sanctuary. Tony's feet dragged along the stone floor and Jamal's face started to turn blue, but soon he had shuffled backwards down the corridor to the deflated raft. Jamal let out a big breath and collapsed to the floor with Tony lying before him.

"Good show, Son!" the professor praised.

"I can only hold my breath for a minute, but I guess it was enough, eh?"

"I should say so," said the professor as he congratulated Jamal with a slap on the back. "Well, Rebecca, it looks as though we were correct about the gas."

Rebecca squatted down next to Jamal. "I'm proud of you, Jamal. That was good thinking."

Dr. Witherspoon stroked his chin. "Hmm. We still have to wait for Tony to recover before we consider leaving."

"I am not going to give *him* mouth to mouth resuscitation," said Jamal.

Dr. Witherspoon chuckled. "You won't have to. He will be awake in a moment...with a nasty headache, I might add."

Rebecca started to pace. "I don't know what's so funny. Those men still have the scuba gear, which means we can't make it to the surface. The gases will rise to the highest points in the sanctuary and eventually drop back down to this area."

Tony opened his eyes and coughed a few times, then sat up rubbing his head. "I should have listened to you, Doc. I didn't even smell a thing."

He looked down at Tony. "It is too late for apologies. We can't leave now anyway, my boy."

"We only have three choices," Rebecca counted with her fingers. "Die trying to swim without our scuba gear, die by a deadly gas, or die by the hand of maniacal thieves."

"They don't have to kill us, because the gas will do it for them," said the professor. "That leaves two choices."

"I don't like any of those choices," said Jamal. "Why is dying our only choice? Rebecca and Tony are great swimmers. What if they go to the surface and send back help."

Rebecca smiled weakly. "We can't hold our breath long enough to even get to the surface, Jamal. If we try to make a rapid ascent from twenty-five-plus meters we'd get the bends for sure without a ship to recover in."

"We should try anyway, Becca," said Tony sitting up.

"That's one in a thousand, Tony, and you know it!"

"Correct me if I'm wrong, Darlin', but isn't one in a thousand better than zero? Cause that's what it'll be if we don't go for help."

"We could try, but I won't leave Jamal and the professor!"

"What are you aimin' to prove by stayin' here, anyway; that you're a strong woman leader in a male-dominated world?"

"No!" She glared back at Tony. "I was left alone in a car when I was three!"

Tony wrinkled his nose. "What?"

"I was kidnapped!" She closed her eyes for a moment, held her head with her hands, and then pushed out a large breath. "It was only for an hour, and they got the man; but when you're three years old and have a big ugly brute breathin' down your neck—" she pinched her face tightly "—and helpless to do anything about it!" Rebecca breathed again and gave Tony a solid stare. "Maybe I'm overprotective, but I promised myself and God that I would do whatever it takes to protect those who can't protect themselves. And this is life and death, Tony. I can't leave them alone…to die!" Her strong outward appearance suddenly shattered, and she covered her face with her hands, heaved, and cried. The others were stunned silent.

Tony stood stiff. "Wow! Where'd this come from? OK, OK. I get it." He moved a toothpick around in his mouth. "So you were kidnapped as a kid, huh. So that's why you ran after some guy in the airport awhile back. To save the girl."

Rebecca pulled her hands away from her face, tears streaming down her cheeks. "I just can't. You go, Tony." She wiped her face with both hands and slid down the wall to a seated position.

The Texan softened and rubbed his head. "Hold on a minute, sweetheart. You don't have to go; I was just throwin' out ideas. To tell you the truth, after getting my lights knocked out, I don't think I could make it anyway."

The professor piped in. "I think…'This sucks big time' is the appropriate phrase."

Rebecca blubbered a laugh, and dabbed at the rest of her tears. "Well now you know my big secret."

Jamal sat down beside Rebecca and put his arm around her. "I think this has made you a stronger person, Rebecca."

She tipped her head to his shoulder with her hands in her lap. "That's what my parents tell me." The tension in her body left her.

It was nice to lean next to a man. It had been a long time, and she missed that feeling. If they ever survived, it would be a dreadful thing to leave this ordeal and never see him again.

Tony threw some stone chips into the water. "I guess we just wait," he grumbled. "The professor is right. This sucks! I wanna do *somethin'*!"

Rebecca knew that Tony was correct; swimming to the surface was the more logical solution. They still may make it and with luck get help before they had any ill effects from the bends. She hated either/or options and with lives at stake wished for another way out. She became somber and stared at her lap. "The 23rd Psalm seems appropriate, right about now," she whispered.

Tony looked over at the professor. "Do you know what she's talking about?"

"I would have to say that the most appropriate section of that particular scripture passage would be, "Yea, though I walk through the valley of the shadow of death, I will fear no evil: For thou art with me.""

CHAPTER 32

THE BERING RETURNS

The *Bering* was still tied to the dock at the port of Turkmenbashi. McCray had spent one and a better part of a second day arguing with the Turkmenistan officials to release the *Bering* and its crew. The Turkmen were adamant about security and territorial rights, and refused to budge. In the end, a large sum of cash donated by Terra Petroleum Industries to the city of Turkmenbashi and an agreed cooperative subfloor oil contract broke the deadlock. Not only did the Turkmenistan Navy release the vessel, but they became a newfound alliance and agreed to escort the ship back to the exploration site.

As the *Bering* circled back to the dive site, Bob McCray sat alone eating his lunch in the mess hall. He still wondered what became of Jamal's rescue plan. Would they get to Rebecca and Harold Witherspoon before something terrible happened? He looked up to see Mary enter the cafeteria. She took slow, timid steps toward him.

"Dr. McCray?" said Mary.

He sipped at his coffee. "Please, call me Bob. Have a seat," he offered.

She sat down across from him. "Mr. Jalil told me that Erol bribed the Turkmen to confiscate your ship. He is such an evil man!"

McCray raised his cup to her. "I can't agree with you more. I suspect he ventured out to the site of the undersea ruins too." McCray stared at his cup a moment, then asked a hard question. "You don't think Erol had something to do with your husband's death do you?"

Mary sat frozen. "I...don't...how did you—"

McCray interrupted. "I'm sorry to be blunt, but I had to ask. Before we left Baku, Harold told me about the ancient box and a connection between your husband, Jamal, and Erol. All arrows eventually point back to Erol. He may be a killer, not just an art thief."

Mary's eyes started to water. "There is still a good chance they may be alive, correct?"

"Rebecca and the others?" McCray scratched his unshaven chin. "There is always a chance," he replied with an unrevealing poker face.

Mary looked down while she nervously played with a napkin. "They are dead, aren't they?"

McCray tried to look her in the eyes, but she evaded him. "Why do you say that?"

"I overheard one of your men talking about the storm and he said, 'It would take a miracle for someone to make it out of there alive.' And with Erol out there too, it is almost certain."

Bob knew she was on the verge of breaking down. He reached over to hold her hand. "No one has ever died under my leadership, and I don't intend on them being the first."

Mary breathed deep and nodded that she understood.

McCray looked over her shoulder to see Mohammad Jalil walking toward them. The Iranian agent had removed his collarless khaki suit, was clean shaven, and dressed in a casual sportcoat and thin black tie. "Excuse me, Dr. McCray." He nodded to Mary.

"Yes, Mohammad? Or is it Officer Jalil?" McCray asked.

"Mohammad will do. If or when we find Erol Chenin, I assume he will be my prisoner?"

McCray leaned back in his chair, relieved of that responsibility. "Have at it. He's all yours. Do you have enough evidence on this guy to put him away?"

"For a very long time…thanks to the Turkmen officials. Erol had convinced them that your ship was spying on them and had official state documents. I presented them with the truth about him and they cooperated."

"The truth?"

"Yes, years of antiquity thefts directly related to him and a museum director named Mr. Damec in Armenia."

"Oh, then I should really be thanking *you*," said McCray.

"Thank me when Erol is in custody," said Mohammad. "May I use your communication equipment to contact Tehran, Dr. McCray?"

"Help yourself." Mohammad bowed his head and McCray watched him leave. "Nice guy. I know nothing about him, but I feel I could trust that guy with my life." He turned back to Mary. "Are you going to be all right?"

She nodded. "I will be patient."

McCray took one last gulp of coffee and decided she could use a diversion. "If you need some company, you can follow me around the ship. I have nothing to do until we get there anyway."

She smiled. "You have been so kind. Yes, I would like that."

He stood up and offered his hand. "Come on, I'll show you my routine."

Mary took McCray's hand and accompanied him on his rounds. The diversion worked well for the both of them. She had something to occupy her mind, other than the potential death of good friends, and McCray had someone to distract him from the duties and responsibilities of work.

The sun was low in the west by the time the *Bering* arrived at the exploration site. The ship slowed down and the forward lookout spotted some Styrofoam and some plastic bottles. Soon they noticed a crudely constructed yellow buoy with a flasher clipped to it. The ship stopped and crewmen went to the dive platform to inspect the float.

"What is that? A buoy or marker?" asked McCray with his hands on his hips. They shrugged their shoulders. "These are the right coordinates, aren't they?"

"Yes, boss."

"Well, pull it out. Let's get a better look."

When the seaman pulled it up, he wrestled with it for a moment because of the attached line. He pulled hard and fell backward onto the platform with it.

"There is a string tied to it." He handed the float up to McCray.

"Anything on the other end?"

"No." He continued to pull up meters of line. He looked a little sheepish. "It might have been attached to something on the seafloor."

McCray scanned the surrounding area, then turned to Joe Hanak, the senior diver. "Hanak, get another man. I want you to go below and check out the bottom. I'll have a few men with glasses checking out topside."

"I'll get right on it, J. Bob," said Hanak.

McCray turned around to see Mary biting her thumbnail. "Mary, why don't you get some rest in your cabin. I'll call you if I have any news." Just in case there was a death, McCray wanted to ensure he could break it to Mary himself.

CHAPTER 33

AN EXPLOSIVE SITUATION

Jamal brightened. "Wait! There still might be a way out of here."

"Really? How?" asked Rebecca.

He stood up and shook his forefinger in the air. "It is so simple! We could steal the scuba gear back from *them*," he said, pointing back to the sanctuary.

Rebecca groaned. "You can't be serious, Jamal. Didn't you see what happened to Tony?"

"Hear me out, Rebecca."

She sighed. "OK, go ahead."

"I saw some statuettes in the treasure room. Remember, they are very greedy men…and will not leave the room until they bring out at least some of the artifacts. I presume that if they are holding the treasure…"

"They can't be holding the knife," finished Tony. "If we work together, this could be quick. Good idea, Raz. Let's do it!"

"I don't know," said Rebecca. You saw how Tony almost died. Do you both want to end up dead?"

"Got a better idea?" asked Tony.

She didn't have an inkling of an idea at the moment. And Tony was right about Erol before. Even if it didn't work, she at

326

least wanted to give them the benefit of the doubt. "Maybe you're right. If the four of us strategically placed ourselves to the side of the treasure room, we should be able to overpower them. But we'll have to work quick, because the oxygen in the sanctuary is only going to last so long."

"That's the Becca I know!" Tony put his hand between them. "OK, team, this may be corny, but all for one and one for all." They sighed and stuck their hands on his.

Dr. Witherspoon agreed. "You're correct, Tony; it's corny."

Erol gazed fanatically at the statuettes, many in gold, all of them adorned with precious stones. The Armenian planned for the Turkmenistan Navy to return in a few hours and retrieve any of the artifacts they had discovered. With small gold statuettes in their hands, the elder soldier and Erol laughed victoriously at their newfound treasure.

Erol suddenly became all business. "We need to get to the surface and locate your people."

The soldier tipped his head toward the entrance. "What about the others?"

"What about them? That big American fell unconscious in seconds. I estimate that it will only be minutes before the others soon follow his demise. It is a perfect solution to my problem. We will be far away by the time the researchers return. This will appear as a dreadful natural gas accident that took their people's lives."

"Then we will split the profits and my country can be honored for the great discovery. Yes?" the soldier suggested.

"Yes. As you can see, we both win. But we must hurry, so we can rendezvous with your military ship."

Erol and the soldier laughed at their good fortune and began to remove the statues from their shelves. One by one they set the artifacts beyond the treasure room opening in the sanctuary. There were still several statuettes left on the shelf when Erol noticed his flashlight starting to dim. Before it could die out completely, he instinctively took out his golden lighter. "Mary, what would I do without you?"

He kissed the lighter and flicked it on. "Oops!" was the last word on the lips of the Armenian.

A brilliant light filled the room. A cacophonous explosion blew the thieves across the room. Before they could get up, the ignited gas consumed them in a suffocating heat and charred their bodies instantly. The explosion sent a rolling fire out of the treasure room and into the sanctuary. The fire then billowed up into the far reaches of the sanctuary, swirled around, and dropped down to the floor.

Rebecca and the men had finalized their game-plan. She was to take the lead with the glowstick in hand, while the others would rush around her and swarm Erol. They stood at the landing and took a large breath before they made their assault.

Rebecca looked forward to see a flash inside the sanctuary. A split second later, there was a loud *WHOOMP!* Before they could say anything, a cloud of fire blasted the large door open. Right behind the blast was an ignited cloud that rumbled along the ceiling with an ugly blue underbelly lined with yellow edges.

"Holy smoke!" uttered Rebecca.

The blazing cloud billowed out into the corridor in slow motion. It rolled and tumbled across the ceiling and down the passage. They were stunned into paralysis for a split second, then instinctually scrambled back around the corner. They tripped over themselves to get down to the bottom of the steps before the fiery onslaught could swallow them. They could feel the heat from the deadly cloud as it turned the corner and pressed downward. They didn't have to debate the fact that their only hope left was to try and make a swim for it.

Tony had one foot in the water, poised to dive, waving the others to hurry, when *poof!*...nothing...silence...darkness. They froze like statues, their muscles taut for action, hearts still pumping madly. All they could make out was a big bright spot in the dark from where the firelight once was.

Finally, after an endless moment, Rebecca broke the silence. "Is everyone OK?" she asked. "Yeah, uh-huh, sure," the men mumbled, stupefied by the abrupt end to the fiery onslaught.

In the blackness the only sounds were their breathing and the lapping of water around Tony's feet. Their eyes adjusted to the darkness and soon they saw the red glowstick floating in the water. "Holy smoke?" Tony critiqued.

"So? It was the first thing that came to my mind."

Jamal sighed. "I am *finally* warm." He fell back on the steps. "And although some of my hair was singed by the fire, God has spared us."

"Amen to that," agreed Rebecca.

Tony bristled. "What are you guys celebratin' for? Can't you smell that stench? And this pocket of air ain't goin' to last forever." He hit the wall with his fist. "If God was so good to us, why would he leave us just to die of asphyxiation?"

"You're such a pessimist, Tony," replied Rebecca. "Be thankful we're alive. In fact, if Jamal hadn't risked his life to save you, you'd be burned alive.

"We were just about to get those S.O.B.s, then this happened. So I should be thankful for this."

"Maybe you should. At least you're alive! Maybe God is giving you one more chance. I believe he's a God of second chances."

"Oh, come on, Darlin'! I'm not a pessimist, I'm a realist. Maybe he's sayin' 'It's up to you, partner, get movin'." Tony snatched the glowstick from the water.

"Believe it or not, the Holy Spirit could be helping and guiding us," she countered.

Tony smacked his forehead. "The what? Oh, yeah, you're a holy roller. The spirit is movin' us to this dead end so we can find a secret batch of oxygen, right? Wait! Before you answer, let me play along with you on this!" He closed his eyes and slapped his hands together. "OK, God, I'm trying this prayer thing for once. If you're for real, send me a cold beer and a side of air."

Tony opened his eyes and looked around. Nothing had changed. "I don't see nothin', Darlin'. Do you see somethin', Raz? How 'bout you, Doc?"

"Knock it off, Tony," Rebecca said. "What I meant—"

"Knock what off? If we're gonna to try and survive, we have to make a swim for it." Tony stepped deeper into the water. "Now are you guys ready to go or what?"

A pregnant pause filled the dirty pocket of air. Dr. Witherspoon coughed a few times, then moved down closer to the water where the oxygen was better. Not another minute of silence went by when a small splash came from the deep end of the water.

Tony jumped back. "Jeez! What the—."

Rebecca took the glowstick from Tony and held it out to see a head of something. "It's…" she leaned forward "…a seal?"

"For a moment, I thought Allah had truly answered you," said Jamal.

"Ha!" Tony pointed. "See! This is what I'm talkin' about. That's the kind of answer I would expect to get from God—a Caspian Seal!"

The animal sniffed the air for a moment, wiggled its whiskers, and then slipped back down into the water.

"That was so weird," said Rebecca.

"I will never forget this as long as I live," said Jamal. The others paused, then gave a painful chuckle.

The professor started to wheeze and then he coughed some more. "I believe the oxygen isn't as good as it once was. I seriously have enjoyed working with all of you and…." No one said a word. They knew what he meant to say.

Tony turned to Rebecca. "We gotta risk swimmin' out of here, sweetheart. There's nothing else to do. Come on, we gotta go."

After a tense moment of silence, another small splash came from the water. Tony groaned. "Oh, not again! What do ya want, ya dumb animal!"

"I came to see if you were all right," said a voice raising a flashlight out of the water and into their eyes.

Tony looked closer, "Joe? Joe Hanak, is that you? I can't believe it! You're a sight for sore eyes, ol' buddy!" He jumped in to hug his crewmate.

"Glad to hear it," Hanak said. He raised his mask and patted Tony's back. After a moment, Hanak peeled Tony off him. "You know, Tony, we broke your tether line to that ad-hoc buoy, so I wasn't sure where to go. But I saw this seal and for some reason decided to follow it in here. It was lucky I did because it was getting dark and I probably wouldn't have made it back till morning."

Rebecca said, jabbing Tony in the ribs, "Yeah…just lucky, I guess." Tony was speechless.

Hanak flashed his light around the space. Fumes and particulates filtered the beam. "This is nasty down here. How did you guys survive?"

"It was a lot more comfortable before the explosion," said Rebecca.

"Explosion?"

She coughed a couple times. "We'll explain later."

Hanak moved his flashlight around to check them for injuries. "If you guys are well enough to swim to the surface, I have a pony tank with me and can take one person now. I'll get some more gear and be back for the rest of you."

They decided that Dr. Witherspoon would be the first to leave the air pocket. By the evening, the other three were safely brought aboard the ship, given hot cups of coffee, and sent to the ship's doctor.

CHAPTER 34

SEPARATE WAYS

McCray and Mary entered the doctor's treatment room just as Tony was buttoning up his shirt. The others were sitting on a bench seat drinking tea, Rebecca with a bandage across her neck. The professor had one on his head, and Jamal had both elbows bandaged. Mary rushed over to Jamal and Dr. Witherspoon to examine their wounds. She hugged her friends and quietly scolded them for participating in dangerous exploits.

McCray addressed the doctor. "How are they doing?"

"Other than a few scrapes and bruises, they're doing pretty well."

McCray smiled at his wounded crew. "Glad to hear it. I was worried sick about you four. How about first thing in the morning we meet in the conference room and you can fill me in on the details of your undersea excursion?"

"We'll be there," said Rebecca. "You wouldn't believe what we have to tell you."

She piqued McCray's interest. "Such as?"

"Such as, waterspouts, an underwater temple full of breathable air, secret chambers with golden artifacts, a gas explosion...that sort of thing."

"You're kidding."

She raised her eyebrows and shook her head.

"Then, this ought to be good." McCray glanced at his watch. "It's getting late, I'll 'debrief' you guys in the morning." McCray started for the door then turned around. "Oh, and Tony, if you want a cold brew, we just received an ice cold case of Bud. See you early tomorrow." He exited the room.

"Did you tell him, Becca?" asked Tony.

"About the beer? I didn't say a word." She raised her hand. "I promise."

"His prayer came true. Praise Allah," whispered Jamal.

Rebecca looked back at Tony and just stared at him. Tony rolled his eyes. "Don't say it, Darlin'."

"I didn't say anything," she replied.

"Oh, yes, you did! It's all in the eyes. Those pretty, sneaky, green little eyes of yours, Becca."

She chuckled. "Tony—"

"Don't!" He interrupted.

She laughed. "Tony! Let me—"

"I don't want to hear it. You were right, I was wrong. I'm going to hell. Simple as that."

The medical doctor was bemused. "What are you people talking about?"

"It's a long story, Doctor," said Rebecca. "But our little talk is not over with, Tony."

"It is for now." Tony got up to leave.

"Oh, by the way," she added.

He stopped at the door. "Yeah?"

"I think you're right; we did make a good team. Like the four Musketeers."

"And you have the sharpest sword of all of us, Sweetheart."

At 0800 in the mess deck, Rebecca, Tony, Jamal, and Dr. Witherspoon reconvened and recounted to McCray all that had happened. They relaxed in soft couches, sipping coffee, and played back the events, each from their own perspective. Dr. McCray took his turn to replay his negotiation nightmare in Turkmenbashi.

The *Bering* was ready to pull up anchor from the dive site and return to port, but McCray suddenly had an inspiration. "If you all are feeling better, I don't see why we have to return to port right away. I could send a dive team down and we can end what we started."

There was a pregnant pause until Dr. Witherspoon spoke up. "I hope you don't mind if we don't assist you in the retrieval of the artifacts, Robert."

McCray chuckled. "I understand perfectly. We'll finish up today and head back to Baku tonight. Fair enough?" They nodded in agreement. McCray stood up and rubbed his hands together. "Well then, I better get Hanak and his team down there. We have some treasure to bring up!" He started for the door then looked back to Rebecca. "Oh, Becca, could I see you a moment?"

She set her cup down and went outside with him. "What's up, Dr. Bob?"

He stopped mid-sentence. "Dr. Bob?"

"It's a name I can live with. It's either that or Julian."

He winced. "You've been talking to Tony, haven't you?" Rebecca nodded her head. "Yeah, I guess "Dr. Bob" sounds fine. Anyway, I wanted to ask you something."

"Shoot."

"Were you the one that found the sanctuary?"

"I was first on the scene."

"And did you save Tony and Jamal from drowning?"

"Really, we saved each other."

"Uh-huh. Well, in any case you seem to be more capable than I thought. I want to keep you around awhile longer; unless of course this little adventure has scared you off."

Rebecca tried to look dubious about the offer. "Hmmm. And what if I am not afraid, but just don't want to stay on?"

McCray was caught off guard. "Um, let me rephrase it. I wish that you would stay on, with an increase in salary, and other negotiables."

"That's better," she agreed. "I'll think about it."

McCray rolled his eyes. "Do you think you can let me know by tomorrow?"

"Why? What's the rush?

"I'm going to be on vacation for a couple weeks, starting the day after tomorrow. I haven't had a vacation in a year and need a break."

Rebecca laughed. "You're not the only one."

"Don't worry, Becca. You'll get plenty of free time when I return.

She looked between McCray and the door to see Mary waiting in the hallway. Rebecca eyed him closely. "Did I hear some rumors about you and Mary?"

McCray glanced back to Mary and gave her a micro-smile and a nod. He turned to Rebecca and lowered his voice. "Let me set things straight. I'm taking Mary to Armenia to clear up some financial loose ends with her deceased husband."

A smile crept up on one side of her face. "So there's nothing between you two? You're just going to escort her to Armenia…as friends?"

"Yes. I'm a nice guy. Don't make such a big deal out of it."

Rebecca could barely hold back a smile. "OK, just asking. I'll hold down the fort while you're gone. Maybe I'll go on my own adventure and check out those ancient cup marks and cart ruts that cab driver told me about. I'm getting pretty good at finding ancient artifacts."

"Suit yourself. But I need you to do me a favor."

"What's that, Dr. Bob?"

"If you have a problem while I'm gone, call the office here in Baku."

She laughed and saluted. "If you say so, chief."

McCray shook his head and glanced at his watch. "I have to get the dive team started." McCray started to walk away, stopped, and then turned back around. "I really am asking you to stay because I have no doubt I can depend on you to handle things. You're a great addition to the team." Before she could respond, he trotted away.

She grinned at the compliment. *Well, if Dr. Robert McCray appreciates my work, I know I've done well.*

At 0900 in Baku, the *Bering* was berthed and receiving shore power. The Azeri authorities were quick to arrive as it set out the gangplank. They wanted to ensure that the newfound antiquities didn't find their way off the boat unescorted. Mohammad Jalil led up the transfer of the artifacts.

Much of the crew was leaving the ship to enjoy some R&R. Rebecca caught the eyes of Dr. McCray and Mary getting into a taxi. She waved to them and they waved back. Rebecca leaned on the railing and heard footsteps behind her. She turned to see Jamal and Dr. Witherspoon with suitcases in their hands. The men set their belongings down.

"My dear, Becca. Take care of yourself and please be careful. Danger has a frightful way of following you," the professor said with a wink.

She gave Dr. Witherspoon a hug. "Thanks, I'll be careful, Professor. Are you headed back to Tehran?"

"Actually, I've been coaxed by the Azerbaijan National Academy of Sciences to assist them in the study of the Tubalite language and the examination of the artifacts. We are only at the cusp of understanding this unknown people group, and it's a capital opportunity."

Rebecca glanced at Jamal staring out over the water. "What about you, Jamal?"

He shrugged, "I need to complete my studies in Tehran."

Dr. Witherspoon saw himself as a third wheel and excused himself. "Pardon me while I say goodbye to the captain."

After the professor left, Rebecca tried to get Jamal to face her. "What are you thinking about?"

He kept his eyes on the sea. "What you said about God."

It had been weeks since she had brought up the subject of religion to him and she was leery about doing it again. "What about him?"

Jamal looked her in the eyes. "Can you really have a personal friendship with him?"

"God?" she asked. Jamal nodded.

"Are you teasing me or do you mean it?" she said with a grin.

His eyes teared up. "I have watched you trust God with your life. Many people do and it is expected. But I also see a peace within you that I do not understand. Allah gives me strength and wisdom...but I know him only from a distance."

Rebecca was caught off guard. She reached out and wrapped her arms around him. "Jesus said, 'Seek, and ye shall find; knock, and it shall be opened unto you.' I will pray for you. But you can pray for me too, Jamal."

He released himself to wipe a tear from his eye. "Why?"

"Before I met you, I had some preconceived ideas of what Muslims were like. You have proven to me that you are more open to the truth than I was."

"Thank you for that. I will miss you, Rebecca. But since I am not a Christian, I trust you will forget me."

"No, I won't. We may live in different worlds, but our friendship can still be close. I can't forget you and you better not forget me," she warned, shaking a finger at him. "Remember, I'm a pushy American who expects big things. I have your email address and I know where you live."

Jamal chuckled. "Goodbye, Rebecca. May Allah—and Jesus—guide you in your life." He picked up his suitcase, caught up with the professor, and gave one last wave back to Rebecca." She waved back and watched them walk down the gangplank to the pier.

"Hey, Rebecca!" Tony called out from the radio room. "Your ma is on the phone. She wants to know if the job has been too boring for you. Ha!"

Rebecca knew that Tony was probably trying to get more information from her mom than she wanted him to know. "I'll be right up!" she shouted. "*Great!* two weeks of Tony," she muttered.

Rebecca stayed on with the Terra Petroleum surveying team in the Caspian and continued with successful hydrocarbon discoveries, but every now and then found herself dwelling on the days in the ancient sanctuary. She pondered the many defenses she built as a protection: her job, her relationships with men, her independence as a modern woman; but she came to realize that the best sanctuary of all is the one that God had built within her heart.

TWO WEEKS LATER

Rebecca stood at the top of the gangplank and looked down to see Dr. McCray exit the taxi. He smiled and waved to her, then climbed the gangway. "Well, look who's back...Dr. Bob." She greeted him with a tip of her baseball cap.

He shook his head with a grin. "Becca, it's nice to see you again. I hope the crew didn't give you a hard time."

"They've been like little angels. I guess it's just my womanly touch. So how was the trip?" she asked with a sly smile.

He set his bags down. "It was fine."

She looked over her nose at him. "Anything else?"

He paused. "And Mary is fine too. She and I are getting along just fine."

"Could you expound on that?"

"Things are progressing just as they should, young lady. Don't you have anybody else to bother?"

She raised her hands. "Oops! Sorry, Boss."

McCray smiled. "There is something I want to tell you." He lowered his voice and looked around. "You wouldn't believe what we found in Mary's husband's safe deposit box."

Rebecca closed her eyes and groaned. "Oh, no! You've got the bug. It's only been two weeks and you've—I don't want to hear it."

He raised his eyebrows. "You have to hear me out on this."

She plugged her fingers into her ears. "I can't hear you." Rebecca turned around and walked away.

McCray called out. "I'm telling you, Becca. This is good stuff!"

She kept walking and talking. "I still can't hear you..."

CHAPTER 1
BOOK III

Shem's breathing was labored as he reached the summit of the ridge. He was older now and his body didn't work the way he wanted it to. He found a boulder with a nice flat surface to rest upon. From the highest point on the plateau, the land and water, east to west, north to south, were clearly visible.

"I will spend the night here and inspect the waters in the morning," he noted to a crow that had followed him on the trail. "This will be my last task before I return home. I can do no more."

In the distance, Shem spotted the large channel of water that connected the great western sea to the black sea. "So this is where people of the valley say the salty water mixes with the sweet. Tomorrow I will find out the truth."

The sun had set and the dark-blue twilight was laid out in splendor above a deep-red horizon. With no moon present, the stars quickly began to brighten. Shem gazed upward and couldn't help but notice a large and long, bright light. He was struck by its size and luminescence. *I have never seen such a star before. It has a tail and runs across the sky as if it fears something. Was this what Father worried of? Is this the time of mankind's doom?*

Millions of miles above Shem, among the celestial lights, lurked the wandering star. However, this was no ordinary star. It was a gigantic comet of loosely-packed chunks of ice, mud, and ore. It was like a small ocean, frozen around house-sized boulders and mucky soil, with snow and ice so loose, only its local sphere of influence kept it from flying apart.

The comet had traveled an eon of time on a trajectory ordained by the gravitational forces of interstellar bodies. Its methodical race throughout the heavens was finally coming to an end. It sped past the outer planets of an average star, called Sun, then through the asteroid belt, shedding fragments of its mass as it clashed with cosmic debris. The comet could have been obliterated by a collision with a rogue asteroid or even into the sun's fiery, hydrogen furnace. Instead, its death would be an impact with the solar system's third inner planet—Earth.

Printed in the United States
96381LV00004BA/1-18/A

9 781414 109220